THE BORROWED OF
MORILEWA

KOLAWOLE OGUNYINKA

MEREO

Mereo Books

1A The Wool Market Dyer Street Cirencester Gloucestershire GL7 2PR
An imprint of Memoirs Books Ltd. www.mereobooks.com

THE BORROWED LIFE OF MORILEWA: 978-1-86151-929-0

First published in Great Britain in 2019
by Mereo Books, an imprint of Memoirs Books Ltd.

The address for Memoirs Books Ltd. can be
found at www.mereobooks.com

Memoirs Books Ltd. Reg. No. 7834348

Typeset in 10/14pt Century Schoolbook
by Wiltshire Associates Ltd.
Printed and bound in Great Britain

Acknowledgements

I extend my thanks to the friends who helped me
to flesh out the words, and I extend love to my
family who had endured listening to the story as
it developed and helped to bring it to life.

Kolawole Ogunyinka
May 2019

OCEAN FRONT

AWOYAYA RIVER

CHAPTER 1

The wealth of Ijowa came from its soil, both above and beneath. Its fertility was as if Onire, the god of harvest, had personally embraced the soils of Ijowa and from its bosoms, had coaxed bounties for the people at every harvest. The blessed soil was constant right across and around the limit of Ijowaland and, given adequate manpower, it could feed her people many times over through the year. Hence the people of Ijowa never wanted for the staple crops of yam, rice, cassava and other household foods. There was also an abundance of fruit-bearing trees which grew naturally, so that it was possible to live on free fruit for days, as there was always a fruit in season, all the year round.

The Awoyaya river flowed across the major town of Ijowa and the villages from east to west and its tributaries ran through the villages in the southern part of Ijowa into the great ocean. The river also passed through Abatanland and Aketeland, but the most productive fishing ground through the whole length of the river was at Kuluso, and the cleanest water was at Oluweri. The plentiful land also supported the kingdom with material resources. Not too deep into the soil of the west of Ijowa were rich deposits of iron ore, and over the past century its extraction had blossomed into a lucrative blacksmithing industry. The neighbouring communities had taken to referring to Ijowa *as* 'the land of friendly spirits', because there had not been a time in current memory when any part of Ijowa had suffered adverse climate or natural disasters like flooding or extreme forest fire, which were almost a yearly experience in other lands.

There were, altogether, eleven major towns and villages under the jurisdiction and control of the *Onijowa* (King of Ijowa). All the families who owned land in Oluweri, Kuluso, Egbejoda and the palace town of Ode-Ijowa were the descendants of those who had arrived and settled with Akinreluku, the first *Onijowa*. The soils of Ode-Ijowa, Oluweri and Egbejoda were the richest in Ijowaland, hence these were the residence of the wealthiest and noblest of the Ijowa people. The palace at Ode-Ijowa was the political headquarters of Ijowaland and, sitting on a throne fashioned from the riches of the land was one of the wealthiest monarchs in the tribe, the *Onijowa*.

The Ijowa population had swollen over the years, not due to internal procreation but the absorption of labour migrants, families and small clans in want of a more economically sustainable environment to settle in. Ijowa was already a land that provided plenty for the hard-working. The founders and pioneers of Ijowa reckoned that it would not be possible to enjoy the richness of Ijowa alone while their neighbours were starving due to gradual depreciation of their land brought about by long periods of harsh climates, and misfortune due to war. So, before their struggling neighbours began to force themselves to a share of the Ijowa soil, the leaders took the initiative of leasing out part of the land which they knew could never be cultivated by many generations yet unborn 'sons of the soil' (that is pure-bred indigenes). The palace at Ode-Ijowa exchanged land for peace and human resources. As a result, over the years, the *Onijowa*, his chiefs and the major landowners of Ijowa had been engaging the abundant labour for the cultivation of cash crops such as palm, kola and cotton.

Migrating communities were allowed to stay peacefully on different parts of the Ijowa soil but had to pay this back with their sweat, which for many seasons in their homeland had been shed for very little, due to drought. The offer was always gratefully welcomed as a very fair bargain by migrants and settlers alike. For the sweat of three adults for half a season every year, or a full season every other year, an extended family, sometimes numbering as many as thirty, could lease sufficient land to cultivate enough food for the family and leave a surplus for sale. The hospitality offered to migrants and settlers by the king and people of Ijowa also helped in maintaining her territorial integrity. As it is a tested truth that one hardly abandons the way that feeds one's stomach, the thousands of able immigrants feeding from the rich soil of Ijowa would resist any attempt by an external force to encroach upon the land leased to them by the king and people of Ijowa.

Other villages like Ayefele, Inukan, Olokoto, Gbemuyona, Gbajumo, Odinjo and Oko-Oba were at different times offered as settlements by successive *Onijowa*. All these villages, including Kuluso, Egbejoda and Oluweri, had their local authorities under a community head with the title of *Baale* who was directly responsible to the *Onijowa*. Although the *Baale* had to be appointed from within the local community, it was vital that whoever the village elders chose to be the *Baale* enjoyed the support of the *Onijowa*.

The market at Oluweri was the most vibrant in the whole of Ijowaland, and of all the four communities that spread along the Awoyaya river in the southern part of Ijowaland, it was only Oluweri that extended across the river. The part of Oluweri on the northern side of Awoyaya which also linked to Ijowa communities on that side was referred to as Upper-Oluweri (Oluweri-*Oke*), while the part on the south of Awoyaya which extended westward to Oko-Oba and southward to the limit of Ijowaland at the seafront was called Lower-Oluweri (Oluweri-*Isale*).

The people of Erebe were the last to be allowed settlement by the king and people of Ijowa. They were forced to migrate from their homeland when an outbreak of disease descended upon their community. The epidemic killed hundreds and rendered hundreds more disabled. No family was spared. The elderly and the young, male and female, all fell to the terrible disease. Within two seasons, Erebe had become more a land of the dead than of the living. As its walls crumbled, so dwindled the morale and willingness of those who were spared to pull the remnants of their tragedy together and develop a fresh community. A once prosperous community had been deserted, leaving only the weak and the disabled who were resigned to their fate.

Those who migrated to neighbouring towns and cities were shocked by the reception they received from those who they had thought would be their friends in need. Their immediate neighbours, in fairness, were willing to help, but the problem was that Erebe people had tribal markings. The neighbours were wary of the future consequences of allowing a mark-bearing community to be established on their territories. It was generally believed that a mark-bearing tribe never entirely integrate with the host community and hence could not be trusted. It had happened in the past; after many years, history would be distorted, and children of immigrants would begin to claim equality with descendants of landowners. The tribal mark was not only a symbol of affluence; it was vital for security and protection in an era of incessant tribal and communal conflicts. Hence those who could not afford the service of the *Onikola* (mark maker) endeavoured to tattoo the mark on their own faces. Though cheaper to administer, tattoos were not permanent and not as elegant as the work of the *Onikola*, who made permanent marks on the skin with sharp knife. The wealth requirement meant, in most families, that only the *Olori-ebi* (the overall family head), and some few elders of lower-class families could afford the service of the *Onikola* to decorate their face with the traditional mark.

The palace at Ode-Ijowa, which was traditionally friendly towards migrants, was unsettled about the people of Erebe. They were far greater in numbers than any group of migrants that had been offered residence in Ijowa and were also the first to be a mark-bearing people. Although it was only in Ijowa that the people of Erebe were given the opportunity to settle and continue to exist as a community, only individual or families without the Erebe tribal mark and those whose marks were removable and who were willing to do so were allowed to stay at all. In what the *Onijowa* described as 'a gesture of friendship from the entire Ijowa people', more than a hundred Erebe families and people without the tribal mark were allowed settlement in a community of their own and with substantial land for cultivation. That meant any Erebe person or family that wished to be settled in Ijowaland would be sacrificing their identity and those of future generations.

Ironically, those without the Erebe tribal mark and those whose marks were not made with the knife of an *onikola* and were willing to remove them in exchange for rights and opportunities equal to that of the Ijowa 'sons of the soil' were mainly families of the peasants in their Erebe homeland. They were without marks not because they wished it to be so, but because they could not afford the *onikola*. They were allowed a community leader with the title and authority of a *Baale*, who was of Erebe flesh and blood, and who enjoyed the same privilege in the palace as the *Baales* of other Ijowa immigrant communities.

The immigrants were offered a homeland on a stretch of land which covered almost a quarter of Ijowa's mangrove frontier to the big ocean on the south-western boundary with Akete, but which the *Onijowa* had already titled as Oko-Oba (meaning 'the king's farm') in anticipation of their arrival and request for settlement.

There were many royal farms across the land, with numerous slaves who were owned by the palace, and the proceeds from them represented a significant source of revenue for the royal families, the titled chiefs and those in the king's personal favour. These farms were only identified in term of the locality of the estate; for example, 'the king's cocoa farm at Egbejoda and the cotton farm at Oluweri', which were among many others owned by the *Onijowa* and were referred to as the 'Oko-Oba at Egbejoda or Oko-Oba at Oluweri.' And in cases where there was more than one Oko-Oba (king's farm) in a particular town or village, the product of the land or the nature of its utilisation would be added to differentiate each of the estates, for example the Eku-Oba (the king's palm oil pit) at Ayefele, or the Agbede-Oba (the king's blacksmithing yard) at Ayefele. It was not tradition, nor had it ever occurred in Ijowa memory that an entire civil community would be called Oko-Oba or have the phrase attached to its identity.

The land upon which the *Onijowa* and the people of Ijowa received and settled the Olodi people was named Odinjo. The land upon which the people of the Muyona and Okoto clans settled were named Gbemuyona and Olokoto respectively, and so on. But the people of Erebe were settled on a land with a name that did not reflect their origin. The naming of the land upon which the *Onijowa* allowed settlement for the Erebe immigrants as Oko-Oba was a tactic by the king and his chiefs to cover their backs and prevent any possibility of losing total control of the land to the immigrants.

Meanwhile, a visitor who was unfortunate enough to arrive in the dead of the night had to contend with whatever was offered by the host. The land upon which they were allowed settlement for 'a very generous annual tribute' compared to what other immigrants remitted to the palace was only good for cultivating short-term crops. The people of Erebe toiled on the land, but each year whatever return they got from the land could hardly sustain them to the next harvest. By the sixth harvest in Oko-Oba, most Erebe families in Ijowa had lost the remainder of their fortune to poor harvests, and an average Erebe family in Oko-Oba had at least five of their kin who engaged in paid labour across Ijowa in order to survive. By their tenth year in Ijowa, many Erebe families in Oko-Oba had been in so much debt that they had to render themselves as bondservants to work out their debt in the households and farms of the feudal lords and *ogunagbongbos* (high-ranking dignitaries) across Ijowa.

In Aketeland, settlers were granted settlement strictly for sheltering purposes and no provision of land for cultivation. All Erebe people, with or without the tribal mark, were allowed to settle anywhere within the existing Akete communities without any condition related to their identity. They would have the opportunity to settle and work wherever they wished but had to negotiate directly with individual *Baale* of the local communities to lease land for farming. About a hundred families stopped at Akete and about half of that number chose to stop in Abatan under the same terms.

The implication of this was that an Erebe person or family in Akete and Abatan would be restricted to cultivating short-term crops that could be harvested at short notice if the landowner suddenly decided to terminate the lease. Those aspiring to own land like any 'son of the soil', and able to cultivate long-term crops of meaningful trade value with traders in big markets, would have to labour for many years, or even across generations, before being able to afford one.

Hence, the best part of the life of an average Erebe person in Ijowa, Akete or Abatan was technically deemed to be spent in bond service. When their parents died, the remaining term would by traditional law and custom be shared by their children and their children's children and so on until the debt was paid for in service, goods, or other miscellaneous value, like giving up the dowry on daughters married into the family of their creditor or landlord.

The Kudaisi family were not so wealthy in their Erebe homeland, and most of the extended family could not afford the service of the *Onikola*. Their tribal marks were merely tattooed on their faces and could be easily wiped away within weeks. But the grandparents of Olubi Kudaisi were among the die-hard patriots who preferred to move on rather than compromise their identity and status in whatever form. For their wilfulness, the family was denied settlement in Ijowa. They were among the first Erebe families to be allowed settlement in Abatan and among many that became impoverished due to the conditions upon which their settlements were granted.

Olubi Kudaisi's father grew up and married in an Abatan village called Igisogba, and that was where Olubi was born and lived until the death of his father. Like the children of most Erebe families in Abatan and Akete, he spent his early years following his parents through the seasons as they laboured for gratitude in various farms across Abatan. The family's permanent settlement was in Igisogba, but the only time they were at home was at the end of the season when there would be almost nothing to do on the farms, and there was little demand for labour until the beginning of the next planting season. That was when all other Erebe families in Akete and Abatan villages would return home to socialise together for about two months before the next planting season began.

The original house of Olubi's family in Igisogba was a

single but fairly large house that had gone through a couple of internal divisions as the family grew and the children got older. By the time Olubi was growing into adolescence, the house which had earlier been divided by palm leaves to make an extra space for the parents' privacy had been redivided to make more space to separate Olubi from his siblings, three girls who were growing into womanhood.

By the time Olubi was ten, farm tools had started going 'missing' under the nose of the landowner. He would trade the missing items for cowries and other articles of value with the *alajapas* (travelling traders) who constantly travelled from one village to another in quest of bargains. His reasoning was simple. If the *oniwofa* (bondmaster) did not care to lavish the sweat of poor peasants on wine, women and praise singers while family bond servants could hardly survive from on season to the other, then he saw no evil in helping himself to whatever he could to aid his family's survival.

His father's ambition before he died was to acquire a family-owned farm and become independent. It was an ambition that led the family into bond service as a faster but more difficult means of becoming a landowner. Unfortunately, Olubi's father died at a very young age, leaving the family in debt. As things were before his father's death, Olubi would need all his own children's sweat before the debt could be paid and the family could claim the land for which three generations had laboured. He had long concluded that it would require more than good luck for his parents' dream to be realised in a lifetime.

Three years after the death of his father, when he was just a little over fourteen, Olubi ran away from the farm of his lord and family creditor. If he was caught and found guilty by the *Baale*, his status could be drastically reduced, from bondservant to slave, and he would be the property of his master for life. However, a runaway bondservant whose status was reduced to slave could in no circumstances be sold or exchanged and was not inheritable; that is, the slave automatically became free on the death of his master. But very few people had the courage to run, to take on the risk in term of security, both material and personal. The *oniwofa* (bondmaster) reported the case to the king's resident *asingba* (debt collector) in Orile-Atan, who sent his men after Olubi. They searched through the nooks and crannies of Orile-Atan and all its surrounding *ileto* (small settlements) but could not find him.

It was common knowledge that runaway bondservants tended to seek refuge in their home villages, so the efforts of the trackers were directed to routes between Orile-Atan and Igisogba. But Olubi knew better than to choose the easy option. He had witnessed many, and heard many more, tales of successful captures of absconders who had chosen their home settlement as the place to hide. Although he would be welcomed and sheltered by fellow Erebe families in other parts of Abatan, he was also aware that the long arm of the king's *asingba* (royal debt collectors) was as effective in all the Abatan villages as it was in the palace town of Orile-Atan. Undeterred, he chose the next available route, to leave Abatan entirely, and headed south with the aim of crossing the border into Gbengbele in Aketeland.

None would have thought that a boy of his age could dare to travel on his own through the jungles and other natural barriers as they made movement between towns and villages very risky for even an adult travelling on his own. These natural frontiers separated communities and effectively set the limits and juridictions of local authorities. The jungle between Abatan and Akete especially was notorious, and even hunters only dared to hunt there in groups. But it was through this jungle that young Olubi chose to escape from the long arm of the *asingba*.

He soon realised the enormity of the challenge he had taken on. By the end of the second day of wandering in the forest, he had been unable to find the right route to get out of Abatan; he also could not be sure of the direction he was coming from. At this rate, he was more likely to find himself in an Abatan village, or, even worse, back in Orile-Atan, than he was to escape into Akete.

He roamed the forest for days, knowing neither his path nor his destination. When he finally managed to get off Abatan soil, it was not into Gbengbele as he had hoped but on the other side, into Gbemuyona. It took him just two days in Gbemuyona to realise that it was not the right place for him to stop. While a mark-bearing Erebe youth was a common sight across Abatan and Akete, it was not so in Ijowa. Gbemuyona was an Ijowa village, and there were only non-mark-bearing Erebe people in Ijowa, their concentration naturally being around their settlement in Oko-Oba. Olubi left Gbemuyona on the third day, but not on foot. He was able to secure a transit to Eti-Osa across the Awoyaya river in exchange for being a load carrier for a canoe man.

In the beginning, he spent his days running errands for persons of questionable character within Eti-Osa and neighbouring settlements and withdrew at night to sleep in one of the many empty fishermen's shacks that lined the Osa lake. Apart from being free, he found that his living standards back in Orile-Atan had been far better than most youths of his age in Eti-Osa. He could see plain desperation written all over the people's faces, and most young people of his age were used to fending for themselves from an early age. Some of the youth of Eti-Osa had given in to other means in their attempt at breaking the cycle. A youth who was determined to at all costs to avoid committing his descendants into bond service on the estate of the landowner had to serve one master during the day and another under the cover of darkness. And for the bold and desperate, fraud, stealing and banditry became promising alternatives. But for the poor majority that were unable to engage in trade and lacked the courage to scavenge on the tough trade routes, hunger and starvation were the order of the day.

One thing however differentiated Olubi from the very young but uncared-for children of Eti-Osa, and that was his exposure in Orile-Atan and his experience in the jungle. Within his first few months in Eti-Osa, he had drawn to himself a small group of equally desperate and frustrated young boys. He made it his duty to arrange secret hideouts for scores of newly-escaped bondservants who poured into Eti-Osa from various farms across Akete and Ijowa at the end of every planting season. Before he was fully grown, he had assembled a small gang of other absconders, mainly of Erebe descent. On random market days, they impersonated the authority of small communities by imposing and collecting illegal tariffs from market traders before the *agbowo ode* (a team of palace law enforcers whose primary and civil responsibility was to ensure effective delivery of the trade tax to the palace at Aromire), arrived to do the rounds.

As his gang grew in numbers and strength, so also did the range and seriousness of their atrocities. For many seasons, and to the discomfiture of communities across the southern part of Akete and Ijowa, from Apete to Seleru, and from Kuluso to Aiyefele, Olubi and his compatriots became a major impediment to traders and travellers alike. But very few people had the courage to run, to take on the risk in term of security, both material and personal. The *oniwofa* (bondmaster) reported the case to the king's resident *asingba* (debt collector) in Orile-Atan, who sent his men after Olubi. They searched through the nooks and crannies of Orile-Atan and all its sorrounding *ileto* (small settlements) but could not find him.

It was common knowledge that runaway bondservants tended to seek refuge in their home villages, so the efforts of the trackers were directed to routes between Orile-Atan and Igisogba. But Olubi knew better than to choose the easy option. He had witnessed many, and heard many more, tales of successful captures of absconders who had chosen their home settlement as the place to hide. Although he would be welcomed and sheltered by fellow Erebe families in other parts of Abatan, he was also aware that the long arm of the king's *asingba* (royal debt collectors) was as effective in all the Abatan villages as it was in the palace town of Orile-Atan. Undeterred, he chose the next available route, to leave Abatan entirely, and headed south with the aim of crossing the border into Gbengbele in Aketeland.

None would have thought that a boy of his age could dare to travel on his own through the jungles and other natural barriers as they made movement between towns and villages very risky for even an adult travelling on his own. These natural frontiers separated communities and effectively set the limits and juridictions of local authorities. The jungle between Abatan and Akete especially was notorious, and even hunters only dared to hunt there in groups. But it was through this jungle that young Olubi chose to escape from the long arm of the *asingba*.

He soon realised the enormity of the challenge he had taken on. By the end of the second day of wandering in the forest, he had been unable to find the right route to get out of Abatan; he also could not be sure of the direction he was coming from. That meant his prospects for escaping into Akete was the same as the unfortunate chance of finding himself in an Abatan village, or even worse, back in Orile-Atan.

He roamed the forest for days, knowing neither his path nor his destination. When he finally managed to get off Abatan soil, it was not into Gbengbele as he had hoped but on the other side, into Gbemuyona. It took him just two days in Gbemuyona to realise that it was not the right place for him to stop. While a mark-bearing Erebe youth was a common sight across Abatan and Akete, it was not so in Ijowa. Gbemuyona was an Ijowa village, and there were only non-mark-bearing Erebe people in Ijowa, their concentration naturally being around their settlement in Oko-Oba. Olubi left Gbemuyona on the third day, but not on foot. He was able to secure a transit to Eti-Osa across the Awoyaya river in exchange for being a load carrier for a canoe man.

In the beginning, he spent his days running errands for persons of questionable character within Eti-Osa and neighbouring settlements and withdrew at night to sleep in one of the many empty fishermen's shacks that lined the Osa lake. Apart from being free, he found that his living standards back in Orile-Atan had been far better than most youths of his age in Eti-Osa. He could see plain desperation written all over the people's faces, and most young people of his age were used to fending for themselves from an early age. Some of the youth of Eti-Osa had given in to other means in their attempt at breaking the cycle. A youth who was determined to at all costs to avoid committing his descendants into bond service on the estate of the landowner had to serve one master during the day and another under the cover of darkness. And for the bold and desperate, fraud, stealing and banditry became promising alternatives. But for the poor majority that were unable to engage in trade and lacked the courage to scavenge on the tough trade routes, hunger and starvation were the order of the day.

One thing however differentiated Olubi from the very young but uncared-for children of Eti-Osa, and that was his exposure in Orile-Atan and his experience in the jungle. Within his first few months in Eti-Osa, he had drawn to himself a small group of equally desperate and frustrated young boys. He made it his duty to arrange secret hideouts for scores of newly-escaped bondservants who poured into Eti-Osa from various farms across Akete and Ijowa at the end of every planting season. Before he was fully grown, he had assembled a small gang of other absconders, mainly of Erebe descent. On random market days, they impersonated the authority of small communities by imposing and collecting illegal tariffs from market traders before the agbowo ode (a team of palace law enforcers whose primary and civil responsibility was to ensure effective delivery of the trade tax to the palace at Aromire), arrived to do the rounds.

As his gang grew in numbers and strength, so also did the range and seriousness of their atrocities. For many seasons, and to the discomfiture of communities across the southern part of Akete and Ijowa, from Apete to Seleru, and from Kuluso to Aiyefele, Olubi and his compatriots became a major impediment to traders and travellers alike.

The period between the last harvest, when the forest began to get less thick due to diminishing rains, and the dry wind that followed was always the best time for riding. Each year, during these periods, young princes of Ijowa, along with friends and personages from equally influential families, often retreated to the royal stable at Egbejoda to ride horses. Each year, about two scores of servants comprising housemaids, cooks and carriers, along with horses loaded with supplies, would arrive in Egbejoda days before the arrival of the royals and their guests to prepare the place for their comfortable stay. Adeyanju was the eldest son of the reigning king of Ijowaland, hence he was the *Aremo-Oba* (crown prince) and heir apparent to the throne of Ijowa. From childhood he had been groomed to embody the glamour of the Ijowa monarch. While the prince's early interest in public affairs was much appreciated by his father, the *Onijowa*, and by Ijowa chiefs and statesmen, an average Ijowa man took pride and comfort in the flamboyancy of Adeyanju, which was well expressed in his favourite sport of riding.

By his fifteenth season, the *Aremo-Oba* had converted ten of the best horses in the royal stable for his sporting activities. Just some months away from his seventeenth season, he was known to be among the best riders in Ijowa. He could entertain on the horse like no one else of his age and was an object of envy to older riders. This season, the prince was planning to make his debut with a public display at the opening of the Orisun race. He would not be competing in the race due to his royal status, but he had been able to persuade the king to let him entertain in the square before the races began.

Six months before the race, Adeyanju approached his father and requested that the palace arrange the service of a foreign horse trainer for him in preparation for the opening ceremony.

'What is wrong with Elesin?' The *Onijowa* asked his son. 'He has been teaching you riding since you were eight years of age.'

Elesin was the head keeper of all the royal stables. He had under his command about twenty royal servants who engaged in the care and maintenance of the king's horses and stables.

'It has nothing to do with Elesin,' replied Adeyanju. 'It is about change. It has always been the same performance, so much that it is difficult to differentiate between the opening displays of one Orisun race and another. The idea of entertaining is to create new excitement. It is the excitement that let memories last longer in the mind.'

'So what new excitements do you intend to learn from a Gambari?'

'I am not employing one of the Gambaris. I want a horse warrior from among the Fulanis to teach me the skill of fighting on horseback. Cavalry warfare is not common among our people, so the display of such skills will be new, creative and entertaining.'

The king consented and ordered one of his chiefs to make arrangements for a foreign trainer. Yahaya, the cavalryman employed by the palace to teach Adeyanju, was a middle-aged Fulani, specially recruited from among the best in the house of Alimi in Ilorin. The Fulani were known for their excellent performance on the horse. Their artistry in this respect was incomparable.

The day after he arrived from Ilorin, the king demanded the presence of Elesin in the palace and formally introduced the trainer to the royal stableman.

'Yahaya will be here until after the Orisun race,' he said. 'While he is here, he will be teaching Adeyanju some skills in cavalry warfare, which my son intends to display at the opening of the race. I want you around the stable to inform me of their progress and concerns, if any.'

The first day at the stable was spent basically discussing the theme of the display and then mapping out the field in the fashion of Ojude-Oba (the kings' square) at Ode-Ijowa where the performance would be taking place. The theme was simple. Adeyanju would be presented as a young hero escaping on a horse. He would be riding one horse while holding onto another carrying a wounded warrior. He would be pursued by half a dozen of the royal horsemen with bows and arrows, and the Fulani would be teaching the prince some basic skills and manoeuvring to outride his 'enemies'. There would be a couple of jumps over fences and ditches, then his pursuers would start using their weapons. After a couple of missed shots, an arrow would hit the horse which Adeyanju was riding. The climax of the display would be when Adeyanju jumped from the wounded and falling horse, still in motion, to the fit one and continued riding without dropping the wounded warrior.

The working relationship between Elesin and Yahaya went sour from the first day at the stable, basically due to a clash of professional responsibilities. Elesin wanted his presence and authority to be recognised by Yahaya. The Fulani warrior did try to accommodate Elesin's intrusion, but by the middle of the day he was beginning to find the royal stableman obstructive to his work, and he complained to the prince about it. On the second day, before the training proper started, Adeyanju called Elesin to his chamber and instructed him to direct all his suggestions to him personally and also to function as an observer only during the training.

'You will just be close enough to perform the task assigned to you by my father,' he told Elesin. From then on it was obvious that the Fulani man had made an enemy, and it would remain so throughout his stay at Ode-Ijowa. For the rest of their first week at the stable, Elesin kept within his limits. He only made verbal contributions when the prince demanded his comment or suggestion; and he made sure his comments were limited to the particular issue on which Adeyanju demanded his opinion.

The first week was spent on improving Adeyanju's skills at steady riding on a single horse and later with another horse, the one he would be holding as he raced to escape. By *ojobo* (the fourth day) of the second week, Adeyanju could confidently ride the two horses at average speed. His training was running well ahead of schedule. Adeyanju wanted to proceed to the next stage right away but, although, the trainer was impressed by Adeyanju's performance, he cautioned the prince not to be too hasty.

'It is too early,' he said. 'You need to be steady in riding before you start jumping the fences, especially when you are jumping with two horses.'

The next stage was scheduled to begin by the fourth

week. Then the prince would be learning the skills that would enable him to jump ditches and fences as he was being pursued. The royal slaves, under the supervision of Elesin, had been working on the field since the second day at Egbejoda. By the seventh day, Elesin and his team had finished with the digging and the fences were all in place. On *abameta* (the sixth day) of the second week at the royal stable, Adeyanju could not wait any longer. He was bored with the routine and he made his intention known to his trainer when he arrived at the field.

'*Sanu yaro seriki,*' Yahaya saluted the prince while crossing his hands across his chest and bending slightly at the knee.

'*Sanu,*' Adeyanju replied casually. 'When will I start trying to jump over the ditches and fences?'

'According to the...' Yahaya began but was sharply interrupted by Adeyanju.

'I am very well aware of what is in the plan and I am not concern about that,' Adeyanju said before the trainer could complete his statement. 'What I am telling you is that I am not waiting until the next *osupa* [new month] before starting the jumping.'

'There are procedures which must be followed before you begin to jump with the horses,' Yahaya protested, but Adeyanju had made up his mind. 'We start the jump next week on *ojoru*, and that is it,' Adeyanju said with finality and left. The stunned Fulani turned to one of the stable hands. 'What day is *ojoru*?' he asked.

'That is the fourth day of the week,' the stable hand replied.

The third week had started in high spirits. Adeyanju and his trainer were pleased with their progress, until an accident brought the excercise to an abrupt end. It was the fifth day of the third week and the sixteenth day of training. On that fateful day, Adeyanju as usual had just finished a spectacular ride round the track to warm up the horse before continuing with his showjumping practice. He jumped the first and shortest post with little effort. His admirers cheer as the young prince raced round the first bend and cleared the second, higher post almost as effortlessly as the first. He then raced to the end of the plains to give himself suitable clearing distance before the third post, which had been raised higher than the second. The prince cleared the third pole, and there was uproar. Yahaya, despite his disapproval of Adeyanju's action, was visibly impressed by the prince's performance.

Adeyanju was really excited. He turned again and began racing to the far end of the field.

'Raise the pole to the next level!' Adeyanju bellowed to the stable hands who lined the track at precise intervals.

'What did your lordship command?' the nearest of the stable hands asked, running along to stay within hearing distance with Adeyanju.

'I said put the pole on the fourth level,' Adeyanju repeated as he raced on.

'The prince commands that the pole be raised to the fourth height,' said the stable hand loudly to the men at the other end of the track.

Yahaya heard the command and knew this was going too far, at least from his present position. He knew Adeyanju was capable of jumping such a height, but his fear was the location of the jump. In order to give the prince a suitable clearing distance, the stable hand had thought it wise to raise the height on the second stake, and that was where the Fulani horseman foresaw a problem. The stake which was raised to the fourth height was on a bend and it would be at a very awkward angle as Adeyanju approached.

Yahaya raced on his horse after Adeyanju to warn him of the danger. The prince saw his trainer racing to catch up with him, and anticipating opposition from the Fulani man, he let the rein go loose and urged the horse to go faster. Yahaya had intended to ride up to the prince and get his horse to stop, but Adeyanju was riding at top speed and was soon approaching the bend.

The horse, despite its strength and agility, was struggling with the demands of the prince. It skidded sideways as it tried to maintain its balance through the bends, its shoes spinning before they caught solid, dry earth. Adeyanju lurched sideways in the other direction, but the impact wrenched his legs out of the stirrup leathers. He fell off the horse and crashed to the ground, landing just before the stallion. The horse was set off balance by the jolt, and as it struggled to regain balance, its left hoof struck the prince's right shoulder. Adeyanju tried to wrench his shoulder free and rolled away from under the horse's hoof, but the sudden twist unsettled the horse even more. The stallion struggled again to regain balance, but the best it could do to avoid dropping its whole weight on the prince was to lean on his exposed right thigh.

'Orooo!' Adeyanju's cry of agony echoed through the jungle as the hoof pressed on a very delicate part of his body.

'*Minini, minini?*' Yahaya shouted in Fulani as he rushed down the middle of the slope towards the fallen prince. He was the first to get to the scene and tried to pull him up, but it hurt the prince's ego to have to be rescued from under a horse. He refused to be assisted and tried to stand up on his own. He slumnped back into the outstretched hands of his trainer.

'*Yeeparipa*! My lord has fainted!' Elesin shouted as he raced down to the scene. From where he stood on the top of the hill, the royal stableman had a good view of the accident and from experience, he feared the worst even before he got to the prince. He knew quite well the possible damage that could be caused by an angry or frustrated horse. He was sure that the prince's body would be bruised or swollen in many places from being trampled upon.

While the royal aides were carrying the unconscious Adeyanju to his chamber, Yahaya rushed down to the shed where afternoon meals were being attended to by the maids and ordered them to put a large pot of water on the fire immediately. He rushed to his knapsack, which he hung on one of the shed posts, then retrieved a short knife and proceeded towards the nearest bush.

Adeyanju's personal minder was already mopping the swollen injured parts of his master before Yahaya returned with some fresh leaves and roots. He was sweating all over as he began mashing the leaves and the roots together in a wooden mortar. He cursed silently as a fragment from the pestle pierced his thumb. Countless times he had warned the prince not to let go of the reins before disengaging his feet from the stirrup. Now the prince's disobedience would make him appear unpleasant in the eyes of a man many times more powerful than him. The king would be furious, and he could not imagine what the reaction of *Olori Agba*, the most senior queen and the prince's mother, would be on hearing of the accident.

The fact that Adeyanju was up and about by the third

day did nothing to ease the fear of the Fulani man. Apart from the bruises and the swollen limbs, there are often serious long-term consequences of riding accidents, and symptoms seldom surface until weeks or even months after the event. His concern was more for Adeyanju's underparts. Yahaya was particularly disturbed by the way the *Aremo-Oba* suddenly went limp as he tried to lean on his left thigh. He advised the prince to cut short his horse-training session and return to Ode-Ijowa for intensive herbal administration, as more damage could have been done than met the eye, but Adeyanju would not hear of it. On the fourth day after the accident, against his trainer's advice, the prince began mounting the horses again.

Although the accident had occurred in full view of his friends and staffs, the official report from his personal minder to all those who witnessed the accident was that the prince had twisted his groin while trying to mount the horse. It was widely known that to be trampled by a horse had cost quite a few riders the use of their manhood. Even men who for other reasons had suffer such a disability were referred to as having been 'trampled by a horse'. Apart from Yahaya, none but his personal minder had seen the injury, and the prince had sworn both men to secrecy about the nature and severity of the injury. For apparent social reasons, the nature of the prince's accident and the extent of his injury were declared classified right from the moment the accident happened.

As Yahaya had feared, the injury worsened a month after he returned from training at Egbejoda. The prince had carelessly ignored the warning signs, the random but sharp pain that went through his loins when about to urinate.

However, when the persistence and intensity of the pain became visible in his walk, his personal minder called the attention of the king to the matter. As expected, despite Adeyanju's insistence that the accident was not in any way due to the instructor's negligence, the king was furious. Oba Adejayi was not altogether pleased with the sight of his son's private parts, which were swollen and smelly.

By the month before the Orisun race, Adeyanju could hardly sit or rise from the mat without assistance and it was apparent that he would not be able to mount a horse on Orisun day. Yahaya, the Fulani instructor, was sent back to Ilorin for failing to report the accident to the palace upon their return from the stable.

The royal herbalist was sent for, and after thorough examination of the wound he requested that the king should allow him to move into the palace, close to the prince, to ensure adequate care and proper monitoring of the healing process. This was approved and the herbalist moved into a chamber within the palace, the one the Fulani instructor had vacated just days before. For six weeks, the herbalist treated and laboured on the wound, which eventually healed, but by then the orisun race had come and gone.

The prince could now stand without being supported and walk without a stick. However, the herbalist was worried about the fluids that kept soaking the dressing on the wound. Even when all the swellings around his manhood had cleared and all the pus had been extracted, the fluid kept coming. He had to keep changing the dressing almost every other day, a procedure which itself was not helpful to the healing process. Already, the herbalist's seemingly endless stay in the palace was becoming embarrassing to him. He could sense that some residents of the palace believed he had stayed longer than necessary. He knew many of the palace aides thought him an opportunist who was deliberately prolonging his residence in the palace for reasons of personal comfort rather than professional need.

'If it takes Ewedairo almost half a season to treat a twisted groin,' murmured one palace maid to another, 'you wonder how long it will take him to treat somebody who is severely wounded in war or attacked by a hyena.' He had overheard such comments frequently enough among the palace staff, and they seemed to be intended for his hearing. He could not blame them. They could all see the prince walking about but were unaware of the nature of the injury underneath the garment, and possibly within the body.

The parent reserves a customary right to choose or at least be in total approval of whoever their daughter-in-law will be. Since the turn of the year when Adeyanju was due to be circumcised and become a 'full man', the prince's mother had already concluded all the necessary underground arrangements and negotiations with the Gbokiki family for the hand of their daughter Omotara in marriage. Birds of a feather flock together, says the adage. The bride chosen for Adeyanju by her mother was from a no less influential family in Ijowa. She was the daughter of Olayiwola Gbokiki, the present Olori-Ebi (family head) of the Gbokiki family. The Gbokiki family had from the time of Akinreluku, the first *Onijowa* of Ijowa, owned up to a tenth of the farmland in Egbejoda. It is not surprising that no fewer than five past *Baales* in the history of Egbejoda had been from the Gbokiki family, and the present *Baale* was a nephew of Olayiwola Gbokiki.

On the day Omotara was taken into the palace as a royal wife and princess, her name was changed to Adetara in line with the tradition to reflect her royal status. All those who attended were well fed. All those who enjoyed drinking got drunk. Most of those who attended for the sake of starting a relationship were not disappointed, as hundreds of guests and families travelled from all corners of Ijowaland and beyond to witness the royal wedding. Ijowa had seen many events and in fairness, many more glamorous events than the marriage between Adeyanju and Adetara, but none in history had recorded such presence or representation of monarchs from far and wide. While the *Alaafin* of Oyo attended in person with all his royal entourage, the rulers of Idomi and Nupe each sent scores of servants bearing gifts for the groom and bride. Since the wedding had been announced, large quantities of foodstuff and cooking materials, carried by scores of men were presented by the *Baales* of Ijowa villages to the palace to support the *Onijowa* in feeding his guests during the ceremony. As there was gin for important guest, so also there was abundant fresh wine from the palm tree for all well-wishers. But despite all the pomp, the unspoken expectation of the palace from the union was clear: a son. The Oriloye dynasty was yet to be assured of its continuous hold on the throne in the next generation but one.

CHAPTER 2

Weeks and months became a year. Soon, three seasons had passed and Adetara was still without a child. Understandably more than anybody else, Adeyanju was extremely concerned. 'Something has to be done,' he lamented to his herbalist.

'Your case might require the service of a diviner, an Ifa priest,' Ewedairo, the royal herbalist, advised. 'In my opinion, the most consistent is Baba Fatunbi, the high priest at Oluweri. In fact, I have consulted him in the past concerning similar cases that I found beyond my practice with herbs and incision. The priest will seek knowledge and wisdom from the oracle on how to go about dealing with difficult ailments concerning conception and birth. If there is anybody capable of looking beyond humanity for an effective solution to a problem of this nature, I can assure you it will be Baba Fatunbi.'

Adeyanju had to wait three months for the most suitable

time to make the journey to Oluweri to seek spiritual guidance for his problem. The royal herbalist advised that the prince should plan the trip to coincide with the popular Ifa festival at Oluweri, in order to avoid negative conjecture. During the two-week long festival, the village would be brimmng with royals and *ogunagbongbos* from across the lands. Ifa diviners and worshippers, enthusiasts, guest and visitors would travel down from as far as Oyo, Ife and the Biniland to witness the festival. The compound of Fatunbi would be brimming with a cross-section of the notable and the nobles. The prince's presence in Oluweri would not seem unusual, and his private session with the Ifa priest, like most of the visiting dignitaries, would not demand any special explanation or attract undue attention.

The week before the Ifa festival, a visitor came to see Fatunbi while the priest was in the middle of one of many meetings with peers in preparation for the coming event. The visitor departed without seeing the priest but left a message.

'A man who called himself Morilewa came to see you while you are with the Ogbonis,' Faturoti, one of the priest's spiritual apprentices, told Fatunbi after he had seen off his peers from the other side of Oluweri. 'He said he had travelled down all the way from Egbejoda purposely to see you, but as it was getting dark, he decided to leave and call back tomorrow as he would be staying overnight in Oluweri.'

Morilewa returned the next morning and asked to see the diviner in private. 'I have a friend and trade associate who used to live across the river in Lower-Oluweri,' Morilewa began. 'We were together on a distant trade

30

to the land of the Ashantis when we were attacked by vicious bandits. What I heard was that he was brought to you during the early months of his illness. There was an agreement involving money between us. The repayment is now due, and I have his money ready, but he is dead.'

'You said your trade associate lived in Lower-Oluweri until his death,' replied Fatunbi. 'My advice is that you try and locate his family and pass on the money.'

'Locating his family is not a problem. I know the house in Lower-Oluweri where he used to live with his wife and son before his death. I have made enquiries and learnt that his widow still lives there with her son. The problem is that it took a long time for me to overcome the trauma of that tragic incident. I saw the bodies of my friends and trade partners, nine of them, strewn about.' Morilewa paused to supress the emotion that was building in him. 'Meeting his wife will take me back to the dark months that followed the incident. That is why I want somebody I can trust to pass on the money to his wife.'

'What was the name of your late trade associate?'

'His name was Iyanda Kekewura and I believe his wife's name is Lalonpe.'

'Oh yes, I remember him. I heard of his passing away about three years ago. Well, because your act is in pursuance of good faith, I will be pleased to deliver your message to his widow. But the annual Ifa festival begins in seven days from tomorrow, and you will understand that it will be difficult for me to leave this side of Oluweri until after the festival. So the soonest will have to be the week after the last day of the festival.'

'That will be no problem at all, Baba. Time is not of any

essence in this case. You can go as at when it is convinient for you. It is not as if the woman is expecting the money.' Morilewa thanked the priest and departed, relieved.

Adeyanju arrived in Oluweri on the third day of the festival. He went only with his personal minder and was personally received by the high priest himself. After he had been entertained in the circle of the most noble and influential dignitaries, the prince managed to secure the privacy of Fatunbi in his shrine. Adeyanju was presented with the customary two half kola nuts, upon which he silently laid bare his trouble and then returned it to the priest. Fatunbi collected the pair of half kola nuts and then retreated alone into an inner room within the shrine for a 'private session with the deities'. When he returned, the priest wasted no words in telling Adeyanju what the oracle had to say to the prince.

'You want to know whether the silence in your yard is due to the woman you marry or your own inadequacy? You are seeking this knowledge before taking another wife because you want to look before you leap. I hope I am speaking from your mind?'

'Yes, Baba Fatunbi, you are on the right track. But I want to believe you can help me out.'

'Let us hope the oracle wishes it to be so,' the priest replied. 'The oracle prescribes that you perform the ritual of truth and all the knowledge you seek shall be revealed.'

'What is the ritual of truth, and what are the materials needed for it?'

"The only way you can know the truth is to have a relationship with another woman in the hope that the affair is fruitful. That is the ritual of truth.'

'*Baba*! Getting a woman is not my problem. If I take a second wife and nothing changes, then people will begin to point their accusing fingers the other way concerning who is to be blame for the silence in my yard and the settled waterpot in my wives' chambers.'

The priest could not help but to agree with the young prince. With or without children, a single wife is not befitting in the yard of the *Aremo-Oba*. In fact, taking a second wife, then a third and a fourth, is more a societal demand and responsibility than the desire of a prince. It would be socially unacceptable for a crown prince, the next in line to the prestigious Ijowa throne, to fill his yard with only one wife for three seasons, especially when she failed to bear children. Even an ordinary townsman would not hesitate to take on a second wife, if the first tarried too long before bearing children. There would be bound to be rumours flying around if eventually the prince took another wife, and again was unable to conceive. Behind the curtains and away from the royal ears, opinion would begin to turn the other way, and the consequences of such alternative thoughts would do no credit to the image of the prince in particular and the royal family in general. The more curious the people became, the more the prince would be prompted to prove to all and sundry that he was well and able by marrying another wife. Infertility was one of the most feared ailments by the nobles. Soon, single maidens would be secretly wary of marrying into the yard of Adeyanju, a royal prince who by birth and destiny had the privilege, and could afford, to live a lifetime amongst the most eligible husbands in the circle of unmarried Ijowa maidens.

'My advice is that you keep the affair secret until you get the desired result from the relationship,' said Fatunbi.

'Secret relationship?' Adeyanju was genuinely surprised by the priest's suggestion. 'Baba, you know that will be very difficult, in fact impossible, for me to keep such an affair out of the public eye.'

'Yes it could be difficult for an *Aremo-Oba* to keep such an affair away from public eye, but it will not be difficulty for an ordinary town person. The only way to go about it is for you to assume a different identity whenever you are engaged in the ritual. You will only need to reveal your true identity to the woman if and when the result of the ritual is what you hope for and is acceptable.'

'Baba, I am sorry if it seems I am being pessimistic. When I said getting a woman to marry is not my problem, I was referring to the royal prince and not an ordinary town person. Getting a woman as a commoner will not be as straightforward especially when I am not even an ordinary town person.'

'Nothing is new any more under the sky. I have helped men with more damaging and distressing circumstances through this kind of ritual in past. Your case is not beyond what could be arranged.'

'Arranged?'

'Yes arranged. Like I said, there is nothing beneath the sky that is new. Although your status as a royal prince will make finding the ideal partner a bit tricky, as we have to be sure that the woman is not someone who had been to Ode-Ijowa before and who, most importantly, is not likely to have seen or meet you before.'

'Hmmm. You are right.'

'I must warn you that it will be tricky and demanding,

but it is not impossible. I will start working on it right away, but one cannot be sure how soon or otherwise it will take to find that suitable partner. Does the king know of the intent of this visit?'

'Nothing beyond witnessing an Ifa festival and of course a complimentary homage to you.'

'Nothing in respect of your concern?'

'None.'

'Who else then is in confidence with you over this issue?'

'None except the royal herbalist who had been treating me since the accident.'

'Not all clothing is fit to be dried under the open sun. Few words, they say, should be enough for the wise; I will let you think that out for yourself. I would advise you to let this matter stay close to your chest. Let not even your herbalist into the true outcome of this visit. He would never think of questioning my wisdom if I said to him that all would be well with you in due course.'

'So what do I need to do now?'

'You will return to Ode-Ijowa when you originally planned to after this festival but be preparing yourself for another trip to Oluweri about sixteen days after the last day of the festival, and many more after that. Within sixteen days, you will receive an *aroko* (coded message) from an anonymous person, asking you to meet another anonymous person in an anonymous place. The anonymous person you will be meeting will be me, and the anonymous place will be the old shrine. You must arrive alone because you will be leaving as an anonymous person. It is common knowledge that once in a while, I retreat to the old shrine for special consultation with Orunmila (the Ifa deity). I will be waiting with the necessary clothing to change you from Adeyanju the *Aremo-Oba* to our new person. I will let the other details wait until then.' The priest having concluded, they returned to join the rest of the dignitaries at the feasting.

True to his word, slightly over a week after the festival, an *aroko* arrived. It was brought by a man who introduced himself as Lagbaja (meaning 'somebody' or 'anybody' in the local language). The coded message was a small calabash, and inside it was a freshly-cooked yam. 'An anonymous person asked me to give this to you, but will appreciate that the *Aremo-Oba* would not mind leaving some leftovers for him,' Lagbaja said and handed the calabash to Adeyanju. That the anonymous person 'would not mind some leftovers' meant that the priest was essentially telling him to respond as quickly as possible. If it took to long to respond, then the 'leftovers' would have been stale and unfit for consumption.

One of the major responsibilities of the *Aremo-Oba* is to maintain healthy and harmonious relationships between the palace and the subordinate communities on one hand, and between surbodinate communities on the other. Except in cases where the eldest son of the king is still too young to assume sensitive roles, the *Aremo-Oba* is usually the king's own treasurer and has the vital responsibility of ensuring that the king's proceeds from subordinate communities are collected and well accounted for. Hence, for proper discharge of his duty, impromptu journeys to villages across Ijowaland were not uncommon in the day-to-day life of an *Aremo-Oba*. This made it easy for Adeyanju, upon receiving the coded message, to depart from Ode-Ijowa the next day at dawn without causing any concern from wife and family. He found this aspect of his responsibility very useful, as it provided him with excuses to travel and engage in his rituals.

'The woman I want you to meet is living across the river in Lower-Oluweri,' Fatunbi told Adeyanju the moment he arrived at the shrine. 'The fewer people you are in contact with, the less the risk. You will have to wait here till about sundown, when most people have finished their daily chores and are resting within their compounds. That is when you will go and visit her at her place. You will change into this while I wait in the yard.' The diviner handed the prince a bundle of cloth. 'Please call out for me when you finish, and I will tell you all the relevant information you need to start a rapport with her.'

Adeyanju changed from his princely attire to the one brought by Fatunbi. It was a decent but moderate outfit, an ideal grade befitting the personality which Fatunbi want him to assume.

'The name of the woman you will be meeting is Lalonpe,' Fatunbi continued. 'She is a widow and her late husband was a trader called Iyanda Kekewura. He died close to four seasons ago due to injuries sustained from an attack by bandits while on a trade transit to Ashanti.'

Fatunbi told Adeyanju all he had learnt about Lalonpe, which would enable the prince to support his claim that he was a long-time friend of her late husband. 'Now remember this very well. To that woman you are Morilewa, a travelling trader from the Omomose compound in Egbejoda.'

'You think there is no way they can meet, or circumstance that might prompt this woman to want to know more about Morilewa?' said Adeyanju. 'It is not only morally responsible but natural that before the relationship is anywhere near the stage that could result in my desire, this woman will seek to know more about Morilewa on her own. The first thing she will do is to go to the Omomose family compound and make enquiries.'

'The two ways they can meet is either Morilewa himself approaches the woman and as you rightly pointed out, she goes to Egbejoda to confirm. As I have explained to you, Morilewa considered my agreement to come between him and Lalonpe to be a great favour, so I don't see any reason why he will want to see her without considering the option of going through me. Meanwhile, if the woman chooses to make personal enquiries, the first thing she will avoid is to come into physical or visual contact with Morilewa while in Egbejoda. Hence, the focus of her inquiries will be limited to Morilewa's personality and the reputation of the Omomose family, and her finding will in no way contradict the little you need to tell her about Morilewa, only to convince her that you are truly her late husband's associate.'

The diviner then escorted the prince from the old shrine along an old and abandoned pathway to a part of the riverbank where he had already moored a canoe. At the riverbank Fatunbi produce a pouch made from animal skin and handed it over to Adeyanju. 'Now it is important that you pass this on to her as I have explained to you. And also remember, for this first visit, you must not give her any other presents of your own apart from this. When you return, just leave the canoe here and I will be waiting for you at the old shrine.' Fatunbi then rowed off across the river towards Lower-Oluweri.

The family of Lalonpe were wealthy in their Erebe homeland

and her father could afford the services of *Onikola* to make the tribal mark for all his children, hence her family was denied settlement in Ijowa. The family moved on to Abatan and resettled on a leased farmland in a peasant-dominated village called Mosinu. Lalonpe grew up in Mosinu and lived there until she met and married Iyanda Kekewura, an Ijowa man from Kuluso.

After marriage, Lalonpe, as expected, left Mosinu to join her husband in Kuluso, and before the turn of the season they were blessed with a baby boy whom they named Ojo. The year after the birth of Ojo, the family left Kuluso to seek better fortune in trade. Iyanda's mother was from Oluweri, and his maternal uncle offered him a place in his maternal family compound in upper Oluweri. Within a couple of years, they had established a flourishing trade in herbs and spices at Oluweri market. By the turn of their fourth year in Oluweri, they had acquired enough wealth to contemplate having a home of their own and being an Ijowa 'son of the soil', Iyanda was able to purchase and build a house for his family across the river in Lower-Oluweri.

The family's ambitions came to a tragic end when Iyanda embarked on a journey with a band of other traders to seek his fortune in the gold mines of the Ashantis. Just over a month after their departure, his crippled form was brought, half dragged and half carried, by four of the adventurers back to Oluweri. The story was that bandits had attacked Iyanda and his fellow travellers between Igbesa and Idomi. Iyanda was suspected of having been struck by an *olonde* (charm), and the result had been the total malfunction of a full half of his body. Although his hearing was intact, Iyanda was brought back to Oluweri without the power of speech, blind in his right eye and stiff in his right hand and leg.

The parents and family of Iyanda had been very supportive materially and emotionally. For fear of making Iyanda's condition deteriorate if he was made to endure another journey from Oluweri to Kuluso, the *Olori-Ebi* (family head) advised, and the family agreed, that it was better to let him rest for a while before arranging such a movement. Furthermore, Lalonpe was three months pregnant with their second child, and it was considered unwise to let her endure such a journey, especially when she was still recovering from the tragedy of her husband. The conception was the factor that had made it both necessary and possible for Iyanda to embark on the trip in the first place. Fortune adventurers and hunters of the big forests embarking on journeys which could span months preferred to leave their wives in that state to avoid the power of temptation. It was immoral for a man to engage in clandestine romance with somebody else's wife, and such an act was considered a serious taboo, which no sane man would contemplate if the woman was pregnant. It was decided that Iyanda would stay in Oluweri until Lalonpe had her baby.

Once a month, the family sent supplies of foodstuffs and cowries to Lalonpe in Oluweri to supplement whatever remained of Iyanda's fortune until he was well enough to be brought back to Kuluso. Her mother-in-law also came over from Kuluso to assist in nursing Iyanda and assist the expectant mother when the time came. But the latter was not to be, as Lalonpe had her baby months before the time was due. It was stillborn.

For three years before Iyanda finally died, apart from

the little assistance that her husband's family could afford to render from Kuluso, Lalonpe struggled alone to meet the demands of her household. She refused the assistance of many willing suitors through the five years that her husband was bedridden, labouring through the day and enduring lonely nights until the death of Iyanda. She earned her living working as a hired hand for various miscellaneous tasks ranging from minor domestic chores to labour-intensive tasks on farms across Ijowa.

Her life took a dramatic turn when on a rainy afternoon a travelling trader from Egbejoda who claimed to be an associate of her late husband visited her at Oluweri.

'I am sorry about the death of your husband,' he said, as rehearsed with Fatunbi. 'I ought to have been on the same journey that claimed his life, but I suffered a guinea worm infestation. It was so severe that I thought I would lose my leg.'

'There is purpose for everything. Maybe if you had made the journey you would not be here today,' Lalonpe reasoned.

'You are quite right there. I consider myself fortunate, as my situation is a price anyone would be glad to pay in exchange for life. But for my leg, I would have loved to travel down and see your husband before he passed away. It is that regret that compelled me to seek you, in hopes of honouring an agreement between me and your husband before he embarked on his tragic journey.' Adeyanju dipped his hand into the pocket of his *agbada* (over garment) and produced the pouch full of cowries which Fatunbi had given him. He placed the sack on the floor between himself and Lalonpe.

'I do not like to bother you with the details, but Inside that pouch is your husband's share of the profit from a trade we were both involved in months before his illness,' Adeyanju said.

Lalonpe was very pleased to see the money, presenting itself as an opportune lifeline. As a token of her appreciation, she made an elaborate meal and insisted that Morilewa must eat before continuing on his trade trip.

'I am not travelling beyond Igbesa, so I hope to be passing this route on my return journey to Egbejoda in about a fortnight. If you don't mind, I will endeavour to pay you another vist then,' Adeyanju promised before leaving.

'You are welcome any time,' Lalonpe answered cheerfully.

Two weeks later, Adeyanju made another visit to Oluweri to see Lalonpe. Because he was supposed to be returning from Igbesa, he had sought the help of Fatunbi to have ready something of value from Awori Market to give to her as a gift, and more importantly, as unspoken evidence that he was returning from Igbesa.

Although by the end of his second visit the message had not been conveyed verbally, Lalonpe was sure that Adeyanju's interest in her was beyond ordinary acquaintance. While she was not altogether surprised when during their next meeting Adeyanju expressed his wish to marry her, she felt a bit uneasy at the speed at which the affair was developing.

'It is barely a month since we first met, and this is just our third meeting,' she said. 'I know very little about you and there's no way I can know all I need to know about you to commit myself to your proposal. The only thing you know about me is my name and that I am a widow, and all

I know about you is what you told me, which, considering what you are asking, amounts to almost nothing.'

'I come from the Omomose family in Egbejoda. Ask even a toddler and he will point to my family's compound. And I am a successful trader on my own account.' He was surprise that he actually felt like the person he was claiming to be.

In the following months Adeyanju made as many clandestine trips as possible to Lower-Oluweri to visit Lalonpe. For every visit, he followed the routine as planned and arranged with Fatunbi, sending a discreet message to the priest advising of his intended passage through Oluweri to, or from, somewhere. This message would prompt the priest to make available a change of clothes at the old shrine for Adeyanju, to keep his princely attire and paraphernalia before proceeding to Lalonpe's home. The diviner of course was handsomely rewarded after every visit.

The problem which Adeyanju had been envisaging arose when he tried making sexual advances to Lalonpe. She absolutely refused to go further with the relationship until 'necessary steps' had been properly observed.

'Listen *ogbeni* (gentleman), and listen very carefully,' she began. 'Yes, I am a widow and I have been a widow close to five years, but I am not starving. I am not going any further in this relationship until the right thing has been done and in the right way, so that the result will be unblemished. I did not fall down from the sky, and neither did you. If you are really serious about taking our friendship further, then you must make preparation to meet my family, and then I will follow you to Egbejoda to meet yours.'

Adeyanju realised that he had to tell her something, but not before she had sworn to keep his secret. Lalonpe obliged. He went out of the hut and came back with an old cutlass he had found lying on the ground. He placed the cutlass in Lalonpe's hand.

'Swear by Ogun, the god of iron that you will never see the dawn if you reveal what I am going to tell you now,' he said. Lalonpe swore and Adeyanju then proceed to tell her everything except his true identity. He was truthful about his accident and the treatment by his herbalist but kept Fatunbi out of it. He was also truthful about his fear due to the accident and his concern that his wife was yet to have a child after over three years of marriage. Everything he said was the truth, except for who he actually was and where he came from.

'It is important that I seek clarification for this nagging suspicion,' he said. 'My mother is restless about my reluctance to take a second wife. But then she does not know my secret and my fear. I will not need to take the third wife before all the townspeople begin pointing their accusing fingers at me concerning who is to be blame for the silence in my yard and the settled water pot in my wives' chambers. The only way to be sure that the situation has nothing to do with myself as a man is to engage with a stranger, but at the same time I must be able to keep my secret if at the end of the day it turns out that the problem is with me and not my wife.' Adeyanju paused to consider Lanlope's reaction. It was already clear what he was suggesting so he had to tread carefully so as not to offend her. Unable to discern her thoughts, he decided to press on. 'That is why I must take a new relationship beyond doubt before making the affair known to friends, associates and families. You are not under any compulsion to cooperate with me on this matter. All I asked, and which you have sworn to respect, is my secret.'

'I will not deny that your generosity to me and my son in the past few weeks has been helpful,' replied Lalonpe, after a brief moment to search her feelings. 'What you are requesting of me is not strange and most women of similar situation like mine would only be too willing to oblige. But I want you to be clear on the exact terms and conditions of this relationship.'

'My proposal to you will be plain but very fair,' replied Adeyanju. 'I will marry you the moment you are pregnant and it is visible to all eyes. However, while we are waiting, I will take care of you and Ojo without reservation. Consider your acceptance of my request as a special favour to me and I promise you will not regret it. If, regretfully, we have to put an end to the relationship for the obvious reason, I promise to continue to support you to the best of my ability. Now that I have told you everything, I want you to give me the answer now, and I will bother you no further on the subject.'

'I have listened well,' said Lalonpe after a long and thoughtful silence. 'However, there is one thing which I will insist upon before giving any thought to your proposal.'

'Tell me what you want me to do and I will do it.'

'I want you to find somebody of affluence either here in Oluweri or within Ijowa who can vouch for your character and who will be a sworn witness to our affair,' Lalonpe replied, and Adeyanju suggested that they invite the *Ifa* priest to be a witness.

'Baba Fatunbi in upper Oluweri has been my long-time

confidant and spiritualist. He knows my family compound in Egbejoda and has met at least two of my relatives whom I have brought to him in the past for one assistant or the other. I don't know if his word in my defence would be enough for you.'

'I know the priest and respect him. Yes, I believe his words should be enough for now.' Lalonpe could not be more assured than that. She reasoned that if her suitor could persuade this priest to bear witness to his promises, if somebody of *Baba* Fatunbi's social and spiritual standing was willing to defend his identity and character, there was no reason to worry.

'Fine, then I will arrange for that to happen during my next visit,' Adeyanju said and left.

'She refused to have any intimacy with me until proper procedure had been followed,' Adeyanju told Fatunbi when he returned to meet the priest at the old shrine. 'I had to tell her part of my story, but she insisted that I must bring a well-known person to be witness to our affair.'

'I had envisaged such a problem. She is a woman of high dignity and I didn't expect things to move more smoothly than this. I am sure it was the background information that has influenced her cooperation so far.'

'I told her you have been the family healer for two generations and capable of vouching for my integrity.'

'That is all right by me except that at this juncture, it becomes my duty to warn you of certain responsibilities and obligations attached to this ritual. If your concern had been for naught and the gods grant your wife the fortune to bear you a child, you are at liberty to end the affair even without the consent of this woman. On the other hand, I must warn you that in no circumstances should you let a person of royal blood be raised outside the palace. To make my words clearer, in the event that your relationship with this woman results in the purpose for which you approach her, you are bound by the sixteen deities of the land to do justice to mother and child. Mark my words, the deities will always ensure that right is done.' Adeyanju committed the priet's warning to memory and thanked him for his time.

On his next visit to Oluweri a week later, Adeyanju informed Lalonpe that he had asked the priest for the favour and had agreed to meet them at the old shrine. They went and the *Ifa* priest confirmed all Adeyanju had said. That night they laid together and Lalonpe gave the comfort of her body to him. Although their bed was a single dry worn-out mat laid on the rough floor, so different from the comfort of the many new mats laid on the smooth floor of his bedchamber at the palace, Adeyanju had never been so content. He basked in the release of the burden he had shouldered through the years. For her part, Lalonpe enjoyed the comfort of a man for the first time in almost five years.

Before leaving the next morning, Adeyanju gave Lalonpe a small sack. It was small enough to be tied on to the waist and hidden under the waist wrapper, but it weighed more than it appeared. Lalonpe's excitement on checking the contents of the sack was a sight to behold. She nearly fainted as she saw inside it, glowing despite the poor illumination from the oil lamp, six gold coins.

'Keep that until I am back,' he told her. 'It is just part of the dowry I intend paying the family of your late husband.'

'I thought you planned this to happen when I was carrying your baby and it was visible for all eyes to see?'

'That is what I meant when I said I would not abandon you no matter your decision. Anyway, something deep in my mind keeps telling me that it will happen sooner than we expected, if not already.'

'I knew you were a successful trader, but I did not know you were also a seer,' she said with a smile.

'You will hail my foresight when by this time next month you have not seen a 'visitor'. Then you will be sure there will be no 'visitor' for you for the next nine months. Then the only person you need to care for is the landlord, and that is me.'

'I hope with all my heart that it is so. By the favour of the deities, so it shall be.'

On the day Adeyanju gave her a mirror, Lalonpe was filled with joy. It was the first time she had ever touched one. The only time she had been allowed to look in a mirror had been when her father had made the family embark on a journey to Aromire specially to see in one. Her father paid in cowries for each member of the family to see through the 'amazing shining panel that turns everything to two'. And now she had her own!

She showed it to her son in the same way she normally displayed the gifts given to her by Adeyanju. For the first time Ojo was privileged to look into the mirror and see his image, his 'second person', as he had never seen it before; not distorted, like looking into a river, but crystal clear from a shiny panel the size of a baby's palm.

On another of his visits, Adeyanju met Ojo sitting in front of the house and playing on an old and wobbly *agidigbo*. The *agidigbo* is a musical instrument whose main components are flexible metal panels screwed on top of a wooden box. The metal panels are screwed in different lengths and positions to give different keys. The *agidigbo* is very popular across the tribes and being able to recognise and understand as many proverbs or adages as possible when played on an *agidigbo* is part of growing up. Most of the popular proverbs played on the *agidigbo* are also parts of folklore stories used to entertain children during the evening by moonlight. Players are expected to communicate with listeners, in rhythms laden with Yoruba proverbs and adages. Hence their performances are rated according to the ability to communicate in many complex Yoruba proverbs and adages through the rhythm of the *agidigbo*.

The *agidigbo* was one of Adeyanju's favourite musical instruments. Its soothing rhythms were his primary respite from princely duties, and he had employed a string of expert players among friends and palace staff for his entertainment. Adeyanju stopped at the doorstep to listen to the young boy playing, not because he expected him to play anything extraordinary but just to flatter him, but he found himself entirely enthralled by his performance and he drew a stool to sit beside Ojo. Although Ojo's performance was nowhere near the performance of boys from his age group who had had the privilege of entertaining in the palace, Adeyanju sensed that given a good *agidigbo* and a proper tutor, Ojo could be groomed into a top player before he was out of adolescence.

'Your son is a born talent on the *agidigbo*. How long has he been playing?' Adeyanju asked Lalonpe inside the house.

'Oh, since the turn of his fourth season, but his ability

is not improving, and I keep telling him that plain rhythms are not enough if he is to get anywhere with it. He needs to work on his adages and proverbs as well.'

'You are right, the rhythm will soon be flat without a regular input of proverbs and adages,' Adeyanju agreed. 'I will teach him some adages, but first he needs a better *agidigbo*. I have a friend at Aromire who is an expert in drums and *agidigbos*. I will ask him to make one suitable for a learner of his age.'

On his next visit, Adeyanju took a small collapsible *agidigbo* made from well-polished mahogany. Each side of the wood and the base of the box were fitted with hinges so that the instrument could be collapsed into just four small panels of woods, packed into a small sack and then re-assembled when needed. It had undoubtedly been made by an expert and was of the highest quality. Ojo was over the moon with excitement when Adeyanju presented him with the musical instrument in a sack.

Before he left, he taught Ojo an adage and promised to teach him more as soon as he was able to master it.

'I expect you to be able to fit this into your rhythms by the time I come back,' he said. 'Then I will teach you another.'

'Igi ti a fehinti, ti ko gba ni duro' (A tree that cannot support one body weight).

'Bowo luni ko le pani,' (it cannot crush one to death) said Ojo.

Ojo promised Adeyanju that he would be very fluent on the *agidigbo* before Adeyanju's next visit.

CHAPTER 3

Trade connections between the people of Akete and white merchants from across the big ocean were via the Saro merchants who travelled down on large canoes from the Ashantiland, and across the waters between Idomiland and Aromire. It was through the many tiny waterways between the seafront and Epetedo that exotic goods from across the ocean entered the major markets of the Akete mainlands, Ijowa, Abatan, Eba-Odan and Ibini. Epetedo was an Akete community, and due to its economic importance to the palace at Aromire, the occupier of the seat of the *Baale* of Epetedo was strictly by the appointment of *Oba* Lagbade, the king of Aketeland.

It was also through these narrow waterways that the first white merchant who was also an explorer arrived on Akete soil. The name of the explorer was Fidel Wontsay, but the locals found it convenient to forge for him a name in the local language that was close to the sound of his name and renamed him Fadahunse which, in Yoruba, literally means 'the oracle is a lone achiever'. But the arrival of Fadahunse was a disappointment of sorts to the king and people of Akete. They were expecting a merchant who would bring articles of trade like those found in the Idomi and Ashanti markets. What they got was not merchants or wealthy seafarers but a band of frail-looking and tired seekers of the unknown places and rare articles of the earth. Their stock included nothing of real trade value. The gifts they brought as a gesture of peace were six muskets and a small barrel of gunpowder, about a hundred yards of textiles and half a dozen bottles of rum, and they did not extend beyond the palace and compounds of a few Akete high chiefs. While the palace at Aromire did not offer sanctuary for the explorer on the palace town, *Oba* Lagbade did not entirely withhold his mercy from the white men.

'I understand that what the white man brings forth is not what we had expected, but I will tell you this,' he said during an emergency consultation on how to deal with the white visitors. 'To shut our eyes in order to avoid seeing bad people risks missing the good ones that pass by. One who wishes his gains to multiply must once in a while be ready to risk the loss of a fraction. To get a profit, you may have to pay for some fakes at the beginning. That is why I will not turn the explorer away. To maintain a safe distance, I have decided to allow the visitors to settle at Iseri.'

Oba Lagbade played a positive role by allowing the settlement of Fidel Wontsay in Iseri. The visitors arrived on the eve of the *Oro* ritual. The *Oro* masquerade was an exclusively male cult and it was taboo for women to see it. The explorer and his people had already crossed from Eti-Osa into Iseri via one of many tributaries of the Awoyaya river that ran through the southern part of Aketeland into the ocean, before the villagers were alerted by the royal messenger that had come with the visitors from Aromire. On hearing this, Orija, the *Baale* of Iseri, quickly ordered fifty strong men to erect a big ban (tent) on the outside edge of the forest that lay between Iseri and the seafront to harbour everybody. Wontsay and the other males were only allowed outside from the third of the day till sundown. The two women among them were barred from leaving the tent throughout the four days and nights left for the conclusion of the seven-night ritual. That was how Fidel Wontsay and his entourage were sheltered and fed while the ritual lasted.

There was one question which none of the elders of Iseri ever bothered to ask, or which they were wise not to ask for fear of risking the anger of the palace at Aromire: 'If Oba Lagbade is so concerned about the welfare of the settlers, why did he not offer them an abode close to the palace on Aromire?' Instead he sent the explorers to Iseri, a minority settlement on the border between Akete and Ijowaland. The elders of Iseri reasoned that while they were not in a position to refuse the orders of Oba Lagbade, they could at least be the ones to decide which part of their land was appropriate for the visitors. They met and agreed to arrange a settlement for the explorer and his people at their present location.

'There is no better way of safeguarding that side of our forest and at the same time being in the good favour of Oba Lagbade than a compound for the white man,' the *Baale* of Iseri had rightly observed.

The side of the forest which the *Baale* and elders of Iseri decided could remain Wontsay's settlement extended to a notorious part of the sea front through which organised gangs randomly entered farms and pillaged crops. However, it was ironically ideal for the visitors because from there, the forest opened up to the Atlantic after a walk from mid-morning to early noon, and far less time on a horse or donkey. The cool breeze from the ocean not only lessened the intensity of the hot dry climate, but blew the mosquitoes far into the hinterland and away from the explorers' settlement.

The month after his arrival and settlement at Iseri, Fidel Wontsay sought an audience with *Oba* Lagbade, and the latter hosted him in the palace at Aromire. During their discussion, at which *Oba* Lagbade only allowed three of his closest allies among the Akete titled chiefs to be present, Wontsay proposed a trading arrangement in which the king would provide the land and people to cultivate cash crops and Wontsay in turn would provide the market and ensure that the palace got the best price for the crops.

'Tell the *oyinbo* (white man) that while I appreciate his gesture, I have yet to see why I need him or his facilities in engaging in this trade,' said *Oba* Lagbade through an interpreter. 'Tell him that I see nothing new in what he has come to say. Tell him that this palace has been cultivating crops for sale across the ocean since the time of my great-grandfather, and the market has not changed.'

'I am here to let the king know that it is possible to open up a market on his own shores rather than having to travel far with goods to other shores or having to rely on a third party to market his produce,' Wontsay explained. 'I know a family with strong interest in a shipping line and they can trigger the emergence of a new market if they are allowed to dock peacefully on your sea front.'

The interpreter relayed Wontsay's words to the king and the titled chiefs present. It was at this juncture that the king became interested. 'Tell the white man that his presence and time spent here in the palace will be worth his while, if indeed he can make possible what he has just said,' *Oba* Lagbade concluded and the meeting ended.

Three months later, Wontsay returned to the palace with the news that all arrangements had been concluded with a shipmaster, and a trade front would eventually be opened on Akete shore.

'I have journeyed down the Akete coast,' he told the king. 'I found Epetedo to be nearest to the most suitable part of the sea front in your territory for a merchant ship to dock.'

By the turn of the fourth month into the relationship and after about seven visits to Lalonpe, Adeyanju went away on a palace assignment to Gbemuyona and then Aiyefele. Because tradition forbade the king from attending funerals, Adeyanju would be representing the *Onijowa* at the seventh day burial rites for the *Baale* of Gbemuyona, who had just passed away. After Gbemuyona, he would be going to Aiyefele to honour an invitation to the opening day of the village's *egungun* (masquerade) festival.

On his return journey, Adeyanju made a detour to see Lalonpe at Lower-Oluweri. He had as usual sent a message to Fatunbi of his intending passage through Oluweri, but the messenger was grounded at Odinjo due to a sudden bout of malaria and was unable to get to Oluweri before Adeyanju.

'I will get men from here in Oluweri to escort me back to Ode-Ijowa,' he told his escorts. But because Fatunbi was not forewarned of Adeyanju's coming, the Ifa priest was away in the bush gathering herbs when the prince arrived. He reckoned that such activity was likely to keep the priest in the bush for longer than he was ready to wait, so he went ahead to the old shrine to make himself ready to visit Lalonpe.

'Tell *Baba* when he returns that I will be waiting for him at the old shrine,' he told one of the priest's apprentices, and left. At the old shrine, because the priest was not expecting him, there was no ordinary clothing for him to change into. He did not always travel in his full regalia, but the event he had just attended required that he should be clad in the full regalia of the *Aremo-Oba*, which was essentially a specially-designed *agbada* (big overgarment) and his *ejigbaileke* (a royal necklace made from exotic beads and precious stones of different sizes, shapes and shades on a single string).

Adeyanju decided to go to Lalonpe's house in his own clothes but without his paraphernalia, so he took off his *agbada* and the *ejigbaileke* and was fairly satisfied with the difference in his appearance. However, when he was within sight of Lalonpe's house he felt a bulge in the pocket of his *sokoto* (trousers) and realised he had forgotten to leave the *ejigbaileke* at the old shrine with his other paraphernalia. He started to look around for a place in the bush to hide it, but it was too late, because young Ojo had already seen him from afar and came running happily down the path to meet him.

In Lalonpe's home, Adeyanju was visibly restless with the beads in his pocket. If Lalonpe found the *ejigbaileke* on him she would immedialtely realise he was more than he let on to be. It was a popular saying across the tribe that 'the crown is for the king, the *ejigbaileke* is for the *Aremo-Oba*'.

Lalonpe noticed his uneasiness and asked what seem to be the problem.

'I think I need to relieve myself,' Adeyanju said, excusing himself and going into the yard, but Ojo lept after him excitedly. At the back of the house, Adeyanju tried to hide the *ejigbaileke* in an unused clay pot in the yard with the intention of picking it up when it was about time to leave, but he failed to notice Ojo, who was taking a keen interest in what he was doing.

'What is that?' Ojo asked, pointing at the pouch in Adeyanju's hand.

'It's a surprise present for your mother. I don't want her to see it until the right time.'

'When will the right time be?' Ojo asked excitedly.

'Very soon,' Adeyanju replied. 'But for now, I want you to promise me that it will be our secret and you will not mention it to your mother.' Ojo promised without hesitation. He felt very proud of himself that such a respected adult should find him worthy of sharing a secret.

At dawn, just after cockcrow, they were apologetically woken by Fatunbi, who had come to seek an urgent and private audience with Adeyanju. When they were alone, the priest informed Adeyanju of the sudden death of his uncle, the younger brother of the *Onijowa*.

'It was very late last night before I heard the news,' he said. 'That is why I set off from upper Oluweri at the crack of dawn to advise that you return to Ode-Ijowa on time for the burial.'

Adeyanju agreed that he should not be outside Ode-Ijowa in such circumstances. He told Lalonpe that he had to return to Egbejoda for an urgent matter but would not be able to explain it until his next visit.

'Fret not my daughter, he only needs to return to Egbejoda to attend to a crucial family matter,' Fatunbi assured Lalonpe. Adeyanju left as soon as he could get away without causing too much panic for Lalonpe.

Adeyanju had long gone before Ojo was awake. He remembered the surprise present hidden in the back yard. He wanted to ask his mother if 'Baba-Kekere' (meaning little father, as his mother had told him to refer to Adeyanju since the *Ifa* priest had become witness to the affair), had given her the present but decided to first have a look. Although he found the sack and its contents as they had left it the night before, he did not bother to examine it. He considered it his responsibilty to keep the surprise alive and hence decided not to tell his mother anything about it but to wait until Baba-Kekere returned to present it to his mother. Until then, he thought it wise to find a more secure place to keep the sack.

Shortly before sunrise, while his mother was away fetching fresh drinking water from the stream, Ojo went to the spot where he and Adeyanju had hidden the sack. He swept away the small layer of sand they had used to cover the half-broken clay pot. He retrieved the sack from the pot but could not resist the urge to have a quick look at the contents and was amazed by what he saw. He had never seen such a collection of shining beads and stones of different sizes and shapes. He covered the shallow hole, took the sack inside the house and put it in his knapsack.

In the evening, while the villagers were resting in groups and enjoying the moonlight, Ojo sneaked away to the community pottery place, found a small clay pot and returned home. He dug a hole in a corner of the back room and placed the pot in the hole. Satisfied that the hole was deep enough to conceal the pot without leaving a mound, he tried squeezing the small sack into the pot without taking out the beads but realised it would take a long time and he risked being surprised by his mother. Instead, he took the *ejigbaileke* out of the small sack and began threading it into the pot. One of the stones came off in the process, and as he was trying to re-attach it he heard his mother coming into the house. He quickly covered the pot with the lid, dragged the earth over it and tied the loose bead in a knot at the edge of his waist wrapper.

Lalonpe knew Adeyanju was not likely to be visiting again for at least two weeks, so she decided to use the time to make the journey she had been delaying for the past months. It was now becoming more imperative as the relationship between herself and 'Morilewa' grew stronger and more promising. She needed to take Ojo to see his father's family in Kuluso. The visit was overdue because he had been only five years old the last time she had taken him there. She also intended to use the opportunity to inform them of the possibility of her getting married again in the very near future.

The journey from Oluweri to Kuluso would take an average traveller two full days on land and river. But mother and child were not average travellers, and the journey was very likely to extend to the early hours of a third day. When Lalonpe set off at dawn with Ojo, her plan was to arrive at Kuluso by noon three days later. They boarded the canoe at Lower-Oluweri and arrived at Olokoto before dusk. The distance between Olokoto and

Gbajumo, where she planned to stop for the second night, was considerably shorter by land than by river.

They left Olokoto at the crack of dawn and began the trek through the pathways and farmlands that lay between Olokoto and Gbajumo in the hope of arriving at their destination before dark. It took mother and son longer than expected due to bad weather. It was raining so hard that they had to seek shelter at a small settlement about midway between Olokoto and Gbajumo and wait for the rain to subside. By the time it finally stopped, it was impossible for them to make it to Gbajumo that day, so they slept at the settlement for the night.

Mother and son set off the next dawn with the aim of bypassing Gbajumo and making it to Kuluso, their final destination, before dark. However, by early evening, when they got to Gbajumo, it was apparent that they would not be able to get anywhere near Kuluso before dark. This time it was not the weather but Lalonpe who was responsible for the delay. She fell sick many times and was so unsteady in her walking that she had to stop many times to rest. It took so long for her to recover that it became impossible for them to continue, so they reverted to her original plan to stop at Gbajumo. She sought and found shelter in the house of Labake, a childhood friend who had left Mosinu to live with her husband in Gbajumo. Labake had a large family of four children of her own plus three belonging to her deceased sister in-law, and she was also nursing her mother in-law, who was so ill that she had to be moved from her home in Gbajumo into a crowded shelter for proper attention and care.

Labake had to ask for a room from her neighbour, who lived about three yards away and was called *Iya* Mojoyin

(Mojoyin's mother) by her peers after her eldest child, but she was popularly known in Gbajumo and beyond as *Iya-Abiye* (the midwife) by virtue of her profession. She was the oldest and most experienced midwife in Gbajumo village, and under her all the midwives there had learnt the trade. *Iya* Mojoyin was a widow and was living alone in a four-room house because her children, all girls, had married and were living with their husbands.

'My dear daughter, you know very well that my house is open to all,' *Iya* Mojoyin told Labake. 'Do you imagine I will ever turn away a stranded visitor? Especially one who is also the family of a nice neighbour.'

Lalonpe and Ojo were made very welcome by the old woman. Labake tarried a little longer to see her friend settled before returning home.

'Are sure you don't want anything to eat?' *Iya* Mojoyin asked after Labake had left.

'No thank you mama, we ate at my friend's house the moment we arrived,' Lalonpe replied.

'What about some dry fish, or are you shy?'

'No mama, it is just that we were well fed at Labake house, and there is no space in my stomach even for a nut,' Lalonpe explained with sincere regret. 'But I will take some water for life.' She did not want to offend the woman by refusing her hospitality. She was too tired, and all she wanted was a place to lie down and sleep.

'If that is the case, then you must lick some honey to add sweetness to the life in the water,' *Iya* Mojoyin insisted.

The next morning, Lalonpe was getting ready to leave Gbajumo for the last lap of their journey to Kuluso when news came that conflict had once again broken out between the fishermen of Akete and those of Ijowa over fishing waters close to Kuluso on the Ijowa side and Seleru on the Akete side. Labake advised her to delay the journey to Kuluso for a few days and assess the situation. 'It is not a good judgement to knowingly plunge into a troubled environment,' she said. 'To be wise, a person with a mobility problem must take full advantage of a warning to get away.' Lalonpe heeded the advice and decided to stay in Gbajumo until the unrest was over.

It was not only the waters of that area that had resulted in confrontations between the border communities, but the lands. The right over an *akuro* (area of dry season farmland) that stretched across the southern boundaries of the Akete and Ijowa villages of Seleru and Kuluso respectively had also been the cause of almost seasonal violent confrontations between the two communities. The possibility of such confrontations was rife in seasons of extreme weather when the rain was either too heavy and incessant or too occasional and scanty. While the former could render the *akuro* unusable for months into the dry season, the latter could result in the gradual loss of over half the fishing grounds before the rain stabilised.

On each and every confrontation, before their anger was spent and the two palaces at Ode-Ijowa and Aromire intervened, both communities would have suffered material loss due to the conflict, as each party must have vandalised the other's canoes, fishermen's shacks and many dry season farmlands along the river. The latest conflict had been building up for close to a fortnight. The news had reached both palaces, but none considered the unrest beyond the usual strong feelings brought about by a threat to both communities' means of survival. But there had never been a time in the past when a single life was lost as a result of such confrontations. Three days before, on a rainy morning, the people of Seleru and other Akete villages along Awoyaya river had been awaken with the news that men believed to be acting in support of Kuluso fishermen had ambushed and taken hostage four Seleru maidens on their way from the river. The eyewitness, a fifth girl who was deliberately let loose after being seriously beaten, was sent with the message that the other girls would not be released until all Seleru fishermen had removed their canoes and all indication of their presence from the disputed fishing area.

'What other action did Agbebi take apart from sending you to the palace?' asked *Oba* Lagbade when a messenger from the *Baale* of Seleru arrived two days later at the palace at Aromire with the latest report. Agbebi was the *Baale* of Seleru.

'Kabiyesi, may the *alales* [deities] let your days be longer than those of your ancestors,' the messenger replied. 'My lord the *Baale* has sent emissaries on behalf of the palace here at Aromire to the palace at Ode-Ijowa, demanding the return of the kidnapped maidens without delay.'

It took the messengers from the *Baale* of Seleru two full days to travel from Seleru to Ode-Ijowa, but they were barely on the way back, and the *Onijowa* was still deliberating with his chiefs on the message from the palace, when news came that two Ijowa traders had been killed and another four seriously wounded at Eti-Osa market by some Akete youths believed to have carried out the deed in retaliation for the kidnapping of Seleru girls. The news of the incident at Eti-Osa got to Oluweri even before it reached the palace at Ode-Ijowa. Before dusk at least twenty Akete traders had had their stalls at Oluweri market looted and burnt to the ground. An eyewitness claimed that an Akete trader who insisted on defending his property was maimed then burnt in the same blaze that destroyed his merchandise.

The hostility had extended to neighbouring settlements on both the Akete and the Ijowa sides even before any of the palaces were able to complete a cycle of communication on the matter. The conflict which many had thought would be resolved in a matter of days, as had been the case with past communal disputes, escalated to the first fully-fledged war between the two palaces just over a week after the first casualty was recorded. This conflict will be remembered as not only responsible for the deaths of many Seleru and Kuluso fishermen, but also the first direct and bloody confrontation between warriors loyal to the palace at Ode-Ijowa and those of Aromire, the deaths of many Ijowa and Akete warriors, and the panic fleeing of many townspeople on both sides of the divide into captivity and enslavement.

Gbajumo was the closest community to Kuluso and the second on the Ijowa side to feel the full impact of the conflict. The attack on Gbajumo came just nine days after the conflict started. It was carried out by a band of Akete warriors sent down from the palace at Aromire specifically to protect the people of Seleru and neighbouring Akete settlements against further attacks. The Akete warriors, led by Eso Akinku (head of battalion), were overwhelmed with emotion on arrival by the extent of the havoc wrought on Seleru by the opposing mob from Kuluso, so much that Eso Akinku took it upon himself to launch a revenge attack on Ijowa soil without consulting the palace at Aromire. Eso Akinku knew full well that the opposing palace at Ode-Ijowa would have taken similar measures by sending reinforcements to protect the people of Kuluso, so in order to ensure maximum casualties, he decided to launch a surprise attack on a totally defenceless Ijowa village.

Almost half the Gbajumo men were away night hunting in the forest when the Akete warriors entered Gbajumo through a small Akete village called Apete. Their entrance was noiseless, and the first person to witness their arrival was a palm wine taper who had stayed late on the farm to make a last check of the gourds he hung on the necks of palm trees, and also to make sure that the sponges used to cover the gourds were still in place. The check was necessary in order to properly reposition them and any sponges that might have been disturbed by the movement of squirrels and rats as they jumped from one palm tree to another looking for ripe palm kernels to eat. If the sponge used to cover a gourd fell off, most of the wine he would expect to be funnelled into it would evaporate as soon as soon as it was deposited. Worse still, if the gourd itself was shaken out of position, the wine would just be dropping away.

He noticed one that needed readjustment, so he climbed up the tree to fix it. He was already at the top of the palm tree when he saw the attackers filing into Gbajumo. He kept rigid, partly hidden by the palm leaves, hoping and praying that he would not be noticed from the ground.

The palm wine tapper did not have the luxury of counting, but he was certain that the invaders were up to fifty in number. A few of them had guns and the rest were armed with either clubs or cutlasses or both. He reasoned that the only way he could help was to get men, and the best for the present situation were those awake, active and armed. He had recently passed a group of hunting youths with slings and urged them to be careful with their shots. He very well remembered that one had assured him that none of his gourds would be disturbed as they were not hunters of rats and rabbits and would not be chasing any game up palm trees. He suspected the youths were after guinea fowl as they followed the southern path, downhill toward the spring where the birds retired at night to drink, rest and prepare themselves for the dawn flight.

So as soon as the warriors had passed, he quickly but as silently as possible climbed down from the palm tree and raced after the hunters. His age was not helping, but he continues until he was able to locate them. He knew there was no limit to what he must endure to get to the youths.

He sighted them beyond the place he envisaged. It was risky to call out for them, so he struggled up the hill to get a wider view of the area. It took all the strength he could draw from his ageing limbs to reach the top of the hill. The boys were in the process of trapping a rabbit when they heard the footsteps of the taper as he rushed down the slope to join them. He was breathing heavily by the time he got to them and it took some time before he could say anything sensible.

The Akete warriors, led by Eso Akinku, sneaked into the village and began raiding houses and compounds. As each household was captured, the people were taken to the outpost in order not to wake the other villagers.

The night had started badly for Labake, the third and youngest wife of Kolapo Alao. On the night her destiny was abruptly redefined, she had declined to honour her husband's invitation to his bedroom, which she was sure was intended for a second intimate session in a day. She complained of aches and begged her husband to let her be, at least for the night. When it was becoming apparent that Kolapo was not intending to let her off easily, she bolted out of the bedroom and out into the front yard, ignoring her husband's order to return to his room immediately. She sat and remained on the front yard while Kolapo's ranting echoed through the yard.

Lalonpe was awake because she needed to relieve herself. Before leaving the room, she gave Ojo a nudge and asked if he needed to urinate, but Ojo said he was fine. As Lalonpe was going to the back of the house, she noticed Labake sitting alone and murmuring in protest. Lalonpe wondered why her friend was sitting outside and alone in the middle of the night. She went across to find out what the trouble was, but it took some persuasion before she was able to make Labake even whisper the cause of the dispute between her and her husband. She told Labake to wait for her and bolted to the back of the compound to avoid soiling herself.

Akete warriors must have been lying in ambush in the yard before Labake stormed out of her husband's hut, and they were ready to pounce when Lalonpe suddenly emerged. Silently the three men pounced upon Labake as soon as Lalonpe had disappeared to the back of the compound. Before Labake could make a noise, her head was covered with a big sack filled with yam flour. She tried to shout from under the big sack, but she choked as dust from the flour filled her throat.

Lalonpe was still in the middle of her natural business when she heard slight commotions coming from where she just left her friend. Her first thought was that Kolapo had decided to push his authority further by physically dragging his wife back into the house. She hurriedly cleaned herself with leaves and returned to see what was going on. She found that the space where she had left her friend just a few moments before was vacant. She thought maybe Labake had returned to the house. The door was still wide open, so she peeped through to check.

'Labake, are you all right?' She called from outside, but there was no response. 'Have you gone back in now?' She called again; still no response.

'Lalonpe, don't worry yourself,' Kolapo replied from within. 'That is her usual way, she will come back inside when she is ready.'

'But she is not here and nowhere about. I just want to be sure she is fine.'

That was the last Kolapo heard of Lalonpe before she suffered the same treatment as her friend at the hands of Akete warriors.

Three compounds had been quietly attacked and about eighteen captives taken before the palm wine tapper could locate the hunting youths. The intention of the invaders was to take as many captives as possible before the villagers were awake, but the alarm was raised earlier than expected, and not from within, but by the youths, who raced into the community brandishing machetes and chanting war songs. Eso Akinku had briefed his men about the next course of action when this unavoidable situation eventually occurred. He had summoned a team that would at the sound of the first alarm begin to set fire to as many houses as possible, while the main combatants began withdrawing with the captives via their entry point.

Ojo was not able to return to sleep after his mother had left the room. He just lay awake on the mat waiting for her to return and was among the first to react to the sudden cacophony of noise that pierced the quiet of the night from different directions. He rushed out to see the first fires that arose from different parts of the village. He looked frantically around for his mother as people began pouring into the street, most confused and still not fully awake enough to comprehend what was going on.

On instinct, Ojo raced to the back of the compound and looked through the bamboo fence used to separate off a private area for adults, but his mother was not there. He then raced back into the compound to look for her as more people began trooping out of their various homes. Some were fully awake, and many were still trying to register what was going on. It was the peak of the tropical dry season, and most adults were in their scanty sleeping clothes, while almost all the children were practically naked as their parents dragged them from their sleep into the open.

Ojo ran into the house to check if his mother had returned, but she was not there. Like other children, Ojo went to sleep in thin underpants. He was about to run out again, then realised he needed to put something on. The clothing he had worn the previous day was still wet as it had been washed by his mother as soon as he was ready for bed. He returned to the room and frantically rummaged through his sack for another cloth, coming out with a *buba* (top) and *sokoto* (trousers). While he was pulling them out, the single bead that had got detached when the string broke as he was trying to stuff the neckbead into the claypot fell out of the sack. He wriggled into his *sokoto*, picked up the single stone and tucked it into the inner pocket of his *sokoto*.

Then in a flash, two of the houses in the compound caught fire. He ran out of the compound to see more houses already on fire and more bursting into flames in quick succession. On instinct, he joined the other villagers as they fled from different directions to the nearest exit out of the village towards the forest. He was hardly in the forest and still struggling with his buba when a strange but strong arm forcibly wrapped it around his head and lifted him off the ground before he could make a sound.

When the lions are on the hunt, the hyenas will never be far away from their trail to pick up the carcasses left behind after the pride has had its fill. As the Akete warriors were marching through the night into Kuluso, on their trail were the hyenas – the opportunists and warmongers. While the Akete warriors were silently ripping through the houses and compounds, gangs of rogues laid ambush at strategic points in the forests surrounding Gbajumo to benefit from the confusion that was bound to follow. They pounced upon fleeing villagers with the aim of taking captives. One such pack of opportunists was a trio of young men called Kudoro, Jebooda and Akodu. The strange but strong arm that lifted Ojo of the ground was that of Jebooda.

Altogether 53 captives were taken by Eso Akinku and his men during the attack on Gbajumo; 13 men, 17 women and 23 children. While it was not an uncommon practice among warriors to take their share of the spoils of war for personal gain before they were officially presented to the king and his council of chief, it was also the normal practice of palaces to have their own intelligence teams, headed by the palace curator, who was answerable to the king alone and responsible for finding out if there was any difference between the actual quantity and value of the spoils that were presented to the palace. One of the basic but crucial tactics used by the fact-finding team was to privately interview the captive and make him tell them (in return for amnesty ranging from deployment to privilege duty while in captivity to unconditional freedom depending on the value of the spoils recovered) if there was anybody they knew or any item of value which they were aware of which was not among the spoils declared to the king's curator.

On the other hand, there were basic but crucial countermeasures taken by warriors to avoid such unfortunate exposure during random questioning by the fact finders. The first was to prioritise captives who were not residents of the pillaged community but had simply been unfortunate enough to be in the village during the raid. Hence, strangers were usually the first to be eligible because they were unlikely to be missed by other captives and residents of the raided community. The second measure was to prevent captives being delivered to the palace from knowing the fate of fellow victims, especially those intended to be sold through the 'back door'. Finally, and most importantly, the captives must be 'made ready for sale'.

As soon as they were well out of Ijowa soil, but before they arrived at any Akete settlement, all the spoils from each invading team were brought together for the first official inventory. The witnesses to the inventory would be selected by the troop commander, and given his agenda, Eso Akinku selected men with whom he had previously conspired to defraud the king of his spoils. Strong young men and beautiful women attracted premium returns at Ojuoro market. So after careful judgement, Lalonpe and

three other young maidens were among nine captives that
Eso Akinku and his fellow conspirators considered eligible
and safe to be removed before they arrived at the palace
on Aromire.

CHAPTER 4

The word 'Ojuoro' literarily means the eye or epicentre of callousness, and the Ojuoro night market was only patronised by the brave and the crafty. The market was on Abatan soil, but it could be accessed directly by both Akete and Ijowa people without transgressing on foreign soil. The people of Ijowa could enter Ojuoro through Gbemuyona village and the people of Akete had access via Gbengbele. The control of the market in principle was supposed to be under the jurisdiction of the *Baale* of Igisogba, who in turn was answerable to the king of Abatan, but in practice Ojuoro was ruled by a blend of rich traders, nobles and degenerate lords of criminal fraternities from across Abatan, Akete and Ijowa.

Ojuoro was a major dumping ground for the 'remnants and waste' resulting from the vices of the rich and the mighty across the tribes. Whenever a treacherous landlord decided to sell off some slaves for personal gain without the knowledge of the *Ajele*, who was the official eye of the crown in the community, or express approval from their respective palaces, the transaction would be done at Ojuoro market. It was often said that there was nothing under the sun that could not be bought or sold there. It was also a common joke that the royal seat of the *Baale* of Igisogba only needed to be moved to the market and it would be sold off many times over within a single market session. This was the place where rare articles could be found and traded in exchange for others.

From livestock raided from farms and villages to looted antiquities from various shrines and palaces, anything could be found in Ojuoro if the price was right. From luxuries like exotic fabrics, gold, silver and beads, guns and gunpowder to articles like the feathers of rare birds, hides of rare animals and elephant tusks, all were readily available in exchange for slaves, and vice versa if you asked the right person. Hence Ojuoro was mainly patronised by rich and mighty traders capable of maintaining minimum but effective force to provide security for their persons and their merchandise.

As the market became popular, so also were more respectable landowners in farming communities around Ojuoro forced to sell or temporarily abandon their property, most of which was taken over by dubious landlords who used them as safe houses for their men and goods. The morning after each night market, it was not uncommon to find dead bodies with mutilated limbs on the site, due to bloody fights between and among rival gangs. Plainly, Ojuoro was a burden placed on the *Baale* and people of Igisogba not only by the king of Abatan to whom the people of Igisogba paid seasonal tribute but also by the kings and *ogunagbongbos* from across Ijowa and Akete.

The night market was held once a fortnight. For a couple of days before every market night, these otherwise quiet communities around Ojuoro market would have been overwhelmed with traders and visitors from as far as Ibadan, Oyo and even Ibini, and it would remain active and buzzing with people until the morning after. Then until the next market, the eight or so communities that had originally established the site as their meeting point for daily trading would use the site for normal day-to-day trading.

To make them 'ready for sale' at Ojuoro, Lalonpe and other captives would be forced to drink a special herb called *amunimuye* to make them lose their memories and general sense of identity. Captives were made to drink *amunimuye* at regular intervals for at least five days and nights for it to be effective. The secret of preparing and admistering it was limited to a very few herbalists and medicine men, and its ingredients were hard to find, so making captives suitable for sale could be very expensive. For ethical reasons, the administration of herbs like *amunimuye* was strictly regulated. There was a consensus amongst herbalists not to administer it without the permission of a king or delegated authority. But there would always be a crooked medicine man willing to do the task via the back door if the reward is right. One such herbalist was called Eweje.

'Eweje will be waiting and ready for you at the agreed place,' Eso Akinku told Lasun, whom he had assigned to lead the transit. 'Fortunately, the next Ojuoro market is still eight days away. That will give the herbalist enough time to complete his task. I don't need to remind you how important it is that you ensure that the herbalist does a complete job. When he is done, look for a prospective buyer and arrange a quick sale. Try and engage in a shrewd bargain without expending too much time, as I want you back with the other warriors before your absence becomes too apparent. I expect you to have sorted things out and rejoined the army before we get to Aromire.'

The agreed place was the abode of Eweje, a herbalist who specialised in the treatment of various kinds of mental illness. The knowledge and administration of herbs for calming restless and aggressive patients was vital for practitioners in this area of medicine. It was Eweje who would prepare and administer the necessary herbs and infusions that would make the captive 'ready for sale' and it was at his place where the captives would be kept for the duration of the therapy and then to Ojuoro for sale. Eweje's place was in the middle of nowhere in the jungle between Gbengbele and Igisogba but had a direct route to Ojuoro. It consisted of a big mud house and many small single-roomed mud houses within a large area of ground which was fortified by bamboo fencing to prevent his patients from wandering away.

The captives had been made to drink *amunimuye* for two full days, but Lalonpe had been unable to keep anything inside her. For two days, she could not eat without vomiting and could only take in little water at a time, and her captors were already doubtful of her survival. Although she was getting weaker due to the sickness, her mental state was unaffected. The herbs and other materials used were not only rare and expensive, their preparation was laborious and time-consuming. Eweje had temporarily but privately discontinued Lalonpe's medication after she vomited up the first two doses. He knew his employers would insist that he continue to forcefeed her, but the infusions he prepared for her while she was vomiting were devoid of the expensive but essential herbs.

Meanwhile, Lalonpe had began to notice the difference between her and the other captives and was sure it was because her vomiting had prevented most of the medication from settling in her blood. The vomiting began to subside on their third day at the herbalist's place and she began to eat without throwing up, so he promptly recommenced the medication and Lalonpe thought it wise to comply, but she always managed to consume as little as possible and secretly dispose of the rest. She reckoned that she stood a better chance of escaping if her captors underestimated her abilities, so she pretended that she was also feeling the impact of the medicine and began behaving like the other captives.

By the end of the fifth day and two clear days before the Ojuoro market, all the captives except Lalonpe were no more than walking corpses. They were so mentally tamed that none of them could remember either their names or their origin, and only responded to new names given to them by Eweje. The guards no longer worried about the possibility of their attempting to escape and they were allowed to wander within the grounds, obediently returning from wherever they had wandered to when called.

Lalonpe was still thinking about how to utilise her comparatively clear mind to escape when an opportunity presented itself. It was already dark, and all the captives had been fed their second and last meal of the day and herded to their sleeping places. Lasun waited till all was quiet and sneaked inside the shed to where the female captives were sleeping. He went straight for Lalonpe and gagged her with thick spongy leaves before she could make a noise while the rest just lay there unconcerned and totally disconnected from reality. He dragged her out of the shed and into an old ban which the herbalist used as a form of conservatory for storing seasonal herbs and roots.

Lalonpe was wide awake on contact and was swift to react as Lasun lustfully pounced on her. She spat at him and Lasun hit her as she made to crawl away from under him. The impact of his open palm on Lalonpe's cheek splashed the second ball of saliva she was gathering in her mouth on both faces. She kicked and scratched and struggled, but Lasun would not let go. He rushed at her, pinioned her to the ground and began to struggle with her wrapper.

Lalonpe sank her teeth onto a fleshy part of her agressor's body as she tried to wriggle out from under him. Lasun groaned in pain and swung a glancing blow at her temple. The impact sent her rolling on the dusty ground. He was upon her in a flash and in blinding fury knocked her back onto the ground as she tried to get on her feet. Lalonpe screamed in agony as he kicked her continuously on the ground and his long toenails cut through her open thigh. She crawled out of range and rolled into a ball in the corner of the barn. He came over to her and jerked her upright, ripping right through the middle of her *iro* (waist wrapper). She stumbled and fell as he tried to drag her back to a relatively smooth spot in the centre of the shed with the end of her robe. He was upon her the moment she was on the floor and Lalonpe, realising she was getting tired and might not be able to hold out for too long, pretended to surrender and saved her last strength for the decisive moment. She found the right time to escape as Lasun tried to deploy one arm to untie the knot around her *iro*. She yanked herself free and bolted out of the ban. Lasun went after her, cursing and panting with lustful anger. Lalonpe headed for the fireplace, picked up a large piece of wood which was burning at one end and turned to face Lasun.

'I will stab your eyes with this if you move any closer!' she threatened. Lasun thought she was bluffing. He moved closer but carefully toward Lalonpe until there were just a few paces between them, then made a sudden leap to grab her. He was not quick enough and Lalonpe was able to step aside. He went flying across and landed face down on the spent ashes around the fireplace. As he turned to stand, Lalonpe was above him, and with blinding fury she pinned him down on the floor with the burning end of the wood. She kept the burning wood pressed upon him and he writhed in pain as he tried to free himself. Lalonpe in her fury was totally deaf to his cries of anguish. She was shocked by the hiss of the flaming end of the wood as it burnt through her aggressor's bare, sweat moistened belly and right into his stomach. She kept the burning end of the wood on Lasun's stomach until he suddenly became still and silent.

She could not say how long it was before the smell of his burning skin brought her out of her burning rage. It was an accident borne out of the strongest instinct to survive. Lalonpe had never intended to do the ultimate damage with the burning wood. Even in defence she could not imagine herself being able to inflict such harm against anybody. She had just wanted to scare him off and find a way to escape.

She dropped the glowing wood and then, as her mind fully registered the damage done to the stomach of the now apparently dead man as he lay in a pool of his own urine and faeces, she vomited. Half of Lasun's middle was roasted. For some time, she felt nothing; only a living fear that clung heavily to her chest. She dragged Lasun's body down to a little shrub to shield it from passers-by. Then she took the belt which held his sheath and dagger and tied it around her waist, keeping it well hidden under her half-torn *iro*.

Her first thought was to get as far away as possible before she was missed, and most importantly before Lasun's body was discovered. She ran as if she was being pursued by the devil himself. The path was very steep, and she often fell and rolled into the undergrowth. In blind panic she raced on, cutting through the thick bushes as she tried to figure out the way out of the forest and hopefully into a friendly community. It was getting dark and she could hardly see her hands before her face, but the terrible fear of being caught drove her on.

She soon began to fell dizzy and was not steady in her stride, so she decided to stop for a brief rest before continuing her flight. She found comfort against a broad, smooth boulder, and within a short period she was asleep.

The lifeless, cold body of Lasun was found in the morning, but the true story behind his death was hushed up by Eso Akinku and his clique. They buried him, and the official report stated that he was either missing or killed in action.

The people of Gbajumo were caught practically defenceless, as none were expecting the conflict to extend beyond the boundaries of the warring communities. It was not until the third day after the Akete warriors had wrought havoc on Gbajumo and gone that help arrived from the palace at Ode-Ijowa. The sudden and unprovoked attack against a peaceful community, whose people so far had not in action or words been involved with the conflict, and the unavoidably late arrival of salvation from Ode Ijowa served as a wake-up call for other Ijowa villages.

In Gbemuyona, the *Baale* and village elders launched an armed vigilante force that would act primarily as a deterrent against surprise attacks, as in Gbajumo. All the able men and youths of Gbemuyona were drafted and engaged on a rota basis to patrol the land and water boundaries between Gbemuyona and the neighbouring Akete village of Gbengbele. At dawn, as a team of vigilantes responsible for patrolling the forest that separated Gbemuyona from Igisogba were concluding their last patrol of the night, one of them found a woman clad in torn clothes sprawled like a dead person on the forest grass made wet by the night dews. After the initial shock, he called the attention of the group to the scene.

Since the attack on Gbajumo, there had been an influx of wounded and displaced persons into Gbemuyona, but no bodies. However, on closer inspection they were relieved to find that the woman was still breathing. The leader of the group bent over, tapped gently on her big toe, and then shook her leg. But Lalonpe, who after her ordeal the night before had fallen into a compulsive slumber, could not be awakened until he held her up and shook her on both shoulders.

Lalonpe could not tell for how long she had been sleeping before she began to feel some presence around her. It was like the sound of a distant gathering filtering into her gentle rest. The instant she felt a hand on her shoulder, she was awake. She looked up to see men standing above her. They seemed like vultures waiting for a wounded animal to die before feasting. Her first thought was that she had been found by Lasun's companions. She screamed and tried to get up, but while her mind was willing, her body was in no way up to the task. The men calmed her down and assured her that she was in friendly hands.

'Where am I?' she asked.

'You are in the middle of the forest.'

'I know that,' Lalonpe said, now fully awake and alert. 'But what is this place, and what am I doing here?'

'You are in Gbemuyona,' Labiran replied. 'As for what you are doing here, I think you are in the best position to answer that question.' He waited for Lalonpe to respond, but the more she tried to concentrate and provide an answer the more confused she seemed to become. Apparently, the few doses of *amunimuye* she had been unable to avoid had finally begun to take effect.

'I cannot remember,' she finally managed to reply.

'Let us start with an easier question. What is your name?' Labiran asked. Lalonpe took her time trying to process the question, and for a brief moment she brightened up as if she had found the right answer, only to go blank again like a lamp extinguished by a sudden gust of wind. Labiran made saveral attempts at getting her to say something meaningful, but soon realised that trying to get anything out of her in her present state was a waste of time.

Labiran beckoned her to rise and follow them, and Lalonpe willingly obliged. They supported her as they walked through the forest and plains into the village and then to the house of the *Baale*. The *Baale* called upon the village herbalist to have a look at her. After careful observation of her behaviour, the herbalist concluded that Lalonpe must have been a victim of one of the conflict zones and rightly suspected that she must have been fed with strong herbs with the aim of selling her.

'She must have been very lucky to find a way of escaping before she took the complete dose of *amunimuye*,' said the herbalist. 'I suspect she did not take enough to cause permanent damage before she escaped. I can place her on regular dose of *isoye*, the antidote, to drain the harmful herbs from her system. It will take some time, but her memory could be revived.'

In slave trading, attacking and physically subduing defenceless victims was far less than half the task. The major challenge was keeping the captives until they found a buyer. The 'hyenas' could not afford the costly clinical process involved in getting captives 'ready for sale'. They basically relied on cruelty and physical aggression to subjugate their victims and keep them in captivity. They employed naked fear as a means of ensuring total compliance from the captives, hence they concentrate their efforts on taking children and women.

Under normal circumstances, the journey from Gbajumo to Ojuoro should not have taken more than a day and half, but it was the best part of two days before Kudoro and Akodu were able to march their captives into the forest and mountains that separated the northern part of Ijowaland from the south of Abatanland, and it was not until cockcrow on the third day that they arrived at their final destination. It had taken a long time to find the way through the dark night and by daylight, the abducted children were already tired and could not be made to move faster than their strength permitted. Furthermore, they had to restrict their movement to the thickest part of the jungle in order to keep as far away as possible from any Ijowa settlement, and also evade routes that were likely to be busy.

Their destination was a farmhouse in one of the tiny farming communities on the edge of Igisogba, which over the years had been gradually taken over by shady characters disguised as farmers whose work was directly linked to Ojuoro. The farmhouse and its grounds, which were on lease to Jebooda for three seasons, were about a thousand heaps from Ojuoro market, but much closer to Igisogba. The farmhouse and similar properties in this area had at one time or another been safe houses for various questionable activities, ranging from keeping stolen goods and livestock to providing safe haven for fugitives on the run on one hand, and for keeping hostages until certain terms had been met.

There were two small sheds strategically located for this purpose at the back of the farmhouse. The sheds were hidden by the farmhouse from the front and the back was made almost inaccessible by rows of trees harbouring thousands of bee colonies. Ojo and the other abducted children were locked up in one of the sheds, and that was where they would be kept and fed till the next Ojuoro market, four days away. At noon, after the captives had been fed and locked in one of the sheds, Jebooda suggested a pre-emptive visit to Igisogba in search of prospective buyers and to make pre-sale negotiations before the market night.

Akodu was considered by the others to be the gullible and weak-willed one, hence all the unsavoury tasks were unfairly passed on to him. Kudoro and Jebooda were able to cajole him into taking the responsibility of looking after the captives while they were away. The truth was that they wanted to go into the village for a session of palm wine drinking. To make their excuse believable, they took Ojo along with them to show a prospective buyer as a sample of the goods and proof of readiness to trade.

'We will be taking you along with us to Igisogba, but I must warn you not to play any trick while we are out there,' Kudoro warned Ojo. 'I will not hesitate to be brutal with you if you try to be smart.'

'And you had better be sure of your success before trying to escape, because if I catch you, you will die,' Jebooda threatened him before they left.

For many reasons, the various wine sheds scattered across Gbengbele, Gbemuyona and Igisogba were strategic locations which anyone intending to trade in the next Ojuoro market should frequent in the days before the night of the market. It was at these places that traders and middlemen engaged in *oja-anosile* (pre-market bargaining), sharing information about the availablility of goods and comparing prices in readiness for market day. It was also at these places that creditors hunted down their debtors, while the latter on the other hand could learn if there was any ambush awaiting them at the market. From shrewd traders to plain opportunists and from *ojara-olosa* (dreaded gangsters) to petty thieves and con men, everyone had to stop to look and listen for at least a day at Igisogba before entering the market at Ojuoro.

Just as they were entering Igisogba, they found a wine shed. There, a drunken traveller who called himself Olowoeyo and claimed to be an Akete man, was successfully sweet-talking the crowd.

'We Akete son of the soil are very stylish by virtue of our long exposure to the white men and all it brings forth,' he said with all the glamour he could demonstrate. 'An Aketeman is like the flying bird. It is only the feathers you can see in a flying bird, you can never get to see its reality, that is the quantity of meat it carries. We are the birds. You can never know our worth, until maybe you fly with us. And flying with us sometimes can be very expensive'. He paused to take a sip from his calabash before continuing. The Aketeman knew he had raised a debatable issue by crediting such a gallant virtue to his townsmen. Olowoeyo was well aware that people were gradually shifting their attention to an elderly man who had been entertaining on the *agidigbo*, so he needed to prove such virtue with at least a reference.

'Recently, an Iloje man was said to have conveniently settled himself, without chains or shackles, aboard what he thought was a merchant ship without realising he was part of the cargo destined for life in the white man's land,' he began after allowing the last draught of palm wine to settle. 'And his seller? Can you imagine he was just an eccentric beachcomber, disguised as a wealthy trader?' The Aketeman paused and induced a belch as his audience drew nearer to listen to what he referred to as the tale of his newest adventure.

'The supposed wealthy trader had earlier promised the Iloje man two bottles of *opalamba* (gin) if he could journey as an interpreter with a shipmaster, a *potoki* [Portuguese] whom he claimed already had some goods to collect down at the seafront of Kotonu. The supposed wealthy trader had earlier told the shipmaster that a friend of his was willing to serve as an apprentice deckhand in return for passage to Kotonu and just ten silver coins.' At this point Olowoeyo was confident that all attention was on him and all ears attentive to what he was saying.

'The *potoki* knowingly agreed, and the beachcomber collected ten silver coins for introducing such a willing deckhand, with which he bought three bottles of *opalamba*.' He paused to take another sip of his palm wine. 'The beachcomber pocketed the remaining silver coins, paid the Iloje interpreter with two bottles of *opalamba*, and kept a bottle for himself. The interpreter majestically boarded the ship, the two bottles of gin tucked in between his elbows. He had drunk up to a quarter of the first bottle even before the journey began and was fast asleep before they were halfway to open water. He was woken up on the deck by the ship master's whip, his hand and leg already chained, and in the middle of the ocean.'

By this time, most of those present were listening to the Aketeman and bellowing with laughter. But the laughter died down, and soon attention was turning towards Ojo, who was sitting among the few people who, despite the growing numbers of Olowoeyo's audience, were not interested in the tales of the Aketeman but continued to listen to the *agidigbo*. Ojo asked for a chance to try his hand on the instrument, and his performance was beyond the expectations of the few listeners. So as soon as the Aketeman seemed to have run out of juicy tales of Aromire and beyond, his listeners began diverting their attention to the *agidigbo* circle and the young boy who seemed to be playing the instrument with rare skill.

Olowoeyo came over to the new circle, and the last of his admirers finally concluded that the Aketeman had exhausted all his juicy tales and joined the gathering, but the Aketeman would not allow the young boy to rob him of his audience so easily. So from his sitting position outside the inner perimeter of the newly-formed circle, he threw a silver coin at the foot of the boy playing the *agidigbo*. The crowd roared with surprise and excitement at such an extravagant gesture. Yes, Ojo was playing the *agidigbo* very well, but the crowd found the value which the Aketeman placed upon his performance to be highly exaggerated.

'Incredible!' shouted a middle-aged man who had taken it upon himself to appraise Ojo's performance. 'I tell you the *majesin* (minor) is an *anjonu* (wizard) on the *agidigbo*. Imagine a silver coin as gratitude from an Aketeman. From somebody who comes from the land brimming with talents on the *agidigbo*!'

The people of Aromire were traditionally known to be very good on the *agidigbo* and it was considered a feat that an Aketeman who was living among the finest hands on the instrument could find Ojo's performance worth a silver coin.

'For this, I am placing a bet of five silver coins on whoever is capable of telling the first six proverbs played by the boy on the *agidigbo*,' Olowoeyo announced. His declaration had the desired result. The crowd cheered the generous challenge. A couple of young men picked up a stool from outside the circle, placed it in the centre and then formally ushered Olowoeyo to the centre. The stylish Aketeman was thus honourably seated close to Ojo. The boy was about to change his rhythm in recognition of the Aketeman when Kudoro intervened.

'The boy is mine, and nobody engages his service without my approval,' Kudoro said directly to the Aketeman.

'How do you mean the boy is yours?' Olowoeyo asked casually.

'He is mine, like he is my own. That is what I mean,' Kudoro replied.

'So how much do you want for your boy to entertain us?' Olowoeyo demanded with the authority of a noble.

'One silver coin will do,' Kudoro replied.

'Then a silver coin you will get,' the Aketeman said with finality, then turned to address the crowd. 'Now who is ready to challenge my boy upon five silver coins?'

While an average Ijowa or Akete person would consider Olowoeyo's challenge a way of winning cheap coins, there was nobody in the crowd reckless or daring enough to risk five silver coins at one go. The closest to the challenge was three silver coins contributed by a consortium of six men who out of rare stupidity nominated a stammerer to take up the contest. The outcome was predictable.

'I think I heard you say the other time that the boy is your slave?' Olowoeyo asked, as Kudoro and Jebooda were about to leave with Ojo.

'Rightly so, in partnership with my friends,' Kudoro replied.

'In that case, I wish to make an offer of three gold coins to buy the boy from you. I want to keep him as my personal entertainer.'

'Well, I don't know for sure. I need to discuss it with my friends,' Kudoro said with sudden interest. Three gold coins was far more than they expected to get for the boy at Ojuoro.

'So where are these friends of yours?'

'One is here, and the other is waiting for us at our post just outside Ojuoro.'

'Well I cannot possibly follow you about and none of my aides are here at present. But I will tell you one thing. Go forth and consult with your friends. If you all agreed to my offer, then I will have the boy.'

'That is nicely said. Be expecting us in while.'

Kudoro told Jebooda about the offer. The latter agreed that it was more than fair but still wanted them to consult Akodu before making the transaction. Shortly afterwards, Kudoro and Jebooda departed. The Aketeman engaged in a short but private dialogue with a younger man whom he called Lagemo.

'I like that boy. I would like to buy him. Can you arrange the purchase?' Olowoeyo asked the young man.

'What do you want to do with such a *majesin*?' Lagemo asked, slightly bewildered.

'I consider the wealth invested in wartime as saving for when the war is over. You will agree that even a *majesin* cannot be acquired so cheaply in peacetime. The boy's performance on the *agidigbo* could fetch a regular income in the Akete markets, and he can be disposed of for a lump sum in the event of need for quick money,' Olowoeyo explained. 'Anyway, I don't intend to pay for the boy.'

'So what do I do to claim him?' Lagemo asked, and Olowoeyo responded by dipping his hands into his pocket and bringing out some coins. He selected three gold coins and handed them to Lagemo.

'You pay with these,' he said as he placed the coins in his palm. 'It should be getting to dusk before you arrived at Ojuoro where the men claimed their partner is waiting. So you should not have any problem paying with that.'

'Yes of course,' Lagemo replied knowingly as he

pocketed the coins. He left to follow the trail of Kudoro and Jebooda, who were already on their way back to Akodu.

The young man introduced himself to Kudoro and Jebooda. 'My name is Lagemo,' he said. 'My lord Olowoeyo asked me to follow you to your friend, with the instruction to make payment and take custody of the boy if all agreed to his offer.'

'You mean your lord asked you to follow us with the money?' Jebooda asked, not quite believing what he was hearing.

'Yes, with three gold coins,' Lagemo replied. 'He said that is what you agreed upon.'

'So you have the money on yourself at this moment?' Kudoro asked.

'Rightly so, and very close to where I keep my gun.' Lagemo mentioned the gun as carelessly as if he was referring to a walking stick. 'You see, my lord thought wisely that your friends could possibly take the money and yet refuse to release the boy. So he asked me to take the gun along. But I personally don't believe that to be true. Such an insinuation is unfair of nice men like you. But my lord believes he is always right, so I had to take the gun. In my own opinion guns are only suitable for hunting animals. I find it degrading killing humans with it. One day, I killed a hyena with a gun and the carcass was very unsightly. I don't wish such an ugly end, even for my enemies.'

Jebooda and Kudoro did not believe what Lagemo had said about not wanting to take a gun along. They were sure that he was far from the peaceful and polite person he was trying to portray. On the contrary they knew he was passing a clear message, something like 'I would not have agreed to follow you if my master had not let me have a gun, and I know how to use it.'

The stranger looked wild, and Jebooda was sure he had used the gun several times before and would use it again at any time. But none of the men showed the fear they felt within.

'I don't like to do this, but I don't know if I can trust you two,' Lagemo began after they had walked on for some distance.

'What is it that you don't like to do?' Jebooda asked. He had been particularly restless from the moment Lagemo had mentioned the gun.

'You see, once in a while I try to take a little care of myself while serving my lord. But then I have to be careful too, as he can be very vicious.'

'How do you take care of yourself, and what has that got to do with you trusting us?' Kudoro asked with some impatience.

'Once in a while, in the course of serving my lord I get to meet intelligent men like you. It is only then I find it safe to try taking care of myself. Because then I can be sure that those with whom we share the secret are respectable not to give me away.'

'So what are you insinuating?' Kudoro said, obviously fed up with the way Lagemo kept dragging his point.

'Now look at it this way,' Lagemo went on. 'I find it ridiculous that you should accept such a price for this boy. His skill on the *agidigbo* is enough to fetch you double that price at Ojuoro, and if you wish I can arrange such an offer for you. Only promise you will not be so careless as to let my lord suspect I had anything to do with the sale, else I could lose a good part of my skin to flogging. However, in the event of a successful transaction, I will have a tenth of the proceeds just to help take care of myself.'

He stopped in his tracks and took a questioning look at the other two in a manner that called for their agreement. Kudoro and Jebooda exchange glances. The first suggested 'let's wait and see' and the second 'what have we got to lose?' Then both turned to Lagemo and nodded in agreement.

'You might be thinking I am stupid making this offer to help,' said Lagemo amiably. 'Yes, you will be wondering why I did not on my own purchase the boy with the money that my lord had agreed upon and of course take all the profit. Truly that is what I could have done if I had my way. But you see, I am well too known with my lord and I'm bound to be noticed at Ojuoro by at least a couple of his peers, and that is where both of you will come in and earn your own pay.'

The way Jebooda and Kudoro became alert and attentive at Lagemo's mention of their own role in the deal showed clearly that they had been unconsciously drawn into a sort of partnership with Lagemo. The men listened on as Lagemo began explaining the details of the transaction as they continued on their way to meet Akodu.

When Kudoro and Jebooda arrived with Lagemo they were surprised that Akodu was not alerted by their approach. They went into the farmhouse thinking he must have fallen asleep on sentry duty but found the place deserted. Jebooda was not at all impressed by Akodu's disregard for security precautions.

'This was exactly my concern about him,' he lamented. 'We have only been away for a few hours and he has already left the place unguarded.'

'Maybe he just nipped into the bush to defecate,' Kudoro said, trying to find a plausible excuse for Akodu's security lapse.

'If so, then why can't he do it in a place where he will have a good view of whatever is happening around here? If we were intruders, we would have had more than enough time to do whatever we wanted.' Jebooda was not in the mood for excuses. But their greatest shock came when they looked into the sheds and found both empty.

As Lagemo sat with Kudoro and Jebooda in the empty shed, his mind was busy trying to add the few pieces together. He had learnt from the men's discussion that the third man was supposed to be watching over four other children. He wondered if the man had simply found a buyer and run away with the proceeds. At the end of the day, having four portions to himself would be better than a third of five portions. He considered this scenario to be more plausible, then became alert. If the third man had chosen to backstab his partners, then he must have been planning it for some time and it was very unlikely that he would risk doing it alone. He suddenly realised he could be in danger himself. Lagemo had been directly involved in quite a few agreements between friends that had ended up in backbiting and betrayal. He had grown and thrived in the wild, fending for himself as early as the age of ten, and one thing he knew for certain was that in such situations the villain must take no prisoners. Maybe the man and his new allies were waiting in ambush with a plot to kill the other two and take the boy but had been surprised by his appearance with a gun in hand. He became restless because he knew he had no defence if the men risked pouncing on them. He had a gun, but no bullets.

Lagemo excused himself on account of the need to answer the call of nature. He left the shed and wandered farther away, pretending to be looking for a comfortable spot. Not far from the shed but well hidden by a shrub, Lagemo noticed the barely-covered body of a man buried in a shallow grave. Then everything became clear; this must be the body of the man they had been waiting for. Lagemo was shocked. Either the third man had been careless and the captives had managed to overpower him and escape, or he had been attacked by a rival gang and robbed of his valuables.

'I don't think I can afford to wait any longer as my lord will be curious and soon he will be suspicious and then restless,' said Lagemo. 'And you see, I don't like it when my lord is restless. It makes my job difficult. I will pay as my lord ordered. Maybe some other time we might be able to trade together.' He paid the agreed sum in gold coins, returned to Igisogba with Ojo and gave an account of what happened back at the shed.

'I think we'd better be going before those men find out I paid them in fake coins,' Lagemo told Olowoeyo.

'This is becoming a bit complicated. I am now beginning to wish I had not bought the boy in the first place. Maybe we should just sell him off and distance ourselves from this situation.'

Then Ojo spoke for the first time since Olowoeyo had taken possession of him. 'Please *oga* [boss], I will pay you handsomely and three times what you could get for me if you can set me free and help me back to Gbajumo.'

'And what have you got to pay us?' Olowoeyo asked sarcastically.

'I have this.' Ojo untied a knot at the edge of his robe and produces the single bead. Lagemo took the bead, examined it briefly but carefully, and then passed it on to Olowoeyo.

'Where did you get this?' Olowoeyo asked with supressed excitement.

'I dug them up in my mother's yard,' Ojo replied calmly.

'Them? Are you telling me that you have not just one of these beads but many?'

'Yes,' Ojo replied confidently. 'That is what I am saying.'

'Now we are hearing a new story,' said Olowoeyo. 'Do you mean to tell me that the soil in your mother's yard is so fertile it grows precious stones?' Olowoeyo began to fill his pipe with tobacco.

'Yes,' Ojo replied.

'So where are the rest of the beads?' Lagemo asked.

'I gave them to my mother,' Ojo lied.

'Your mother has the rest of them, right?' Olowoeyo queried

'Yes, that's right.'

'And you live in Gbajumo village?'

'No, we live in Oluweri, but we got stranded in Gbajumo due to the conflict.'

'So the last time you saw your mother was in Gbajumo?'
'Yes.'

'If you really want me to help you, then you will have to be more forthcoming with the truth,' Olowoeyo said.

'That is the truth, I swear,' Ojo replied.

'Do I look like somebody who would believe that this stone could be dug up by a *majesin* [minor]?' Olowoeyo asked menacingly, his countenance suddenly changed from that of a sympathetic and kind helper to a vicious master.

'No baba!' Ojo stammered. The little boy was visibly shaken by Olowoeyo's sudden change of attitude.

'So I want you to begin by telling me exactly where this stone came from and if there are truly more in your mother's possession.' He spoke in a tone that left no doubt in Ojo's mind that nothing but the truth would save him.

'I did not dig them up.' Ojo confessed. 'They were a gift to my mother.'

'What is the name of the person who gave them to your mother, and how do you happen to be in possession of this bead?'

Ojo explained how the bead had got to him through 'Baba Morilewa' and how he had kept one, saying the rest were still with his mother.

'So what are we going to do now?' Lagemo asked Olowoeyo, after he was sure that Ojo has divulged all he knew about the bead.

'We are going to look for his mother. My problem is what we are going to do with him for now.' Olowoeyo put out his pipe and began to wipe off the powder on his face, revealing a tattooed Erebe tribal mark.

'We might as well take him along with us while searching for his mother,' Lagemo suggested, but felt Olowoeyo's silent disapproval and realised his folly. Taking Ojo with them would be as good as freeing the boy.

'No, we cannot take him with us. He will remain in the care of Morountodun in Igisogba while we go looking for his mother and also see what we can get for the bead at Ojuoro. I am sure that it would keep us going for a while.' Morountodun was Olowoeyo's soon to be third wife.

The real identity of the supposed Aketeman was not Olowoeyo, and he was not an Akete son of the soil. He was Olubi Kudaisi, the boy who had run away from Igisogba when he was fourteen years old. Olowoeyo was just one of the names he was known by in the underworld, and which he assumed whenever he was in places like Ojuoro.

CHAPTER 5

In the search for Lalonpe, Olubi's first point of enquiry was Gbajumo. But while Lalonpe was receiving treatment in Gbemuyona, she was believed by the survivors in Gbajumo to have been taken captive by Akete warriors.

'She was a neighbour of mine in Oluweri. She sent a message to me that she was stranded here with her son on their way to Kuluso due to the conflict,' Olubi explained. 'She said she sought refuge at her friend's place, but we have not heard from her since the attack on this village, so we came down to look for her.'

'What is the name of the person your neighbour was staying with?'

'She was staying with somebody called *Iya* Soju (Soju's mother).'

'*Iya* Soju, *Iya* Soju...' The villager repeated the name but could not put a face to it. 'Do you know any *Iya* Soju?' He asked his friend, who was also listening,

'I think I have heard that name before, but there is more than one Soju in this village.'

'If you take us to the one you know, that will be a step forward,' Olubi suggested. 'If she is not the one we are looking for, she will most likely know other women with that identity.'

'The only *Iya* Soju I know is Kolapo's second wife, Labake,' said the man.

'Which Kolapo?'

'Kolapo the cotton farmer,' the other man replied. 'But you will have to be very cautious in asking, as Kolapo himself is still grieving because I heard his compound also lost some of their own to the invaders.' He gave them the directions to Kolapo's house.

When Olubi and Lagemo arrived at Kolapo's place, the tense atmosphere within the compound confirmed what they had been told.

'Yes, she was here with her son,' Kolapo replied. 'Lalonpe and my wife were among the first casualties of this unnecessary and avoidable conflict,' he added before breaking down in tears. 'His son Ojo was running about looking for her as the house were burning. That was the last time I saw him.'

Now he knew Lalonpe was also a victim of the attack on Gbajumo village, Olubi moved on to the only other means of finding her. Like other impoverished indigenes of Akete, there were some men of Erebe descent who found the conflict an opportunity to earn some income and signed on to fight alongside the Akete warriors. He travelled to Aromire and linked up with an Erebe man who was with the Akete warriors during the attack on Gbajumo. The man, whose name was Akilapa, told Olubi that none of the captives taken to the palace at Aromire from Gbajumo fitted the description of the person he was looking for. Akilapa went further, saying he had heard on the grapevine that some captives had been separated off by Eso Akinku and secretly sold at Ojuoro. Olubi concluded that Lalonpe must be among the latter.

It took until another market day at Ojuoro for Olubi to find out what had become of the captives Akilapa was talking about. He was told that they had all been sold to a single buyer who was a normad from across the desert and had since taken them to an undisclosed destination. This effectively put an end to the search for Lalonpe. Olubi withdrew his men from the field, collected Ojo from Morountodun at Igisogba and returned with him to Eti-Osa.

Olubi's immediate family in Eti-Osa consisted of two wives with seven children between them. However, the residents of Olubi's compound were rarely limited to this number. There were always visiting relatives, ranging from brothers or sisters to maternal third cousins or paternal grand-uncles, depending on the age and gender of the visitor. The duration of the supposed visits ranged from two weeks to six months or a year. The status of the visiting relatives varied. While some would appear to have been running away from a war-torn community, some came in the manner of visiting princes or princesses and the standard of lodging and attention given to a 'relative' during the period spent in Olubi's compound was usually commensurate with their first appearance in the village. There was hardly a time when Olubi did not have at least eight visiting relatives, yet none of them had ever travelled down to the village to seek his house in the usual manner.

On the contrary, the visiting relatives were always brought into the village by Olubi himself. The elders and decision makers at Eti-Osa chose not to see anything unusual about Olubi's endless stream of visitors, but Ojo was the first visitor Olubi had brought into the village and introduced as his biological child, and the only visiting relative who eventually became a permanent resident.

On arrival, as the communal rule demands across villages, Olubi took Ojo to the house of the *Baale* and introduced him to the village leader as his son by another woman living in Oluweri.

'He was living with his mother in Oluweri until the war began,' he explained. 'Since then it has been difficult to trace his mother, so I have brought him here to live with me. For how long depends on how soon we are able to find his mother.' As usual the *Baale* had no scruples concerning who Olubi's visitors were or whether his story was true or not.

'What is the name of your son?' the *Baale* asked.

'With all due respect, Baba *Baale*, I would say it before you ask, but it is a name which is despised by many families and compounds in this village. Therefore, I have decided that he should be referred to as Omo-Olubi' (meaning the son of Olubi).

'That is very thoughtful of you,' the *Baale* replied understandingly. Eti-Osa was basically an immigrant settlement and the Ijebu people were by far the largest immigrants there and were very influential in the commercial circle. The name 'Ojo' was not popular among the Ijebus because of their bitter experience at the hands of an Ibadan warlord during one of the many incessant wars within the tribe. The warlord was popularly known as Ojo Ibadan. He was so despised among the Ijebus that they wold not carry out the customary naming of children born with the umbilical cord round their necks like other Yoruba clans. Across the tribe all male children born this way were called Ojo, while the females were called Aina, but the Ijebus choose to call both genders with such births Aina. So in Eti-Osa, Ojo, now called Omolubi, was known to all and sundry as the son of Olubi from his former wife who had remarried and was living somewhere between Abatan, Ijowa and Akete. As far as Olubi was concerned, it was only Ojo and Lagemo who knew the simple truth. He knew his story would not hold water in presence of the *Baale*, his own wives and the few townspeople, so he could not be bothered. His wives were used to accepting whatever family status he chose to accord his visitors. However, counterfeit or genuine, the paternal factor which Olubi attached to his relationship with Ojo made his wives uneasy.

'My concern is, why must he introduce this boy as his son?' That was Olubi's second wife Banke expressing her dissatisfaction to the senior wife, Kofo.

'Well what can we do about it? For all we know, the poor mother might be running about looking for ways to rectify whatever compelled our husband to take her son from her,' Kofo replied, apparently not as bothered as the younger wife.

'I am not bothered about whatever made him take the boy from his mother. My point is why must he introduce him as a son? Why not a cousin, nephew or stepbrother like previous visitors?'

'I am not bothered about who he claimed the boy to be in

front of the *Baale*. To me it does not make any difference.'

'Very soon he will come home with a former sister-in-law and expect us to keep quiet.'

'My concern is that the issue that brought the boy should be reconciled as soon as possible, because that is when our husband gets rewarded. The truth is that the boy is not his son and will soon be returned to wherever he comes from.'

'That is the problem with you, Kofo. You always let our husband's excesses go unchallenged. That is why he always take us for granted,' Banke fumed.

'Well, say whatever you wish. However, remember before you start accusing me of being complacent that you were initially introduced to me as a niece by our husband,' Kofo said sarcastically and walked away, leaving the younger wife shocked and speechless.

But Banke would not accept the story without making any effort at finding the truth. In the first month of his arrival, she employed various tactics, from hostility to hospitality, in order to squeeze the truth from Ojo, but without success.

It took over two weeks of treatment from the herbalist before Lalonpe fully regained her memory. 'My name is Lalonpe,' she said. 'I lived in Oluweri and I was travelling to Kuluso with my son when the conflict started, so we had to stop at Gbajumo. There I was captured by Akete warriors, but luckily I escaped. I don't know what has become of my son.' She told the herbalist about the attack on Gbajumo, her ordeal at the hands of her abductors and how she was nearly sold away at Ojuoro, but she was careful not to mention the death of Lasun. 'I was trying to find my way to

Gbajumo to seek my son when I gradually began to lose the ability to think coherently,' she said. 'I have no idea how I ended up where I was found.'

'You should thank your creator that you ended up on friendly ground and were not eaten by wild animals during the night. Given the state you were in when you were brought into the village, you would have been easy prey to a lone wolf. I can see you have regained your mental capacity, but you only started eating normally yesterday so I advise you to rest for a couple of days to regain your strength.'

'How long have I been here?'

'You have recovered much faster than expected. On average it takes at least a month before victims of *amunimuye* recover, but you have only been here for sixteen days.'

'Sixteen days?' She was alarmed to have been away from reality for such a long time. 'I am fine now,' she said with certainty. 'My only worry is my son's safety and wellbeing. I must return to Gbajumo at once. I need to go and look for my son.' Lalonpe was defiant, but the herbalist had no intention of persuading or compelling her to stay longer than she was willing.

'I have nothing against that if you are sure you are fit for the journey,' he said. 'It is only natural that your first priority is your son's safety. In fact, reuniting with your son is also essential for total recovery from the trauma you have been through.'

'I hid my money and valuables away in Gbajumo on the night of the attack before I went to sleep, and I am sure nobody could stumble upon it accidentally,' said Lalonpe. 'I promise to return and show my appreciation for your help and support.'

'That will not be necessary. The *Baale* and the elders decided that the village should bear the cost of the herbs and other material for your treatment. As for my service charge, just take it as a sympathetic gesture from me. I wish you to return to Gbajumo and find your son to be safe and well.' The herbalist said. 'My assignment will be concluded when I hand you over to the *Baale*. Meanwhile I have a nephew who is a canoeman and who fortunately will be rowing down Awoyaya river as far as Olokoto. He will be setting off tommorow at dawn. I will talk to him and hope he should be able to help you up to the part of the river that is nearest to Gbajumo.'

That evening, the herbalist took Lalonpe to the *Baale's* house and then to each of the village elders so that she could express her gratitude for the support given to her. The next morning, she began the two-day journey to Gbajumo, hoping to find her son. Labiran the canoeman was at the herbalist's place before daybreak and Lalonpe was ready and eager to leave. The latest news was that the confrontations were tending to spread southward, so it took much longer for Labiran to fill his canoe with passengers, because he would be rowing towards the conflict, while most people were naturally travelling away.

It was mid-morning before they could set off, and even then, Labiran had to leave with a half-filled canoe. As they rode south, they came across many more displaced people travelling in the opposite direction as they fled the conflict. By late noon, when they were about halfway between Gbemuyona and Kuluso, it was apparent that continuing past Kuluso to Gbajumo would not only be risky but stupid. So instead of rowing to Kuluso, they spent the night midway, with other displaced people travelling in the other direction who were also stopping and resting before continuing the next day.

At dawn the next morning, Labiran and Lalonpe, along with a few others travelling southward, continued their journey on foot to bypass Kuluso. They arrived at Gbajumo before noon and the canoeman endeavoured to escort her through the forest up to the king's plantain field on the edge of Gbajumo, which was nearly a quarter the size of the whole of Gbajumo's farmland.

'My fair woman, this is as far as I can go with you,' said Labiran. 'You should be through the plantain field and into Gbajumo before it is dark. I would not have minded seeing you through the rest of the journey, but it will be difficult to find my way back through the dark fields. The big banana leaves will block whatever daylight remains.' He began his journey back to his canoe by the riverside.

Lalonpe set off for Gbajumo immediately, and as the canoeman had predicted, she was out of the plantain field before the evening sun had gone down. It was close to a month since the night of the attack, and the survivors of the raid were still struggling to come to terms with their losses. Except for the elderly and children, the captives had cut across gender and families.

She went directly to *Iya* Mojoyin's house, which was among the few that had not been vandalised or totally destroyed by the invaders. Before the attack, it had usually been quiet and devoid of people, but with many houses temporarily unfit to live in, *Iya* Mojoyin, like others whose property had been untouched, felt obliged to accommodate as many homeless neighbours as possible. She now shared her house with the families of her long-time peer Jibike and her cousin Ajike.

Jibike was the only female herbalist in Gbajumo, a profession which she had grown into and inherited from her father. He had been the only herbalist in the growing village, but all his children were female. Rather than passing his knowledge to a male successor, he groomed Jibike, his eldest daughter, to continue the work after him. His choice of Jibike was not particularly due to the fact that she was the eldest. From as early as her fifth year, Jibike had been known to have the ability to identify, and differentiate between, many similar medicinal leafs and roots. By adolescence, she had mastered the use of more than two hundred herbs and medicinal concoctions, and before adulthood she had been credited with the discovery of five new plants and their potentials. Although she was born with only one good eye, she was a keen observer of nature and events. It was a popular saying among villagers that she could see with one eye twice as much as others saw with two.

Abike was *Iya* Mojoyin's cousin from her mother's side, and the youngest of the three. She was a successful trader and arguably among the wealthiest in Gbajumo village. Her trading interests spanned Ijowa and beyond, and not less than a score of Gbajumo women had, under her tutelage, found good fortune in trading. Although she had lost fortune in goods due to the destruction of her property by the invaders, this meant very little to her as she had more valuable trade goods in store houses at Ode-Ijowa and four other Ijowa villages

Both women were with *Iya* Mojoyin when Lalonpe arrived. Their joy at her safe return dissipated when asked of Ojo.

'We have not seen your son since the attack,' *Iya* Mojoyin said, confirming Lalonpe's worst fears. 'About the fifth day after the attack, two men who said they were mandated by your neighbours at Oluweri came down from Kuluso in search of you and Ojo.'

'My neighbours?' Lalonpe was visibly surprised to hear this. 'How did they know I was here?'

'They said they had been to Kuluso and were told that you had not got there before the uprising began. They suspected you might be stranded here, so they decided to come and look for you,' *Iya* Mojoyin explained. Although Lalonpe had told her neighbours that she was travelling to Kuluso, she had never expected them to be so concerned as to send men to look for her.

'Your friend Labake was also taken by the Akete warriors,' *Iya* Mojoyin went on. 'The *Baale* has been able to get the names of all those being held at Akete and has passed them on to the palace at Ode-Ijowa. Hopefully they will be freed through hostage exchange between the two palaces, but that will only be when the conflict has been resolved.' She told her.

'I guessed as much. She must have been taken just before me,' Lalonpe said. She told *Iya* Mojoyin about the last time she had seen her friend. Lalonpe was about to excuse herself to search for her valuables when *Iya* Mojoyin dipped her hand into a large basket made from raffia and produce a sack, which she handed over to Lalonpe.

'Those are the belongings you left behind,' *Iya* Mojoyin said as she passed the sack over to Lalonpe.

'Ojo was not among the captives taken by the Akete warriors, so he must have been abducted by opportunists,' said Lalonpe. 'Ojuoro is the place to look for people abducted by traders of the spoils of war. I intend to go and look for my son at the next Ojuoro night market and buy him.' She took a brief look inside the sack and confirmed that nothing was missing and thanked *Iya* Mojoyin. At this juncture, Jibike asked Lalonpe to examine her palm, and she obliged.

'You need to stay here in Gbajumo,' she said after a brief study of Lalonpe's left palm. 'It will be a safe haven for you and your son.'

'Well, I will need to find him first before thinking about a place to live,' Lalonpe replied. The three women exchanged glances and laughed.

'I am not referring to the missing son, but that which must not be missing,' said Jibike.

'I have only one son and I have neither seen nor heard of him in almost a month,' Lalonpe said, visibly confused.

'What about the one in your stomach?' Jibike asked, but with no intention of waiting for a reply she continued, 'That is the one that must not be missing.' Then, turning to *Iya* Mojoyin, she asked, 'Am I right?'

'Quite right, my friend,' *Iya* Mojoyin replied.

'Yes, you are quite right,' Ajike agreed.

'Which one is in my stomach?' Lalonpe was bewildered.

'With my only this left eye, I am sure that what I noticed rumbling in your stomach is not an *omolangidi* (piece of dry wood) but a life turning in its slumber,' Jibike said with pride as she indicated to the one working eye she had been born with.

'How do you know I am pregnant? I mean, what makes you think that?'

'If Jibike says you are pregnant, then you must be pregnant,' *Iya* Mojoyin assured her. 'You see our friend here, she is very nosy.' Jibike obviously took her friend's comment as a compliment and acknowledged it with a large grin, but this made her look more as if she was about to cry rather than smile. The poor old woman sincerely intended to be pleasant with her smile, but her effort was thwarted by an expanse of coloured gums, the result of chewing lots of kolanut, and many missing teeth.

'She could identify a pregnant snail within its shell,' Ajike confirmed

'And even count the of eggs in its belly,' *Iya* Mojoyin added with pride.

'She could tell the moment a woman is pregnant,' Ajike said.

'And long before the bearer realises it,' *Iya* Mojoyin boasted. Then Jibike took another look at her left palm.

'You shall be united with your missing son,' Jibike said with an air of confidence and assurance. 'When, I cannot tell. It is here in Gbajumo that your son was separated from you, and it is here that you shall be reunited.'

'What my friend is saying is that here in Gbajumo your son will come looking for you,' Ajike explained, with emphasis on 'here in Gbajumo'.

'My daughter, I advise that you heed to the words of this 'wretched, half blind, old woman',' *Iya* Mojoyin jested. 'You will not find your missing son in Ojuoro even if you make a thousand trips there.'

'And neither will you be able to pay for the value placed upon him even if you have a house full of horses to offer,' added Ajike.

'But if she says you shall live to see your son again, so it shall be,' *Iya* Mojoyin assured Lalonpe.

'I will never be at peace with myself and my conscience

until I am convinced that I have done enough to find my son,' she replied defiantly.

'My daughter, big shoulder bones and money are not often enough to ensure a safe entry into Ojuoro, and trading there is even more dangerous,' *Iya* Mojoyin warned. 'It is the people you know that matter. Entering Ojuoro market is not an easy task, but not as difficult as finding your son to buy at the market. It has been reported on many occasions that even freemen who went to trade in the market had left the market as somebody else's property.' Lalonpe was unconvinced but felt it laborious to push the subject further at the time. Once she regained her strength then she would resolve to seek out Ojo nonetheless.

However, by the sixth day after Lalonpe's return to Gbajumo, she had grown certain that she was indeed pregnant. 'Mama, your friend was right. I am sure I am pregnant. What should I do?' She asked *Iya* Mojoyin.

'I find that to be a very strange question. What should a pregnant woman do than to wait until her term is due and then give birth?' *Iya* Mojoyin replied.

'It is not as simple as that, mama.'

'It will remain as simple as that unless you tell me what is difficult about a woman being pregnant.'

They talked well into the dead of the night. Lalonpe did most of the talking while the old woman listenned. She told *Iya* Mojoyin her story right from the tragedy that had befallen Ojo's father to her secret relationship with a trader from Egbejoda called Morilewa, but without the part which she had sworn to keep secret.

'You see where my problem lies, mama. Our only meeting place was Lower-Oluweri and as I heard, it is presently under siege by the Akete army. Even if Morilewa, the father of my unborn child, risked entering Oluweri to look for me, it would be very difficult and dangerous for me to go waiting for him there. It would be like returning into captivity with my eyes wide open.'

'I see no problem with that. Since he has already told you his name and family compound at Egbejoda and Fatunbi confirmed it to be so, all you have to do is to journey to Egbejoda when things have quietened down and seek him.'

'I have thought of that. No one can predict when this war will be over, but the pregnancy is growing. It would be more ideal if he knows before the baby is born.'

'That is true. However, it is the saying of our elders that knowing where one is going is half the task done. The other half of the task is finding a means of getting there. There is time. The war will not go on forever, but Egbejoda will still be there and so also will be the people.'

Lalonpe slept all through the morning and did not awaken until when the sun was right up. *Iya* Mojoyin and her friends were in the compound when she came out of the house. She went over to greet them, kneeling in turn in front of each of the elderly women and thanking them individually for their hospitality. After each of them had responded to her appreciation, *Iya* Mojoyin asked Lalonpe to take her seat on the only vacant seat, a square-shaped bamboo stool. Lalonpe sensed that the women had something to tell her and must have been waiting all morning for that purpose.

'I have told my friends just a little of our discussion last night and they understood even beyond what you told me,' said *Iya* Mojoyin. 'Their advice is the same as mine.'

'You must understand that there is no way you can

travel to Egbejoda to look for Morilewa in your condition and with battle still going on in not few fronts between here and Eti-Osa,' said Ajike. 'That means you might not be able to make the journey until after you have had your baby.' Lalonpe agreed. The memory of her previous miscarriage stung, for the sake of the child she carried, she could do nothing but wait. And so as to not let grief overcome her in stagnance, she resolved to wait until after reuniting with Morilewa and had regained some stability before finding Ojo. She clung to the thought as a lifeline.

The almost seasonal communal dispute, which many had thought would be resolved quickly by the palaces the way they had in the past, escalated into a fully-fledged war within weeks of the first fatality. Adeyanju's visits to Lalonpe in peacetime had required meticulous planning, but such adventures were practically impossible in wartime. Moreover, anybody who was somebody in Ijowa was totally engaged by the conflict. The speed at which it had escalated was unprecedented, and it caught all those involved, especially on the Ijowa side, by surprise.

Adeyanju sent an underground contact to Baba Fatunbi's to seek information about the welfare of Lalonpe, but the messenger came back to tell him that she and her son had left Oluweri before the war started and were yet to return. Since then, he had been sending coded messages every other day to Fatunbi about Lalonpe, and the reply had always been 'the chicken is yet to come back home to roost.' When it was apparent that Oba Lagbade was poised to send the Akete army into Oluweri, Adeyanju remembered the *ejigbaileke* he had left at Lalonpe's place. He decided he had to do something before it was too late.

On the one hand, he thought Ojo might have told his mother about the bead and Lalonpe had retrieved it. He feared that if the war entered Oluweri, it would be a long time before he would either be able to communicate with the priest or travel down to collect it. On the other hand, he was counting on the possibility that Ojo had forgotten about the beads and they could still be where he had left them.

The next morning after reports emerged that Oluweri was in danger, Adeyanju risked a quiet dash out of Ode-Ijowa at the crack of the dawn. He arrived at Oluweri and the old shrine just before dusk and change into one of his Morilewa outfits that Fatunbi ensured he replenished personally. He knew Lalonpe was not likely to be back, else the priest would have sent a message to that effect, so he had no option but to find a means of getting across to Fatunbi to warn him of the urgency of the situation.

While it would be risky for the fake 'Morilewa' to breach Lalonpe's compound in her absence, that would not be the case with Fatunbi. Being an influential person in Oluweri, the priest would not be challenged by any of Lalonpe's neighbours if he was noticed rummaging under a shrub in her yard. An average person would assume that the priest must be searching for certain herbs and roots for medicinal purposes.

He waited patiently on the plains close to the shrine for somebody he could send to Fatunbi, as he normally did whenever he needed to see the priest during his clandestine visits to Oluweri without forewarning. This part of Oluweri was not known to be a favoured route to anywhere, so it would take a while before Adeyanju found somebody going towards the village who was willing to deliver his message to the priest.

'Please tell *Baba* Fatunbi that his friend Morilewa is waiting for him at the old shrine.'

The stranger expressed his doubt about Adeyanju's request. 'My brother, this is a difficult time and the priest must be very busy. I am not sure he will be able to attend to this kind of call.'

'My purpose here is also about this difficult time and I am sure the priest will be delighted to see me. He sent me on an errand, and he is awaiting the reply, which has to be given to him in private,' Adeyanju explained passionately, but the man was still reluctant to take the errand, until he produced a couple of silver coins. The man was visibly impressed.

'You don't have to give me this. I was going to deliver your message anyway,' the man said, but not before he had collected the coins and tucked them away in his *agbada*. 'What did you say your name was again?'

'Morilewa.'

'Just Morilewa?'

'Yes, just Morilewa, and he will understand,' Adeyanju replied.

The man looked Adeyanju up and down. He saw nothing special in his appearance to suggest that he was an *ogunagbongbo* (noble person) of any sort.

'I will surely deliver your message, but the priest must really be expecting you to make it down here at this crucial time,' the man said and went away.

Fatunbi went as soon as it was convenient to excuse himself from the crisis meeting he was having with some elders over the possibility of an attack on Oluweri. When he arrived at the old shrine, Adeyanju told him why he had had to rush down to Oluweri again without prior notice.

'I would not have bothered you at this crucial time if it was not very important,' Adeyanju apologised. 'I mistakenly took my royal neckbead with me on my last visit to Lalonpe. I hid it in the back of the house, but then forget to retrieve it before leaving the next morning.' Adeyanju reminded the priest of his hurried departure from Oluweri during his last visit. He told Fatunbi how Ojo had got to know about the beads, and what he had told the young boy about them. He then gave the priest a detailed description of where he had hidden them.

'I will forever be grateful to you, *Baba*, if you can make a quick journey to Lower-Oluweri and collect the beads while I wait for you here,' Adeyanju pleaded. 'If the beads were not in the place I just described to you, then Ojo must have taken them and given them to his mother. I will rely on you to find a convincing explanation for taking them back from her as soon as she returns to Oluweri, even if you have to disclose my true identity. Just make sure you collect them and keep them safe until I come personally to collect them. Meanwhile, I will be sending somebody down from Ode-Ijowa every other day to check on progress.'

Fatunbi asked Adeyanju to wait while he returned to the house and quickly concluded his meeting with the elders. Moments after the priest left, Adeyanju heard a loud gunshot followed by the anguished cry of the priest, which was almost drowned by the sound of the shot echoing through the forest. He raced towards the sound and found the priest lying face down in his own blood. He turned him over, but he did not need a second opinion to know that the priest was dead. He had been shot in the chest, probably at very close range, and the bullet had ripped through from one side of his ribs to the other. The wound was so unsightly that Adeyanju felt instantly sick.

Then he suddenly realised the terrible consequences of being found in such circumstances. He looked around and quickly plucked some large leaves, which he used to cover Fatunbi's face. Then he returned to the shrine, collected all the clothing and other things he had kept there for use as Morilewa and bolted. He was back in Ode-Ijowa before the following dawn.

The lifeless body of the priest was found later at dusk by concerned family members who were wondering what was keeping him so late at the shrine. The four elderly and respected members of Oluweri who had been with Fatunbi when the spiritualist was called away were consistent in their claim that the message that took the priest to the old shrine and his death was from a person called Morilewa. The priest's family and aides testified to the fact that the deceased truly had an associate by that name and that he was from Egbejoda.

Morilewa was reported to have been the last person to see Fatunbi alive. The circumstances that led to the tragic death of the priest got to the palace and the king ordered the arrest of the culprit. Adeyanju was hoping that Morilewa would not only be home when the *ilari* (civil enforcers) sent down to Ode-Ijowa arrived, but that he would be proven to have been home over the past few days. Egbejoda was quite a distance to Lower-Oluweri and Morilewa would have enough defence to prove his innocence.

Three days after the death of Fatunbi, the *ilaris* from the palace at Ode-Ijowa arrived in Egbejoda. But Morilewa was neither at his family compound nor anywhere in Egbejoda when they arrived, and the first statements taken from members of his family indicated that he had not been in Egbejoda as at the time of Fatunbi's death. The palace enforcers laid seige to Morilewa's compound and made his family prisoners in their homes in order to compel Morilewa to give himself up.

Upon his return, Morilewa was arrested and taken to Ode-Ijowa, where he was charged and convicted with treason. Morilewa had no defence, as he could not provide credible witnesses to support his activities while away from Egbejoda and his whereabouts at the time of Fatunbi's death. There was no way Morilewa could absolve himself from the charges. Members of Fatunbi's household identified him as the person who had recently visited the priest a couple of times. The supposed messenger whom Morilewa hoped would at least be able to identify the actual person who had sent him to the spiritualist did not turn up when publicly requested by the palace to come and identify the suspect.

In Oluweri the priest's family were mourning the passing of their dear one, while in Egbejoda the Omomose family were trying to come to terms with the unfortunate situation in which one of their members found himself. But in Gbajumo, Lalonpe was in agony, not only over her missing son but over the death of the priest by the hand of someone who was supposed to be the father of her unborn baby.

'I have lost a son, and now the father of the child in my womb is being held by the palace at Ode-Ijowa for the death of a respected priest,' Lalonpe lamented when he learnt about the circumstances sorrounding the death of Fatunbi. 'Even if the war ended tomorrow, there is no way I can return to Oluweri. How can I face my neighbours with such scandal on my doorstep?'

'You can stay here and live with us as long as you wish until you find a comfortable place to settle within Gbajumo,' said *Iya* Mojoyin, trying to reassure the crestfallen Lalonpe. 'The most important thing for you to do now is to make yourself strong and ready for your baby. As for Morilewa, there is nothing you can do about it than to hope he survives his ordeal.'

The conflict continued to spread across both Akete and Ijowa land. More and more communities become inaccessible, vibrant markets become deserted, and survival became difficult for the average town resident. There were reports of daily confrontations between Akete and Ijowa warriors, right from Lower-Oluweri in the south to Kuluso in the north on Ijowa side, and from Isale-Eko in the south to Gbengbele in the north on the Akete side. There were reports of attacks and counter-attacks by both armies of the divide. From Kuluso, the Ijowa army crossed the river into the Akete side, overran Seleru and held onto it for almost a month before they were pushed back by reinforcements sent from the palace at Aromire, but not before many farms had been pillaged and many prisoners taken.

The following month, Akete warriors launched a retaliatory offensive on Olokoto from Iseri. Then Ijowa warriors entered Aketeland from Oko-Oba and took over Isale-Eko for almost two months before it was liberated by the Akete army.

CHAPTER 6

While rare stones were considered to be of high value at Ojuoro market, finding someone to buy even the single precious stone was not as easy as Olubi had imagined. The glittering metal which he had thought would bring a considerable fortune eventually became what could be likened to the king's *kakaaki* (flute), as he who stole the royal flute would very soon discover that he had risked his life for nothing, because he would find nowhere to blow it without arousing the curiosity of the nearest townsman. None of Olubi's regular buyers of questionable goods at the market was willing to buy the stone, until he presented it to Goje Salaji.

It is an accepted fact that as there must be men in any community, there also must be women. As there must be elderly people, there also must be children. As there must be criminals, so also must exist comemendable townspeople. As there were many generations of Erebe families in Ijowa made impoverished due to harsh soils of Oko-Oba, so also were a few Erebe families who could afford to feed their extended families and still have some to share around. They were those families who were quick to realise that the soil of Oko-Oba was of no use beyond subsistence farming, and as soon as they arrived, they had abandoned farming altogether and risked what remained of their dwindling wealth in trading. One such was the Salaji family.

From adolescence, Goje Salaji had craved a life of luxury, and on attaining manhood, he persuaded his father to let him seek a more rewarding trade outside Ijowa.

'I heard from a person whose father had traded along Awoyaya to the big ocean that one could trade steadily into fortune even in places as near as Aromire and Idomi,' Goje told his father.

'It is no secret that these are lucrative trading sites,' his father replied. 'The problem with them is safety. On more than a few occasions traders have gone missing while journeying between these markets. None were ever found, dead or alive. The whole of Aketeland is becoming polluted by an influx of desperate fortune seekers.' Yet Goje's mind was dead set on seeking his fortune beyond Ijowa. He managed to get the blessing of his father to seek a settlement outside Oko-Oba, but his father insisted he must promise not to trade beyond Aketeland.

Goje kept his promise to his father and settled at Isale-Eko. However he fell into dispute with his parents over issues of greater consequence by marrying a non-Erebe woman, despite his parents' disapproval. Goje's wife, Bibiola, was the daughter of Alawiye, the *Akigbe* (royal poet) of the palace at Aromire. He belonged to a class of nobles popularly referred to as *Oloye Tasere* (minor or lesser chiefs). The *Akigbe* was the palace poet and also entertained at royal functions. After marriage, and upon the influence of his father in-law, Goje was able to set up his family home in an environment that befitted his new status at Aromire, the seat of the palace of the king of Aketeland.

The nobility of Alawiye was solely a matter of professional privilege, because he gained access to the gathering of the richest and the mightiest of Aketeland not by birth but by virtue of his voice. The day the palace *Akigbe* begins to lose the sweetness of his voice either due to ill health or eventually old age, marked a significant beginning of the change from grace to grass. But Goje was a smart opportunist. While his father-in-law was alive and able, he had been able to exploit his access to Alawiye's circle of (albeit minor) nobles to mingle with wealthy Akete traders and sons of the soil. During that time, he had created for himself an informal position among those who would not have socialised with him if he had not been an in-law to the palace poet. Soon he began to draw upon the influence of his father in-law to engage in trade with people who would not have traded with him if he had been just an ordinary son of the soil in Aketeland. As his trade took him to larger markets, he worked his way into the circle of *ogunagbongbos* in communities across Akete and mastered the act of managing in-betweens. That was how he met influential traders from Idomi, Kotonu and beyond.

Goje's father in-law enjoyed a comparatively long term as the *Akigbe* because he became the palace poet at a comparatively young age, in fact the youngest in known history, but he was not blessed with a comparatively longer life. The death of Alawiye dealt a major setback to Goje's ambition. His aim was to establish his own personal and direct influence with the *ogunagbongbos* of Aketeland, to the point where he would not need his relationship with his in-law to get what he wanted. The *Akigbe* died when Goje was just beginning to launch himself into the personage of high chiefs of Aketeland. Those whose title and position at the palace at Aromire, unlike the *Akigbe*, were guaranteed by heredity and tradition, and not by 'the king's favour'.

For Goje, the death of Alawiye was as if a vital lifeline had been severed. While he was not at all poor in term of material needs and could continue to provide for the needs of his young family from the proceed of his fledgling trade, he was unable to maintain on long-term the extravagant life his wife was used to, which was basically funded on the influence of his father-in-law, the *Akigbe*. Just over six months after the death of her father, Bibiola packed her things and left Goje's house without Ojuolape, the only child of the union, who was just five years old. About four months after she left Goje, Bibilola remarried. She became the fifth wife of Parakoyi, a high-ranking Akete chief who was known to have close to fifty slaves and scores of bondservants in his service. The incident was humiliating for Goje, so much so that he found the environment at Aromire very uncomfortable, so he left Aromire and returned to Isale-Eko with Ojuolape.

Close to two months after he had bought the bead from Olubi, Goje travelled to Eti-Osa and Olubi's house with unexpected feedback about its value.

'I could not find a buyer for that stone until I got to Ashanti,' he said. 'But when I did find one, the proceeds were beyond my imagination. Although it is not widely sought for, the value is about ten times the value of gold of the same size.' He paused in anticipation of Olubi's reaction, but the latter remained silent. Goje was expecting Olubi to be excited and wondered if he had not heard him right.

'Are you with me?' Goje asked, but there was still no response from the other man, until he gave him a slight nudge. Then he realised that Olubi was far more stunned than he had imagined he would be. The disclosure had clearly put him off balance. He had been dealing with the likes of Olubi and knew that it was very unusual for somebody of his track record to carelessly expose his emotion the way he just had. He would have loved to indulge himself in the luxury of seeing how Olubi would react if he disclosed the actual value he had got for the stone. But such indulgence would be extravagant and stupid, to say the least.

'Yes, I am with you all right. I heard all you said,' Olubi replied hastily. Goje was right, Olubi was shocked to know the worth of the stones, but that was not what had got him carried away. Olubi was mentally calculating the difference between what he had got from Goje for the stone and what the latter said he got for it at Ashanti.

'You said the value is ten times the value of a piece of gold of the same size?' he asked.

'Yes, that is what I said,' Goje confirmed.

'That is incredible!' Olubi shouted excitedly, but Goje was not happy with his reaction because he knew that Olubi was acting.

'Then you must be wondering why I told you this,' said Goje. He did not wait for Olubi's reply but proceeded to address the issue he rightly guessed was brewing in Olubi's mind. 'Yes, I know that by revealing this to you will put me in certain financial obligation to you, but I just cannot afford not to share the excitement with you,' Goje said and then dipped his hand into the inner pocket of his *agbada*. The hand came out as a clenched fist. Olubi understood and opened his palm, and Goje placed a gold coin on it. He instantly closed it. Although there was nobody with them in the room, the contents of Goje's palm disappeared so quickly that someone watching would never have known anything had changed hands.

'This is very kind of you,' Olubi said. He fetched a small metal box which was well hidden between the beams of the roof. He opened his palm and for the first time briefly glimpsed the contents before carefully placing it into the box. 'Very few people would be fair enough to share such bounty.'

'I am sure you must be expecting certain questions from me,' Goje said after Olubi had replaced the metal box.

'Yes,' Olubi replied. 'I assume you want to know the real source of the bead.' Goje nodded and Olubi told him how he had come across the precious stone, the little he knew about the source, and all the efforts he had made to trace Lalonpe without success. But Goje was not ready to give up until he had explored the one and only remaining link with the valuable stone.

'The boy said the beads were a present to his mother by a man. If we cannot find the woman, why not let us try and find the man?' Goje suggested. 'If he can give not one but many of those stones to a lover, then he must have more in his possession.' Olubi wondered why he had not thought of this.

'Hmmm. You are right,' Olubi replied thoughtfully. 'That angle is worth looking into. I will set about doing that right away and let you know as soon as there is something positive to report.'

Later, after his guest had departed, Olubi asked Ojo to join him in the front room where he had just been talking with Goje.

'Your *Baba* Morilewa, does he live in Oluweri as well?' he asked Ojo. 'Being a good friend of your mother, he should be very supportive in the search for her.'

'No, he lives in Egbejoda. He is a trader and only stops in Oluweri whenever he happens to trading along that route.' The prospect of being reunited with Morilewa was the first good news he had had since his separation from his mother.

'What is the name of his compound in Oluweri?'

'I don't know,' Ojo replied sincerely.

'Now you are going to do something for me. You are going to take your time and give me a detailed description of your Baba Morilewa as best as you can,' Olubi said. He motioned Ojo to sit on the mat that had been spread for Goje. Ojo sat down as instructed.

'Does he have any distinguishing feature like a tribal mark, scar or birthmark?' asked Olubi.

'He has no tribal mark or visible scar and as far as I can tell, he has no birthmark, but he limps slightly on his left leg like somebody with a permanent spell of *pajapaja* (cramps).'

Two days later, Olubi was on his way to Egbejoda. He told his wife he could be away for at least ten days but was back after only five. The third day after Olubi returned from Egbejoda and just eight days after his last visit, Goje was back at Olubi's house. He claimed he was on his way to Apete and had decided to use the opportunity to check if there had been any development since their last meeting.

'Yes, I have traced the man,' replied Olubi. 'I have been to Egbejoda and back, but I am afraid the outcome is a fish and not a crab.' He could see the disappointment written all over his guest's face. 'The man in question is out of reach, and he could be for a long time, or even forever.'

'How?'

'You must have heard about the death of the Ifa priest at Oluweri?'

'Yes, I heard about it.'

'Well, the man in question is at the centre of what is generally believed to be the conspiracy that led to the death of Fatunbi, the priest. His name is Morilewa and he is presently in confinement at Ode-Ijowa pending his trial.'

Morilewa was tried for murdering the *Ifa* priest and found guilty by the palace. He faced between twenty years to life in servitude in the king's farm, depending on the discretion of the *Onijowa*. There was a possibility of parole in the event of war, when he would have the choice of being conscripted with other inmates convicted of similar crimes to fight for the king wherever the battle was thickest. The tradition was for the king to pardon all convicts who fought or partook in a successful battle.

One could say that Morilewa was fortunate that there was a war on. He could be free as soon as it ended, if he chose to fight for the king and hopefully survive the war. But Morilewa chose not to do this. His decision was not due to cowardice but upon principle. He would rather serve his term and maintain his innocence than fight for the king and be pardoned.

As the king's enforcers were taking Morilewa to begin his term on the king's farm they were ambushed by an armed gang between Ode Ijowa and Ayefele. They were overpowered, and along with Morilewa, they were blindfolded and led deep into the forest. It was a long walk and the sun had set before they arrived at their destination. It was a small clearing in the middle of the forest with just a small hut which, from the freshness of the bamboo frames and palm leaves at the top, must have been erected just a few days earlier and probably for this purpose. The king's men, still blindfolded and with hands tied behind their backs, were sat on the damp grass, while Morilewa was led to the hut, where a man in hood, apparently the leader of the gang, was waiting. The leader asked his men to take off the blindfold and leave them together.

'I am here to free you,' said the leader, 'but there are certain items I want from you in exchange for that favour. As you are well aware, the guards who were supposed to be taking you to serve time on the king's farm are still being held by my men, and I will not hesitate to retract my favour by returning you to them if I am not satisfied by your response.' He voiced his threat clearly but calmly. 'The item which I believe you have in your possession is made of a kind of rare and precious metal. It is not gold. They are rarer and more valuable than gold. The *oyinbos* (white men) called it 'dayamon'. If you can let me have a few of them, then you can rest assured that you will not be proceeding on your original journey. You will be going to a safe place, away from the reach of the king and the people of Ijowa.'

'Precious metals? I don't have any precious metal in my possession. I don't even have a single silver coin,' Morilewa replied with passion and fear.

'I can see you are not too keen on swapping your possessions for your freedom,' the leader said in a cold but still tone. 'But you are deceiving yourself if you assume that I will not try everything, while making sure you are alive to spend your sentence on the king's farm, before letting you off.'

'I am not lying. I don't have any danyamo, or whatever you call it. I have not even seen one before. I have only tried once to trade in gold, and it ended in disaster.'

'Do you know a woman called Lalonpe?'

'Lalonpe. Lalonpeee... That name is familiar but I cannot put a face on it at the moment.'

'I can help you with that. She lives in Oluweri and she is the woman you gave that precious metal to as a gift.'

'Ah yes! I know a woman by that name in Oluweri. She is a widow and her late husband was a trade associate of mine until his death. The last time I saw her was about five years ago, just before her husband and myself went on the journey to Ashanti in quest for gold. That was my one and only attempt at trading in precious metals, and it ended in tragedy.'

'What you are telling me now is that you never had anything to do with the woman after that?'

'Not exactly. About six months ago, to be precise just before the last Ifa festival in Oluweri, I went there purposely to repay a debt I owed her husband. But I could not bear to face her, as the memory of the tragic event still haunts me today. So I approached Baba Fatunbi, who is now deceased and whose death is the root of my present predicament, to help pass the cowries to her.'

'Lalonpe has some dayamon in her possession. She said you gave them to her at about the time you said you sent the priest to her, and his son attests to that,' the man said, looking Morilewa directly in the eye.

'Somebody whom I have never met claimed I sent her to the priest, and that the last time the family saw him alive was when he left the house for the forest in response to my message. The priest was found dead close to the shrine,' Morilewa lamented. 'I will be glad if you can arrange a meeting between Lalonpe and myself and see if she can tell me to my face that I gave her anything like that or have even seen her physically since the death of her husband.'

'That I will surely do in good time. Meanwhile, I will take you along with me, but I must warn you not to play tricks with me. If at any point in my investigation I find out you have been lying, or trying to be smart, I can assure you that you will wish you had continued on your journey to the king's farm.'

'I promise to cooperate with you to the best of my knowledge. I don't know whom I have wronged but I am sure there is somebody out there bent on destroying my life,' Morilewa lamented.

Morilewa was reported to have suffered a strange illness after his trial, but before it was time to move him from Ode-Ijowa to the king's blacksmithing farms in Ayefele to begin his sentence. The illness made him lose his mind and he began to make a string of incoherent confessions about his involvement in the death of the priest. Ewedairo, the royal herbalist and medicine man, was called upon to 'observe Morilewa and make a verdict on his mental state.' Ewedairo confirmed that Morilewa was 'not stable in the mind and dangerously insane.' He went further, declaring that Morilewa must have been afflicted by a mysterious and possibly infectious disease. The herbalist's verdict was well received by the priest's family and general public as being a sign that the spirit of Fatunbi is haunting his killer.

Morilewa was referred to *Igbodudu* (meaning 'the dark forest'), an open asylum in the heart of many mountains where people with acute mental illness were taken to be cured or to wander for the rest of their lives. *Igbodudu* was not a labour farm, and its occupants were neither slaves nor criminals, so families of inmates had unrestricted but supported access to their sick kin. But this privilege was not extended to Morilewa, as he was considered a criminal who just happened to be in Igbodudu because he was sick. So on arriving at *Igbodudu*, he was put in solitary confinement, barred from having contact with other inmates and denied visits from friends and family.

'Morilewa is not like any other inmates of *Igbodudu*. He is first of all a convicted criminal and there is a strict directive from the king that he must be treated as such.' That was the head keeper and resident healer's first instruction to the guards about Morilewa when he arrived at the forest. So like the convicts on the king's farms, Morilewa was denied visual or physical contact with visitors, and all communication between him and his visiting family had to be through the guards.

Since learning of Morilewa's crime and predicaments, Olubi had abandoned any possibility of getting closer to the source of the precious stone through Morilewa. But his hope was rekindled when he learnt that Morilewa had been taken to *Igbodudu* instead of the king's farm.

Lagemo was a childhood friend of Dagunro, the head keeper at *Igbodudu*. He was later relocated from Eti-Osa by his father to live with and support his aged grandfather, who had been living alone in Inukan since the death of his last and youngest wife. It was at Inukan that he began an apprenticeship in the knowledge and skill of treating and managing people with different kinds of mental issues. Dagunro was quick to learn, and by the time his grandfather passed six years later, he had impressed his mentor so much that he willingly gave his blessing for Dagunro to practise independently and had since drawn patients from across Ijowa and beyond. The head keeper at Igbodudu died three years after Dagunro began his private practice. Atlthough he was still young compared to the past keepers, many agreed that he merited the decision by the *Onijowa* to appoint him as the new head keeper.

Lagemo took Olubi to Igbodudu and introduced him to Dagunro as a close friend who was desperate to have a private conversation with one of his patients.

'Dagunro, I know how difficult the favour I am asking could be for you,' he said. 'But I would not have asked if it is not a matter of life and death for my friend. One of your patients recommended a herb for my friend's chronic ailment, and it works wonderfully. He neither charged my friend nor receive any gratitude for his help and also did not reveal the secret of the medication, but he insisted that my friend would have to keep coming back about every three to four months for follow-up doses.'

'What makes you think this patient would not have forgotten about the prescription or even you, due to his mental state?' Dagunro warned.

'We thought of that, but there is no harm in trying and hoping that he will remember.'

'What are you going to do in the event of his death?'

'He told me all the necessary herbs and roots he uses for the medicine,' Olubi interjected. 'In fact I have been getting them myself since he first made for me. But he warned that while he is alive, the medicine will not be effective until I have taken the already prepared medication to him for blessing.'

'I can understand that,' Dagunro replied. He could not fault Olubi's story, as it was common practice for herbalists and medicine men to attach such clauses and conditions to their prescriptions. 'But there is no herbalist or person of similar vocation among my patients that I know.'

'He is not a herbalist or anything of such nature. He claimed the secret of the herb was given to him as a reward for a favour he did to a medicine man, and the conditions attach to its dispensation were not his own making, but from the source.'

'What is his name them.'

'That is the difficult part. He was brought here from the palace as a criminal.'

'Oh, you mean Morilewa.'

'That is right, my friend,' Olubi replied hopefully. 'I know the conditions of his stay here must be different from your regular patients, but I am ready to swear by all deities that my meeting with him will not go beyond the three of us here.'

'Now listen to me carefully,' Dagunro began after Olubi had been sworn to secrecy. 'None of my workers know this, but I will tell you this in private and you can be certain that I will deny having this conversation with you in the presence of any other person.' Dagunro began whispering. 'Morilewa's case is very sensitive. He was never sick in

134

the head and never stepped into this forest. There was recently a failed rescue attempt by armed men believed to be friends of Morilewa during transit to the king's farm at Ayefele. The Ijowa chiefs considered the attempt a vital warning signal that such attempts might be made again in Ayefele or any of the king's farms. There had been word already going around that some powerful men were behind the death of the *Ifa* priest and Morilewa is just being used as the sacrificial lamb. They feared that Morilewa's escape while in custody would be very embarrassing to the crown and would outrage the Ogboni fraternity and the general public. So as a precautionary measure, the chiefs advised the *Onijowa* to swap an *alanganran* (mentally unstable person) for Morilewa. Ordinary people will have no access to him as a result. Whereas, people of influence and the Ogboni fraternity have been advised of his true location, which is an undisclosed king's farm, where he will serve his time. They did not specify which in case the information leaked to Morilewa's friends again.'

'So where is Morilewa now?'

'Your guess is as good as mine,' Dagunro replied. 'Like I said, I do not know which kings farm he is at. But I can assure you that this place will be like a palace compared to where he is being held.'

While Olubi was away at *Igbodudu*, a messenger from Goje arrived at his house in Eti-Osa requesting Ojo to come down to his compound in Isale-Eko. He needed him to entertain some important but unexpected guests from Ajase who, according to the messenger, were eager to hear the youngster play the *agidigbo*. Olubi was not at home in Eti-Osa when the messenger got there and was not

135

expected back for few days. Knowing the esteem in which their husband held Goje and knowing the messenger to be a close aide of Goje, Olubi's wives agreed to allow Ojo to honour the invitation.

For two evenings, Ojo entertained Goje's guest. The five men from Ajase were individually praised by Ojo in his lyrics. They all enjoy the young boy's performance and responded very kindly.

'Correct me if I am wrong, little boy, but your face seems familiar,' one of the guests, Ekisola, asked Ojo. It was the second evening, just before the start of the performance and in the presence of two other guests. Ojo looked at the man but was certain that if he had met him before he had no recollection of it.

'I don't think so Baba,' Ojo replied. 'You travelled down from far away Ajase and I have never been anywhere outside Ijowa and Akete in my life.'

'I am sure I have seen you somewhere before, and I don't mean in Ajase,' Ekisola insisted. 'I often visited Oluweri whenever I happen to be in Ijowa. Do you know anybody in Oluweri, or have you ever been to Oluweri?' Ojo's reaction to the mention of Oluweri was unmissable.

'I was born in Oluweri and that is where I lived all my life!' Ojo replied excitedly. 'I would have been there now if not for the war.'

'That is it. That is be where I must have seen you before,' Ekisola said triumphantly. 'Are you sure you have no recollection of my face?'

'It is possible you might know me, but I cannot remember seeing your face before,' Ojo replied with certainty.

'Ha ha! Ekisola, leave the poor boy alone,' Goje interrupted as he emerged from within the house. 'He said he cannot remember your face, or do you have something to benefit from being recognised?' He stopped Ekisola from probing further.

Later in the evening, Goje was with the two other guests who were present when Ekisola was chatting with Ojo.

'What do you think about this evening?' he asked no one in particular.

'I think he is telling the truth. The boy definitely had not seen him before,' one of the guests replied.

'There is no doubt about it. Neither of them had ever seen each other before,' the other added in agreement.

The conflict lasted for eight full months. At the peak of the confrontation, the Akete warriors were able to inflict considerable havoc on the people and properties of the Ijowa villages that lay along the boundary between Ijowa and Aketeland, like Kuluso, Gbajumo, Olokoto and Oko-Oba. Ijowa warriors were able to do the same to Akete villages like Apete, Iseri, Isale-Eko and of course Seleru. Then, just when the battle could be adjudged to be going slightly in favour of Aketeland, the *Akogun* (supreme warlord), of the Akete warriors suddenly ordered his men to retreat from all other fronts and concentrate all efforts at occupying the entire seafront of Oluweri for as long as possible.

The battle of Oluweri was the last of the conflict, and the most severe. The Akete army entered Lower-Oluweri and twelve days later, the whole of Oluweri fell into the hands of the invaders. The general belief was that Oluweri would not have been easily overrun if Fatunbi had been alive. Some went further to claim that the death of the

powerful and respected spiritualist was part of a larger
conspiracy by Oba Lagbade to invade and occupy Oluweri.

Lalonpe had her baby when it was due. The birth of her
son, whom she named Bogunde, was remembered as the
day after Oluweri and its sorrounding settlements finally
fell into the hands of the Akete warriors, and the seafront
of Oluweri was no longer under the control of *Onijowa* and
the palace at Ode-Ijowa.

The invasion and consequent occupation of Oluweri might
have been a rude shock to the *Onijowa* and people of Ijowa,
but the reason behind it was known to those closest to
the king of Aketeland. Although the conflict between the
fishermen of Seleru and Kuluso and the escalation of the
feud into a fully-fledged war was not by design, there was
a clear motivation for the occupation of Oluweri.

Fidel Wontsay had originally chosen Epetedo among
other Akete communities on the seafront as most suitable
for a merchant ship to dock. But about the fourth month
into the war, he received a visitor in Iseri, another
explorer, called Goldigger. He brought with him the single
stone from the *ejigbaileke* which Ojo had given to Olubi,
and which the latter had sold to Goje Salaji. Within two
months, the stone had been traded and retraded until it
got to a market in Kotonu, and finally into the hands of
Goldigger. In order to be able to sell the stone even to the
shrewdest of traders at Ojuoro, Goje needed to back up his
ownership and right to sell it with a story. Any story would
do, as both buyer and seller knew the process was just a
formality. The buyer knew that the seller would not even
believe his own story and would not be likely to remember
the detail after a few weeks. Goje's story was that he had

inherited it from his father, whom he claimed had found it in the belly of a fish he had caught while fishing in the Oluweri part of the Awoyaya river.

As the stone travelled around and the story was passed from one buyer to another, it accumulated added tales and mystery. By the time the stone got to Goldigger, the story was that the original owner had got it from his father, who had found it at the bottom of the deepest and clearest part of the Awoyaya river at Oluweri. Wontsay visited the palace at Aromire with what he called an 'urgent issue' which could be best resolved while there was a war on. Wontsay explained that due to the position of Akala, which he had regretfully failed to take into consideration, Aromire and Epetedo, the two Akete communities with vibrant markets on the seafront, would not be suitable for merchant ships to dock.

'It is unfortunate that Akala Island has screened most of Akete's deepest and widest seafront and the rest are too far from existing markets,' Wontsay told the king in council. 'The nearest feasible shore that can hold trade ships and at the same time falls along the existing trade route into the hinterlands is that of Oluweri.'

Oba Lagbade made Wontsay understand that taking over Oluweri and holding on to it would require enormous resources, but the latter pledged to provide all the support needed by the Akete army to achieve the task. Whilst *Oba* Lagbade's decision to occupy Oluweri was to take control of a future trading front, Wontsay's change of location from Epetedo to Oluweri had nothing to do with the suitability of the Epetedo seafront.

Relying on the advantage of newly-acquired firearms, the warriors of Akete had dreamt of a profitable campaign in term of spoils of war, but the ease with which they overran the Ijowa army at Lower-Oluweri boosted their moral to the brim and the warriors did not hesitate when Akintokun, the *Agba-Eso* (battalion commander) who had led the Akete army in the conquest of Lower-Oluweri ordered his men to cross the Awoyaya and march upon the stronghold of the Ijowa army at upper Oluweri. By the time the clash between the forces of Ijowa and Akete had run its full cycle, it was Ijowa that had suffered most of the losses with very little gain in return. On the other side, the palace at Aromire suffered minimal casualties and gained an enormous fortune in terms of human captives and material loot. The fall of Oluweri effectively ended the war. At the end of the conflict, it was the king and people of Ijowa who suffered the greatest loss of the war; the commercial nerve centre of the entirety of Ijowaland, the market at Lower-Oluweri.

The seeming truce between the palace at Ode-Ijowa and its counterpart at Aromire was largely due to the strategic withdrawal of Ijowa warriors from the front line to avoid total humiliation. Unlike other fronts, where bullets and gunpowder were strictly rationed on both sides based on urgency, Ijowa warriors were surprised and suppressed in Oluweri by an army that seemed to have an endless supply of firearms.

To redeem the occupied Oluweri, the palace at Aromire knowingly demanded what they knew the Ijowa people would not be willing to pay. *Oba* Lagbade decreed that the *Onijowa* must for the next twenty seasons submit twenty bondservants at the beginning every season, to serve *Oba* Lagbade in his palace at Aromire. In the event of non-compliance by the *Onijowa*, *Oba* Lagbade would at the end of each and every season that the bond servants failed to report at the palace at Aromire, convert a quarter of the next harvest from the residents of Lower-Oluweri for the use of the king and chiefs of Aketeland.

The *Onijowa* and his chiefs deliberated on the issue and as expected, they concluded that it would amount to a great insult on the head that bore the crown if the *Onijowa* conceded to such a condition. They considered that having to send young Ijowas to serve the king of Akete for twenty years in order to retrieve what rightly belonged to Ijowa was humiliating. It was not the first time that territories had been taken over due to war, and it was not unusual for an occupying palace to demand one price or levy as penalty before territories taken during war were returned. What was unusual, and what any monarch across the tribes would find humiliating, was to be subjected to a continual reminder of its woes over such a long time.

The refusal was not about cost, but ego. If he conceded to such a demand, the *Onijowa* would be looked upon by other monarchs as a weak ruler, and his chiefs would be the subject of mockery among circles of nobles. So the king did what was expected, and what most monarchs would do in such a situation – he stood on his pride. By refusing to comply, the message was that *Onijowa* had only taken a tactical retreat and the Akete army would neither be able to afford to sleep nor slumber in occupied Oluweri, as Ijowa could launch an offensive at any time to reclaim it. So in response to the condition, the reply from the palace at Ode-Ijowa was plain and simple: 'The Ijowa people will reclaim that which rightly belongs to them, even if it has to be in the manner by which it was taken. The *Onijowa* will recover what rightly belongs to his forefathers when he is ready and without condition.'

The response from the palace at Ode-Ijowa was as *Oba* Lagbade has hoped and expected, and he was quick to take the action he had planned in anticipation of such a response from Ode-Ijowa. The *Baale* of Oluweri was exiled from Lower-Oluweri, and *Oba* Lagbade appointed an *Ajele* (sole administrator) to fill the void.

'The king demands me to ensure that his annual tributes are remitted to the palace at Aromire as at when due and in the right quantity,' the Ajele appointed by Oba Lagbade upon his arrival told the Ijowa residents who had chosen to remain in occupied Oluweri. 'The king demands of me to make it clear to you all that even a year's default in the annual tribute to the palace would compel him to send down his own *Asingba* (administrator of defaults) to take whatever quantity of your harvest the king decides to be his rightful dues.'

The *Onijowa* refused to send bondservants to the palace at Aromire, but the Ajele put in place by Oba Lagbade, in the same spirit, ensured that a quarter of all the last harvest in Lower-Oluweri at the end of the season was duly tranported to the palace at Aromire. Furthermore, a tenth of the returns on all transactions at Oluweri market every fortnight were duly remitted to the *Akapo* (palace treasury) of Oba Lagbade. In his concluding action and amidst fierce protests by the palace at Ode-Ijowa, Oba Lagbade moved the settlement of Fidel Wontsay from Iseri to Lower-Oluweri. The explorer and his staff were resettled in a location which the people of Akete quickly (amidst further disapproval by the Ijowa people) referred to as Ago-Oyinbo (the abode of the white man).

The *Onijowa* and his chiefs considered the resettlement of Wontsay in occupied Oluweri to be a breach of the peace agreement. In pursuance of justice, the case was taken by the king and people of Ijowa to Oyo town, and presented before the supreme council of Yoruba chiefs, known as the Oyomesi. For its own part the palace at Aromire insisted that it had not broken the agreement which guaranteed the return of Lower-Oluweri to the palace at Ode-Ijowa after twenty seasons. The palace claimed that the settlement of Fidel Wontsay at Oluweri would not extend beyond the duration of the occupation.

The Oyomesi sat, but decided in favour of Akete. They urged the *Onijowa* 'in the interests of peace' to allow the time specified in the agreement to run its course.

While the *Onijowa* and his chiefs were seething over the development at Oluweri concerning Ago-Oyinbo, Adeyanju's own anger was mixed with anxiety. This was because the men he sent to occupied Oluweri came with depressing news. Lalonpe's house was among many that were vandalised during the battle for Oluweri and the ruins were now within the perimeter of Ago-Oyinbo. This meant that his only link to Lalonpe has been broken, and all his labour over the ritual of truth had come to naught. Furthermore, and of equal importance, the possibility of accessing the site to look for the beads was close to naught.

Adeyanju decided to take the bold step of learning the truth the conventional way by marrying a second wife. He married Gbemisola, the youngest daughter of the *Iyaloja* (the titled chief in charge of market affairs) of Ijowaland.

On a rainy dawn, about five months after she was married into the palace, Gbemisola (now called Gbemisade to reflect her new status as member of the royal family) suddenly fell sick. She complained of dizziness and later vomited. The royal herbalist was immediately sent for. He arrived in the palace with a variety of fresh herbs he thought might be useful, based on the messenger's description of Gbemisade's condition. Meanwhile, he advised the prince to invite Agbomola, the royal midwife, to have a look at the woman. Agbomola later sought a private audience with the prince and broke the good news to him that Gbemisade was pregnant.

Gbemisade had her baby when it was due, and the palace was full of unspoken relief that it was a boy. The youngest prince of Ijowa was named Baderin, and his birth was recorded by the palace historian as having taken place at the beginning of the second harvest after the fall of Oluweri.

CHAPTER 7

Although the Ijowa/Akete conflict had come and gone, the hostility between the two palaces would continue as long as Lower-Oluweri remained occupied, and the distress suffered by an average Akete and Ijowa resident would linger for many seasons. During those periods, there were acute shortages of food, synonymous with the aftermath of a war. There was nothing to scavenge upon. The market at Eti-Osa, which had been considered the second most vibrant on the Akete mainland, was deserted for a whole season. Throughout the year following the war, all the 'fertile' trade routes from which the likes of Olubi's gang collected security grants were taken over by idle warriors who were reluctant to return to their peacetime occupations. As a result, the farmers of villages bordering Awoyaya on both the Akete and Ijowa territories were unable to work on the farms in fear of sudden attacks from either side.

The fortune from the single stone which Olubi had collected from Ojo had come at the right time, but it only lasted for a few months as it was all Olubi and his household (which now included Ojo) had to depend on. Although spending was lavish while it lasted, every stomach was affected when the fortune was exhausted.

As soon as relative peace began to reign across the Akete and Ijowa town and villages, Ojo was made to earn something for the 'family' by playing the *agidigbo* to entertain on market days, and sometimes as an uninvited performer at social functions. There were times when the memories of the comfort due to the proceeds from the stone nearly tempted him to considered confessing to Olubi about the rest of the stones and beads, but the thought of his mother, and the possibility of the owner of the beads coming back for it, prevented him. However, he kept the hope that one day he would be able to journey to Oluweri and retrieve the *ejigbaileke* without Olubi's knowledge.

Very much like the inmates of the king's farm, visual interaction was strictly disallowed between Morilewa and his visitors. Communication between him and his family had to be directed through the guards, along with all supplies. This privilege, however, was restricted to important family news like births and bereavements, and for inmates with chronic ailments having access to a regular supply of herbs and medications provided by their families. For obvious precautionary reasons, herbs, medication and other edibles had to be tasted by the bearer, and if they were for external use, they had to be tested on the bearer before being passed on to the inmate.

Morilewa had been in confinement for almost two years and Lalonpe had made two journeys to *Igbodudu*, but the response from the other end had alway been the same:

'Morilewa is still not in his right mind and can neither comprehend the message nor make a sensible response,' as she was told by the guards on her first visit.

On her second visit she was told, 'Morilewa's mental state has so deteriorated since arriving at *Igbodudu* that sending messages to him or expecting a sensible reply is a waste of time.' On each journey, she took with her supplies like fresh clothing, sun-dried meat and fish in considerable quantity to support Morilewa until her next visit. On her third and last journey to *Igbodudu*, the guards on sentry duty declined to take the supplies she had brought for him. Lalonpe got the message and burst into tears. She was still sobbing as she began the first leg of her return journey to Kuluso, when she was cornered by one of the guards - an old man who looked so frail that she wondered how he could be of any use as a guard in such a place.

'What are you to Morilewa?' The old man asked.

'I am his friend. A very close friend. We are the kind of friends you could refer to as family,' Lalonpe replied amidst tears.

'If you are that close, I expect you should have learnt something from his family.'

'Well, I don't live in Egbejoda. I live in Gbajumo and I am not so well known by his family,' Lalonpe replied, and the old man rightly understood the kind of friendship that existed between Lalonpe and Morilewa.

'My fair woman, I don't know if what I am going to say will be of any consolation to you, but I sincerely believe that Morilewa is better dead than continuing with life as he was. His mental and physical state has deteriorated considerably since arriving at *Igbodudu*. He rarely sleeps and goes for days without eating, just drinking water. Most of the consumables you brought were not used by Morilewa but shared among the guard before they turned bad. They refused to take the items you brought this time around because they were not comfortable with robbing the dead. That is a taboo.'

It was a little over two years after the war that the much-anticipated trade ship finally sailed round Akala Island and docked on the seafront of Oluweri. For years, the people of the Akete and Ijowa communities on the seafront would gather by the shore for hours watching, in the far distance, large ships as they occasionally sailed across the far end of Akala Island and then disappeared. Under normal circumstances, the palace at Ode-Ijowa was supposed to be the authority to deal with the captain of the merchant ship that docks on this waterfront, and the sons of the soil of Oluweri were supposed to be the major beneficiaries of the goodness that came with the new trading front. But because Oluweri and its surrounding lands all the way to the seafront were still under occupation, it was the palace at Aromire that singularly took charge of all communication and transactions with the ship's master.

Before news of the merchant ship reached the palace at Aromire, the *Ajele* (an Akete high chief who was also privy to the underlying reason for the occupation of Oluweri) appointed by *Oba* Lagbade to be the 'eye of the king' on the occupied Oluweri had taken the responsibility of calling upon Wontsay to broker peace with the captain. In their first communication via Wontsay to the captain, the Ajele insisted that for peace to be assured, the merchant and all his crew must remain aboard until *Oba* Lagbade had been formally told of their presence. This news and the action taken by the *Ajele* was immediately conveyed via messengers on horseback to the palace at Aromire, and the messengers returned with a definite reply from the king that the captain and all his crew must present themselves, without arms, to the palace within three days.

The captain and his crew, as decreed by the palace, were mounted on fourteen horses to be escorted to Aromire. The name of the captain was Tettlestone, and his ship was filled with all that the king and the Akete chiefs desired. The outcome of the meeting was pleasing to both parties. Tettlestone and his crew were granted the right to dock and trade on that waterfront, on the condition that his cargo must be made known beforehand, and all trading must be done through the king's representative for the purpose of trade tax.

Captain Tettlestone's ship was the first of many to dock on the seafront of Oluweri, and the beginning of a flourishing partnership between the palace at Aromire and many ship captains and merchants to come. As ants are attracted to honey, the Akete royals, high chiefs and wealthy sons of the soil were the first to benefit from the arrival of the merchant ship and those that followed it. But there is a saying among the elders that 'the squirrel that enjoys the sweetness of banana should also be aware that sweet things have been the cause of many a downfall.'

The occupation of Oluweri greatly affected the livelihood of the average Ijowa person. Oluweri was the major market where traders from across Ijowa's towns and villages met and traded with their counterparts from other tribes and kingdoms. It was at Oluweri that produce from the rich soils of Ijowa was traded for goods from as far away as the Idomi and Ashanti lands and even beyond.

Due to the occupation of Oluweri, all trade tax previously collected by the palace at Ode-Ijowa from traders at every Oluweri market, and the passage tariffs collected from traders and commuters using the many tributaries of Awoyaya at Oluweri into the big ocean to access Isale-Eko and other parts of Aketeland, were now being collected and remitted to the palace at Aromire. The once-busy markets of Ijowa's towns and villages were becoming more and more isolated. Communities became impoverished, and unrest grew. The palace at Ode-Ijowa had withdrawn half its military presence in the countryside due to shortages in the palace revenue, rendering the routes into upper Oluweri and other Ijowa markets like Egbejoda unsafe and traders more vulnerable to attack.

For many generations, Ijowa had remained the largest concentration of labour in the whole tribe. Hundreds of families were employed to work on various cotton farms across Ijowa, and many more at the mines on the north frontier. Moreover, because of the richness of her soil which enabled profitable trade, an average Ijowa man did not have to engage in extremely physical or stressful labour to survive.

But unfortunate tides were beginning to blow upon Ijowa on both the commercial and political fronts. The downturn in its economy was not only due to a change in trade that favoured the emerging alternative trade route down south to the big oceans, but also to poor weather conditions which had been affecting local produce for the past four seasons. Hence labour, which was the nucleus of Ijowa's economy, began to move the other way, down across Awoyaya to serve wealthy merchants at Akete or to go seeking gold in the mines of the Ashanti people.

The loom yards were becoming deserted due to decreasing patronage, as lighter textiles, more suitable for the tropical climate than local textiles were coming through Lower-Oluweri into the markets at Eti-Osa and Aromire. All these goods were being traded in quantities which would have been unimaginable before the first ship docked in Oluweri. The blacksmithing yards across Ijowa and Akete were producing far below capacity and losing craftsmen because lighter and more durable farm tools and other hardware were coming into the Ijowa market from traders, who now travelled through the numerous waterways that had now opened up. The immediate result of this development was a trade tax collected by the palace from both the buyers and sellers who passed through Ode-Ijowa from across the tribes.

The unfortunate tide that was blowing the fortunes of Ijowa away across the Awoyaya river was blowing a fairer one from the big ocean upon the towns and villages that had their backyards on the seafront. Notable among these were the waterfronts of Idomi, Ibini and the new port at Oluweri. Merchant ships from across the oceans now frequently docked and traded in Oluweri, each ship laden with articles of value in quantities far larger than any brought by the many trade caravans by the Arabs through the north. Merchants from big cities, who had previously had to endure the difficult task of having to cross the Awoyaya river and then travelling through Ode-Ijowa and further north of Ijowaland to meet and trade with the Arabs, began travelling in the opposite direction.

The economic advantage enjoyed by the palace at Aromire since the first merchant ship had docked on the seafront at Oluweri was beyond all the king's expectations.

At Aromire, one could earn up to three silver coins a day merely by fanning mosquitoes away from nobles, white merchants and seafarers. Better still, you could get yards of textile, enough to make a *dandogo* (oversized garment) in three days by helping the merchants to carry goods to the coast from the hinterland. The rich landlords of southern Ijowa were the first to feel the impact of such movement. Their labourers no longer wanted to stay on the farms; their focus was now on trading on the coast. Ijowa landowners and slave owners were finding it more profitable to lease out the land and put their slaves into bond service than to use or keep it for production.

In anticipation of many more merchant ships to come after Tettlestone's, Oba Lagbade and his chiefs realised the need to increase production to meet the future demand for cash crops. The relationship between the palace at Aromire and her subjects suffered a serious setback when *Oba* Lagbade decreed that henceforth, any of his subjects whose activity or inactivity 'provoked the king's anger' would be sent to Akala Island.

The pronouncement came from the palace a few months after Tettlestone's ship departed from Oluweri. According to the palace spokesman, the king's pronouncement was not a new one but an extension of an existing law. The new pronouncement was an extension in the sense that the range of criminals or crimes purnishable by deportation to Akala was extended to include those found guilty of being 'incorrigible criminals'.

In the past, securing access to and exit from Akala had not been in any way a security priority to the palace at Aromire. However, after the new pronouncements by the king, the only navigable access to Akala from the Akete mainland at Aromire was under the watchful eyes of the king's army. The rest of the island's frontier was with the open ocean, which was only navigable by big ships. The architects of the idea knew what they were doing by introducing the clause 'incorrigible criminals' in the king's pronouncement. It is clear that score of petty cases were brought to the palace and local authorities on a daily basis, while trials for major crime could 'provoke the king's anger'.

According to palace sources, the phrase 'incorrigible criminals' was what influenced the king to make the new pronouncement. The king's new pronouncement would affect only those who refused to change after several convictions, explained the title chief mandated by the king to promote public approval of the decision. However, the message is very well understood by the analogy of the crying baby and the pacifying mother. The pronouncement was a calculated measure to draft more men into the king's plantation at Akala. This meant that a hungry peasant convicted four times for petty crimes would automatically be sent to Akala. But a first offender, who robbed and killed in a single criminal act, would only be taken if he 'provoked the king's anger'.

Soon petty crimes became less profitable, as the spoils did not justify the retribution. Why steal three silver coins at different times and risk deportation to Akala when you can steal a sack of gold in a single crime and can get away with less than four seasons on the king's farm on the Akete mainland? At the same time, few people have the courage and bravery to engage in violent robbery; hence at the end of the day, there were still many petty criminals whose motive for stealing was little more than the need to survive the next day. In daring gangs like that of Olubi, already convicted inmates were kept away from risky assignments to avoid running out of chances at the palace court and ending up in the Akala.

Convictions became speedy, and the trips to Akala became more frequent as the palace started amending laws to be less tolerant to offenders. Convictions for rape were amended and extended, applying to the moment it was proven that the accused had seen the nakedness of his victim, as against there being carnal contact. Then punishment for 'incorrigible rapists' was extended from five to ten years on Akala Island. Convictions for rape were rare before the amendment, as many victims were too ashamed and afraid of ridicule to even admit to the jury that the accused had had intercourse with them. But within weeks of the amendment taking effect, convictions had trebled. This was because it was less damaging for a victim to claim that the accused had only seen her nakedness than that he had gone all the way. This way the victim could retain her crucial dignity and still get justice.

On every market day and in all markets, fresh news of rape convictions was shared daily by market women from different towns and villages across Aketeland. The whole of Akete were alarmed at the number of 'evil men' that lived among them. The women argued that recent developments indicated that the palace had for long been insensitive to the plight of women. The topic sparked new consciousness among women activists, who began to question the responsibility of *Iyalode* of Aketeland. *Iyalode* was the king's adviser on women's affairs in general. She was the official voice of women in the palace, and also the 'king's eye' in the market.

'That shows the level of indifference at the palace to the

plight of ordinary woman,' one activist commented.

'You're right. The palace has been for a long time insensitive to our suffering,' a second agreed.

'But tell me, what can one voice be among eight? *Iyalode* is the only female voice in the palace. We are supposed to be thankful to her for ensuring that such crimes against women are included among those purnishable by Akala,' said a third.

The controversy compelled *Iyalode* to appeal to the king, saying that in order to 'further protect our women' there should be a compensation scheme for victims of rape and domestic violence. The popularity of *Iyalode* among townswomen was at an all-time high due to the compensation scheme. *Oba* Lagbade and the Akete chiefs on the other hand were delighted by the result, as there was a daily increase in the number of accusations, charges and conviction.

Three months later, she made another proposal to the king which further lowered the crown's tolerance to assaults on women. She argued, and the king agreed, to further amend the Akala pronouncement so that rape would be established the moment it was proven that the accused had touched either the breast or the bottom of the victim. The conviction was the same, but the compensation increased according to the extent to which the victim had been assaulted. Hence, a victim would get more if she had been assaulted on both the breast and the bottom than just one of the two but less than a victim who had been stripped of any part of her clothing before she was rescued. A maiden who was bold enough to admit in public to having been carnally assaulted would get a premium compensation.

While Ojo could not be said to be enslaved to Olubi, and the latter had not at any point considered himself his owner, he was not entirely free to range on his own. He was enslaved by age and maturity, which together are a vital prerequisite for security and freedom. A boy of his age would not be able to travel alone beyond the next community before his identity and mission would be questioned. Ojo's comfort or deprivation since Olubi took custody of him, like that of other children of Olubi, largely depended upon the circumstances of the head of the family. Whenever Olubi's fortune soared, Ojo would automatically begin to enjoy a life like that of a son. In those times Olubi seldom engaged Ojo in any productive activity, so the boy stayed in Olubi's compound and engaged in domestic chores, and in the evening he entertained Olubi and his friends on the *agidigbo*. But whenever Olubi needed to be outside Eti-Osa, Ojo was everything to Olubi except a slave or servant. While Ojo's living conditions at a particular time basically depended upon the fortunes of Olubi, his status in the presence of 'his father' outside Eti-Osa at any time depended on the nature of the task he was engaged in, and the circumstances. Sometimes Olubi referred to him as just 'a dependant' and at other times he would tell whoever was concerned that Ojo was his nephew, cousin, stepbrother, half-brother etcetera, but never his child. Although Olubi also engaged his children as hired hands to work in farms in the same way he did with Ojo, he never referred to them as anything but his children. Only his daughters were old enough to work. His only son from his second wife was just eight months old when Ojo joined the family. Then, to be fair, Olubi could not engage his girls in farms outside Eti-Osa as it was socially unacceptable that unmarried girls should be made to live away from their parents or guardian, especially when such migration was for economic purposes. Young girls were not supposed to trade outside their community except under supervision.

The first time Ojo attempted to retrieve the *ejigbaileke* ended in disaster. It was close to five years after he had left Oluweri with his mother. One afternoon, he was mentioned as a blood relation to a friend whom Olubi met at idi-odan. The odan is a tree with broad shade that provides soothing cover from the tropical sun, and its surrounding ground is generally referred to as the *idi-odan* (meaning under the odan tree). The idi-odan was very popular among communities as a place for evening recreation after a hard day's work on the farm, and there is hardly a community or settlement without *odan* trees in their common grounds. It was under the odan tree that men used to get together in the evening to chat, drink and play games. At the *idi-odan* there was always something to keep minds, mouths and hands busy. He who did not drink would eat kola and chat, as there would always be a chatterbox to start a gossip and many more to keep it going.

That same evening, before he left Idi-Odan, Olubi had concluded a bargain over Ojo.

'But you told me he was your nephew?' the planter asked with total disbelief when Olubi offered his 'nephew' to be an *iwofa* (bondservant) in the melon farm, knowing fully well the kind of task such an *iwofa* would be engaged in.

'Whatever direction pleases the wind, that is where it bends the treetops. The kind of errand I send my nephew on is none of your concern,' Olubi replied to the planter.

So by cockcrow the next dawn, Ojo was on his way to a

melon farm in upper Oluweri as a bondservant. He could not grumble, for he was sure there would be at least two solid and regular meals every day, and Olubi for his own part could use some regular cowries to survive till the next windfall.

Although Lower-Oluweri was under occupation, it was still united with the other Ijowa communities by the market at Oluweri. Every fortnight, the markets on both sides of the river at lower and upper Oluweri were the meeting points for both communities. As early as cockcrow, farmers and produce traders from Gbemuyona, Inukan, Gbajumo, Egbejoda and Ode-Ijowa would converge on the market in upper Oluweri, while their counterparts from Ayefele, Odinjo, Olokoto, Oko-Oba and Kuluso would converge on the market in Lower-Oluweri. The Awoyaya river was at its narrowest between upper and Lower-Oluweri, so traders and buyer often made numerous shuttles across the river before a transaction could be completed. The only difference was that the market tariffs collected on each side of the river went to the treasury of the palace in control there. However, in order to avoid paying trade tax to any of the palaces, more than two thirds of all transactions on every Oluweri market day were conducted aboard canoes on the river.

Three months after he arrived at upper Oluweri, Ojo found the opportunity to cross the Awoyaya into Lower-Oluweri. He was very depressed by what he found. Even more than four years after the war, the havoc wrought upon that side of Oluweri was still visible in every corner. The potters worksheds had gone, and in their place was the newly-built compound of the Ajele (administrator) of Oba Lagbade in occupied Oluweri.

It took a while before he could locate his former home, as the entire building was now within the grounds of Ago-Oyinbo. Although almost half the building had collapsed, he was relieved that the back room of the house and the area where he had buried the beads were still standing.

He climbed over the bamboo fencing into the outer part of Ago-Oyinbo and walked quietly towards the old house. He was trying as much as possible to avoid stepping on the dry leaves that covered most of the ground at that season. It was painful to see the state of what used to be his home. Half the walls had crumbled, apparently due to fire. He ventured into what remained of the sleeping room, and it was evident that the house had been looted before it was set on fire. But his presence was noticed as he sneaked into the part of the building he believe to be the back room. In an attempt to cover his real intentions, he stooped and pretended to be relieving himself.

Ojo was arrested, taken to the court of the *Ajele* and charge with tresspassing and vandalism. He got fifty lashes and lay in pain for a full week due to his injuries. He was unable to work on the farm, which drew the anger of the melon farmer as it was the middle of harvesting.

In the fourth month after he had leased Ojo away, Olubi found a compelling reason to redeem him from bond service at upper Oluweri. It was at the peak of harvesting and the busiest time on the melon farm. Despite the fact that Olubi offered to pay all he owed for Ojo in full, and was ready to consider the four months of labour which Ojo had put into the service of the planter as interest, the melon planter was not at all happy with Ojo leaving.

'We will need to see the *Baale* about this,' he said with an air of formality.

'The *Baale* was not called as a witness to our agreement, so why do we have to see him now?' Olubi asked.

'We need to see the *Baale* because I deserve compensation for the sudden change in agreement. Where do you expect me to find a free hand to work the farm at this time of the season?'

'But I am offering to ignore the four months which my nephew worked on your farm,' Olubi explained.

'It does not work that way, my brother. What you are offering would amount to nothing compared to the value of the melons that will rot on my farm if not harvested on time.' Olubi, however, was visibly rushed; very unlike the man that had sent 'his nephew' on bond service a few months earlier. Moreover, he had a new sharpness about his presentation, and was dressed in a manner which suggested he had left purposely to make this particular journey.

Before now, the appearance of Olubi had never been in any way a reflection of his pocket. Rich or poor, he had never bothered about the state of his appearance. It was obvious even to the melon planter that Olubi at that moment was the focus of what seemed to be a smiling god. Olubi chose not to pursue the matter with the village authority but paid what the farmer was asking in compensation and left with Ojo. Olubi had needed only to wait for another month for the season to be over. By then, Ojo would have served the term of the bond, and he would not need to return the original debt or pay any compensation. Ojo knew there must be a very good reason for Olubi's action.

The next morning before cockcrow, Olubi left upper Oluweri with Ojo. They were joined by Lagemo on the outskirts of Oluweri. He had with him two horses and a bundle of fine clothing. Before they set off, Olubi revealed their intended destination to be Elewe-eran. On their way, he explained in detail the purpose of their journey and Ojo's role in his scheme.

They stopped when they were nearing Elewe-eran. It was getting to noon and Olubi asked Ojo to change into the fine clothing and mount one of the horses, while Lagemo led the other. This time around, Olubi's need for Ojo demanded a total reversal of roles. On arriving at Elewe-eran, Olubi and Lagemo introduced Ojo as their landlord's son in the presence of a band of Fulani nomads who were seeking good pasture for their herd of cattle. Olubi was able to convince the Fulanis that an uncultivated stretch of grassland bordering a recently vacated *ahere* (farmhouse) belonged to Ojo's father and that the boy had his blessing to lease it out for such purpose. After a long session of haggling and passionate pleading by the Fulani for a moderate charge, Olubi collected five cows and ten horses from the nine Fulani families and disappeared with Ojo.

Close to eighty years after departing from their homeland, almost all the well-to-do Erebe people in Ijowa, Akete and even Abatan were either directly or indirectly, genuinely or otherwise, connected to trading. While an average well-to-do Erebe family in Oko-Oba engaged in trade across town and villages of Ijowa, Abatan and Akete, the preoccupation of the average less well-to-do Erebe person in Akete was the disruption of trade. The trade routes that extended across the major commercial hubs of Idomi, Ibini and Ashanti lands were the most precarious, an area of trade which many Ijowa, Abatan and even Oyo traders found too risky to justify the profit. Meanwhile, traders of Erebe origin travelled to and from these big markets without fear for themselves or their goods. This was because the major hindrance to this trade was basically the activity of bandits, most of which were headed by an Erebeman and largely constituted Erebe youth across Ijowa, Akete and Abatan.

The emerging generation of Erebe traders were not unaware of the factor that enhanced their success in trading across boundaries, and did not mind indirectly investing part of their profit in maintaining the status quo. They established a clandestine channel through which contributions in term of money, goods and other valuables, popularly referred to by the donors as *owo-olona* (passage tariff), were given to major bandits that plied these trade routes, for two purposes. The first was to continue to spare Erebe traders while travelling along the notorious route and the second, equally important, was to step up attacks on non-Erebe traders along the same routes. Hence, the popular slogan within the circle of Erebe *alajapas* (travelling/normadic traders) was 'treading the dark night could be fatal for the rats, but it is no barrier even to a baby python'. An equally popular but derogatory slogan by the adversaries of Erebe people was 'a wealthy Erebeman is either an *alajapa* (travellng trader) or an *onisunmomi* (bandit or conman).

Olubi's outfit started as what could be described as a kind of 'banditry for beginners'. They plied the minor routes, holding up small traders and travellers on their way between local farms and markets. However, after swindling the Fulanis, the outfit soon developed into a more sophisticated and organised gang with a few horses to their credit, and the scope of their activities enlarged to include some semi-legal trades and occupations. He now engaged his horses and men to provide security for wealthy traders and their goods through difficult terrains along the trade routes. Those were the limit of legal activities carried out by Olubi's new outfit. But in the cover of darkness, Olowoeyo still provided the service of a private debt collector. He engaged his men in many clandestine activities, ranging from forceful recovery of debt or property and seizing and holding goods against default on rent or bond service to acting as witness to pledges and enforcement of pledges. However, none of this, legal or otherwise, was without an element of intimidation, threat and violence, and both Olubi and Olowoeyo's names were very popular in their respective fronts. While Olubi's security outfit was among the most sought after by rich traders and travellers, the men of Olowoeyo were the most dreadful among the *asingba* (debt collectors or pledge enforcers).

The trading concern of Goje Salaji was among the major contributors to the *owo-olona* (passage tariff). Olubi Kudaisi was the major channel through which the security grants collected from traders of Erebe origin were distributed to various Erebe bandits, and the gang of Olowoeyo was one of the receipients of the largest share of *owo-olona*.

CHAPTER 8

It was not unusual once in while for communities to wake up to the news of a young girl running away with a man. Each case followed the same general pattern. The incident usually began with the girl stupidly losing her virginity to the wrong man, one whom the girl's parent for one reason or the other would never accept as a son-in-law. In extreme circumstances, the families or communities of the lovers, due to long-standing disputes, would never agree to the relationship.

In most cases, the girls were adolescents who had matured too quickly, and whose parents had failed to recognise the warning signs and take necessary precautions before the girl fell for the scheming of an admirer. In some cases an older man with two or more wives already in his compound would lure the innocent girl into sex before marriage with cheap gifts. After that there was no turning back, because no maiden would be prepared to face the humiliation of the wedding night when the groom discovered that the bride was not a virgin. The girl's only choice was to find a way of eventually marrying the opportunist.

However, in typical cases of true love between teenagers, the couple, while hoping to eventually marry each other, would religiously hide their secret. The crucial step was when the lovers officially disclosed their desire by asking for the blessing of their parents to begin courting. In random cases when parents accepted their choice of spouse, and the union was mutually supported by both sets of parents, then nobody would be the wiser concerning the virginity of the new wife. It was considered a great dishonour upon the bride's family, and very humiliating for a groom, to discover on the wedding night that his new bride was after all not so new. There would be no traditional bloodstained cloth to display at dawn following the wedding night. The groom would have no 'proof of conquest' for peers who had been through similar experiences. For the unfortunate one for whom one or both parents disapproved of the relationship, the only option was to elope without their blessing

The story of Goje's daughter Ojuolape follows this typical pattern but with a slight variation. Just before her seventeenth year, Ojuolape and Adigun, the eldest son of Olayera, had been each other's favourite for close to a year, and it took a short time for their parents to be aware of the association. It was apparent that both parents had in principle agreed to the relationship and what it was intended to develop into. Otherwise, their children would have been made to stop seeing each other within the first two weeks of their friendship, by either or both of the families. Although each had been a frequent visitor to the other's house, it was strictly under the watchful eyes of the parents or an elder. Ojuolape was well accepted by all that matters in the Olayera family, and because the signal from Goje concerning the association was favourable, Olayera and his wife decided to assist their son in taking the relationship to the next level and began to make arrangements for a visit to Salaji's family on behalf of their son Adigun.

According to custom, the families of the prospective bride would not recognise or address the suitor and his family in term of the relationship between their daughter and son until the family of the prospective groom had made a formal introductory visit, commonly referred to as *ijoko momi-nmoo*, to the family of the potential bride. This aspect of tradition was made popular by the dramatic effect that went with it. Although the groom's family would be expected visitors, and the purpose of their visit common knowledge, the bride's family would ridicule the guest by pretending not to be aware of the visit until all the *iyawo-ile* (an informal association of women already married into the bride's extended family) had taxed the visitor to a pre-budgeted limit of their pocket or more. The family seeking a wife would on this day be reprimanded and charged with as many bogus but laughable anti-social 'offences' as possible. The more ridiculous the charge, the more it would empty the guest's pocket. Then after the visit the future bride would become officially engaged to the future groom. Then the husband would officially be free to discuss the bride's future with her parents, and the girl for her part could freely relate with her future mother in-law. After due consultation between representatives of both families, and all inconveniences on both sides had been considered, the visit was agreed to take place in the months following *Lakaaye* festival in Oko-Oba.

The Yoruba religion was based on two levels of faith. Every Yoruba man, irrespective of his creed, believed in Olodumare (the supreme deity) as the creator of heaven and earth. Olodumare in Yoruba language literarily means 'the custodian of ultimate wisdom'. The second level of the Yoruba religion was the attachment to one or more of the lesser deities, through which Olodumare 'dispensed wisdom and prosperity to his creations'. Sango, the god of lightning, was believed to be the deity that Olodumare sent forth with the secret of fire and general illumination. Oya was the river goddess and commonly worshipped by fishermen, seafarers and other inhabitants of riverfronts whose livelihoods, directly or indirectly, were linked to the river. Ogun, the god of iron, was the deity through whom the Yoruba people believed that Olodumare dispensed the wisdom and benefit of iron and metal work. In the long run, almost all Yoruba communities had Ogun worshippers in their midst as it was difficult to find anyone who did not make use of iron and iron products, either for work, trade or domestic purposes. Hence, Ogun was regarded as a universal deity, and the festival of the god of iron was referred to as *Lakaaye* (universal) festival.

Since departing from their Erebe homeland, Oko-Oba had been the only place Erebe people considered as an alternative homeland, and the annual *Lakaaye* festival there was the rallying point for all Erebe people across Ijowa, Akete and Abatan. It was during the *Lakaaye* festival in Oko-Oba that Erebe people looked forward to reuniting and socialising with their fellow tribesmen who travelled down from their various settlements.

Ojo and Ojuolape had met twice before the *Lakaaye* festival. The first time was during Ojo's early days in Olubi's household when he went to entertain her father's guest from Ajase. He remembered the little girl that sat beside him all through his performances. During his brief stay, she kept pestering him at every opportunity to teach her to play the *agidigbo*. Then he was still nursing the pain of the sudden separation from his mother and only struggled to be polite and yield to her plea when there were people around.

The house of Goje Salaji in Isale-Eko was their first destination after Olubi and Lagemo conned the nomad Fulanis out of their livestock. By this time, they were both in early puberty and he was struck by her beauty from the time he set his eye on her. They had stayed for two days and nights, and he had the opportunity to spend some time to chat with her in the presence of other peers. He wished he could have a woman as beautiful as Ojuolape for himself alone, as a wife, but he would never dream of such a thing happening, for two reasons. One had to do with Ojuolape's noble background, which she made sure Ojo was aware of through her unending tales of her life at Aromire, and the second was that Goje and Olubi seemed to be somehow related, and as Ojo was the 'son of Olubi' it was unacceptable for them to associate beyond certain limits.

Goje, his wives, Ojuolape and her siblings had been in Oko-Oba since the week before the festival. Olubi and his family arrived four days before it. They were received and hosted for the duration of the festival by Goje in the Salaji family compound in Oko-Oba. Olubi's grandparents had never settled in Oko-Oba. The family were not qualified for settlement because they refused to drop their identity by removing their tattooed tribal markings. However, since his fortune had begun to soar, Olubi had through the help of Goje Salaji, and of course the *Baale*, been able to secure a piece of land, upon which a moderate house was almost completed.

Ojuolape and Ojo had been on good terms since Olubi's family arrived in the Salaji compound. Although Ojuolape has never lived in Oko-Oba, she had been a regular visitor to the village until the death of her paternal grandfather three years before, and her father decided to bring her grandmother down to live with the family in Isale-Eko. So she considered it her duty to show Ojo around the village. They were seen together in almost every place of interest in the village. She introduced him to her friends in Oko-Oba, but Ojuolape was always quick to make them aware that Ojo was her cousin to avoid undue speculation, and she kept away from questionable places and circumstances that might lead to misinterpretation or misconception concerning her relationship with Ojo.

About three years into his manhood, Ojo had become someone a woman could hardly pass without noticing. He was big for his age and moderately handsome. His charm lay in the way he moved his large but shapely figure. Whenever he stopped by the stream for a bath and swam bare-chested, maidens washing by the river, regardless of their soapy hands, would hurriedly wipe their faces in admiration.

Adigun was away trading in Ibini. He was supposed to be back before the *Lakaaye* festival to join Ojuolape in Oko-Oba, but thought it wise to make a quick detour to Idomi in order to purchase beautiful ornaments and clothings for the coming wedding ceremony. Two days before *Lakaaye*, a messenger from Adigun arrived at the compound of Salaji in Oko-Oba, bearing news for Ojuolape that Adigun would unfortunately not be able to make it to the festival, so Ojuolape accepted Ojo's invitation to be his companion on the eve of the festival.

The eve of the *Lakaaye* festival was the peak of the excitement, especially for youths and adolescents. The festival day itself was essentially about spiritual activities, like rituals and sacrifices to appease Ogun (the god of iron) and seek his guidance in the utilisation of iron for prosperity, and also his protection against the dangers associated with the use of metals and metal works. Hence, the events of the festival day proper were understandably not as popular among the young people as the night before. The eve of the festival was always full of fun and ceremony, a night when the village slept late, and most young men did not sleep at all. The night was always filled with entertainment and performances by the young people, and there would be lots of drinking, dancing, flirting and romance. New and secret affections would develop.

The unusual friendship between Ojo and Ojuolape started two days before the *Lakaaye* festival, and it took a sweet but risky turn on the festival eve. It continued through the week after the festival until most of Kekewura's family who had travelled down to Oko-Oba returned to Isale-Eko, but not before irreparable 'damage' had been done.

It was getting towards early evening when Ojo and Ojuolape arrived in the *ojude* (village square). The gathering at the square was still about a quarter of its usual capacity on *Lakaaye* eve. It would have been dark but for a bright moon.

'What a good night this *Lakaaye* eve falls upon,' Ojuolape observed as she looked up at the bright moon in the sky.

'Yes, it is a good night, especially for lovers who wish to live together for the rest of their lives.'

'My meaning of a good night is not in that sense.'

'In what sense do you mean then?' Ojo asked

'I mean in the simplest sense, and not the typical interpretation of a youth like you. A bright night enhances proper relaxation in the festive gathering compared to a cloudy or rainy night.'

'So what is the typical interpretation of a youth like me?'

'On a night like this, the only pleasure that a youth like you will find in this beauty of nature is the opportunity to lure a maiden into an affair which most will regret the moment it started. Now tell me, am I wrong?' Ojuolape asked almost accusingly.

'Yes you are, because on this particular night, my opinion about it being a good night has nothing to do with flirtation or infatuation. It extends beyond all you have just said. It is spiritual.'

'How do you mean?'

'On a night like this, when the moon is at its brightest, it is not common to see so many bright stars in the sky. But it is only on such a night that the *alatilehin* would be visible.'

'What is the *alatilehin*?'

'It is a unique star,' Ojo replied. 'Look around that moon.' He turned Ojuolape's head towards the sky. 'Can you see a very bright star, the closest to it?' He pointed.

'Yes '

'That is the *alatilehin*. It is the only star among the many in the sky that has a fixed location. It is always close to the moon.'

'So what is spiritual about the *alatilehin*?'

'Just as the name suggests, it is 'the follower'. It is believed that only death can tear asunder the love which is wished upon the closeness between *alatilehin* and the moon. So you see what I mean when I said it is a good night for lovers.'

'When you said I was wrong, I never thought you would mention anything like love or lovers in defending your so-called spiritual reason for this night to be a good one.'

'Well, I cannot think of any other expression that would justify all the beauty around me.'

'I cannot see anything beautiful around you.'

'There is the moon for a start.'

'Apart from the moon, what are the others?'

'There are no others, except just one, the most beautiful of all.'

'And which is that?'

'You, of course.'

'Oh no. I will not be flattered.'

'Look in my eyes. What do you see?'

'Nothing.'

'Take a closer look into my eyeballs, there must be something there.'

'I cannot see anything except my own face staring back at me.'

'That is exactly what I mean. Beauty is in the eye of the beholder. That is why your face is the other thing in my eye apart from the reflection of the moon.'

'Can't you be serious for a moment?' Ojuolape teased. 'I

thought you had a fly trapped in your eye.'

'Well your beauty does the same as a fly in the eye. It makes me shed tears, but with a difference.'

'So what is the difference?'

'When you are in my eyes I shed tears of love, not the tears of discomfort caused by a fly.'

'You certainly know how to flatter a girl,' she murmured huskily.

'I love you so much, Ojuolape, that I will chase you to the moon if necessary,' replied Ojo. He drew Ojuolape closer to him and she snuggled herself to the warmth from his body. At that moment she realised with a shock of excitement how emotionally attached to Ojo she had become in the short time they had known each other. Even before his hand touched her shoulders she was lying against him, and then his hands moved gradually down to her chest, just above the top of her *buba* (blouse). Ojo managed to squeeze his right palm through the neck of the blouse and began probing inside. He suddenly held her away from him and looked at her face with a tenderness that made her heart beat faster as he loosened the tie on the upper edge of her *iro* (wrapper). She shivered from head to foot as Ojo's warm palm found and explored her most sensitive part. Her limbs were totally weakened by his touches, so much that she let her whole body rest upon his shoulder. She found herself being lulled into an ecstatic state by his tender fingers, which now extended to the lower part of her back. He moved his hands slowly across her abdomen and down the outsides of her thighs. She raised her eyes to search his face and was greeted by an overwhelming emotion that would suffocate her as heartbeat rose and it felt as if her ribs would collapse into themselves.

Ojuolape could not tell how they got there, but she found herself lying on her back under the natural protection of a mango tree. When his weight came on to her, she experienced something that made her eyes open wide, for she was feeling a part of a male that she had never been so close to before in her life, and for a moment, a wave of fear swept through her. She thought of rising but her hands she pressed against his chest defied her better judgment and swam around his body to his back.

'We must not' she whispered feebly, drawing him closer as she did.

'It is all right, my love, I would never hurt you, not ever,' Ojo said calmly, but his hands remained on her naked breast. She tried to rise and recalled pressing her hands against his chest as her body tried to heave upwards. One moment she was almost struggling to free herself, and the next she was as submissive as a lamb.

Then many things happened in quick succession. The pain of her initiation into womanhood was overtaken by a tickling sensation as Ojo pushed gently but deeply into her. Then her muscles softened as she succumbed to an overpowering urge from within herself. She felt herself being gradually elevated to a strange realm, one which she had never before visited. While the heat lasted, she experienced the bliss of her life.

The mouth wishes to retain the savour of well-roasted meat, but the pull from the belly will not let it stay there. So when both their urges had been spent, Ojuolape came to her senses, not in the gradual and exciting manner by which she had been overtaken by ecstasy but with sudden and shocking realization of the implications of what had just happened. She had lost her virginity, to the wrong man. Not Adigun Olayera, the man who had already been arranged as her future husband, but to a 'cousin' who could never be her husband.

'What have you done? By the head of my mother, what have you led me into?' Ojuolape cried in anguish. She flung Ojo's arm away from where it rested across her breast and sat upright. 'What do you except me to do now?' she cried. 'I am supposed to marry Adigun, but now you have shamed me. What will I say on my wedding night when Adigun discovers my folly? Oh, I am done for! You have killed me and left my corpse unburied, for all and sundry to see the shameful cause of my death.' Tears flowed freely down her cheeks.

'Ojuolape stop crying, there is always a way out,' said Ojo. 'I love you, and you need not marry Adigun. You could be my wife.'

'Oh stop it. Please stop it now! What do you mean marry me? It is not possible. I am betrothed to Adigun. It is going to be a great disappointment to my parents and this surely will kill my *iya agba'* (grandma).

'What if I promise you that I can make my father supportive of the union?'

'You are going to do what? Ask your father to condone an abomination? I will curse you if this stupid mistake gets to the hearing of any soul.'

'You will have to do more than to curse me, because that is exactly what I am going to do. I am going to tell my father, and in return I promise you his support,' Ojo said confidently.

'You must be the greatest clown of our time, and a selfish one too. I will tell you this, if your father is for whatever reason ready to trample upon custom by supporting such a union, mine will never agree to it. Marry my cousin? Impossible.' Ojuolape replied indignantly.

'Impossible? For whom it is impossible, you or your parents?'

'It does not make any difference.'

'Yes it does. I plead of you to speak for yourself. I am ready to trample upon any custom and tradition to live with you forever. I am asking if you can you do the same for me.'

'But you have already spoken on behalf of your father when you said he would agree to such a union,' Ojuolape argued.

'No, I did not speak for him. I only promise to make him agree to it, and even make him persuade your parents to agree to the union.'

'So how do you come about this *mayehun* [hypnotism] that you so believe could work on anybody? Because it seems I am the only person concerned in this matter that you have yet to cast your spell upon,' Ojuolape said with mock disbelief.

'On the contrary, you are the first to fall for my spell,' Ojo said, taking a deliberate glance towards the spot where they had both lain a few moments before. He wanted to laugh, but stopped as she clearly was not finding it funny.

'It is all right for you to make it a laughing matter. It is not your shame, but mine. And on a very serious note, I still maintain that none of what happened tonight must be known to anyone. What we did was against custom. It must never happen again, and it never will!'

'No, it is not against custom, because we are not in any way related by blood,' Ojo replied boldly.

'Yes we are, because I have heard your father refer to my father as brother, and likewise.'

'That is not new. Almost every Erebe person outside Oko-Oba refers to each other as family, but many are not related by blood.'

'Almost, but not all. According to my father, our grandparents were born and grew in the same compound, so that makes us cousins and such a relationship is against the custom. I will not fantasize over a deed that will lead to greater abomination.'

'Even if that is the case, we are still not related, because the man you believe to be your uncle is not my father.'

'Your father is not your father?' Ojuolape asked, in genuine disbelief.

'He is not.'

'So who are you, and what is your father... I mean my uncle, as you call him, to you?'

'He is supposed to be my owner, but most of the time our relationship has been the equal of a blood relationship. He does not keep slaves, he is against it. But I am no doubt his only and of course most favoured dependant.' At the mention of slave, Ojuolape jumped and moved further away from him as if she had just discovered that he had an infectious disease. That made the situation more unthinkable. The wife of a slave is equally a slave, and so also will be the fate of their children.

'*Kasa*! Upon the head of my mother, I have been robbed. How could my grandfather in his grave have fallen into such slumber and let me suffer this irrevocable loss.' She bit her finger in bitter regret as tears flowed freely down her cheek.

'Over time, I have saved considerable wealth in gold and silver coins,' Ojo began, ignoring Ojuolape's hysteria. 'I am old and wise enough to be on my own and to properly approach your parents for your hand in marriage' He spoke with true compassion and made to hold her.

'Don't touch me!' she screamed, cringing away from him. 'And don't ever come near me again?' She spat at his foot and walked away angrily.

'Please wait and let us sort this matter out in a sensible manner,' Ojo said, running after her.

'No. There is nothing to sort out. Do you hear me? Nothing!' Ojuolape shouted. 'And leave me alone.' She started running towards home.

'Remember that either absent or dead, a slave was once fathered by a man, and even if unknown or unreachable, he does belong to a family,' He called after her, almost shouting. But Ojuolape would not listen. Instead she proceeded hurriedly towards home. Ojo tried to catch up with her, but decided to retreat. He thought it wise not to provoke a scene that might make people want to ask questions.

It was towards the end of the ninth season since he had been so rudely separated from his mother. Apart from her, Ojuolape was the first and only person he felt comfortable to tell the truth to about himself. She rekindled the memory of his mother, the memory he had kept alive in his mind all through his struggle and whatever came across his way. As he remembered her, he also remembered the *ejigbaileke* and the painful end to his attempt at retrieving it. Although, the post-war tension between Akete and Ijowa had simmered and the activities of the Akete army of occupation in Oluweri had relaxed, he had not found any compelling reason that worth risking another attempt. But having met Ojuolape, he found a good reason to retrieve it and put the precious stones to use. He comforted himself with the thought that he would be spending the fortune on something his mother would have approved of if she were around. He could start his own family and begin a respectable life. He was sure that with moderate wealth, a woman like Ojuolape as a wife could make him a decent man.

Ojuolape on her part struggled to find sleep that night so she cried in its place. Her folly would trouble her incessantly until daybreak. How would she explain her circumstances to Adigun on her wedding night? She wished she could turn back time and decline her father's invitation to attend the *Lakaaye* festival.

The next morning she made sure to avoid Ojo by any means. It would not be difficult as the Salaji compound, like the rest of Oko-Oba, busied itself with final festival preparations. At noon she went with the family to wash some dirty clothing in the river. Ojo was also at the river enjoying the rising heat of the afternoon sun as it blended with the cooling effect of the flowing water. At the first opportunity, he swam up to Ojuolape and whispered into her ear, not minding if she was listening or not.

'I have been thinking all night, and I have been able to find a solution which I am sure you will be happy to hear,' he said. 'At sundown, I will be waiting for you by the *odan* tree. I mean the one by the clearing on the way to the blacksmith's shed. Meet me there and we will talk it through.' He quickly swam away before Ojuolape could decline.

Ojo had been waiting by the *odan* tree since the

afternoon meal. It was not that he expected Ojuolape to be that early for their meeting. He knew that even if she was anxious to hear what he had to say, she would not want to admit it even to herself, and being deliberately late was one way of expressing this. Ojo decided to be there long before her in order not to make their meeting looked pre-planned or unusual.

By the time Ojuolape arrived, the crowd under the *odan* tree was almost at its largest. He intended to do the talking while she did the listening. He was sure that she would be more reasonable when there were so many people within hearing distance.

'After the way you behaved last night, it seems to me that the only reason why you would not marry me is because I am nobody, and your husband to be is a son of somebody,' began Ojo. 'I am not taking any offence from that, because I know you cannot decide to abandon Adigun on your own. I know it is a fantasy to think of humiliating a family like that of Adigun on such a sensitive issue without the support of your family. Now I am going to ask you. If I make myself somebody today, I mean overnight, would you marry me?'

'What do you mean, make yourself somebody? I beg of you please to spare me these riddles and make your point,' Ojuolape said curtly.

'I think the best thing to do is to tell you my story from the beginning, then at least you will know who I really am, and you will be well informed when making your decision.'

Ojo told Ojuolape everything he knew about himself. 'First of all, my real name is Ojo and not Omolubi. I will explain how and why I became Omolubi later.' He told Ojuloape about his mother, and the very little he knew about his father. He talked about the short acquitance with Morilewa, his generosity, and how he had come to be in possession of valuable stones. He told her how he had been captured with his mother in Gbajumo on their way to Kuluso, how he had become part of Olubi's family, and the reason for his change in identity. He told her about the fortune realised from the single stone he had given Olubi, and rounded off his story with his failed attempt at retrieving the rest of the beads from Ago-Oyinbo.

Ojuolape listened wide-eyed. 'Now you intend to go back for the beads after what happened during your first attempt?' she asked.

'I made avoidable mistakes during that attempt, due to my age and inexperience.'

'So now you are old and experienced enough to risk another attempt? And if you do manage to get the beads, how are you going to sell them and protect your fortune?' Ojuolape was beginning to listen and reason, and Ojo was happy with his progress.

'Since living with your uncle, I have become wise enough to trade with and manage such fortune. All it will require is a well-planned journey to Aromire, or worse still, Ojuoro market. Come to think of it, I should have gone back to Oluweri for the beads. Given my experience during the first time and my age now, it would have been easy. But I had no compelling reason to do so. Somehow I felt no need for such wealth. But now I have a reason.'

'I am still not comfortable without a clear identity. I mean being the son of whom you are not.'

'I beg your pardon,' Ojo replied, 'I have never been without an identity. I know who my parents are, and the name given to me by my parents. Those are identities.' For the first time since she had known him, Ojuolape detected a note of anger. She sensed that she had said something he found most displeasing.

'I am sorry if I said something wrong,' she began. 'I was only…' but she could not continue, and tears began flowing down her cheeks.

'Never mind,' Ojo said, drawing her to him and drying off her tears. 'My father, I mean your uncle, had never considered himself as my owner in the first place. He personally detests the idea of enslavement. He admitted to me that he had purchased me with bogus coins, and deemed it unfair to claim my ownership. I must admit that he does treat me better than most fathers treat their children when his fortunes are good, but I am always the first person to feel the crunch when he is on the wrong side of fortune.' He stopped to mimic Olubi. 'You, *majesin*, (adolescent) are the major threat to my wealth. What you consume of my fortune is enough to make a man engage in prosperous trading, and that is exactly what I am going to make you do for me.' He turned to Ojuolape. 'And for sure within three days, I would have been or should be on the way to a farm, as a bondservant, until his good fortune returns, which could be any time from a month to a whole season.' Then he softened up and smiled. 'Come to think of it, you might be right, in a sense. I was bought with coins which cannot be honoured in the market, and if a person is of no value in public, then he is nothing.' He smiled. 'But my beads are not fake. They are of great value in big markets, and the fortune I am going to make from them will be spectacular. I am going to leap from a nobody to a somebody.'

Despite her situation, Ojuolape smiled for the first time.

She admired the way he had prevented her from spoiling what was turning out to be another beautiful evening with her unguided utterances.

'You said you felt no compelling reason to sell the beads until now. What is your reason now?'

'You are my reason. Since I met you, I believe you are a person that deserves to share my fortune – if you choose to marry me, of course.'

'Choice, my dear friend, is what you denied me last night,' Ojuolape said weakly.

'I am very please to hear that.'

'You had better be.' She smiled. 'What you said was only as easy as saying it. I truly believe your story. Yes, we are not related, and you could be rich, then what next?'

'Money and wealth bring power, and power makes a person somebody. By the time I return from Aromire Market, I will have in my possession enough wealth to make your father value my friendship more than that of Adigun's family.'

'I still cannot see how all this will compel my father to agree to our union and jeopardise his friendship with Adigun's family.'

'I will tell you this. There are two ways to get to the top of a tree. You can either climb the tree or you can cut it down.'

'Meaning?'

'Meaning if we cannot get your father's blessing to be husband and wife, we could run away until time cools his anger. We could hide at your mother's place.'

'Then you will have to make this journey as soon as possible. The *ijoko momi-nmoo* [introductory family visit] is less than two months away.'

'Oluweri is not far from here, and if I have my way I will set off tomorrow. My father – I mean your uncle! – has ceased questioning my movements and personal affairs for some time now. I had a prior arrangement with him for when we return to Eti-Osa the day after tomorrow, but that will not delay me for more than a day. So I will definitely be leaving Eti-Osa for Oluweri before, or in six days.' Ojo spoke with assurance and determination.

'How long do you think it will take you to retrieve the beads and then travel to Aromire to sell them?'

'It is difficult to say, but whatever happens, I will make sure to call on you at Isale-Eko not later than two weeks' hence, even if I have to stop on my return journey from Oluweri to assure you before going to Aromire.'

'It seems you have already looked into all possibilities. You make me feel like I don't need to bother myself thinking.'

'I hardly slept all through last night,' Ojo confessed.

'Neither did I, but all I did was cry and curse myself.'

'I don't blame you. That's what all women do best in these circumstances, lamenting and crying upon what can never be reversed. Never mind, leave the men to do the thinking.'

Olubi and Ojo left Oko-Oba for Eti-Osa the third day after the *Lakaaye* festival. Three days later, Ojuolape, her stepmothers and most of the Salaji family who had travelled down to Oko-Oba for the *Lakaaye* festival returned to Isale-Eko. Goje had to stay behind for a few days after the festival to delibrate with other notable Erebe men, who had also stayed behind to discuss matters concerning Erebe people in the diaspora.

It took Ojo the best part of a day to travel on horseback

from Eti-Osa to Okoloto. He stopped at Olokoto to buy the things he would need for his mission in Oluweri, and stayed the night. The next morning, he left his horse in the custody of a horse minder, hired a canoe and continued his journey to Oluweri via the Awoyaya river. He was well past midway between Olokoto and Oluweri before it was too dark to continue, so he stopped for the night. He arrived at Lower-Oluweri just as the sun was setting and headed directly to Ago-Oyinbo. He had no specific plan for how to accomplish the task ahead, but one thing he was certain of was that he would not rush into any action that could result in him being humiliated and punished as he had before.

The Ago-Oyinbo had changed considerably since his last visit. The first thing he noticed as he get close was that there were more people around and more was going on, but this made it easier to observe without arousing any suspicion. There had been many changes. There had been only one fence around Ago-Oyinbo during his first attempt, but now a second had been erected within to separate Wontsay's personal quarters from the rest of the ground. His old home remained as it had been during his last mission to Oluweri, but now there were new homes around which Ojo reckoned must be the residences of Wontsay's greatly-increased staff.

On his first attempt, the entire area had been restricted and was almost always deserted, but now only the inner perimeter that surrounded Wontsay's personal residence was restricted. The outer perimeter was full of activity as residents were going about their daily chores and restricting access to this section would have been almost impossible.

All these changes and developments promised to make the task easier for Ojo, because he did not have to jump over any fences to gain access. He could see that his now decrepit old house was isolated from the rest in the outer perimeter. So all he had to do was wait until there was less traffic around his dilapidated old home, mingle with people going in and out of Ago-Oyinbo, and then casually proceed to his target. The rest was easy.

CHAPTER 9

A lump that is determined to disfigure the face will find the tip of the nose the best vantage spot to pop out from. So it was with Ojuolape. The day after they returned to Isale-Eko, her grandmother Ajiun discovered that half her cowries had gone missing while she was away for the *Lakaaye* festival. The first thing she did was to consult Yeye Olomi, the river priestess, about the matter.

'I know your schedules are tight, but it is a matter of utmost urgency which I will be very uncomfortable to leave unattended for too long,' she told Yeye Olomi.

'Tell me, what is the nature of this matter, so that I can prepare myself?' Yeye Olomi asked with genuine concern.

'While I was away to Oko-Oba for the *Lakaaye* festival, somebody went to where I keep my valuables and made away with almost every cowrie I have saved since I got married.'

'The person must be stronger than a mule to move such

a heavy load within your compound unnoticed,' Yeye Olomi commented sarcastically.

'Yeye, this is not a joking matter,' Ajiun declared, obviously not in the mood for the priestess's joke. 'It would be appreciated if you would promise to find time within the next few days to call at my compound and perform a divination that will reveal the identity of the thief.'

'I'm sorry if you are offended, I was just wondering how...'

'There is nothing to wonder about,' Ajiun interrupted, 'and you very well understand what I meant by 'all I had been saving since I got married'.'

'Anyway, I will be at your compound before noon, the day after tomorrow. Meanwhile you will need to get ready a fresh calabash, one which has neither been dried in the sun nor used before. Most importantly, we need a young girl who has not known a man, or a boy who has not been with a woman before. Finally we will need a small pot full of *omi-okun* (ocean water). I hope all those will not be a problem.'

'Except for the *omi-okun*, I do not think there should be any problem with the rest. Even with reasonable notice, it will take time to get those who trade in ocean water to deliver.'

'That will be no problem either. I always keep some for situations like this, and I will use that for now. I will not be asking you to pay for the water, but you will replace it as soon as you find a reliable traveller to fetch more from the ocean.'

'Then there is nothing else to worry about. I have plenty of untouched *majesin* [minors] of both sexes in my care,' Ajiun assured the priest. 'The calabash, how big should it be?'

'Just big enough to bath a new baby.'

When she arrived, Yeye Olomi filled the calabash with ocean water and then placed it in the outstretched hands of Ojuolape, whom her grandmother had nominated for the assignment. Then the river priestess began to recite a lengthy incantation. If all went accordingly, Ojuolape was expected to see a clear, indisputable image of the person or persons who had stolen her grandmother's savings. But the girl saw nothing. Ojuolape wished that like the flame of a spent oil lamp placed against the wind she could fade out of the scene, but at the insistence of her grandmother she kept her eye fixed on the water pot until it was shedding tears, without seeing a thing.

'This is strange, the gods have never failed me in this act before, nor have they failed my predecessors. I wonder what could have gone wrong,' The river priestess lamented with frustration.

'Maybe the water has been contaminated,' Ajiun suggested.

'It cannot be so. The man who fetches this water from the ocean has been performing the task for me for ages, and he is very well aware of its purpose and how to handle the water. It could not have been contaminated.' The priestess took a glance at Ojuolape and then asked her to leave her alone with Ajiun.

'Are you suggesting...' Ajiun began, then stopped. She could guess what the priestess might be insinuating by asking Ojuolape to vacate the room, but found the suggestion ridiculous and unbelievable.

'I am not drawing any conclusion, but there is no harm in removing all benefit of doubt,' said Yeye. 'Have you any other girl within your compound whom you are equally sure to be a virgin and whom you can trust with this task?'

'I am sure Ojuolape is a virgin,' Ajiun replied. 'But if you insist, there are other younger girls in the compound that I can call upon.' The conclusion which the priestess was reluctant to make, and which Ajiun dreaded, was made apparent when the other girl presented by Ajiun looked in the calabash and was able not only to reveal the culprit but to give a detailed account of how the deed was performed.

'What you have seen is a delicate issue and should be handled by elders,' the priestess warned the girl before she left the room. 'In no circumstances must you disclose what you have just seen to anyone outside this room.'

Ajiun was stunned as she tries to comprehend what was happening. The implications of what she had just witnessed were too much for her and she broke down in tears as soon as the little girl was out of the room.

'This girl has shamed me!' she lamented. 'She has shamed her father and tainted the name of the family. I wonder why our children nowadays prefer to rush things unnecessarily. I see no reason why Adigun had to rush Ojuolape into disrespecting her father, especially when both families have already agreed to meet formally in matter of weeks.'

'Who is Adigun?'

'Adigun is the person she is engaged to marry,' Ajiun replied.

'Well if Adigun is the partner in this deed, I see no reason for you to be alarmed. But it is better you have a serious talk with your granddaughter and confirm that it was him. Meanwhile, what are you going to do about the thieves?'

'I will deal with that later. My priority is how to deal with Ojuolape's situation.'

'Now or later, there will be nothing to deal with,' Yeye Olomi said. 'On the contrary, I will be advising you not to do anything at all.'

'Why?' Ajiun asked despite herself.

'Would you have known about Ojuolape if your money had not been stolen?'

'No.'

'I appreciate your loss, but would you have minded willingly parting with the money in exchange for learning about the state of your granddaughter before the wedding day?'

Ajiun understood what the priestess was implying. 'No, I would not have minded,' she replied reluctantly.

'There you are. Those men were wrong to steal your money, but they will be fortunate to get away with it this time. They were thieves all right, but it is the wish of the gods that they will not be purnished for this crime. You will consider whatever taken as a ritual to the gods, and that is why I will not charge you a single cowrie for my service. Even the replacement of the ocean water will not be necessary. That is how the gods want it to be and that is how I will advise you to let it remain.'

That evening, Ajiun summoned Ojuolape to her room.

'Do you agree with the saying that it is impossible for a corpse to hide its nakedness from the undertaker?' Ajiun asked her granddaughter, and Ojuolape nodded in affirmation.

'So if you agreed to that, then it is only wise that you tell me the truth, and only the truth, about what I am going to ask you. I think I am making myself clear.'

Ojuolape again nodded.

'According to what happened this afternoon, it is my suspicion that you are no longer a virgin. But I want to be sure.'

This time Ojuolape made no response. She just sat rigid, her eyes fixed to the ground.

'Am I deaf or are you dumb, because I cannot hear any reply to my question. Have you known a man or not?'

'Yes,' Ojuolape replied in a very muted voice.

'I cannot hear you properly. And I want you to look at me straight in the face when answering my question. Have you known a man or not?'

'Yes, I have.'

'Hmmmm. Now tell me who is the man you have known?'

Silence.

'You have started playing dumb with me again. I ask you, who is this man that you have been with?'

Ojuolape remain silent.

'Is it Adigun?'

'No,' Ojuolape replied.

'Then who is the man? You cannot tell me you don't know the person who made you a woman.'

Ojuolape remained silent. She was determined not to bring Ojo into the open until he was ready with his plan. Her grandmother probed into the night, but Ojuolape refuse to give any response to the question. Ajiun threatened, swore and pleaded, but without success. She gave up when she realised that Ojuolape was not only determined to remain silent but was falling asleep in the middle of the interrogation.

The next dawn, before cockcrow, Ajiun was at her

granddaughter's side asking once again who had taken her virginity. When by daybreak Ojuolape still remain unbroken, Ajiun took her to Yeye Olomi for further counselling.

'She confessed to be no longer a maiden, but I am afraid that the partner in deed was not Adigun as I had hoped,' Ajiun began.

'Who did she say is responsible?' Yeye Olomi asked.

'I have tried my best to make her say, but so far she refuses to tell me,' Ajiun replied. Yeye asked Ojuolape to leave the room while she spoke with her grandmother.

'Ajiun, I think the most important question was answered when the girl said it was not Adigun,' Yeye Olomi began after Ojuolape had left the room. 'Whoever it was, the situation is the same. The question now is, what are you going to do about it? You can be sure that Adigun will ask questions if your granddaughter falls short of natural expectations on her wedding night.'

'Yeye, you are right, the problem has been identified. It is the solution to the problem that is the issue.'

'In my experience, there are three ways of going about solving this kind of problem. The first is to find a way of getting Adigun to your side. Tell a story that will convince Adigun that your granddaughter was a victim, a story of woe that will make Adigun sympathetic to Ojuolape's situation. Then it will not come as surprise to him on the wedding night.'

'How does one convince a buyer to accept a half measure for the price of a full measure? Yeye, that is difficult!' Ajiun lamented.

'The second option is to find a means of breaking the engagement and let your granddaughter marry her partner in this deed. In my experience, girls who refuse to reveal their partner's identity in affairs of this nature were usually willing partners in the deed and not victims.'

'Breaking the engagement is out of the question. Her father must never hear about that. Many relationships will be ruined. The *ijoko momi nmoo* has been arranged to take place in about six weeks. Adigun's father is a high-ranking Akete noble and must have informed and invited friends to grace the occasion. He will not take lightly such humiliation upon his family. Until his death, Ojuolape's maternal grandfather held the title of *Akigbe* in the palace at Aromire. Goje's experience in Aromire ended in shame and he would not approve of anything that will worsen the standing he has struggled to regain,' Ajiun went on.

'If that is the case, then we have to look into the third option.'

'Which is?'

'To seek the help of those who hold the secret of how such a defect in a bride can be repaired so that the groom will never be any wiser. I hope you understand what I mean.'

'Yes I do.'

'Now, apart from the cost of getting this service, there is another important issue that must be resolved. That is to either make her reveal the identity of her partner or to find out by ourselves.'

'What does the partner have to do with it?'

'He has a lot to do with it if we are going to pursue this third option. He knows what we know, and he is a partner in secret with your daughter. As I said, it could be that your granddaughter is a very willing partner and even prefers him to Adigun. Even if all our efforts turn out as expected, and Adigun suspects nothing, we must ensure that whoever he is, he is kept away from your granddaughter and keeps his mouth shut about the affair. We will be putting ourselves in a vulnerable position if he is not willing to let go. He will be like the masquerade under the veil. He can see us and know what we are up to, while we are unable to see him.'

'Yeye, with all due respect, there is little time on my side as the marriage is just weeks away. I think Ojuolape is dead set on keeping the secret. Embarking on a fact-finding mission will take time, and might raise some suspicion. Before we chase the foxes away, we must first make our chicken pen secure.'

'When I said we must find out by ourselves, I don't intend to go on a fact-finding mission, as you called it. I intend to put her under a spell and make her speak despite herself. What do you think about that?'

'That is all right by me, Yeye. Whatever is needed to avert this shame is very welcome.'

The river priestess asked to be left alone with Ojuolape while she performed the task. She prepared a mixture of herbs and roots, which she asked Ojuolape to drink. Within minutes, the girl was fast asleep. While in slumber, Yeye Olomi asked Ojuolape the necessary questions, and she was unable to hold back on her answers. She did not only name the boy responsible but revealed when and where it had happened. When she was satisfied that Ojuolape had answered all the vital questions, Yeye Olomi let her continue with her slumber and left the room to join Ajiun, who was eagerly waiting in the front yard.

'Did you manage to learn anything?' Ajiun asked the moment the priestess stepped out of the house.

'Yes I did. I know all I need to know,' Yeye Olomi replied. 'Omolubi. Do you know anyone by that name?'

'Omolubi... I think I have heard the name before, but I cannot remember where. But I can assure you that I will soon find out,' Ajiun promised

'In that case, prepare yourself and your granddaughter for a nine-day stay in Gbajumo village. We will leave as soon as you are ready.'

'Why Gbajumo village? I thought everything would be done here.'

'Oh no, nothing can be done here. I am taking your daughter to those who have knowledge of solving this kind of problem.'

'Yes, so you said, but I thought they lived here in Isale-Eko?'

'No, there are only two people alive that I know who are truly capable of performing such a feat. You are even fortunate that one lives in Gbajumo. The other is in Ile-Ife.'

'Please don't consider me ungrateful, but is it possible to bring the person down to Isale-Eko, even at extra cost? My main problem is that I intend to keep all this away from her father. How will I explain both our absences for nine days, especially when we have just returned from Oko-Oba?'

'I am sorry, but that will be impossible, and it has nothing to do with money. The woman is very busy within the community. It will take a matter of life and death to get her out of Gbajumo for even three days. In fact, I will be drawing heavily on my friendship with her in order to make her treat this case as an emergency.'

'If we have to stay in Gbajumo for that long, then I must wait for her father to return from Oko-Oba. It is imperative that Goje is involved in the matter,' Ajiun replied. 'He should be back in two days' time. When do you want us to leave?'

'Let me know whenever it is convenient for you, and we will set off.'

'We should be ready within five days. Is that well with you Yeye?'

'That will be fine by me,' Yeye Olomi replied.

Upon his return to Eti-Osa, Ajiun told her son all that had happened in the past four days. Goje was furious.

'Who is Omolubi? Have you heard the name before?' she asked.

'Yes mama, I know him. But you don't need to worry about the boy. I will sort him out.' Goje spoke calmly, but his mother knew he was fuming inside. 'I just want you to concern yourself with Ojuolape,' he went on. 'Take her to the woman in Gbajumo as advised by Yeye Olomi. Do everything required, and spare no expense to right the wrong.'

After this news Goje refused to see Ojuolape or talk to her, as he could not trust himself to control his emotions. He feared his anger might make him act in a way he would regret later.

Just over a week after she had returned to Isale-Eko, Ajiun and Ojuolape were on their way to Gbajumo. It took a full day and half to reach Gbajumo. The river priestess took them directly to *Iya* Mojoyin's house.

Apart from being childhood friends, the relationship between Iya Mojoyin and Jibike was further strengthened by their professional callings. Health practitioners such as midwives, psychiatrists and healers of general ailments found Jibike's knowledge of herbs and plants invaluable to their practice. While *Iya* Mojoyin could detect immediate and future complications in pregnancies, she relied on her friend for the prescription and administration of the right medications for her diagnosis. On quite a few occasions *Iya* Mojoyin had asked her friend to be present during a difficult childbirth.

Iya Mojoyin and Jibike were returning to Gbajumo that noon when Yeye Olomi arrived with Ajiun and Ojuolape. They had been away for three days on an emergency visit to Kuluso village, to support the local midwife in delivering triplets.

'*E nle onile o*,' Yeye Olomi greeted *Iya* Mojoyin from the doorstep.

'*E rora o, e ma wole*,' *Iya* Mojoyin replied from within. After they had exchanged pleasantries and the women were comfortably seated, Yeye Olomi informed *Iya* Mojoyin of Ojuolape's situation and the reason why she had travelled down to Gbajumo to see them.

'The foretelling of an invasion is a treasure for whoever is serious about survival. That is why I bring this woman and her granddaughter to you, the wise and knowledgeable ones, to help her out of the situation, to save the girl and her family from the humiliation of the wedding night.' When the river priestess had finished, *Iya* Mojoyin asked for her friend's opinion, but Jibike was only half listening. From the moment the guests had entered the house, her focus had been on Ojuolape. She asked the guests to allow them some space while she engaged in a brief discussion with her friend.

'My friend, this is no longer a matter of a foretold invasion because in this case, the invasion has come and passed. The territory has been occupied,' Jibike told *Iya* Mojoyin when they were alone.

'Are you saying that the girl has not only been deflowered but is pregnant?'

'That is what I am telling you. Do I need an eye at all to find a pregnant woman among many virgins?'

'I know you don't need your eye even to see the gender of the foetus.'

'Even if I shut my eye, the odour from the young girl tells me not only that she has been deflowered, but she is at least a week overdue for her monthly routine.'

'Are you sure?'

'As sure as I can tell that the light coming into your house this afternoon is from the sun and not the moon,' Jibike replied confidently. 'I wonder if the girl herself is aware of her condition. I can give away my bedtime meal to see the reaction of her grandmother when she realises how far her granddaughter has gone into womanhood.'

They called Yeye Olomi back into the room and told her of the development.

'I think it will be better if her grandmother hears this directly from your lips,' Yeye Olomi suggested.

'We have a very serious concern about your daughter's situation,' *Iya* Mojoyin began after Ajiun had entered and seated.

'What else could be of more concern about her than what you have told me? If your concern is about her safety, I will tell you categorically that she can as well drown herself in Awoyaya river, because I don't care,' Ajiun replied in anger.

'Maybe you will need to calm down and listen,' Yeye Olomi cautioned Ajiun. 'If you keep going on like this, I might have to wait until we return to Isale-Eko before further discussion with you on this issue.' She was not impressed by Ajiun's unchecked outburst. 'I am really surprised at the way you are taking this matter. Sad as it may be, at our age we must have got used to these things happening.'

'Please accept my apology,' Ajiun pleaded. 'But what else is your concern about her?'

'Our major concern is that your little girl has not only ceased to be a maiden, she is already a proven woman. I believe you well understand my meaning.'

'No, I don't understand what you mean, or rather I ask you to speak plainly to me. Are you saying that Ojuolape is pregnant?' Ajiun was both shocked and bewildered.

'Yes, and given this situation, it is impossible to proceed with what you requested of us without destroying the life inside her,' *Iya* Mojoyin explained.

'We are the mothers with big robes. Our robes are big enough to protect a thousand infants from cold. Ours is to protect life, never to destroy,' Jibike added.

'And while we are on that topic, I must warn you not to attempt anything of such nature yourself, because it will end in disaster,' *Iya* Mojoyin said and the gathering was effectively put to an end.

Meanwhile in Isale-Eko, Goje was engaging the service of an *asingba* (debt collector) to abduct Ojo and keep him in confinement.

'I am beginning to suspect that one of my debtors is taking advantage of my good nature,' he said. 'I have given him a respite of two years, and I guess he is contemplating begging for another year.'

'*Oloye* (honourable), I don't see any problem with that. You know the procedure. All you have to do is to inform the *Baale* of your intention and let me know the debtor.'

'Yes I know the procedure, but for reasons which I will explain to you, this assignment needs to be done in strict confidence, hence I don't want the *Baale* to be privy to it. The defaulter is a close relative and that is why I have been very flexible with the debt. I would not have minded giving him more time but for a hint I heard on the grapevine. I am reliably informed that this close relative is engaging the service of a spiritualist to make me forget that he ever owed me money. I want to prove to him and his spiritualist that they are wasting their time. That is why I want to ensure that the debt is paid. Engaging a debt collector to recover debt from the family will not be good for my image and that of the family. It is impossible to make everybody understand why I have to set a debt collector after my own flesh and blood. That is why I want to keep my action private, and that is why I don't want to involve the *Baale*.'

'Even if you don't involve the *Baale*, it is bound to come into the open. When I put pressure on your relative to pay his debt, the first thing he will do is to send family and friends to you, begging you to get us off his back.'

'The way I planned to go about it, even the debtor will not know that he has paid his debt.'

'How do you intend to achieve that?'

'That is where you and your men will come in. I want you to abduct his son and take him to Akala. The palace at Aromire is paying a good price through the back door for his almost endless need for labourers on Akala Island. I am sure the going rate for three years labour by an able and strong youth like the person in question will be enough to pay for your service and cover the debt.'

'Hmmm, if that is how you want it done, so be it. Just tell us how to find the person and the work is as good as done.'

'His name is Omolubi, and he lives in the Kudaisi compound in Eti-Osa.'

The notorious crime which not only made even Eti-Osa too hot and hostile for Olubi to live in but also made him a wanted man by the palaces at Aromire was committed the week after he returned from Oko-Oba for the *Lakaaye* festival. The crime took place at a small weavers' settlement close to Paramole, and it was classified as sacrilegious, hence unpardonable. Olubi was relaxing in his yard on a clear evening when he was visited by a man who brought with him a large gourd of palm wine. Introducing himself as Lagbaja, meaning somebody or anybody in the local language, the visitor said he needed to get in contact with Olowoeyo and had heard from certain quarters at the recently-concluded festival at Oko-Oba that Olubi could lead him to him.

'I cannot tell you exactly when I might stumble into him,' Olubi replied with his standard precautionary approach. 'Olowoeyo is wanted for strings of offences, not only by the palaces at Aromire but by many individuals, most of whom he cannot recall or remember. So he must be cautious about the extent to which he claims to have access to him. What have you got to tell him in case I stumble upon him?'

'Please, if ever you 'stumble' on him [the visitor deliberately emphasised the word stumble], 'tell him that the Fulani cattlemen are willing to extend their stay at Elewe-Eran.' Olubi then relaxed, as he was sure that Lagbaja had been sent to him by one of the very few from the underworld who knew about the link between the Fulani issue and Olowoeyo.

Olubi looked around to be sure none of his wife or children were within hearing distance. 'Now tell me what is it that you actually want to tell Olowoeyo?' he asked, and it was the turn of the visitor to let out a sigh of relief. Lagbaja told Olubi that he had been privy to a certain transaction between an Awori trader and some weavers from Paramole.

'Going by the little I could learn from the bargain, it seems the work is enormous and certainly the payment should be likewise,' he said. 'More importantly, I was able to learn from my friend that the *asansile* [deposit] had been paid when the party met in the last Aromire market three days ago.'

The next day, Olubi went out with Lagemo and two other outlaws named Odeku and Baoku. They were outlawed in the sense that the four of them not only had strings of pending cases in the palace at Aromire, but each already had two convictions to their credit. This meant that the next conviction would automatically land them in Akala. Due to the nature of the crime they were planning, it was imperative that they should leave the village as quickly as possible. So it was agreed that there should be a horse for every member of the gang. Though Olubi was never short of men willing to 'work' with him, he took along with him only eight of his regular men and their acceptance was strictly on the condition that each must find a means of securing a horse for their quick exit.

It was getting close to dusk before Olubi and his men got to the weavers' settlement. On the outskirts they split into two groups, and each group entered the small community from the only two entrances to the village. They left their horses by the exits, and none of the villagers were aware of the intruders until they had taken strategic positions around the village. After the inhabitants of the small and defenceless community of about twenty families had been rounded up and bound, the community head, was singled out and questioned by Olubi.

'Where is the money you received in Aromire during the last market?'

'I did not come back to the village with the money,' the *Baale* replied.

'Why?'

'Because I was afraid of being attacked on the way by thieves.'

Olubi thought he was lying, so he asked his men to set fire to one of the village looms, but the *Baale* was not lying. The money which Olubi sought, the payment for two hundred lines of *aso-oke* (hand woven textile), had actually been collected at Aromire during the last market. But the *Baale*, due to the fear of bandits along his route, had given the money to one of his trusted apprentices, whom he had asked to wait until the fifth day after the market before journeying down to the village.

'Where then do you keep the community treasure?' Olubi barked at the now visibly shaken old man.

'We don't have any joint treasure,' the *Baale* replied. Now Olubi was convinced that he was lying. It is almost impossible to find a community without a common treasury kept in reserve, designed to service many of the community's obligations, like the seasonal tribute to the palaces and other unforeseen communal expenses.

'Set fire to the second loom,' Olubi commanded his men without hesitation.

'Please don't! It is our only source of income,' The *Baale* pleaded, but Olubi was in no mood for sympathy, so his men set fire to the second loom.

'I will ask you again, and if you refuse to part with the treasury I will set fire to the third loom, and I will continue until you tell the truth.' His men began making preparation to light up the third loom. By now the *Baale* was convinced that Olubi was not the kind who is given to wasting words, and he was sure Olubi would not hesitate to destroy all six looms, so he confessed and led Lagemo to the place where he kept the community reserves. But it was too late to prevent greater destruction, because the wind came and blew the flame from the burning looms onto the Obatala shrine. The sacred ground was burnt to the last snail tied to the shrine posts.

While waiting for the *Baale* to co-operate, one of the villagers, who had been relieving himself in the bushes when Olubi and his men had entered the village, sneaked away unnoticed and sought help from Paramole. The gang had to take a hurried exit when they were surprised by Paramole's volunteer vigilantes. Baoku and two others were caught and overpowered by the villagers before they could get to their horses. Olubi, Odeku, Lagemo and three others made good their escape and rode southward towards Epetedo.

The magnitude of their crime was soon made clearer to them when they were ambushed in the forest, just on the outskirts of Paramole, by a combined team of hunters who happened to be on night hunting and volunteers from Paramole. In the confrontations that ensued, Odeku and another man were killed, and Lagemo and another were captured alive. Only Olubi and one of his regular men, Dehinde, escaped.

From his hiding place, Olubi watched as his compatriots, each tied to a mule, were dragged about on rough farm terrain. The intention of the angry mob was to drag them about till they died, and they would have done so had it not been for the timely arrival of the *Ilaris* (civil enforcers) of the *Baale* of Paramole, who took charge of the criminals and escorted forcefully to the *Baale's* compound. Olubi was so shocked by the incident that he stayed in his hiding place for hours, waiting until he was sure that the forest was clear of all vigilantes.

He crept out of his hiding place, just before daybreak. He knew better than to attempt returning to Eti-Osa immediately. Given the way the captured men had been handled by the angry mob, he was sure that at least one of them would be more than willing to talk in order to prevent further torture and humiliation. So instead of continuing towards Epetedo, he changed course and headed east, hoping to find his way through the dark forest on a long journey to Isale-Eko, to the only one person within the gradually enclosing perimeter of the long arm of the palace at Aromire where there could be any hope of assistance.

On his return journey, Ojo took a detour to Iseri to see a friend and seek advice on where and how to sell the beads. His name was Molaja, and he was popular among his peers, having been in the service of rich merchants and travelled far and wide.

'Your best bet is the land of the Ashanti,' Molaja advised. 'The soils of the Ashanti is known to be rich in precious stones and that is where buyers travel for trade. You will be surprised how many rich traders of different shades and colours will be willing to buy those beads off you and pay in articles of your choice, from widely-valued coins to hardware and even guns. You only need to ask for your favoured form of payment and you will get it. Half of the *Oyinbos* (Europeans) and the *Larubawas* (Arabian) merchants in Ashanti are there for just one purpose, and that is to collect gold and other precious stones.'

'How long will it take to make the journey to Ashanti?'

'I have never been there. The farthest I have travelled in that direction was to Idomiland. However, friends who have frequented the place say the shortest route is via the ocean. Given a favourable wind, they claim it will take between two to three days on the sea from Aromire to arrive at the shores of the Ashanti.'

'That means it will be possible to make the journey, sell the beads and be back in Aromire in less than sixteen days.'

'Yes, I think that should be a safe estimate.'

'Will you be ready and able to embark on this journey with me in about five days? I need to sort a few things out at Eti-Osa, but I will be back in three to four days. I want you to find a suitable canoe and a crew of two to travel with us. Meanwhile, I will give you this as part payment for your efforts.' Ojo placed a small sack on the mat between them. Molaja took the sack and empty the contents on the mat. They were silver coins. He counted them as he returned them to the sack.

'This should cover the cost of hiring a canoe that will

be big and strong enough to withstand the ocean tides, and the service of four rowers,' Molaja said as he put the last of the coins in the sack. 'But you will have to make provision for our feeding and other needs as we go.'

It was getting towards dusk before Ojo returned to Eti-Osa. His plan was to rest the night and wait till the next morning before journeying to Isale-Eko to share the story of his successful trip with Ojuolape and update her about the next step. Although tired, he was too excited to sleep, so he decided to spend some time getting together things he would be needing for the journey to Ashantiland. He inserted the beads in the hole of the leather waistband he had bought at Olokoto specifically to carry them, then tied it on his waist to see how well concealed it would be under his clothing. Satisfied, he removed the waistband and looked around his room for a temporary place to hide it. After moments of indecision, he finally chose to put it underneath the big clay water pot in his hut. He dug a small hole in the ground and placed the waistband inside it, but paused as he was about to drag the pot over it. He reckoned Ojuolape would need all the assurance she could get in this situation, and showing her the beads would help, but he thought it unwise to take all of them to her. A sample, he believed, would be sufficient to give her the necessary assurance. So he retrieved one shining stone from the waistband, then dragged the waterpot over the hole. He wrapped the stone in a small piece of cloth and put it in the inside pocket of his undershorts. He then continued getting things together for journey, but moments later he fell asleep on the mat, with all his clothes on.

The men sent by Goje to abduct Ojo had been loitering

around Olubi's compound for three days before Ojo finally returned to Eti-Osa. On their third day on the watch, they were delighted to see Olubi depart with some men at dawn, in a manner that suggested he would be away from home for some time. Ojo returned later in the evening, but they decided to wait until the dead of the night to carry out their task. It took little time and effort for the three men to sneak into Kudaisi compound, then into Ojo's hut and overpower him. Ojo had been blindfolded and his hands tied behind his back before he was fully in control of his senses.

'Now listen very carefully,' one of the men whispered into Ojo's hear. 'Our intention is to take you out of this compound quietly. To achieve that, it is essential that you cooperate with us and do exactly as we tell you. If you try to be smart, you will be dead before whatever action you take has any impact. Do you understand?'

'Yes I do,' Ojo replied.

The men led Ojo out of the house as silently as they had entered. Ojo's first thought was that he had been betrayed by his friend Molaja, whom he had intended to travel with. He became confused when after a long and eerily silent walk into the dark night none of his aggressors asked question relating to the beads. Despite being blindfolded, he could sense that they were going deeper into the forest.

After taking long detours around settlements and risky passages through unavoidable communal areas, and having to keep to difficult but deserted terrains between Seleru, Apete and Eti-Osa, Olubi was able to make it to the outskirts of Isale-Eko at about sundown of the second day after the crime had been committed. He waited in the forest until it was very dark before sneaking into the compound of Goje Salaji at Isale-Eko. At the Salaji compound, Olubi was told that Goje was not likely to return to Isale-Eko until after the next Aromire market. That was four days away, but Olubi had no choice but to wait. Most of the residents of Salaji's compound knew Olubi and he was readily allowed to stay in the compound while waiting for Goje.

The news of the incident at the weavers' settlement and the identity of the culprit reached Isale-Eko the day after Olubi sneaked into the compound. As he had feared, the captured men talked freely. They did not only confess but did so in a manner that made matters worse for Olubi. In their attempt to evade Akala, the captured men did not mention Olowoeyo as part of the gang. By their reasoning, mentioning him would make them accomplices to Olowoeyo's many prior crime, and they would automatically be bound for Akala. Instead they identified the escaped member of the gang by his true identity, Olubi. The adult members of the Salaji family in Isale-Eko did not have to be told that Olubi's presence must be kept between as few as possible. They cautioned him to limit his movement to certain areas of the compound and make himself totally invisible, especially to children.

Five days later, Goje returned to Isale-Eko. Although he had heard about Olubi's crime, he was not expecting Olubi to still be within Aketeland, and most disturbing of all places - inside his compound in Isale-Eko. Goje's plan before finding Olubi in his compound was to rest for a couple of days before setting off for Gbajumo to check on his mother and daughter.

Despite his personal predicament, Goje had to stay for a few days to help Olubi before travelling to Gbajumo. In the context of his latest crime, Goje for his part did not agree with the people that Olubi had sinned. A criminal, yes, but not a sinner, because he had never intended to burn the shrine and his crime was not directed against the gods. According to all the eyewitnesses, he had ordered the burning of the loom and not the Obatala shrine. Goje believed Olubi was wanted by the king and not by the gods, else he would not have bothered to offer any help, because you can run from the kings but never from the gods.

'If the king wants you dead, then you should die,' Goje advised Olubi.

'What do you mean?' Olubi asked in astonishment.

'Die by your own hand rather than giving the palace the credit for your demise.'

'May the gods forbid such an end for me!' said Olubi, more in anger than surprise. How could Goje of all people suggest such an option? 'I am a properly born and well-bred Erebeman, I will never give in to cowardice,' he said. 'And may I remind you, in case you have forgotten, that suicide is the worst form of cowardice, and a route which no true Erebeman must seek. I would rather spend the rest of my life in Akala than take my life with my own hands.'

Goje remained silent and still. 'If you cease to be an Erebeman, what will you be then?' he asked after Olubi had finished.

'Dead,' Olubi replied.

'You see, you have just said it. Dead! That is what you will be when your tattooed tribal marks is removed, and I arrange your exit from Aketeland to Ijowa right on the nose of your pursuers. You are a wanted man and in hiding, not because you have committed a crime, but because you are a criminal with the Erebe tribal mark. There are many criminals with greater offences than yours, roaming freely across Akete villages simply because they are not identified with Erebe people.'

Olubi nodded. He knew Goje was right and found it very strange that he had never thought of an escape route from that angle. The Akete army would not take a second look at him if he had the right tribal mark, or none at all. In the past years, many mark-bearing Erebe men had been arrested during the search for 'Olowoeyo' and on not a few occasions mark-bearing Erebe women had been taken from the market into custody to be stripped naked by female patriots to confirm their sexuality, because they were suspected of having been the 'elusive Olowoeyo' disguised as a woman.

'So do you want to die by your own hand, or do you want *Oba* Lagbade to boost his fame by displaying the body of the after all not-so-elusive Olubi in the market square?' asked Goje.

'Yes, my dear brother,' Olubi replied calmly. 'I would rather kill myself than let *Oba* Lagbade add such a feat to his achievements.' He shivered at the thought of being captured and tied to a stake like a sacrificial dog. That would mean the end of 'elusive Olowoeyo' and the beginning of a person destined to bid the world farewell. He could not suppress the excitement that was fast replacing the anger that had been building up in him just moments ago. He made to embrace Goje, but Goje deliberately ignored the gesture. He had too much on his mind to engage in any display of emotion.

'I will send somebody down tonight to escort you out of town to a safe place where your tribal mark will be done, and then arrange your safe exit from Aketeland,' said

Goje. 'From there you can find your way to Oko-Oba and the Salaji compound. I have sent a message to my brother Lagori, whom you know very well, and he will be expecting you. I don't have to tell you that you must keep yourself strictly within the family compound until I am able to travel down and introduce you to the *Baale* to discuss the terms and condition upon which your stay in Oko-Oba will be granted.' He left the room without saying goodbye, while Olubi remained on the spot like a statue, his outstretched hand still hanging. He wondered why Goje was being so cold towards him. He had had disagreements with him in the past, but they had never parted in such a way, even after a heated argument.

That same night, Olubi was escorted out of the Salaji compound to a safe house in the forest on the outskirts of Isale-Eko.

Having committed a crime against the deities, Olubi accepted that his banishment from Aketeland was certain. He did not have to be told that he had crossed a dangerous boundary by violating the sanctity of a deity like Obatala. It was an unpardonable crime, which the palace could not ignore, as it readily enjoyed public support in making culprits answer for their crimes. It had been easy when his concern was evading the so-called long arms of the king, but Olubi's crime had widened his enemies to the masses, as every town person considered it a duty to assist in bringing to justice whoever was responsible for the destruction of the shrine of Obatala.

On the ninth day after Olubi's actions had led to the destruction of the shrine, a convergence of high priests of the 'sixteen deities' in Aketeland met at Aromire, and as expected the issue of the burnt shrine was prominent on their agenda. After the meeting, a high-powered delegation headed by the *Oluwo* (highest priest) and comprising the eight Obatala high priests from the eight villages of Akete (including Eti-Osa) was mandated to conduct a ritual, invoking the gods to inflict great tragedy upon any household that harboured Olubi in Eti-Osa, or any part of Aketeland.

Meanwhile, the consequences of the crime had reached Olubi's family in Eti-Osa. His compound was ransacked and burnt to the ground by angry villagers, who insisted on making it clear to Olubi that he must never return to their community. His wives and children had sensed the tension before it boiled over and fled Eti-Osa the day before an angry mob attacked, fortunate not to be lynched. Olubi's senior wife, Kofo, was an Akete woman and her family compound was in Iseri. That was where they went to seek temporary shelter, but their entry into the village caused bad feeling. Their sudden departure from Eti-Osa, the stress of a full day and half's journey to Iseri, their wretched appearance and their numbers made their entrance very noticeable, so everybody knew who they were and why they were in the village.

They arrived at Iseri at noon, but their stay was bound to be shorter than they had anticipated. At sundown, a messenger came from the *Baale* asking to see the host immediately. Upon his return from the *Baale's* compound, Kofo's uncle Gbamu sadly informed his guests that the *Baale* and elders had denied the family a stay in Iseri due to the nature of Olubi's crime. They feared that the curse placed upon him by the high priests of Aketeland could extend to his offspring and consequently the community. They were given five days to leave the village.

It took nine days to get Olubi's tattooed tribal mark completely removed. It was not until the day he was due to leave the safe house and be taken out of Aketeland that he learnt of his family's predicament. The tattoo remover was kind enough to keep him updated and tell him what had happened.

'I want you to do a favour for me for which I will reward you handsomely,' Olubi said to Somolu, the tattoo remover. 'I want you to get this message across to my in-law in Iseri. His name is Gbamu and the name of the compound is Alasan. Tell Gbamu to arrange their journey to Oko-Oba. When they get there, he should go directly to the Salaji compound, ask for Lagori and tell him that they are from Olubi. He will take it from there.'

The men Goje engaged to abduct Ojo had their work made easy when, due to the public interest and emotion generated by the destruction of a sacrilegeous place, the palace at Aromire placed a substantial bounty on anyone providing assistance or information leading to the arrest of Olubi and any member of his gang. An even larger amount was placed on Olubi himself. Those who initially were neither concerned about Olubi's crime nor particularly offended by the assault on a religious place joined the hunt for the sake of the bounty. So instead of going through the relatively long process of sending Ojo to Akala via the 'back door', the men sent by Goje simply delivered him to the palace at Aromire, claiming he was part of the gang, and collected the bounty.

Meanwhile, having learnt that Ojuolape was pregnant, Goje realised that there had to be a change of plan. Even in his anger and disappointment, he had to accept the reality; that Ojo would in due course be the father of his first grandchild. He needed to get Ojo back, but he soon found out that while it was easy to plot his path to Akala, events since then had put him practically beyond his influence. Even Goje's friend among the minor nobles of Akete could do nothing to help. Goje's situation was like someone who breaks a calabash, only to find that putting the pieces back together is an impossible task. In order to keep Ojo away from his daughter, Goje had masterminded an event intended to keep him in Akala for at least two seasons. Now he was unable to get him out for his daughter.

After due consideration, Goje and Ajiun decided that the only option to avoid shame was to declare Ojuolape missing until she had had her baby. In order to keep her well away from the public, it was arranged that she should stay with the old women in Gbajumo until she had had her baby. Ojuolape had been living with the older women for two weeks before meeting Lalonpe, who had been away trading in Ijaye, and as usual left Bogunde in the care of *Iya* Mojoyin.

On their first meeting, Lalonpe took no particular interest in Ojuolape, as such guests were not uncommon in *Iya* Mojoyin's house. She had been a beneficiary of the support the old woman gave to maidens and women with various female problems. During and after her stay in *Iya* Mojoyin's house, many had come and stayed for different durations depending on the nature of their problem and the support required. She never probed, but on a few occasions *Iya* Mojoyin had told her the issues that had brought individuals to her house.

CHAPTER 10

By the time Ojo and the rest of Olubi's gang were brought to Akala Island, there were more than four hundred 'incorrigible criminals' serving terms for crimes ranging from petty stealing to arm banditry. The minimum penalty for any convict at Akala was three years, and before the arrival of Ojo and the gang, the maximum sentence served by any convict had been ten years. Hence, Olubi's gang received the longest sentence so far, and it was one of the very few verdicts in which public opinion was completely in favour of the palace. Lagemo, Baoku and all the six men directly involved in the crime were each sentenced to twenty years. Athough Lagemo and Baoku testified in the palace that Ojo had not been involved in the crime, he was given ten years just for being the son of Olubi.

Ojo was naturally enraged and bitter that he was being punished for a crime he knew nothing about. But despite his bitterness, the thought of Ojuolape and the incident that had preceded his appearance as a criminal took priority in his mind. He would not have been judged along with Olubi's compatriots in the crime that had led to the destruction of the shrine if he had not been abducted in the first place. According to the little he learnt before arriving at Akala, all residents of Olubi's compound had vacated the premises since the news of the tragedy and personalities involved reached Eti-Osa. That was three clear days after he had been abducted and six days before the angry mob descended on the Kudaisi compound. Hence, apart from the real culprits, he was the only resident of the compound that appeared in the palace and then taken to Akala. He was sure his abduction had happened before the crime had even been committed. So why had he been abducted, and what was the initial intention of his abductors before they changed their minds and handed him over to the palace?

He knew Ojuolape would have heard of the incident and was likely to believe that he was really involved, and the thought stung him. He wished he could tell her his own version of the story. His abductors claimed that they had caught him trying to escape to Abatan through Gbengbele, and that was what the palace and the general public accepted as the truth.

Since the first set of convicts had arrived at Akala, there had been ten escape attempts. Eight of them were the conventional type, whereby inmates tried to sneak past the numerous well-armed guards who patrolled the walkable part of the cliff around the island, which also led to the only part of the ocean between Akala and Aromire which could be swum across. In five attempts, the escapees were cornered before they could cover the sand between the base of the island and the water. All were returned alive to the plantation after being well beaten. Three manage to get to the ocean, but the guards on each occasion were able to carry out the last measure to stop escapees from Akala, as instructed by the palace - gunning them down.

The details of the two remaining attempts were known only to a few inmates of Akala, and to a great extent the guards believed them to have been the only successful escapes so far. On each occasion, men were beaten and tortured in order to find the truth, but none confessed. The attempts were made by desperate inmates daring to go via the very steep cliff, which even the guards did not dare to patrol, due to the high risk of tripping over the edge. On one attempt, the escaping inmate made it right to the bottom of the cliff with the intention of swimming halfway round the edge of Akala to the water between Akala and Aromire. The escapee was reported to have been swept away by the ocean currents the moment his body touched the water. The second attempt, which probably put an end to all further thoughts of escaping via the unguarded part of the cliff, was by a young Ilaje man who slipped and fell to his death from the middle of the cliff. The fatal accident happened at noon, and all the other inmates watched from above as his body was consumed to the last toenail before sundown by a combined team of vultures and hyenas.

Ojuolape had her baby shortly before the time was due, according to Jibike's estimate. But the baby, a boy, was healthy at birth. He was named Malaolu and his birth was recorded in the seventh month after the burning of the Obatala shrine. Malaolu was almost six months old before his maternal grandmother Bibiola came to Kuluso for the first time to see the mother and child. She put pressure on her daughter to leave Malaolu as soon as he stopped breast feeding, leave him in the care of Ajiun in Isale-Eko and return with her to Aromire to start life afresh. But Ojuolape declined, and declared that her intention was to wait in Gbajumo for Ojo to return from Akala.

'You want to wait for him to get out of Akala?' said Bibiola. 'You want to wait for nine years for an outcast? You seem to forget that his crime was not only against the king but also against a deity. Tell me, where will he live after Akala? Because there will definitely be no place for him in Aketeland.'

'Akete is not the only place on earth. We will find a place to live here in Ijowa or even Abatan.'

'I cannot believe you just said that. You want to spend the rest of your life with an outlaw, a criminal?'

'If he is good enough to be the father of my son, then he is good enough to be my husband,' Ojuolape insisted. She discussed her problem with Lalonpe and asked for her advice.

'You know him better than anybody else,' she said. 'If you are sure he is worth waiting for, then I will encourage you to do so. Then you will be able to take care of your son by yourself, and be there to see him growing up.' But Lalonpe advised that if she really intended to wait for Omolubi and at the same time retain her dignity as a single woman, she must remain under the roof and care of *Iya* Mojoyin. Ojuolape agreed and chose to remain in *Iya* Mojoyin's house, where she had been since her arrival in Gbajumo.

By the middle of his second season in Akala, Ojo had lost all hope of leaving the island until he had served his term. Apart from cultivating the land for crops to be exported, the inmates of Akala were also engaged in loading the produce onto wagons at the plantation. Others were tasked with clearing and levelling the wagon route between the hinterlands of Akala and the seafront. Under the watchful eyes of armed guards, convicts would be marched along with the wagons to the seafront, where the produce was loaded onto large canoes that ferried them to the storage house at the seafront of Oluweri, in readiness for the next merchant ship. On occasion, Wontsay and some crewmen would oversee the delivery from Akala at the seafront to facilitate coordination between the guards on the island and the outpost at lower Oluweri.

It took, on average, from dawn to noon for a transit of cargo to travel between the hinterland of Akala Island to the shore. None of the convicts, and very few regular natives in the service of Fadahunse, were allowed into the canoes.

On one occasion, Ojo was part of the team responsible for delivering produce to the seafront, then to bring supplies brought by the ship meant for Akala back via the same wagons. On their way back to the hinterlands of Akala, both convicts and guards were beset by herds of wild monkeys, In recent years, the convoys were been increasingly troubled by the primates. There had been tremendous increase in the activities on Akala since the first ship docked at Oluweri, and the cconsequent increase in traffic through their habitation had been unsettling to the monkeys. They were used to chasing them away but the numbers they were suddenly faced with this time did not give them much hope of fending them off with the few men that they were.

The screech of the monkeys drowned out the forest as missiles of faeces, rotten fruits and coconuts were launched from atop trees. Terrified, Wontsay's men drew their guns and fired into the sky but this only hastened their undoing. Contrary to their expectations, the gunshots did not repel the monkeys, but instead attracted reinforcements as it echoed through jungle. Hundreds of enraged monkeys began descending on the convoy from the forest trees like a swarm of giant white-maned rodents.

In the chaos, one of Wontsay's men along with two king's guard were killed. Many of the king's guard who tried to brave the situation with their cutlasses, suffered the brunt of the attacks. Bite marks on their legs and arms and blunt force bruises on their heads and backs were evidence of their struggle. Few who managed to escaped with slight injury, owed their fortune to the brief head start they gained while the monkeys were distracted by the gunshots.

Throughout the ordeal Ojo, who had been near the front of the convoy, remained transfixed by an apprehensive calm, with Fidel Wontsay, who had clung to him in terror. When the pack began its attacked, Ojo instinctively leaped to the nearest tree and sat with his back to it. To outrun monkeys in a forest was folly and his prior encounters had taught him they were more readily thieves than brawlers. Wontsay had stumbled to Ojo's side as he watched his colleagues battered and his legs surrendered in fear.

They sat there, unmoving, even as the others fled and some of the troop chased after them. All through the commotion, the monkeys just passed by Ojo and Fadahunse, or maybe ignored. It was as if they were not there. Fadahunse was threatened only once, when he tried taking advantage of a seeming escape route and disengaged from Ojo. He quickly changed his mind after the first two steps, due to spontaneous reaction by a couple of monkeys to his sudden movement. It took a long time before the monkeys finally decided there were no more threats about and moved on. Long enough for each of the men to have at least twice urinated on themselves and each other in order not to risk a movement that would attract the monkeys.

It was getting dark by the time Fadahunse and Ojo decided it was safe to leave their sanctuary. Because they were closer to the seafront than to the base of Akala Island, and because the monkeys' departure route was into Akala, they both deemed it wise to return to the seafront and look for an empty canoe or hitch a ride to Lower-Oluweri before it was too dark. They made it to the seafront without further attack from the monkeys. At the shore, they soon found a vacant canoe and set off for Lower-Oluweri. They rowed through the dark night until they arrived at one of the many fishermen's shacks scattered across the shoreline between Akala and Oluweri.

In the dark, Wontsay rummaged through his knapsack and was able to find his matches. They made a fire, and after a quick survey of their environment to make sure they were safe, Wontsay dipped again into his knapsack and brought out a small bottle of rum. He drank a little and passed the bottle to Ojo.

It has been close to nine years since Wontsay had first stepped on the soil of Aketeland, and his command of the language was now well above average. He asked the question which Ojo had been anticipating; what power had enabled Ojo to survive the attack? Ojo told Wontsay that their survival was due to a charm he had tied above his left elbow. Called *owo* or *isora*. The charm, as Ojo explained to Wontsay, was made from the hunch of a hunchbacked squirrel. 'It is very rare to find such a squirrel,' he said. 'Finding and capturing a squirrel with such a deformity is a task that requires not only experience but spiritual support. That part of the squirrel, when combined with other materials, including a portion of hair cut from the centre of the user's head, with the necessary incantation invoked by a truly knowledgeable spiritualist, ensures protection against attack from any animal with hair. That is why we were never attacked by the monkeys.'

Ojo in turn inquired about the significance of the pendant that Wontsay had hung on his neck.

'The crucifix and the man that was staked upon it are capable of performing miracles,' Wontsay explained.

'What do you mean by miracles?' Ojo asked.

'It is the ability to make the impossible possible, like raising the dead, curing diseases like leprosy, barrenness and similar ailments.'

'I see,' Ojo said in admiration. 'My tribesmen have a similar charm. Its infusion is prepared from very rare materials, rarer than those which the charm I gave you was made from, and its preparation and administration are known to very few. It is called *gbogbonise ajebidan*, and it is believed to have the ability to cure numerous diseases and ailments. The secret of *gbogbonise ajebidan* is known to very few herbalists, but no charm has been known to bring the dead back to life. To create life, yes, but not to reverse death, like the one you have just revealed to me.'

Wontsay was visibly impressed and excited by what he had learnt from Ojo about the charm. Had he not been for the incident which had saved their lives, he would have dismissed such ideas as nonsense. So the explorer made an offer, and the outlaw accepted. The crucifix was swapped for the charm, but not before Ojo told Wontsay about the condition which according to his medicine man could render the charm impotent. 'Avoiding fear – that is the antidote,' he said. 'You must not be afraid or make any move that could be interpreted as an attempt to retreat or to attack. Just remain calm.'

Wontsay then asked how and why Ojo had got to Akala.

'I have not committed any crime and I have not the slightest idea what led to my being there,' Ojo replied, and went on to narrate the circumstances that had led him to Akala.

'You might have been indicted as an accomplice to the crime.'

'No that is not possible. I had already been abducted the day before the crime was committed.'

'Actually neither your crime nor your innocence is of any relevance now,' Wontsay said. 'What is relevant to me is that you saved my life, and the least I can do is to ensure your freedom. Given the nature of the crime, taking you to the palace to prove your innocence could be tricky, so I suggest we pretend you are among the dead in the jungle.'

Wontsay offered to help and Ojo graciously accepted. 'The only problem is that you will definitely not be able to return Eti-Osa, and if you are going to stop anywhere under the jurisdiction of the king at Aromire, you might need to change your identity,' Wontsay advised. 'If you decide to change your name, I can allow you to remain within Ago-Oyinbo and be one of my employees.'

For obvious personal reasons which were unknown to Wontsay, the need to change his name was an added bonus, not a sacrifice. He was delighted at the prospect of reverting to his original name from Omolubi, so Ojo was the name he suggested.

'That is settled then. But while this incident is still fresh in people's memory, you will need keep a very low profile. It will be up to you to avoid undue attention and restrict your movement to within Ago-Oyinbo.'

They set off at the crack of dawn and were able to make it to Oluweri by early morning. The news of the attack had not yet spread beyond Akala, and the residents of Ago-Oyinbo had not been expecting Wontsay for a few more days. They were shocked by the state he was in on arrival. He told them about the incident and how he alone had been lucky enough to escape. He said Ojo was a canoeman who had helped him from the shore of Akala to Oluweri.

'I asked what I could do for him as a reward for his good deed, and he asked to be one of my employees,' he said. 'I have granted his request and he will henceforth be living inside Ago-Oyinbo. He will be sleeping in the produce store until I can find a better shelter for him.' The stranger introduced himself to the residents as Ojo.

Three days later, Ojo approached Wontsay concerning his accommodation. Without disclosing his childhood residency in what was now Ago-Oyinbo, he requested permission to rebuild his old home. It was granted, and by his second week in Ago-Oyinbo he had been able to renovate the least damaged of the rooms and move out of the storage house.

It was the tragic news that Omolubi was among the victims of the attack in the jungle at Akala that brought Lalonpe closer to Ojuolape.

'My daughter, I know very well the way you must be feeling right now. I was pregnant with our second child, when disaster struck and my husband remain invalid till his death,' said Lalonpe, trying to console Ojuolape.

'It is just so sad that my son will never know his father.'Ojuolape sobbed.

'Yes very sad indeed. But still, life must go on. If it is true that you love him the way you have proven in the past two years and half, then you should be thankful that you have a son of his to keep his memory fresh in your mind.'

Athough Malaolu was still a babe in arms when Ojuolape got the tragic news, tradition demanded that Omolubi's passage be celebrated, and his funeral (even in the absence of the corpse) had to be performed in a manner that befitted one who had left a child behind. So the onus was on Ojuolape to observe all the due rites in honour of her son. On the day of the final burial rites, Ojuolape insisted that the deceased father of her son should be addressed not by his adopted name, but by his real name, Ojo.

Later in the evening, Lalonpe, out of curiosity, visited Ojuolape to learn more about who the father of her son had been and how he had come to change his name from Ojo to Omolubi. Lalonpe fainted even before Ojuolape was halfway into her story. She had just been to the funeral of her own son without realising it. *Iya* Mojoyin and Jibike were by her side when she finally came round. Having listened to the account Ojuolape had given, they were able to put the pieces together and understand what had happened.

'You assured me that it was here in Gbajumo that my son would come seeking me. But you did not tell me that it is the ghost of my son that will be coming!' Lalonpe lamented to Jibike. 'To think my son has been living in Eti-

Osa all these years, and I never met or heard of him until his death.'

Lalonpe's tears would come for many weeks after, even when she wished it would not. Her grief felt like it would never subside in its intensity. She found herself unable to supress her heavy heart when she learnt of her son's struggles through Ojuolape. At the times she remembered the manner of his death, as a convict accused of sacrilege, or the agony of their separation, it was as though all his tribulations flowed through her at once. The only consolation that stayed with her lay in Iya Mojoyin's words that though they may not reunite physically, his spirit is with her through Malaolu. That he had grown into a man worthy of Ojuolape's sacrifice reassured her further. After many moons, some calm returned to her heart; becoming more comfortable in the thought that, though misfortune befell him, he had internalised her love and was a man capable of passing it on.

Then three months after the final funeral rites of the father of her son, Ojuolape realised she had to face the reality of a future without Ojo, and finally yielded to her mother's wish to leave Gbajumo. Since the revelation, Lalonpe had assumed the role of paternal grandmother to Malaolu. Ojuolape waited another three months to wean Malaolu off breastfeeding. She then left him in the care of his willing paternal grandmother and returned to Aromire.

In Ago-Oyinbo, native residents in the service of Wontsay were engaged in various labour-intensive tasks, ranging from digging under different parts of the Awoyaya river around Oluweri to breaking rocks across Aketeland looking for precious stones and rare metals. There seemed to be no end to which Wontsay would not go to explore the jungle and the clear waters of the Awoyaya under the jurisdiction of Oba Lagbade in search of these materials. Wontsay was also a collector of elephant tusks and the hides of various wild animals like leopards, lions, crocodiles and snakes. He regularly sponsored large-scale hunting expeditions into the thickest part of the jungle for this purpose. Scores of metal boxes, filled with Wontsay's collections and other goods, were carried at regular intervals to the shore, loaded onto canoes and ferried to the big ship.

Few of the natives of Ago-Oyinbo were allowed into the inner perimeter. There were some whose language or accent Ojo could not place. They had lighter skins, but it was clear that they were not from any familiar tribe, and they communicated very well with the white men. These were the natives who were often permitted to follow the canoe to the big ship or be present when Wontsay was meeting or entertaining guests in the inner chambers of Ago-Oyinbo.

Ojo's relationship with Wontsay, and his status within Ago-Oyinbo, took another leap the day Wontsay heard him playing the *agidigbo*. The first thing Ojo had missed while in Akala was his *agidigbo*, but he missed it even more in Ago-Oyinbo because his tasks there were less tedious, and now he was a free man. Although he had witnessed performances by many of the best *agidigbo* players during his numerous visits to the palace at Aromire, Wontsay found Ojo's performance to be nothing like he had ever heard before.

The entire ground of Ago-Oyinbo was shielded from the rest of Lower-Oluweri by tall bamboo fencing, and internally demarcated into an inner and outer perimeter by short bamboo fencing. Wontsay's quarters were in the inner perimeter, and other residents were housed within the outer perimeter. Due to the social barrier, Wontsay initially had to be content with listening within the inner perimeter whenever Ojo was playing to residents on the outer ground of Ago-Oyinbo. But the more Ojo played, the more Wontsay found the urge to get closer to the source irresistible. Instead of breaching the inner perimeter of Ago-Oyinbo to mingle with the natives, he invited Ojo to play for him alone in his private grounds. That was the first time Ojo was allowed into the inner grounds of Ago-Oyinbo and the first time he had fully seen Wontsay's private residence.

Wontsay was not only a lover of music, he also was very good on the accordion. He soon began experimenting with creating rhythms from a blend of *agidigbo* and accordion. He also began learning from Ojo how to play the *agidigbo*, and in return he taught Ojo how to play the accordion. The month after Ojo first played for Wontsay in the inner perimeter, he was redeployed to serve there. Within the next three months, Wontsay had acquired more than four top range *agidigbos* and a second accordion for Ojo.

The first time Ojo had the rare privilege of being invited into the main house which was Wontsay's private residence was also the day Wontsay announced that 'the Lord was born.' He invited Ojo into his home to entertain his guests and the fellow explorers who had chosen to stop there to celebrate the day the Christian Lord was born. Very few of the native residents were privileged to be present in the inner chamber of Ago-Oyinbo on occasions like this. The other times were when the same Lord, according to Wontsay, rose from the grave after he had sacrificed his life in order to set his people free. Ojo thought it was intriguing how different peoples deified ancestors had braved similar trials.

'There existed among my people too a selfless hero, called Ela Oluorogbo,' he told Wontsay that evening. 'He was the only son of Moremi. History told us that Ela Oluorogbo was rendered for sacrifice by his mother in order to protect her people, who were our ancestors back in Ile-Ife, from the horrors of the invaders.'

One day Wontsay proudly showed Ojo his collections of artefacts and valued treasure. 'All these here are my special possessions, and I would never think of parting with them. These, and whatever else I can add, will assure me the best of life when I am old and back in the good old country.' Wontsay gleefully went through each of the articles. While Ojo found some of the collections worthy of value, he considered most of the articles which Wontsay held in high esteem, and would not risk be shipped without him, as commonplace.

About eight months after *ijamba-obo* (the monkey tragedy), as the incident was now popularly referred to, Ojo was convinced that it was safe to leave Ago-Oyinbo. In those eight months he had only been able to update himself on general events when he had been inside Akala, and knew nothing about the fate of Olubi and his family. He had been careful not to ask too many questions of native residents of Ago-Oyinbo in order to prevent anybody linking him with the sacrilegious crime for which he had spent time on Akala. He was sure that even the friends he had made inside Ago-Oyinbo in the last eight months would reconsider their association with him if they knew he had had something to do with the destruction of a sacred place. It was not because such knowledge would make them hostile to him, but they would want to avoid him for personal safety, against the spiritual consequences of associating with an accursed person.

When he decided that it was time to move on, his first intention was to clear his mind of the situation he had been dealing with before he was abducted. He needed to know what had become of Ojuolape, and then he intended to seek information about the fate of Olubi and the rest of the family. Of equal importance was eventually to find out the reason for his abduction. To fulfil any of these aims, he knew he would have to begin from Eti-Osa.

He decided to risk a dead of night visit to the ruins of Olubi's compound in Eti-Osa, in the hope of recovering the beads. He found it peculiar that this was the second time he had had to retrieve the beads from a ruined building that was supposed to have been his home. It was as if destruction was following the beads everywhere.

His aim was to look for the large clay pot under which he kept the beads. The fact that he was supposed to be dead proved to be both an advantage and at the same time a disadvantage. It was an advantage in the sense that nobody was looking for him, and that included both friends and foes. Hence it would be easier for him to conduct his business in Eti-Osa without fear of being recognised and possibly molested by foes. The disadvantage was that nobody wants or wishes to see a ghost, and that includes friends and foes alike. As such it was difficult and risky to contact even trusted friends who might be able to help him with information about his family. To cap it all, differentiating friends from foes could prove a challenge. So for now, he would have to work alone.

Ojo did not stay inside Eti-Osa. Instead, he camped in the forest, on the outskirts. The next morning, he spent his first day at Eti-Osa discreetly walking around, avoiding personal contact with anybody. He went past the ruins of Olubi's compound and was relieved by what he saw. While the entire compound was in total ruin and the main house had been burnt down, he could clearly see the large waterpot among the debris, under one of the fallen roofs.

That same night, he returned to the ruins. Finding his way through was easier than expected, as the moon was high. The waterpot under which he had placed the *ejigbaileke* was undisturbed and the beads were just as he had left them.

It was not until he had been walking around Eti-Osa for six days that Ojo was fortunate enough to stumble upon some information that would lead him to Olubi and the rest of the family.

The sun was high overhead as Ojo rode into Oko-Oba. He kept his horse at walking pace as he approached the village square. It had been more than three years since he had been here for the *Lakaaye* festival, but nothing had changed. It seemed only yesterday that he had been sitting with Ojuolape in the same square, plotting their future together.

There were quite a number of people on the paths and in the open stalls, and also a fair few women and children. In general it looked peaceful and calm, which would give a stranger the impression that there was a capable *Baale* in charge of village affairs.

At the edge of the square, he found a tree trunk to which he tied his horse. In a shed nearby, a woman was selling food. He had no idea what it was, but he was past caring as he was very hungry, and anything would do. He also needed a break to study the environment before beginning to enquire after Olubi. By the time he was ten paces from the food seller, Ojo could rightly confirm from the aroma oozing out of the steaming pot, as the woman tended to a moderately restless queue of customers, that it was boiled yam. Hot yam would not be bad at all, he thought, especially at this time of the year when the harvesting of fresh yams was at its peak.

He waited his turn and collected his meal, which was served in a broad leaf, and settled himself in a vacant space at the end of the bamboo bench. The third morsel of yam was approaching his open mouth when he heard a commotion not far away. He saw a group of six men led by a short stocky man with balding head. The short man was wearing a *dansiki* atop an undersized *sokoto*, and his awkward stride reflected hidden discomfort. He calmly returned the hot yam back to the leaf as he realised the group was heading toward the shed. When it was obvious that their destination was his position, he stood up.

'What is your mission here, stranger? Are you looking for work or just passing by? We have a peaceful settlement here, there is no work and we don't welcome strangers,' said the short man, all in quick succession, as if he had rehearsed the statement beforehand, or had said it to quite a number of people in recent times. Ojo let a slow grin spread across his face, but his eyes were bleak and unsmiling.

'Where I come from, nobody asks personal questions in such a manner, unless he is the *Baale*, or the *Ajele*,' he said, 'and from what I can see, in my presence you are no such person.' The short man flushed and those around him groaned angrily, but Ojo ignored them.

'I am asking in the name of the *Baale*,' the short man said. He produced a short stick, beaded around each end and in the middle. 'And you had better have the right answers.'

'Or?' drawled Ojo. He was balanced on his heel with the legs slightly apart, deceptively casual. 'I have answers to all your questions, if and when you decide to ask them properly. However, whether they are right or wrong is for you to judge, and it bothers me not at all.'

'*Ogbeni*!' the short man barked. 'When *Bopo*, the *ilari* [civil enforcer] of this village asks questions, men answer, and without hesitation!'

'So your name is Bopo, and you are the *ilari* of this village,' Ojo said, more in the manner of a statement than a question, and raised his hat in recognition of the short man's position. Bopo took this gesture as mockery rather than courtesy. 'Well to be fair Bopo, I guess that information entitles you to some information from me. My name is Ojo, and I am an Erebe man. I have just ridden in from a long way off. And my mission? That is my concern, it is very personal.' He saw a reflex action in Bopo, and knew he was about to pull a weapon from under his *dansiki*, anything from a knife to an *olonde* (juju or charm). Ojo drew his knife and in a flash, the tip was pressing on Bopo's protruding belly before he could reach for whatever he had under his *dansiki*. Bopo froze and wisely kept his hand where it was. Onlookers were beginning to gather, watching and waiting.

'You were saying?' Ojo asked, as if it had all the while been a civil dialogue, and not a confrontation that was on the brink of violence. Bopo remained frozen for a moment, then he slowly drew back his arm. Ojo relaxed, and with eye-defying speed, his knife went back to wherever it had come from, out of sight.

Visibly humiliated and with red eyes, Bopo turned his back on Ojo and stomped away, followed at his heels by his adjutants. The small crowd that had formed dispersed as quickly as they had gathered, and everybody went back to what they were doing before the diversion. Their reaction would have been different if the tables had been turned, and Ojo had backed down. They would have cheered and laughed, but none dared to express the slightest excitement due to the humiliation of the *ilari*.

Ojo calmly returned to his seat and continued with his food as if nothing unusual had happened. He took his time to finish it and then approached the food seller.

'Which way is it to the Kudaisi compound?' he asked the woman.

'Who are you seeking there?' she asked suspiciously.

'I am here to see *Baba* Olubi,' Ojo replied calmly. 'I believe he is the head of the family.'

'You are seeking the Kudaisi compound, and to see *Baba* Olubi, the head of the family?' the yam monger asked, still eyeing Ojo suspiciously.

'Yes, that is what I asked for. The Kudaisi compound and *Baba* Olubi,' Ojo replied with clarity.

'Kudaisi compound is on the other side of the market. You cannot miss it. Just follow the well-paved path on the other side of the village square until you come to a big *ayunre* tree. The compound is directly opposite the tree,' the woman replied, then added. 'If you are looking for *Baba* Olubi, then you should not be quarrelling with his men.'

'I did not know that *Baba* Olubi was now the *Baale* of Oko-Oba,' said Ojo.

'Oh no, he is not the *Baale*. He is just the *Seriki*, but he is the closest to the *Baale* among the village elders. Whatever *Baba* Olubi says in this village is agreeable to the *Baale* and vice-versa. They were like this.' The yam seller locked her fingers to indicate the strong bond between the *Baale* and *Baba* Olubi. She paused, looked around briefly and then continued in a whisper, 'The *Baale* and the elders make the law, but the *Seriki* and his men enforce it, and the *Baale* is very pleased with him. Without the help of *Baba* Olubi and his men, this village would long have been without order. Without the *Seriki*, this community would have been overrun by criminals and outlaws.'

The yam seller was obviously far better at gossiping than giving directions because finding Olubi's house was not as straightforward as she had led him to believe, but he got there eventually.

'The last news I heard of you was that you were dead!' Olubi managed to say after the initial shock of seeing Ojo alive. 'I thought you were killed in the monkey tragedy in the jungle.'

'That is the general belief, but here I am, alive and well,' Ojo replied. He told Olubi what had actually happened and how Wontsay had sheltered him. 'Now you must no longer call me Omolubi. Fadahunse advised me to change my identity in order to stay in Ago-Oyinbo, so I reverted to my original name, Ojo. That is what they call me in Oluweri.' He concluded his story, and Olubi in turn told him about the incident that had led to the destruction of the shrine, and how he had managed to escape from Aketeland with the help of Goje Salaji.

'I was surprised when I heard you were not with the family in Iseri,' said Olubi. 'I thought you too had deserted me until I began to hear from the grapevine that you were wrongly accused with my men, and had been taken to Akala.'

'*Baba*, I must confess to you. The event that led to my being taken to Akala is still a mystery to me. I was abducted the day before the tragedy of the Obatala shrine, days before you were declared wanted. The reason behind my abduction, and why my abductors decided to turn me over to the palace and collect the bounty, still eludes me.'

'That is certainly a mystery. I would have been getting to the root of the matter if it had not been for my condition. Aketeland has been off limits to me since then. Apart from Goje Salaji, none of my associates in Akete would have anything to do with me. They are all afraid of the curse inflicted on me by the Obatala priests. Goje explored all his little influence in Aromire to free you but failed. He then masterminded an escape plan to free you and others, but the unfortunate news of your death came just when all was set. He bribed the families of the guards in charge of overseeing you to turn a blind eye on a night where you and others would escape to the shoreline where a boat would meet you. It was the same scheme that got Lagemo and two others out of Akala."

'Are you telling me that Lagemo is no longer in Akala?'

'Yes, Lagemo and Baoku escaped Akala shortly after you were pronounced dead. In fact, he is here with me in Oko-Oba. He only went on an errand for me to Odinjo. He should be back by noon tomorrow.'

Later in the evening, after he had washed and eaten, Ojo

sat chatting with Olubi in the open space in the front of the house to catch up on the missed months. He tactically steered the discussion towards Goje Salaji with the aim of eventually getting to Ojuolape.

'It is very impressive the way *Baba* Goje responded when asked for help,' he began. 'Very few people will respond to their kinsmen in their time of need.'

'Yes, you are right. Very few people will respond to a friend the way Goje did in time of need. But you will have to be in a situation to know who will stand by you.'

'What about her daughter? She must be long married now,' Ojo asked as casually as he could. 'She could not stop talking about it the last time we met here, during the *Lakaaye* festival.'

'That is another sad story,' Olubi began, and Ojo's heart skipped a beat. 'She was reported to be very ill shortly after that same *Lakaaye* festival. Her illness as I understood was so serious that they had to put off the wedding.'

'Oh, that is sad indeed. I hope she is better now.'

'I don't think so. Goje and the family choose to be very discreet about it. What I heard from the grapevine was that her illness had something to do with her brain, and she was taken to a woman in Gbajumo for healing.'

'You mean she has not recovered from the illness?'

"The last time I asked her father was about a year ago, and all he said was that she was getting better. But in my experience, such ailments seldom get cured totally.'

'That is a pity. I would have liked to see her and wish her well. But how does one find out where exactly she is being treated in Gbajumo?'

'That should not be difficult, but I don't think Goje will be pleased with that. It is clear that he meant to keep her daughter's situation as private as possible. I don't think she will be pleased either.'

'Don't worry *baba*, I will make my visit very short. I will leave the moment I have the feeling that Ojuolape is not comfortable about my presence.'

'The woman looking after her is very popular in Gbajumo. They call her *Iya-Abiye*. Even a toddler will show you where her place is.'

'Did you say *Iya-Abiye*?'

'Yes.'

'But that is a title for midwives.' Ojo was visibly confused. 'You said her sickness had to do with her brain.'

'Yes, I thought so myself, but when I inquired, I learnt that *Iya-Abiye* is knowledgeable in treatment of ailments peculiar to women, but midwifery is her primary practice.'

CHAPTER 11

Ojo could not contain his excitement over the possibility of seeing Ojuolape again. Gbajumo was less than two days on horseback from Oko-Oba. He would have loved to set off right away, but such a move would arouse undue attention and questions from Olubi, so he waited restlessly for another day before leaving. He left Oko-Oba on horseback at cockcrow and arrived at Gbajumo the next day, just as the sun was high overhead. Olubi was right; *Iya-Abiye* was very popular in Gbajumo and he had no problem finding her house. He knocked on the door, but there was no answer. He looked around the house to see if there was anybody around to ask, but the compound was deserted.

He was about to go to the next house to enquire when a woman emerged from a compound opposite. She introduced herself as Gbekeyide, and Ojo told her he had come all the way from Oluweri to see *Iya-Abiye*.

'She is not at home at the moment, and I don't think she will be back until late this evening,' Gbekeyide told him. 'You can leave a message if you like, and I will surely pass it on.'

'Actually, I am here in respect of a certain young maiden whom I believe was brought down here for treatment about three years ago. Her name is Ojuolape.'

'Ah, Ojuolape! I know her very well. She was here but she left about four months ago.'

'Did she get better before leaving?'

'She was fine as far as the eye could tell. She left after the sudden death of her husband.'

'She lost her husband? I did not hear about that.' Ojo was not only shocked but hurt to hear that Ojuolape had married. He was also slightly ashamed by the brief feelings of hope he had felt upon hearing that she was now a widow.

'Yes, her husband died in a tragic incident about nine months ago. That was when she decided to leave Gbajumo and return to Aromire.'

'How I wish I had come earlier. Well, I am glad to hear she has been cured of her illness.'

'There was nothing special about her condition anyway. But if you want to know more about Ojuolape, the best person to see is *Iya* Bogunde. They have been exceptionally close since she lost her husband.'

Ojo asked how he could find his way to *Iya* Bogunde and Gbekeyide willingly directed him. Ojo thanked her and left.

He arrived at the place as describe by Gbekeyide without difficulty. The front of the house was deserted, but he noticed a woman by the fireplace at the back of the house. He guessed that it was the woman Gbekeyide was referring to as *Iya* Bogunde and went around to meet her.

'I hope you woke up well, mama,' he said.

'Good morning,' Lalonpe replied. 'Who is it?' She turned around to look at the person greeting her.

'I am very sorry to disturb you at this moment. My name is Ojo and I am here on behalf of a...' Ojo began, but he stopped when he saw the change in Lalonpe. In that same moment he recognised the person standing before him as his mother. On hearing his words Lalonpe had slowly but fearfully stepped back towards the fireplace. She searched with her leg and her heel came in contact with a piece of dead firewood. Without taking her eyes off Ojo, she bent down, drew a handful of cold ash from the fireplace and threw it at Ojo.

'Mama, you don't have to do that. I am not a ghost. I am alive and real,' said Ojo, wiping away ash and tears. It is believed that ghosts will fade away upon contact with ashes or dust. He regained his vision just in time to catch Lalonpe as she fell backwards, disorientated.

Ojo quickly removed his top, bent over his mother, and was fanning her vigorously when Bogunde came through the door. He saw his mother lying on the floor, and a young man bending over her, and thought she was being attacked. He drew a piece of wood from a pile he had been gathering to build a goat shed. He rushed at Ojo, and in a flash he had thrown him on the floor.

'What have you done to my mother?' Bogunde yelled, thrusting the pointed end of the stick into Ojo's chest.

'I have done her no harm,' Ojo quickly replied. 'She is my mother too.' But it was obvious that Bogunde was not listening.'

'I am asking you, what have done to my mother?' he asked again, his weapon still pinning Ojo to the ground. The sharp end of the wood was pressing dangerously into his chest. Then Lalonpe began to come around and coughed, causing Bogunde to take his attention away from Ojo. In that brief moment, Ojo wriggled away and got swiftly onto his feet.

'Please hold on and listen to what I have to say,' Ojo pleaded as Bogunde made to strike him with the wood. 'I mean no harm to either you or your mother.' But Bogunde angrily chased him about the compound with the intention of striking him. Ojo soon realised that it would take more than words to calm Bogunde down. He suddenly stopped, and when Bogunde rushed again at him, he stepped aside, causing Bogunde to miss and lose his balance. In the brief moment while he was trying to regain his balance, Ojo moved in, disarmed Bogunde, and forced him to the floor. By this time Lalonpe was struggling to get on her feet.

'Tell him, mama, that I am your son and that I mean no harm to you!' Ojo shouted across the yard to Lalonpe, while keeping a tight hold on Bogunde.

'Ojo! Ojo! Is it you or am I dreaming? Please tell me I am not dreaming!' Lalonpe burst into tears. Ojo could sense that Bogunde was taking in what his mother had said, as he suddenly stopped struggling. Ojo released his hold on him and ran across to Lalonpe.

'Mama, I am really here,' Ojo replied as he helped his mother up and supported her into the house, leaving Bogunde on the ground still perplexed.

'Where have you been? I mean, what has happened to you?' Lalonpe asked. Understandably she had many questions to ask a son who had been separated from her for almost fifteen years, and whom she had believed to be dead.

'Mama, all I can say for the moment is that I am

happier than the happiest person on earth. I know how you are feeling, but all your questions will be answered in good time. I have many questions to ask you myself but answering them all could take months.'

'The last and only time I heard anything about you was at the funeral rite held for you by Ojuolape,' said Lalonpe.

'The woman who directed me to you said you were close to Ojuolape.'

'Ojuolape lived here in Gbajumo for three years, but I did not have any idea you were connected to her until the day of the funeral rites. She insisted that the deceased, the father of her son, should be addressed by the true name given to him by his parents, and that was Ojo. I later questioned her and all I learnt from her convinced me it was you she was talking about.'

'You mean Ojuolape had a son by me?'

'Yes. Didn't you know?'

'Mama, I had no idea. *Olodumare*! To think I had intended to risk going to Isale-Eko to spy on her father's compound in hopes of learning something about her. I made enquiries in Oko-Oba, and it was only three days ago that I learnt she had been ill for a long time and was brought down to Gbajumo to be treated for an undisclosed illness. I was told she was being treated by *Iya Abiye*. It was there that a woman directed me to your house. I did not know that Ojuolape was pregnant or nursing my child.'

'She was not suffering from any illness. That story was fabricated by her family to cover the shame brought about by your secret affair with her. Her father kept her away from Isale-Eko, and she was here all through her pregnancy. She had her baby here and stayed here waiting for you to complete your term. Then came the news of your death. All the while I did not know that she was nursing my grandson. I did not know that it was you, my son, she was waiting for.'

'I am hearing all this for the first time. I had no idea she was waiting here for me to return.'

'Yes, she was waiting for you. She refused to yield to her mother's pressure to abandon you until the unfortunate news of your death.'

'But mama, we only misbehaved once. I mean how can it be?'

'She said the same in your defence. But once can be enough, my son.'

'The woman who directed me to this place said she had returned to Aromire. I would like to see her and let her know that I am alive. You need to help me.'

'I will seriously advise that you keep away from her.'

'Why?'

'I'm sorry my son, she has recently been wedded to another man in Aromire, and I supported her in that decision. Your presence will not be any good to her at this crucial stage of her relationship. It will be unfair to tempt her into another scandal by your return.'

Ojo sat there for a moment, dejected by the news. The events of the past few days, finding the *ejigbaileke*, reconnecting with Olubi, and now reuniting with his mother, had led him to believe that the gods were finally relieving him of the misfortune that plagues him. That he would not be able to fulfil his promises to Ojuolape and start a family with her reminded him of his reality.

'How about my son? I need to see him,' Ojo spoke, rising from his misery.

'His name is Malaolu, and he is here with me in

Gbajumo. I successfully claimed custody of him as his paternal grandmother.'

'Where is he now?'

'He has gone to play with his friend in the next compound. He will soon be hungry and come home for his lunch.'

'I am so excited. I cannot wait to see him. Does he look like me?' Ojo was plainly struggling to cope with the excitement of suddenly realising that he was a father. 'Who is the *majesin* who almost threw me into the fire because of you?'

'Bogunde is your brother,' Lalonpe replied casually. 'Do you remember that generous man who used to visit our house shortly before the war?'

'Do you mean *Baba* Morilewa?'

'Yes, that is him. Morilewa is the father of Bogunde. Although I did not know it then, I was already pregnant before the war started and before we were separated. And the result is Bogunde.'

'I see... and where is Baba Morilewa? I would like to see him too,' Ojo said excitedly.

'He is not here, and I don't think he will ever be anywhere again.'

'What do you mean?' Ojo asked, and Lalonpe told him about Morilewa and the death of the priest.

'Immediately after the war, I went on a fact-finding trip to his family compound at Egbejoda,' said Lalonpe. 'I was told that the father of the child I had on my back was responsible for the death of Fatunbi, and consequently the loss of Oluweri.' That was as far as she got before she burst into tears. 'It was a good thing *Iya-Abiye* accompanied me to Egbejoda. After what I heard, I cannot imagine how I will be able to cope with a return journey alone. He was sentenced to twenty-five years on the king's farm,' she continued amid sobs. 'He suffered a mental breakdown during the trial and was taken to Igbodudu to be healed before commencing his time on the labour farm. He died two years later inside Igbodudu.'

'Do you really believe that *Baba* Morilewa killed the priest?' Ojo asked. 'I can't imagine him hurting anybody.'

'We heard that he confessed to the crime. But I have a strong belief that Morilewa had nothing whatsoever to do with the murder. He was used as a sacrificial goat to calm the people's agitation and satisfy their demand for justice.'

'Did you tell Bogunde about this?'

'No, I cannot tell him who his father was. After the fall of Oluweri, there was renewed anger over the crime Morilewa was accused of. So I told him his father had died during the war, and that is what everybody believed, except *Iya-Abiye* and her peers. They were the first to know that I was pregnant. Now tell me about yourself. What has been happening to you. Where have you been?'

'I spent most of the time in Eti-Osa, in the care of a man called Olubi. He bought me at Ojuoro and took me to Eti-Osa. He introduced me to the *Baale* as his son by another woman. By the way he treated me, except for his immediate family and his close associate who was with him when he bought me at Ojuoro, everybody believed I was truly his son.' Ojo told his mother how he had been adopted and why his name had had to be changed to Omolubi.

'May he be well rewarded for his good gesture,' said Lalonpe. 'It must have been the spirit of your father that brought him to your aid. Kind people like that are hard to come by.'

'Well, I will agree that I am fortunate that he took me into his household, rather than selling me off for maximum profit. He confessed to having bought me with fake coins.' Ojo laughed.

Later in the evening, after Ojo had eaten and got better acquainted with his son and new-found brother, Lalonpe took Ojo to *Iya* Mojoyin's place.

'*Mama*, I want you to guess who is here,' Lalonpe said to her from the doorstep.

'It is you of course. I don't have to guess, your voice is the giveaway,' *Iya* Mojoyin replied sarcastically from inside the house.

'*Mama*, you know I am not talking about me. I mean can you guess who I brought to your house on this peaceful evening?' Lalonpe and Ojo entered the dim room where *Iya* Mojoyin was lying on a mat.

'Now you are talking,' *Iya* Mojoyin, lifting herself up into a sitting position to have a good look at Ojo. 'Then the answer is yes,' she replied. 'This is Ojo, your missing son, who my friend Jibike said would be reunited with you here in Gbajumo. May the deities soften the earth under which she was buried.' Jibike died about five years after the war.

'How do you know it is him? You only saw him once and that was almost fifteen years ago.'

'To you it is fifteen years, but to me it is like fifteen months,' *Iya* Mojoyin replied.

'Yes mama, your friend was right and I am wrong. My son is alive and had truly come here to Gbajumo.'

'To think you have been in Gbajumo all these years and I have been just days away in Eti-Osa,' Ojo said in amazement.

'Yes, I have been here all the time. I actually came

back purposely to pick up my valuables, which I intended to sell and use the proceeds to reclaim you at Ojuoro at any cost. Then *Iya* Mojoyin and her friends convinced me that such a venture would be futile. *Mama* Jibike, may the deities soften the earth in which her body was wrapped, and her rest be even more comfortable. She predicted that the only way I would ever see you again was if I remained in Gbajumo. 'Here in Gbajumo will your son come seeking for you.' Those were her exact words'

'And it has truly come to pass,' *Iya* Mojoyin said.

'Yes, it has truly come to pass,' Ojo agreed.

By the turn of his fourth season in the service of Wontsay, Ojo had been fully integrated into the community and had become part of the fabric of Ago-Oyinbo. In four years, his status there had been elevated from that of an 'odd job person' to one of the closest aides of Wontsay, and arguably the closest among the native residents. In three years he had risen from being an ordinary resident of Ago-Oyinbo to a domestic servant within the inner perimeter, with access to Wontsay's private quarters. He had been elevated from being just one of many labourers that Wontsay engaged in moving contents between Ago-Oyinbo and the seafront to part of the crew, with privileged access to the ships. In the last two years, he had travelled with Wontsay aboard different merchant ships to places as far as a week away across open water.

One clear evening, Ojo was sitting in front of his home enjoying the evening breeze when he saw a man enter the outer perimeter. Ojo had the feeling that he had seen the face somewhere before but could not place it. His first thought was that the stranger was visiting one of the regular residents and workers of Wontsay. From his frontage, he could see the path that led to the entrance of the inner ground and Wontsay's private residence. He became more interested in the visitor when he saw him being led along the path and inside the inner fence by one of Wontsay's domestic servants. Apart from the inner chamber, which he had only entered on a few occasions at Wontsay's invitation, he now had unrestricted access to every part of Ago-Oyinbo. He decided to wait for the return of the servant who had led the visitor to Wontsay.

'I have never seen him before,' said the servant. 'He said he had something in his possession which would be of great interest to Fadahunse.'

'Do you have any idea what it is?' Ojo asked. He was trying to solve the nagging riddle of where he had seen the man before.

'No I don't, but he must have been certain that Fadahunse would be interested in it. He was initially refused audience, but then he sent me back with an object wrapped in a dark piece of cloth and asked me to take it to Fadahunse. He was sure the *oyinbo* would be very willing to see him if he glimpsed the contents.'

'You did look to see what was inside the cloth, didn't you?' Ojo asked knowingly, and the servant smiled.

'I would have done, but Fadahunse was at the front of the house and he was watching,' the servant replied regretfully.

'What was Fadahunse's response when he saw the contents?' Ojo asked.

'I could not tell, because he did not unwrap the object in my presence. He took it into his inner chamber before unwrapping it, and it was wrapped again when he came out. But one thing was certain, he was very eager to see the man afterwards.'

Ojo could not contain his desire to know more about the the visitor. He decided to go through into the inner perimeter, on the pretence that he had come to see if Wontsay might be interested in a session of *agidigbo*. Wontsay and the visitor were coming out of the inner chamber as Ojo was entering the inner perimeter. It seemed the business the visitor had come for had been concluded. The object still wrapped in the dark cloth was in Wontsay's hand, but the visitor was holding a small sack which Ojo presumed contained the proceeds from the sale. As he passed him, Ojo took a closer look at the visitor but was still unable to place where he recognised him from.

Later, Ojo was let into the secret of the cloth's contents as soon as the visitor had gone. Wontsay invited him into his inner chamber and laid out on the table were about a hundred beads and precious stones of different shades and colours. Wontsay then unwrapped the object he had collected from the visitor, exposing yet another stone. He handed it to Ojo and ask him to have a careful look before collecting it and putting it among the many already on the table.

'Many of these stones are of no significant value beyond their appearance,' he said, turning to Ojo. 'Some of them are rare and put together they could bring a moderate fortune, like the one I just showed you. Only about ten of them are worth a sizeable fortune on their own. However, there is one that stands out from the rest, and it has been verified as worth an enormous fortune anywhere in the world. Can you pick it out from this lot?'

After a careful but brief look across the beads, despite the poor illumination from the single oil lamp in the room, Ojo could clearly recognise the single stone which had got detached from the rest and which he had given to Olubi years back, as it sparkled through the dimly lit room. He picked it up and handed it to Wontsay.

'Excellent! That is the one, but it is not a bead. It is a very rare gemstone called a diamond. That is what has been keeping me in this part of the world for all these years. For over ten years I have been searching beneath the waters of the Awoyaya river, leading men to dig inside mountains and spending months in the jungles and forests across Akete and Ijowa. I have yet to come across any other like it.' Wontsay shook his head to indicate his frustration and defeat.

'How did you come across this then, and what makes you think they are from around here?' Ojo asked, feigning ignorance.

'My friend named it the Sun of the African Coast. It was bought at the port of Kotonou about thirteen years ago by a friend who was also an explorer but with lots of money to throw around, as he was in the service of a king. My friend managed to trace the source of the stones to around Oluweri. He left the stone with me as an aid in finding its source, and of course to explore the ground for more. He died months later at sea.' Wontsay lifted his cap in respect for the departed.

'This stone you are talking about, how valuable is it?' Ojo asked casually.

'The Sun of the African Coast, or any other in its category, could be traded for a shipload of any produce, from sugar cane to tobacco. That is how valuable it can be. I have witnessed a transaction whereby a whole ship with all its cargo was traded for a stone of the same class, but much bigger.'

'That is very valuable indeed. That means two or three of those beads could be worth the value of a merchant ship.'

'Certainly.'

For the first time since the beads had been in his possession, Ojo was able to have an idea of their real value, and more importantly he had a direct link to a premium buyer. Since his first voyage with Wontsay, Ojo had been certain that seafaring was his future, and he intended to travel as far across the ocean with Wontsay or any ship's captain who would be kind to employ him as a deckhand. The more opportunity he had to sailed with Wontsay, the more he envied the captains for their unlimited access to ships and the open water. He viewed the ship as a moving island, and the captain as the owner of a mobile piece of land with an almost unlimited choice of places to dwell. He had once told a friend in Ago-Oyinbo that, given the choice, he would choose to be a ship's captain rather than a king.

'A ship's captain can move his island away from hostile ground, but a king must either make his kingdom habitable or vacate it,' he argued. Although he secretly fantasised about the idea of being a shipowner, he had at the same time conditioned his mind to accept the idea for what it was – fantasy. That, he thought excitedly, was about to change, and the prospect of becoming a shipowner suddenly became feasible. But he was not deceiving himself that owning a merchant ship was as easy as just having the means to buy one.

Because his association with the beads had always

been marred by undesirable ends, Ojo had been very wary, even afraid of having anything to do with them again. In his experience, his encounters with the beads had always been followed by disappointment and disaster. The first time he had seen them was the last time he saw Morilewa, the man who, from their short period of acquaintance, was everything he would have wanted from his own father, but whom he had never really known. Then came the war and he had been separated from his mother. An attempt to retrieve the beads had earned him fifty lashes at Lower-Oluweri, leaving marks on his backside that would remain with him for life. When he had finally been able to retrieve the beads, with high hopes of starting a new life with the woman of his dreams, he had ended up in Akala for a crime he did not commit.

Although he had now retrieved the beads, he had done so for only one reason, to keep them in a safer and more accessible place. While he admitted that the chance of meeting Morilewa again was slim, he wanted the beads to be available in case of such an event. But now that Morilewa was dead and Wontsay had told him the real value of the beads, and he had seen a possibility of getting what he had always wanted and even more from them, the temptation to trade was too compelling to ignore. Meanwhile, the unexplained and persistence urge to free his mind about the visitor forced him to digress from the main discussion.

'What is the name of the man who brought the last bead?' he asked. 'I'm sure I have seen him somewhere before.'

'I don't ask for names. It is a waste of time as I hardly remember most of them,' Wontsay replied. 'He is just a messenger from an associate called Salaji. But I can guess he travelled down from Isale-Eko, because that is where Salaji lives, and that is where I believe he will be returning tomorrow.'

Ojo was not sure whether it was due to his short affair with Ojuolape, but the instinct to know more about the visitor became even stronger when Wontsay mentioned 'Salaji'.

The next morning, he left Oluweri for Gbajumo to see his mother. *Iya* Mojoyin was with Lalonpe when Ojo got there. He did not bother to wait until they were alone before telling his mother the purpose of his visit. He knew from experience that there were no secrets between his mother and the old woman.

'Mama, do you remember the last time *Baba* Morilewa came to our house?' Ojo asked after he had settled down.

'Yes. He had to leave in a hurry the next dawn. According to him and *Baba* Fatunbi, he had to return to Egbejoda immediately due to some family issue. That was the last I ever saw of him.'

'That evening, before we all went to sleep, he asked me to keep something for him,' said Ojo. 'He said it was a surprise present for you, but he intended to hide it from you until the right moment. But as you remember, he left in a hurry. He also forgot to collect the item. I would have told you about it, but I did not want to spoil the surprise. So I decided to keep our secret, but how was I to know that there would be a war and I would be separated from you for so long? The item he left in my custody has been instrumental in my destiny. To be precise, my survival, my relationship with my guardian, or rather my foster father, and my reunion with you after so many years, have been strongly influenced by it.'

'What was it?'

'It was an *ejigbaileke*, a necklace made from a collection of rare and precious stones. I found it difficult to understand why somebody would leave such a valuable item in the care of a child, and unbelievable that he forgot to collect it before leaving. Meanwhile, all my attempts at retrieving or selling the beads ended in disaster. Each time the stakes got higher, and so did the risks and the consequences of failure.'

Ojo told his mother how he had tried to retrieve the beads while in bondservice at Oluweri, how he had met Ojuolape, his successful attempt at retrieving them and the circumstances that had led to his imprisonment on Akala island.

'You should see my back after the fifty lashes with a horsetail whip I was given at the *Ajele's* compound in Oluweri,' he said. 'My next attempt at retrieving the beads was successful, but I found myself in Akala before I could use them for the purpose that made me take the risk. I kept the stones for so many years, hoping that one day I would come across either you or him, and pass them over. But I had forgotten about them until a few days ago when I came across a single stone I gave to my foster father which had ended up in Fadahunse's collection. When the *Oyinbo* told me their worth, the temptation to trade was too much for me to resist, so I decided I would have to tell you about it.'

'What is so special about the beads anyway?'

'That has also been a mystery to me. They look beautiful, but not extraordinary.'

'Where are the beads?' *Iya* Mojoyin asked. 'Let me have a look.'

'I only have one of them here, mama.' Ojo dipped into his sack and handed the stone to *Iya* Mojoyin. 'I hid the rest in a secret place in the jungle.'

'Why in the jungle?' *Iya* Mojoyin asked.

'That is due to another mystery about the beads. My experience had taught me not to keep them in a house. The two houses where I had hidden the beads were burnt down. That is why I have been reluctant to pass them on to you.'

Ojo made reference to their old house in Oluweri, and briefly told them about the events that had led to the burning of Olubi's compound in Eti-Osa. 'Do you not feel that the war, our separation, the loss of our home and the occupation of Lower-Oluweri might all have something to do with those beads?'

'We all know the war was caused by the conflict between the fishermen of Seleru and Kuluso,' Lalonpe argued.

'*Mama*, such conflicts happen almost every year between communities. But none has escalated to war before that, and none have since. It was the quest for these beads, which were believed to have originated from Oluweri, that made Fadahunse armed Akete's warrior.'

Ojo told his mother how the single stone he had given to Olubi had got to Wontsay and why the explorer believed the beads were from beneath the Awoyaya river around Oluweri.

'These are not ordinary beads. In fact, they are not beads at all,' *Iya* Mojoyin said after careful examination. 'They are precious stones indeed. They are very rare and expensive, but they are not from anywhere around here. History has it that such stones originated from far-away lands and were brought to this part of the world by *Larubawa* (Arabian) traders. When I was little, my father used to mention this material in stories about the *Larubawa*. He calls it *ajio*.'

'You are right mama. Fadahunse also has a name for them, but I cannot remember it now. According to him, that single bead you are holding could be worth more than hundred horses.'

'I wonder where Morilewa got it from?'

'You are not the only one who has been wondering about that. For fourteen years, Fadahunse had been trying to find the source of the single stone he had with him. He is on the verge of giving up and return to his homeland.'

'So what do you want us to do with it?' Lalonpe asked.

'That is for you to decide. *Baba* Morilewa said it was meant for you. But if you want to trade it, I can arrange a meeting with Fadahunse.'

'What do I want with a hundred horses?'

'There are many other things you can trade them for. Fadahunse only mentioned horses to give me an idea of the worth of the beads. For a start, the smallest of them could be worth hundreds of gold coins and many more in copper, and there are endless goods and valuables like hardwares, tools, textiles and general goods that you can trade for.'

'How do we go about it? You are the one who knows the *Oyinbo* and understands his language and ways. I will leave it to you to do all that is necessary,' Lalonpe said.

'No *mama*, it will not work that way. You will need to play the leading part in this arrangement, because it is important that he does not know I have anything to do with the beads. I will only introduce you to him as their owner. He must not know that we are related in any way or even had a prior relationship before now. I don't want Fadahunse to suspect that I have other interests in this matter beyond his own. But in order to be sure that I am included, you will insist on speaking in the Erebe dialect. Fadahunse's communication is limited to the common dialect, so naturally he will ask me to interpret for him. That is as far as we are going to let him believe I am involved.'

Ojo returned to Ago-Oyinbo and approached Wontsay as agreed with Lalonpe. 'The precious stone we were talking about days ago,' he began. 'I know how disappointed you were at wasting such a long time in Oluweri in the hope of finding more. So I have travelled to few places and made enquiry about the beads, and I can confidently say to you that I met someone with similar stones, and most of them are even bigger than the one you have.'

'Have you now?' Wontsay responded with very little interest. 'I have heard that many times, and most of the time, the best I have got are all you have seen. None has come with a pure diamond like the Sun of the African Coast.'

'I have seen them, and I am sure they were the same as the one I singled out from the rest.'

'You are sure they were like the one you singled out?'

'Yes,' Ojo replied confidently. 'Remember you challenged me to pick it out of the rest, and I got it right the first time?'

'Be careful of what you say boy. Are you telling me you know someone who claims to have more of those beads?'

'Now let me say it clearly to you. The person did not just claim to have them, I saw the beads with my own eyes. I did not count them, but I touched them and I would not be far away if I guessed there were twenty of them,' Ojo replied with assurance

'Twenty?'

'Yes, at least twenty, if not more.'

'I will not discuss this further until I meet this man and see the stones myself, to see if they are what you thought they were.'

'She is a woman, but she wishes to remain anonymous until she has met you personally.'

'How did the woman say she came about so many of them?'

'I did not ask, because I was sure she would not tell me.'

'And she is willing to trade them?'

'Yes, she is willing to trade with you if the bargain is right. Those were her exact words.'

'So where do I come in? What does she want for the stones?'

'She said she would discuss that with you personally if you are interested.'

'Of course I am interested,' Wontsay replied, 'Did you tell her I was interested?'

'I said I was sure you would be interested in them.'

'Tell the woman that I am ready to meet her anytime, at her convenience.'

On the tenth day after Ojo returned from his mother's place at Gbajumo, Lalonpe arrived as planned in Ago-Oyinbo with Bogunde, and they were introduced to Wontsay as the wife and son respectively of the owner of the beads. They were received by Wontsay in the innermost chamber in Ago-Oyinbo, where he had made ready a lavish reception for them. Ojo made to leave even before Lalonpe spoke, but Wontsay asked Ojo to stay and be a witness to their discussion. Lalonpe wasted no time in telling Wontsay what he had been waiting to hear.

'My late husband was a hunter and during his hunting years, he travelled deep into the jungle, to places that have been trodden upon only by a very few people,' she began, as previously rehearsed in detail with Ojo. 'While hunting very deep in the forest, he came across an ancient mine which he said was so rich that digging to extract those stones demanded no more sweat than the work between sundown and dusk on the farm. He came back with a small sack containing these rare stones, but was unable to find a buyer before his death. He told me where the mine was, and the secret has remained with me since then.' Lalonpe paused, supposedly to drink some water, but her intention was to gauge Wontsay's reaction. The latter was listening attentively, like a child being told a fairytale.

Although Wontsay was certain that she was not telling the truth about the source, he did not show it. The diamond they were talking about had been processed, as against those obtained in their natural state, as claimed by Lalonpe. But the mine was the least of his concerns at the moment. His primary interest was getting the stones which were in Lalonpe's possession.

'The stone you have in your possession is just one of those from the mine,' Lalonpe continued. 'He gave it to a friend to sell, but what happened to it afterwards he did not know, because his friend never came back. My husband guessed his friend sold it and decided to run away with the proceeds. It did not bother him as he knew where they came from, but then none of us had any idea that the stone could bring such enormous wealth, until this young man came asking questions about them.' Although Lalonpe sensed that Wontsay understood most of what she said, she paused to allow Ojo to interpret for Wontsay before she continued.

'He said you have an interest in buying the beads?' said Lalonpe.

'Yes, I am interested,' Wontsay replied excitedly.

'I am willing to trade the beads. That is why I am here today with my son.' Lalonpe untied a knot at the end of her waist cloth to expose a small sack made from antelope hide. She untied the sack and emptied a single stone onto the table. 'That is one of the stones my husband left in my keeping just before his death over twelve years ago,' she said. 'I want you to examine it carefully and be sure it is the type you are after.' Lalonpe moved a step away from the table to give Wontsay enough space to have a proper look. The latter examined the stone closely.

'It is exactly the type I am looking for,' Wontsay finally managed to say. His voice was shaking as he returned the diamond to Lalonpe. 'What do I have to give in exchange for them?' He spoke in a quiet and very serious tone.

'I have just one offer to make for now,' Lalonpe began, but this time she did not wait for Ojo to interpret for Wontsay, as he seemed to be catching on quite well. 'My son loves the sea, and it has been his desire from childhood to roam the ocean as widely as his father roamed the forest. He wants a ship, a trading ship. I am willing to give you two of these stones in exchange for a merchant ship worthy of travelling on the sea as far as there is water. That is my offer.'

Lalonpe paused again to gauge Wontsay's reaction. This time, she liked what she got.

'Of course, I don't expect you to provide a ship right away' she said. 'All I want to know is your willingness to trade upon these terms.'

'A ship I can get, but whether what you are offering will suffice depends on the ship,' Wontsay replied, barely managing to contain his excitement. 'So in that light, I am accepting your offer in principle.' He was sure he stood to make a bounty out of the deal. If he played it right, the woman could be persuaded to add one or two more diamonds to the offer.

'I will leave this one stone as a deposit for the ship, and the balance will be available upon delivery,' said Lalonpe. I hope that is well with you?'

'That is fine with me. Absolutely fine,' Wontsay replied.

Two days later, Wontsay called Ojo into his private chamber to discuss his plan with him.

'I want to set about meeting her demands as soon as possible because I believe she has more to trade with, and the earlier I get this over with the better,' he said. 'So in a few days, I will be leaving this part of the ocean for this purpose. You will not be travelling with me this time. I want you to stay here and take charge at Ago-Oyinbo while I am away. I might be away for months, but I want my departure to be quiet. If there is any call for me from the palace, tell them I have gone to Ashanti to see Capitán Plata. The king will understand my message.'

Five days later, Wontsay left Oluweri in pursuance of a merchant ship for Lalonpe.

CHAPTER 12

The *Onijowa* had been ill for some time, and his health was deteriorating, not only due to his ailment but to his age. This compelled Adeyanju to officially begin taking an active role in the affairs of the palace. Ijowa's continuing economic downturn was beginning to cause unbearable restlessness between the different social classes of Ijowa. It began with the rain, which ceased in the middle of the planting season and did not return until after harvest. The next rain did not come until well into the next planting season, and when it did come, it was as if the gods intended to wash away all the soil of Ijowa. The harvest was again drastically poor that year, and the next. Now for over two seasons, there had been nothing like rain, only scores of tiny short showers throughout the year. The drought had been so bad that there had been little or nothing to do on most of the farms since the beginning of the planting season.

On one morning when it was raining, about two

months after Wontsay left Oluweri, cries of sorrow rang
through the palace town of Ode-Ijowa. People rushed out
and gathered to share the sad news of the passing away
of the *Onijowa*, who had died in the early hours of the
morning. His death came as a rude shock to members of
the royal family, because only about five days before his
death, the *Onijowa* had suddenly bounced back from the
illness that had kept him almost inactive for over a year.
Even the night before his death, he was reported to have
been quite healthy before retiring to his chamber and was
even said to have left his bedchamber in the middle of the
night to answer the call of nature.

The situation which Adeyanju and the Ijowa chiefs had
been dreading since *Onijowa* fell ill was now staring them
in the face. With the passing of the king, the normal thing
was to proceed with the necessary traditional rituals and
procedure associated with the coronation of a new *Onijowa*.
According to tradition, one of the last duties of an *Aremo-
Oba* (heir apparent to the throne) before becoming the king
was to proceed on a kind of 'familiarisation tour' across
Ijowa's towns and villages. It was believed that upon
mounting the throne, the new *Onijowa* would be too busy
engaging in important affairs of the kingdom for regular
interaction with his many subjects. The purpose of this
journey was to enable the *Aremo-Oba* to offer final respects
to people and elders across Ijowaland, in a manner which
nobody would expect of him after he ascended the throne.

The familiarisation tour was the concluding part
of the coronation process. The rest of it was more about
dance and general merriment, and very little in the way
of ritual or spiritual activities. The tour was the only
part of the coronation process in which every Ijowa 'son

of the soil', immigrants and well wishers, felt a sense of involvement. Not a single *Onijowa* in known history had mounted the throne without performing the tour. Going by the agreement brokered by the *Alaafin* of Oyo and the *Oyomesi*, the occupation of Oluweri was not due to end for another two and a half seasons. The coronation ritual could not be concluded until the *Aremo-Oba* had returned to Ode-Ijowa from the tours of the ten Ijowa communities that made up Ijowaland, including Oluweri. Apart from the fact that Adeyanju would be the first *Aremo-Oba* to avoid any of part of Ijowaland during his familiarisation tour, a failure by the *Aremo-Oba* to visit Oluweri of all Ijowa towns during this important occasion would amount to a mockery of tradition. It was like admitting that Oluweri was no longer part of Ijowaland.

Since *Onijowa's* illness had begun, the palace at Aromire had envisaged the possibility of renewed agitation for the return of Oluweri in the event of the passing of the ageing Ijowa king. Akete, on the contrary, had experienced continuously rich harvests for the last four seasons, and proceeds from the trade had been so good that *Oba* Lagbade and the Akete chiefs began to reconsider the decision to return Oluweri to Ijowa at the expiration of the term agreed with *Alaafin* and the *Oyomesi* at the start of the occupation. So the king and the Akete chiefs had taken a proactive step by approaching Wontsay for assistance. The explorer in turn introduced the Akete rulers to a merchant of 'general goods and hardware' and a ship owner called Capitán Plata. The name of his ship was *La Felicidad*. The palace at Aromire made advance payments in the form of huge quantities of sugar cane and tobacco for fresh supplies of arms.

Five months after *La Felicidad*'s departure from Oluweri, news came that the ship bearing new guns, bullets and barrels of gunpowder for the palace at Aromire had on its return journey met with stormy weather and run aground on the coast not far from the seafront of Kotonou. The king and chiefs of Akete approached Wontsay to help salvage the cargo of the grounded ship. The latter was willing to help but needed funding to journey to the site in another chartered ship to move the cargo of *La Felicidad* to Oluweri. Although *Oba* Lagbade had two ships at his command, neither was fit for the high seas due to neglect and lack of maintenance. The next harvest was still very far away, and the palace had invested most of its reserves in the grounded cargo.

The palace entered into an agreement with Wontsay by which the latter would bear the cost of salvaging the cargo and the payment would amount to a quarter of all the produce of Akala in the coming harvest. Wontsay agreed, but said he could not be precise about the time it would take to complete the task until he had been to the site. A week later he journeyed to the coast of Kotonou, where he met and discussed the matter with Capitán Plata. There he learned the truth about *La Felicidad*. The ship had not met with stormy weather, and had not run aground. Capitán Plata was only holding on to the cargo in order to extract more value for it.

'What I have here is worth far more than I agreed with the king,' he told Wontsay. 'The palace negotiated for muskets which are presently short in production. Most factories now make revolvers. There is no way I am going to give away revolvers for that value. The king will have to wait until I have stocks that match our agreement.'

Wontsay negotiated with Capitán Plata. He paid the balance of the difference in value, which the merchant finally agreed upon, and took delivery of the arms. However he kept the arms in Ago-Oyinbo, with the intention of recovering the charges for the rescue operation. He returned to Aromire and inform the palace that the task could not be done until the stormy season was over. While every investment in arms by *Oba* Lagbade was always given maximum publicity by the palace, for obvious strategic reasons, the unfortunate news of the arms shipment, also for obvious strategic reasons, was kept within the confines of the palace.

Seven days after the the passing of the *Onijowa*, the Ijowa chiefs and kingmakers sent emissaries to the palace at Aromire requesting that the occupation be ended immediately, to enable Adeyanju a dignified and peaceful passage through Oluweri as part of the traditional requirement before ascending the throne of his ancestors. For obvious security reasons, *Oba* Lagbade was not at ease with the passage of such a high-profile procession through Oluweri.

'Your highness, I suggest we make an offer, a condition upon which Oluweri will be returned peacefully,' said Oluperi, the Akete titled chief assigned by his peers to brief the king on what they believe to be the right action to take. 'The offer will be made not with the aim of leading to any conclusions, but to have an insight into the aims and plans of Adeyanju and the Ijowa chiefs.'

'What kind of offer?' Oba Lagbade asked.

'We are thinking of asking the *Aremo-Oba* to release another territory on the seafront in exchange for Oluweri,' Oluperi replied cautiously, not sure what the king's response might be. 'We could ask for somewhere like Oko-Oba, or even Odinjo.'

'If the response from Ode-Ijowa indicates that they are giving the least consideration to the offer, then we can be sure that our fears are unfounded,' said Baruwa, another titled chief. 'Otherwise it will be certain that Ijowa warlords are getting ready for war.'

'What happens if the offer is accepted?' *Oba* Lagbade asked.

'Your highness, our aim is to gain time. The time needed to consider, deliberate and respond by *Aremo* Adeyanju and Ijowa chiefs before the offer is accepted, or even rejected, will enable us to prepare for war,' Oluperi explained. The king reluctantly agreed, and five days later, Odule, the palace messenger, delivered a message to Adeyanju.

'The message from my lord the king of Akete is simple but clear,' he said, as instructed by the Akete chiefs. 'The palace at Ode-Ijowa will regain control of the land and waters of Oluweri without a shot being fired, on the condition that it will be willing in the same vein to relinquish ownership and control of the land and waters of Odinjo.'

The *Aremo-Oba* and Ijowa chiefs were not only shocked by the the offer but felt insulted. They considered having to make a formal request to *Oba* Lagbade before the *Aremo-Oba* could pass through his ancestral land in aid of a statutory traditional duty to be very humiliating. During the meeting, which was chaired by Adeyanju, the call to reclaim Oluweri by whatever it took, meaning war, was overwhelming. All the chiefs except the *Iyalode* believed that the only way by which *Aremo* Adeyanju could pass through Oluweri during his familiarisation tour was through the use of force. The *Iyalode* insisted that the struggle to reclaim Oluweri should be pursued diplomatically, via the *Alaafin* of Oyo and the *Oyomesi*.

'In my opinion, this message is worth nothing more than the bearer, and the offer is too simplistic to be possible,' said the *Otun*.

'I believe the messenger is from the palace at Aromire,' said the *Iyalode*, cautiously disagreeing with the *Otun*. 'This is *Oba* Lagbade indirectly offering an alternative to war in resolving the issue.'

'Alternative to war?' the *Otun* interupted. 'With due respect to the head that may soon bear the crown, the winning side does not provide an initiative for peace. It is usually the other way around. At present, *Oba* Lagbade and the Akete army are the occupying force in Oluweri, so they are the winning side. We would be deceiving ourselves if we believed that *Oba* Lagbade would offer such a truce without an underlying motive. It is against good judgement to plunge into an agreement without knowing the reason behind *Oba* Lagbade's offer. It would be like walking into a dark tunnel with our eyes closed.'

'It was a good thing that the *Alaafin* and the *Oyomesi* were witnesses to *Oba* Lagbade's pledge to return Oluweri to the *Onijowa* after twenty years of occupation,' said the *Iyalode*. 'If there is anybody that can persuade *Oba* Lagbade to give special consideration to tradition, it is the *Alaafin* of Oyo. The point of waiting this long to reclaim what rightly belongs to the Ijowa people is to explore the path of peace in settlement of the dispute. Even if in the end our efforts fail, it is wise to be on the good side of the *Alaafin* and the *Oyomesi* before going to war. If there is any force that can dislodge the Akete army from Oluweri, it will be the army from the palace at Oyo.'

'What will happen if we have to take the matter to Oyo?' the *Ajiroba* asked. He was not expecting an answer from *Iyalode* and did not wait for one. 'The *Alaafin* will send a team from among the *Oyomesi* to Aromire, then they will go back to tell him what *Oba* Lagbade has already told us, and which the *Alaafin* must have expected even before his delegates set off. Now let us assume the *Alaafin* is truly angered by *Oba* Lagbade's respond. What will he do?' Again he did not wait for an answer but continued. 'He will send back the *Oyomesi* to Aromire, to at best give the mandatory notice of one season for *Oba* Lagbade to vacate Oluweri before considering the use of force.'

'I don't think a year is too long, compared to the fifteen years we have endured,' said *Iyalode*.

'I said a season before considering the use of force, not actually using force. After the expiration of the ultimatum, and while considering the use of force, the *Alaafin* will keep sending the *Oyomesi* back and forth to Aromire on our behalf and at our expense. Do you know how much it will cost this palace to fund a return journey of the *Oyomesi* to Aketeland?' This time, the *Ajiroba* did not bother to answer his own question, but seemed to have rested his case.

'Even a year is too long for Ijowa to be without a king, unless the *Aremo-Oba* will be satisfied with a familiarisation tour without passing through Oluweri,' said the *Asipa*. 'Meanwhile, make no mistake about it, if that happens we might as well forget Oluweri and its seafront forever.'

'Even if the *Alaafin* himself has the genuine intention of seeing justice done, I doubt if the *Oyomesi* will ever advise the *Alaafin* to march against Akete warriors in

Oluweri,' said the *Otunba*. 'We all know that in the past fourteen years most of the *Oyomesi* and Oyo nobles have established flourishing trading interests in Oluweri. If they oppose the use of force to secure justice, there is nothing the *Alaafin* can do other than to keep giving ultimatum upon ultimatum.'

'Oluweri will be reclaimed the way it was taken,' declared the *Balogun*. 'That has been *Oba* Adejayi's position since the occupation. That is the way of my ancestors, and that is the way it is going to be while I am still alive, and while, by the blessing of the deities, I remain the *Balogun* of Ijowaland.' *Balogun* Odebode, the grand commander of the Ijowa warriors, was generally known to be a man of few words. While his support for the use of force could be said to be solely due to sentiment and national pride, the position of his peers was greatly influenced by their material losses through the occupation of Oluweri. Almost a quarter of the lands in occupied Oluweri had, since the first *Onijowa*, been dedicated to the ancestors of titled chiefs. and had remained with their families until the occupation.

'What have we got to confront Akete army with?' challenged the *Iyalode*. 'What have we got to make us think we stand a chance of winning a war with Oluweri in the first place? We should not let egotism and impatience lead us to unnecessary bloodshed and further loss.'

'Our strength and our success in this offensive will depend upon how close we are to the enemy before they have the slightest idea that a war is on,' *Balogun* Odebode told his fellow chiefs. 'That is why I strongly advise that we don't make any comment or take any action that reflects our determination to take over Oluweri at all costs. Even though I quite agree with *Ajiroba's* analysis of the futility of going through the *Alaafin*, it will be wise to direct our activity towards that line in order to deceive *Oba* Lagbade about our real plan of action.'

'The effect of our surprise attack on Oluweri, even if it's successful, will only last until fresh warriors from the palace at Aromire march from Eti-Osa to Oluweri,' the *Iyalode* warned. 'They will not be relying on retaking Oluweri by surprise, but on the abundant arms at their disposal.' But it was clear that her concerns were now falling on unwilling ears.

'That is where you are wrong!' the *Balogun* interjected. '*Oba* Lagbade is presently not capable, and will not be launching a counter-attack. It is almost a year since any ship docked at Oluweri. The palace at Aromire just used up a considerable chunk of its gunpowder reserve in quelling the Ilaje uprising. At present, the Akete army is low in arms and the palace at Aromire will not be expecting fresh supplies soon. So to get the desired result, there is no better time to strike than now.'

'If we can reclaim control of Oluweri, and hold it until the next ship arrive, which is most likely to have arms to trade, then the shipmaster will have no choice but to trade with us,' added the *Asipa*.

'As far as I am concerned, I see no wisdom in starting a war when your only strategy is to surprise the enemy,' insisted the *Iyalode*.

As Adeyanju was just an *obalola* (king in waiting), his role was limited to listening to both sides of the argument, then finding a common ground which was agreeable to all. As an *obalola*, he could neither take a unilateral decision nor veto a collective decision by the chiefs. But Adeyanju was in a dilemma. While he truly agreed that the *Alaafin* and the *Oyomesi* route would never bring back Oluweri, and that *Oba* Lagbade would never release it without the use of force, it would be unwise to go to war against the wishes and political support of the *Alaafin*. Moreover, he had no confidence in a strategy that depended solely on the extent to which the Akete army would be taken by surprise.

'Whether *Oba* Lagbade is serious with the offer is a secondary issue,' Adeyanju argued. 'The primary issue is whether we are willing to trade Odinjo for Oluweri, but I can assure you that I will never be a party to such agreement. Meanwhile, in order to retain our element of surprise, I think the best thing to do is to pretend to be considering the offer. By ignoring the messenger and the offer right away, we would be sending a strong signal that we are bent on fighting to regain Oluweri. Such a signal would be contrary to our strategy. Our preparedness for war is supposed to be classified, as our chances of reclaiming Oluweri largely depend on a surprise attack.'

While the offer was unanimously rejected, the chiefs agreed with Adeyanju that it would be unwise to respond in a manner that would make their intentions easy for Aromire to anticipate. So, in response, the Ijowa chief replied that the Aremo-Oba would need time to consider the offer.

To the relief of everybody involved at the palace at Aromire, the response from Ode-Ijowa was as *Oba* Lagbade and his advisers had hoped. But in a matter of days, the meeting between Adeyanju and the Ijowa high chief on one hand, and the messenger from the palace at Aromire on the other, was no longer news anywhere in Ijowa or Akete. The news that the palace at Ode-Ijowa was considering giving away the land and waters of Odinjo in return for occupied

Oluweri caused widespread anger among the people of Odinjo. They considered the inclusion of their habitation, their livelihood and their future in a negotiation without consulting them as a gross disregard for their feeling and existence.

The young people were the most restless and would not be calmed, until the *Baale* sent a fact-finding team of Odinjo elders to Ode-Ijowa to confirm the story or otherwise make an official disclaimer. At the palace at Ode-Ijowa, the Odinjo elders were told that Adeyanju was at present very occupied with the affairs of the palace, and unfortunately would not be able to attend to them. In order to have something to report, the delegates proceed to the compound of *Balogun* Odebode for clarification.

'The *Aremo-Oba* has no knowledge of such an offer and the Ijowa chiefs never deliberated on such a matter. It is all rumours,' *Balogun* Odebode assured the delegates.

Like the people of Odinjo, but for different reasons, the news of the offer of Oluweri in exchange for Odinjo by the palace at Aromire caused panic and anxiety for Ojo. The news comfirmed his fear that the Akete army was not ready for any confrontation. If the offer was accepted, it was certain that the landlord and occupants of Ago-Oyinbo would have to leave, along with the occupying army. In the few years that he had been residing in Ago-Oyinbo, he had been a known figure associated with Fadahunse and Akete's administrators of occupation. But unlike other residents of Ago-Oyinbo, apart from losing his trading influence on the seafront of Oluweri, he also stood to lose the childhood home which he had rebuilt. Ojo was visiting Olubi at Oko-Oba when the news broke.

'*Baba*, I think there is a problem here,' said Ojo to Olubi. 'At present I have unfettered access to the seafront of Oluweri due to my good relationship with Fadahunse and consequently the palace at Aromire. That privilege will cease if Oluweri is back under the control of *Onijowa*. I don't care who owns or control Odinjo, but Lower-Oluweri is very important to me. Apart from Oluweri being my place of birth and only true home, the port at Oluweri is essential for my dream.'

'Calm down, my son. For one thing, I doubt if the messenger was acting on behalf of the palace at Aromire. And if the offer indeed comes from Oba Lagbade, I don't think he is sincere about it.'

'I wish there was something I could do on my part to protect my interests,' Ojo replied. 'I just don't think it is right that my breakthrough, and my future, have to depend on people I cannot reach. Even if *Oba* Lagbade is not sincere about it, the *Aremo-Oba* cannot stomach the humiliation of a familiarisation tour that does not pass through Oluweri. The Ijowa people cannot bear to be without a king until the end of the occupation. There will come a time when something has to give, and I have a feeling that that time is very near.'

'I don't see the need to fret. The motive to go to war is not the same as the ability to win it. I very much doubt if Ijowa is ready for war at this moment. The occupying forces, if anything, are much stronger than they were seventeen years ago. The only way *Onijowa* can reclaim Lower-Oluweri is via the support of the *Alaafin* of Oyo, and I don't see that happening soon, because like you, most of the Oyo chiefs now have considerable trading interests on the seafront of Oluweri, and will be reluctant to support any action directed at changing the status quo.' But it was clear that Ojo was not at all comforted by his optimism.

'Is there anything else bothering you, son?' asked Olubi. 'You don't seem to be at ease.'

'There is, and it is still about Oluweri. There is more to it than it seems.'

'Tell me, what more is there?' Olubi asked.

'Even if Ijowa is not planning to attack for now, there are other issues which are restricted to the confines of the palace at Aromire, but which I happen to know by chance, and which if known to the decision makers at Ode-Ijowa, will make reclaiming Oluweri easy for the Ijowa army, or any invading army for that matter. That is my greatest fear.'

'What other issues?'

'Apart from me, only *Oba* Lagbade and few high-ranking Akete chiefs are aware of this. Given the present state of the Akete warriors, in the event of an attack it is not only likely but certain that the *Onijowa* will reclaim occupied Oluweri.'

'What is wrong with the present state of the Akete warriors?' Olubi asked. Ojo told him about the ship bearing the consignment of arms meant for Akete warriors which had met with disaster due to stormy weather.

'Fadahunse was called upon to assist,' replied Ojo. 'His story was that the task cannot be done until the stormy season is over, but he had actually emptied the grounded ship of its cargo of arms and must have delayed delivery for certain reasons. Although *Oba* Lagbade and Akete chiefs are unaware of it, the cache of guns and bullets have been in Fadahunse's private quarters for the past eight months.'

'You mean the the offer of Oluweri for Odinjo was

a delay tactic by *Oba* Lagbade to prevent Ijowa from attacking while he is sorting out the security problem?'

'Exactly.'

'Hmmmm. This is a tricky situation,' Olubi said after a fairly long spell of thought. 'While calling the attention of the palace at Aromire to the arms could ensure that the status quo at Oluweri remains unchanged, you would be betraying Fadahunse by making such a disclosure without his consent. On the other hand, if you keep quiet about the weapons and Ijowa decides to attack before Fadahunse returns, the seafront of Oluweri will fall back to the palace at Ode-Ijowa.'

'Now you can see my dilemma and understand my reason for concern,' replied Ojo.

'Young man, I see no reason why you should be worried. On the contrary, I see an opportunity for you to be somebody without Fadahunse, and outside the roof of Ago-Oyinbo, but with a time limit. If you ask me, I will tell you that your time is now.'

'How?'

'By dealing with any of the palaces with neither the name of Fadahunse nor Ago-Oyinbo connected to it, but from a private source. It is against good judgement not to utilise bargaining power when it is at a premium. The information you have, and your knowledge of the inside of the Akete security structure in Oluweri, gives you a greater bargaining strength against Ode-Ijowa than with Aromire.'

'You mean I should abandon Akete and shift to the Ijowa side?'

'That is what I mean,' Olubi replied bluntly. 'Reclaiming Oluweri has never been of greater importance to the palace at Ode-Ijowa than it is now. The Ijowa kingmakers needed to complete the rituals involve in the coronation of the new *Onijowa*, but the *Aremo-Oba* is presently being denied access through Oluweri for his familiarisation tour.'

'*Baba*, don't make any mistake about this. You don't detest *Oba* Lagbade more than I do. I have suffered injustices that have caused me lots of pain due to decisions made by the palace at Aromire. But my resentment of the late *Onijowa* and his chiefs is deeper than that. I would rather lose everything by sticking with Akete than gain everything by helping *Onijowa* to reclaim Oluweri.'

'You need to grow up son. You might be young, but you must accept the fact that you are at this moment walking a path reserved for the bold and the ruthless. This is not a path to be trod with sentiment.' He was a little taken aback by Ojo's sudden outburst. 'My advice to shift to the Ijowa side may be influenced by my bitter experience at the hands of the Akete rulers, but I am just being realistic. The reality of the near future is that *Oba* Lagbade cannot forever hold on to what does not rightly belong to him. The *Alaafin* and Oyo chiefs will eventually insist that *Oba* Lagbade to honours the agreement to return Oluweri to the Ijowa people after the expiration of twenty years, which is only three years away. What have you got against the *Onijowa* anyway?'

'The *Onijowa* and his chiefs were responsible for the death of somebody very dear to me.'

'What was this person to you, if I may ask. A relation?'

'Yes, he was like a stepfather, the father of my younger brother Bogunde. He was accused of murder, and died while serving a lengthy sentence on the king's farm for a crime I am certain he did not commit.'

'For murder? What was the name of this person?'

'His name was Morilewa.'

'Are you by any means referring to the Morilewa who was held for the death of the high priest at Oluweri during the war?'

'Yes, that was the one.'

'The one you said gave your mother those precious stones?'

'Yes,' Ojo replied. He deliberately had not mentioned the beads, but it seemed time would never erase them from Olubi's mind. It was the next thing he had asked after congratulating him for finding his mother. His reply then had been that his mother had left the beads in Oluweri and the house had been looted during the war and all her mother's valuables taken away.

'Well in that case you will find what I am going to tell you very welcoming and refreshing. I can assure you that the Morilewa held responsible for the death of the priest is still alive, although without his freedom,' Olubi said authoritatively.

'That cannot be true. What my mother told me was that he suffered a mental breakdown in middle of his trial, and had to be taken to Igbodudu for treatment. He died two years later while undergoing treatment.'

'Yes, he was declared sick in the head due to his utterances during the trial. But the truth is that Morilewa was never sick in the head. Yes, he was said to have been sent to Igbodudu for treatment. The truth is that Morilewa never stepped into that forest.'

'But my mother said she journeyed to Igbodudu more than twice to visit him. She learnt of his death directly from the guards at Igbodudu, and it was confirmed by his family at Egbejoda.'

'Did your mother see Morilewa at all during her visits to Igbodudu?'

'No, she did not. The directive from the palace was that Morilewa should be treated as a convict and not a patient. Hence he was allowed no visitors.'

'Now let me tell you what you don't know. Morilewa was convicted and sentenced to twenty-five years of labour on the king's farm. But there was a failed attempt to rescue him during his journey there, which if it had been successful would have cause serious embarrassment to the *Onijowa*, and seriously angered the Ogboni cult of which the late priest was the patron. In order to prevent anyone from attempting to rescue him again, an *alanganran* (deranged person) was taken to Igbodudu and presented as Morilewa, then subsequently declared deceased. The real, sane Morilewa arrived at one of the king's farms the following month to serve the time for his crime under a new identity. That is why the rule at the king's farm was extended to the replacement at Igbodudu. The *alanganran* was put in solitary confinement and barred from meeting visitors. Very few of the guards were let into the secret. Even the head guard at the king's farm was not let into the true identity of the prisoner. Morilewa was generally believed to be dead once the *alanganran* died two years later.'

'How did they make *Baba* Morilewa agree to an arrangement that would make it difficult for his friends to rescue him?'

'They did not have to make him,' Olubi smirked. 'He was even grateful for it. While his friends were plotting to free him, the friends and devotees of the late priest were demanding the ultimate justice, meaning death. If presented with the opportunity, many would be more than willing to see justice done themselves, and the king's farms were anything but a safe haven against such an attack.'

'How do you know about this?' Ojo asked.

'Birds don't sit on a rooftop only due to idleness. They were eavesdropping,' Olubi replied with pride.

'Which of the king's farms, and how can I see him?'

'That I don't know, and don't ask me the name because I don't know that either.'

'Are you sure *Baba* Morilewa is still serving time on the king's farms?'

'As sure as the day. You don't have to take my word for it. If Morilewa is as dear to as you as it seems, there is no better opportunity for you to help him become a free man again.'

'How?'

'The only way Morilewa can ever be free in a real sense is by a royal pardon. If there is one thing that can compel the *Aremo-Oba* and Ijowa chiefs to do that, it will be an offer relating to the prospect of reclaiming Oluweri. Remember, the crime of Morilewa was also believed to be largely responsible for the loss of Oluweri.'

Ojo reckoned that if what he had just learnt about *Baba* Morilewa is true and he was indeed still alive, then there was no better time to help him than now. But it would be very difficult.

'That is easier said than done,' he said. 'Getting access to people in those high places is one thing, but there is a risk that they will stab you in the back. I cannot trust the prince and the chiefs to honour our agreement after Oluweri has been reclaimed.'

'Not if we do it the right way,' Olubi replied confidently. 'Meanwhile, if what you said about the state of the Akete army is true, then there is no guarantee that such information has not reached Ode-Ijowa. That means an attack could be sooner than anybody expected. If that happens, you will have to leave not only Ago-Oyinbo and Oluweri but the whole of Ijowaland, and in a hurry. It is a long way and such a journey cannot be done with sacks of guns and bullets weighing on your shoulder. The beneficiary will most likely be the palace at Ode-Ijowa. So the first thing I will advise is that you get the weapons out of Oluweri as soon as possible.'

'That makes sense, but my concern is that Fadahunse might return before the conflict breaks out. He does not know that I am aware of the arms in his private chamber, so I want him to find them undisturbed.'

'Ago-Oyinbo and the fort are going to be the prime targets in event of confrontation, and the control of those two places will determine who is victorious in this war,' replied Olubi. 'Your best option is to move them to a place outside Ago-Oyinbo but within Oluweri, where you have easy access in the unfortunate event of a successful reclamation of Oluweri. Fadahunse will not step into Oluweri without first stopping at the palace at Aromire. That mean you can rely on at least a day's notice to return them before he gets to Oluweri.'

CHAPTER 13

Except in defence against external aggression, tradition demanded that the oracle was consulted before the palace launched an offensive mission. Adeyanju and the Ijowa high chief summoned Fakorede, the palace diviner, to consult the oracle. After due consultation with the oracle, the priest told his audience that the solution lay entirely with the *Aremo-Oba*.

'The lands and waters of occupied Oluweri can never be reclaimed until the *Aremo-Oba* has been through an *Ebo-Adaru* (self-administered ritual),' Fakorede said. He recited the message from the oracle, then waited for the prince and the chiefs to absorb the message, to leave significant time between the recital and his own comment.

'The gods are demanding an *Ebo-Adaru* from the *Aremo-Oba* before Oluweri can be reclaimed,' he said. 'The oracle reveals that any attempt at reclaiming Oluweri without performing the ritual will end in disaster.'

When asked what the ritual entailed, the *Ifa* priest

explained that due to the nature of the ritual, it was essential that only the *Aremo-Oba* was privy to the process and procedure of it.

The priest waited for the chiefs to leave, then turned to Adeyanju. 'What the oracle reveals is a case of an abandoned ritual,' he said. 'The gods are asking if *Aremo* Adeyanju knows the truth behind the issue upon which he set on the ritual of truth, and has fulfilled all obligations and responsibilities due to the ritual of truth. Do you know anything about a ritual of truth? Does it mean anything to you?'

'I have been involved in a ritual of truth, but I am hearing the *ebo-adaru* for the first time,' said Adeyanju.

'If you have been involved in a ritual of truth, then it must have been an *ebo-edaru* [self-administered ritual], as the purest truths are the most private. The rituals are similar but not the same. The difference is that all rituals of truth must be self-administered, and they are always prescribed for problems that are very personal and private. An *ebo-adaru*, on the other hand, does not have to be performed in aid of personal or private problems, and its execution does not have to be kept secret. The only similarity is that both must be performed by the individual at the centre of a problem, or the one that is supposed to be most concerned or affected. However, the important thing now is that the oracle forbids any attempt at reclaiming Oluweri by force until the ritual of truth has been concluded.'

Adeyanju took a very deep breath before replying.

'You are right, *baba*. But my need for the ritual, as the oracle rightly revealed, and which you also agree, was personal, and it was truly self-administered. I fail to see how completing a personal ritual could have anything to do with the liberation of Oluweri.'

'I was not privy to your ritual of truth, so it is impossible for me to reason on how its completion will translate to regaining Oluweri. But have you been able to find the truth behind the issue upon which you conducted the ritual?'

'Yes, *baba*. To the best of my knowledge, I have found out all I wanted to know,' Adeyanju replied confidently.

'If indeed it is true that you knew the truth upon which you set out to perform the ritual, have you concluded the ritual as prescribed by the oracle? Your diviner must have told you of certain responsibities that you must fulfil before the ritual can be concluded.'

'Also to the best of my knowledge, I have fulfilled all my obligations and responsibilities due to the ritual. Maybe you could appeal on my behalf to the gods to shed more light on my responsibilities.'

'Well let me try,' the priest said, and placed a kolanut on the prince's left palm. Adeyanju enclosed it in his palm, whispered his concerns and troubles to the closed palm and then gave the kolanut back to Fakorede.

'The oracle reveals that there is something of the royal family and which belongs within the confines of the palace that was left behind during the course of the ritual,' said Fakorede. 'If whatever it is can be found and taken to the palace, then and only then will the gods accept the ritual as concluded.'

'Something left behind during the course of the ritual that belongs within the confines to the palace?' Adeyanju asked.

'Yes. Does that have any meaning to you?'

'Yes it does,' Adeyanju muttered thoughtfully. 'I

accidentally left it behind during a visit to Oluweri shortly before the war. My only faint hope of recovering the item is if my host at Oluweri removed it before the war got there. I said faint because my host's family were displaced during the war, and I have neither seen nor heard of them since. The house where I left the item was destroyed during the war, and of all places in Lower-Oluweri, *Oba* Lagbade chose the site to be the abode of the *oyinbo*.'

'There are three steps to recovering an item that is not supposed to be missing. The first step is to look where you left it. If the item is not where you left it, then the next step is to ask the person with whom you share knowledge of the place you left the item. If the item is not with the other person, then the next step is to return to the place and search again.'

'Twice I risked the lives of trusted aides in an attempt to penetrate Ago-Oyinbo and search for the item, but failed.'

'I understand that it is not only difficult but very risky for you to enter occupied Oluweri unnoticed. But you cannot recover the item by sending somebody. That is why the ritual was self-administered.'

'Do you really think that it is possible that the item will still be in the place I kept it after all these years? That is if I can even recognise the place after so much destruction.'

'I can assure you that the oracle would not have prescribe this if the item cannot be recovered. And the deities would not have insisted, if returning the item to the palace had no link with the liberation of Oluweri.'

So in order to complete the ritual as prescribed by the oracle, Adeyanju would have to either risk a journey to enemy territory or find Ojo.

The unrest at the palace at Aromire was at an all-time high when *Oba* Lagbade got information that the Ijowa cabinet had consulted the oracle concerning the decision to go to war in order to regain Oluweri. Although the outcome of the consultation remained shrouded, *Oba* Lagbade and the Akete chiefs were concerned that the unfortunate incident that had befallen *La Felicidad* and its cargo, and the poor state of the Akete army, may have leaked to their counterpart at Ode-Ijowa. The king's strategist at Aromire advised *Oba* Lagbade that it was essential to project the image that his army were fully equipped and ready for any confrontation.

Since the end of the war and the agreement between the *Onijowa* and *Oba* Lagbade over Oluweri had been sorted and sealed in the presence of *Alaafin* and the Oyo chiefs, the military presence along the borders between Lower-Oluweri and the rest of Ijowa had been gradually reduced, then finally limited to entry through the Awoyaya river. By the end of the second season after the occupation of Lower-Oluweri, after about seven ships had docked on Oluweri seafront, the market by the riverside at Oluweri had lost its vibrancy. Trading was now concentrated on the seafront. Consequently, the protection and security of the seafront took greater priority in the palace at Aromire than communal Oluweri. From the turn of the fifth season into the occupation, communal Oluweri and the market by Awoyaya river had been devoid of Akete warriors. The administration of law and order in the whole of communal Oluweri had been handed over to the *Ajele* (king's sole administrator) and his team of *Ilaris* (civil enforcers).

At the time of the passing of the *Onijowa*, the security and defence infrastructure of Akete warriors in Oluweri was basically the fort on the seafront. Akete warriors stationed in Oluweri numbered no more than a hundred at any particular time and were always headed by an *Agba-Eso* (warlord). An *Agba-Eso* was directly responsible to the *Akogun* (supreme warlord of the Akete army), who in turn was directly responsible to the king alone. In line with the recommendation of his war strategist, *Oba* Lagbade displayed a clear show of force by deploying a fresh reinforcement corps of four hundred men to Oluweri. The king further instructed the *Akogun* to temporarily relocate from Aromire to Oluweri and take direct command of the Akete warriors.

Olubi and Ojo rode into Ode-Ijowa on two distinctive horses. Both were stallions, and the way they were groomed and dressed drew considerable attention as they rode through the streets. It gave the average townsman the impression that the riders were not ordinary people. That was the impression Olubi wanted to portray, and he was satisfied. They did not stop to ask for directions but proceed directly to the compound of the *Balogun*. This was on the third day after the oracle was consulted.

'We are here to see the *Aremo-Oba*, but given the situation in the palace, we know the prince is still in mourning and it will be difficult to have a private discussion with him,' Olubi told the *Balogun*. 'So we thought the best thing was to come to you.'

'As you already understand, the *Aremo-Oba* is very busy at the moment and will certainly not be able to attend to minor issues, especially without prior arrangement,' said the *Balogun*.

'I believe he will not regret finding time to meet us.

We rely on you to do all within you means to persuade the prince to spare some time with us.'

'What makes you think I will be willing to do that?' the *Balogun* asked. He was beginning to get irritated by the arrogance of this stranger who thought he could just walk into his compound and tell him what to do.

'As I said earlier, the prince will not regret making time for this meeting,' said Olubi. 'If you decline to facilitate it, we will try our luck at the palace at Aromire, but you will be the one to shoulder all the responsibilities and regrets due to our inability to talk with *Aremo-Oba.*'

The mention of the palace at Aromire got the intended response from the *Balogun*. 'What do you want to see the prince about?' he asked.

'It is about Oluweri and his familiarisation tour.'

'Such an ambiguous statement will not be enough to convince him. You will have to be clearer than that.'

'I'm sorry, but that's all I am allowed to say without the prince in attendance.'

'Allowed? By whom?'

'I am afraid the answer to your question will have to wait until I have seen the *Aremo-Oba,*' Olubi replied in a decisive tone. The *Balogun*, in his true element, was far from the kind of person that would be fazed by Olubi's calm but sinister style of discussion, but he was also a man of enormous experience and could tell when a man was speaking with conviction. He decided not to probe further, but asked for a few moments to change into a proper garment for the palace. He advised that they should leave their horses in his compound in order to avoid undue excitement. Olubi obliged. As far as he was concerned, the efforts made in preparing the horses had been justified.

When they arrived at the palace, *Balogun* Odebode asked them to wait outside while he went in to inform the prince of their presence. He returned a moment later to tell them that the prince was engaged in a meeting, and it could take a while. Olubi told him they were not in any hurry. The Balogun offered them seats under the shade of an *iroko* tree by the east entrance to the palace. While waiting, they were offered palm wine, which they declined, but accepted water and kolanut. Olubi suggest that Ojo should play on his *agidigbo* to ease the tension.

After he had been playing for a while, the *Balogun* returned to inform them that the *Aremo-Oba* had concluded his meeting and was seeing off his visitors. Ojo had just begun to play the rhythm he had learnt from Morilewa when the prince emerged with his guests. They exited from the east side and came within hearing distance.

Bowo luni ko le pani (It cannot crush one to death)

Igi ti a fehinti, ti ko gba ni duro (A tree that cannot support one body weight)

Bowo luni ko le pani (It cannot crush one to death)

The *Aremo-Oba* only walked with his guest as far as the main courtyard, but heard the music. Ojo finished the verse that was the common limit of the use of the adage on *agidigbo* and then moved to another verse which had been Adeyanju's own composition, and which he had taught to Ojo.

Ajekun iya ni o je (Such will be served with a premium beating)

Eniti ko to ni lu, to n'dena deni (He who dare to lay ambush against a stronger man)

Ajekun iya ni o je (Such will be served with a premium thrashing)

Adeyanju heard Ojo playing the added verse, and did not miss the peculiarity of the rhythm. His added composition was not as popular among *agidigbo* players as he would have wished, and he had not heard his lyric played by a stranger for a long time. The natural instinct to hear the rhythm through before returning to the palace made him stop, while pretending to be removing a speck from his eye. The added rhythm was perfectly timed to blend with the original, so much that Adeyanju adjudged it to be smoother than he had ever played it. He was curious to know more about the player, and then he recognised Ojo. It was a good thing he had chosen to stay at a fair distance. His sudden recognition of the person on the *agidigbo* made him perspire so much and so suddenly that the sweat on his brow was visible to his aides. They urged him to leave the open sun and retreat to the cool of the palace.

The *Balogun* waited until Adeyanju had recovered from his sudden shock and was certain he could cope with another possibly lengthy discussion before telling him about the visitors and the little they had disclosed about their mission.

'They don't seem to be in a hurry. I can lodge them for the night in my compound and bring them in the morning, to give you more time to recover,' *Balogun* Odebode suggested, but Adeyanju dismissed the idea.

'I am feeling better now, but the sudden heat and perspiration has left me feeling a bit cold around the head,' he said. He doubted if Ojo could ever connect his face with that of the Morilewa he knew, whom he would probably believe to be dead, but considered it wise to do whatever possible to prevent him from noticing any resemblance between *Aremo-Oba* and Morilewa.

'What I need is a thicker hat to keep my head warm, and I'll be ready to see them,' Adeyanju said. He asked one of his aides to fetch his *abeti-aja* (a hat with sideways extensions to cover the ears), while *Balogun* Odebode went to fetch the visitors to speak with the prince who would be sat in the meeting room.

'We are here on behalf of a lord and patron who prays to remain anonymous for now, but who in turn is acting on behalf of friends of Morilewa,' Olubi began. 'The task entrusted upon us is clear and simple. We are here to inform you that friends of Morilewa are willing to enter into a negotiation that will guarantee the return of the occupied part of Oluweri to the *Onijowa*.' Olubi spoke in a manner which suggested that his words were specifically chosen by his sender.

Before Adeyanju could respond, Olubi made a gesture to Ojo, who humbly placed a wooden box in his hand. Olubi in turn passed the box to *Balogun* Odebode. The warlord took a cautious look at the prince, seeking approval to open the box, and Adeyanju's body language told him to carry on. The *Balogun* opened the box, took a brief look at the contents and then passed the box to Adeyanju.

'The gun you have in your hand can fire six times without reloading and it will take just six blinks of the eye to load another six rounds,' Olubi told Adeyanju with pride. 'My lord said that you should be assured that friends of Morilewa have seventy of those, with abundant ammunition at their disposal. The arms, along with some useful information, will be made available to the Ijowa army on two conditions.' Olubi humbly took two steps backwards to indicate that he had nothing more to say but was waiting for the prince to ask the obvious question.

Adeyanju carried out a brief but careful appraisal of the contents of the box, closed it and return it to *Balogun* Odebode.

'What are the conditions?' Adeyanju asked calmly.

'The first is that Morilewa be granted a royal pardon. That he be freed and able to return safely to his family home in Egbejoda. The second is that upon the liberation of Oluweri, the Fadahunse settlement will remain valid in Ago-Oyinbo.'

'You will understand that meeting your second condition solely depends on the successful takeover of Oluweri, which in turn partly depends on the quality of support that the friends of Morilewa are able to provide. Now to your first condition. The case of Morilewa is very peculiar, and the decision to free him cannot be taken entirely within the confines of this palace. The late priest was very influential in the occult circle, and it will require serious consultation with the Ogboni fraternity before his freedom can be granted.'

'Fortunately, the bi-annual convergence of the Ogbonis all over Ijowa is scheduled to begin in just under a month,' the *Balogun* interjected, and immediately regretted it. He knew he had overstepped his boundary by making a comment that could infringe on the prince's right to a unilateral decision. Adeyanju's body language showed unmistakable disapproval of the warlord's impudence.

'Yes, the Ogboni convergence is around the corner,' Adeyanju reluctantly admitted. 'That will give me the opportunity to pacify them into accepting the decision to free Morilewa.' He was not at all pleased that the *Balogun* had limited the time frame by stupidly mentioning the coming Ogboni convergence. It was within his power as the

Obalola (king-in-waiting) to pardon and free any prisoner, and the Ogbonis had no say whatever on to whom the palace chose to grant the royal pardon. He was only looking for an excuse to gain time, and the Ogboni fraternity just happened to be the first that came to mind.

'Actually, it not within our mandate to give an ultimatum,' Olubi told Adeyanju. 'The friends of Morilewa will only consider their offer to have been accepted the moment Morilewa is granted the royal pardon and is able to return to his family home in Egbejoda. If the prince wishes to have further communication with the friends of Morilewa on the matter, it can be done through a man called Ojo in Oluweri, and his place is very easy to find. Your messenger, whom we suggest will be known as Tekobo, will travel down to Oluweri and seek the house of Ojo Kekewura inside Ago-Oyinbo.'

The meeting was over and they left Ode-Ijowa that same evening, but stopped for the night at a small settlement just outside Ode-Ijowa. They were both tired and did not have the energy to review their meeting with the *Aremo-Oba* until the next morning.

'You have been fairly quiet since we left Ode-Ijowa,' Olubi said at dawn, as they were about to set off for the last part of their return journey to Oko-Oba. 'I know you have something on your mind when you are like this.'

'Yes, I have something on my mind, and I must confess I have serious concerns about our arrangement with the *Aremo-Oba* and the Ijowa chiefs.'

'What is your concern?'

'I am worried about having to rely on the word of the *Aremo-Oba* concerning our future in liberated Oluweri.'

Olubi grinned. 'I knew you would be worried. I was

only waiting to see how long it would take you to complain. I already have a plan that will be sufficient to calm your concerns. We are not going to hand over the weapon to the *Aremo-Oba*. That would be stupid. All they will ever get hold of is the single *akerekoro* we presented to the prince, but that is necessary to convince them that we have the capacity to deliver.'

'What do you have in mind?' Ojo asked, mounting his horse.

Olubi did the same before replying. 'The weapons are our only bargaining assets, and the only way to safeguard our position is to hold on them. I have men capable of using them to support *Aremo-Oba* in his effort to reclaim Oluweri. That is what we are going to do when the time comes to deliver.'

'But that is not what we agreed with the *Aremo-Oba*.'

'Young man, we are having this discussion because you are concerned about trust. I can assure you that the first issues the prince and the Ijowa chiefs will be trying to sort out will centre around trust. They will want to safeguard themselves against our distrust, and at the same time find ways of shortchanging us after we have delivered.'

There were many things which the prince learnt from the unexpected meeting, but they were far beyond the imagination of both the messenger and the supposed sender on one part, and the *Balogun* on the other. It was like the case of the masquerade that can see his admirers, but the admirers are unable to see or recognise the person behind the mask. While the messengers, whom Adeyanju guessed could be the friends of Morilewa, were unknowingly negotiating for the freedom of the wrong person, the *Balogun* had no idea that the *Aremo-Oba* had at a particular time before the war been known by certain persons in Lower-Oluweri as Morilewa of the Omomose compound at Egbejoda.

That evening there was an emergency meeting of the Ijowa cabinet, which continued late into the night. Adeyanju and *Balogun* Odebode shared their discussion with Olubi and Ojo with the other chiefs.

'They said they were here on behalf of a group called friends of Morilewa,' said Adeyanju. 'They are offering to provide enough arms to make dislodging the Akete army from Oluweri easier than we would ever have expected. They claim to have a secret that will make it very easy to reclaim Oluweri, if this palace agrees on certain conditions.'

'What conditions?' the *Ajiroba* asked.

'They made two demands. The first is that Morilewa must be freed and allowed a safe return to his ancestral home in Egbejoda. Second, they want this palace to agree that in the event of a successful takeover of Oluweri, Fadahunse's settlement will remain valid in Ago-Oyinbo. I assume you all remember the Morilewa that was supposed to be serving time on the king's farm for the death of Fatunbi, the *ifa* priest at Oluweri?' The chiefs nodded in acknowledgment. 'I have neither accepted nor rejected their offers but made them understand that there is no way we can meet the second demand until they have provided the arms and we have retaken Oluweri.'

'If I remember correctly, the Morilewa they were asking to be freed escaped on the way to the king's farm,' *Iyalode* observed.

'Yes, but it is evident that the Omomose family have been very forthcoming in their agreement, so much that even valued friends of Morilewa were unaware that he is no longer in our custody, else they will not include his freedom as part of their demands.'

'They believe that Morilewa is still being held on one of the king's farms,' *Balogun* clarified. 'Their ignorance is our advantage. All we need to do is find Morilewa and make his freedom official,' He added.

'I don't see any need to find Morilewa. He will come into the open the moment we announce that he has been pardoned and is safe to return to his family home in Egbejoda,' said the *Ajiroba*.

'It is not as simple as that. It would be unwise to announce Morilewa's pardon until we can physically free him,' *Balogun* pointed out.

'The quickest way to find Morilewa is through his family in Egbejoda. We had a secret pact with the elders of the Omomose family that we would not pursue Morilewa if he kept his escape secret. I am sure his family will be willing to cooperate if we promise to grant him a royal pardon.' the *Ajiroba* explained..

All the chiefs agreed except the Otun. 'This seems too good to be true,' he said. 'We have to be careful about our response. We don't even know the true identity of those behind this proposal. There is no reason to believe that anybody apart from the palaces has the ability to deliver what is being offered.'

'They brought this along.' Adeyanju produced the gun Olubi had left behind. 'They said it is a gift for me, but I take it as proof of their ability to deliver.'

'*Olodumare oooo!*' The Ajiroba responded excitedly on seeing the gun. 'This is an *akerekoro!*'

'*Akerekoro?*' echoed the Otun.

'Yes, with six chambers, and they claimed to have seventy of them and abundant bullets which can be made available for the Ijowa army if we agree to those conditions,' said the *Balogun*.

'What is an *akerekoro*?' the *Iyalode* asked eagerly.

'A small gun that can be hidden in the pocket. An *akerekoro* can fire up to six shots and kill or wound at least four men before being reloaded. It does not need gunpowder, only bullets, and they are new!' the *Balogun* said with pride. 'A good warrior with one of them stands a better chance against twenty warriors with long guns.'

'I would still advise that we should be very cautious about this,' said the *Otun*. 'We need to give the the matter much thought. Remember the words of the oracle, that we dare not attempt to reclaim Oluweri by force until the *Aremo-Oba* has been through the ritual.' He was still sceptical about the whole development.

'This is like a blessing from the gods. We have nothing to lose by agreeing to this offer,' *Ajiroba* countered.

'We are in a time when all matters should be given due attention,' said *Balogun* Odebode. 'Urgent issues cannot be left unresolved while we slumber. A decision must be made, and at the right time.' He was beginning to get irritated by the *Otun's* pessimism. Although all the chiefs, except the *Otun*, agreed that Ijowa had nothing to lose by agreeing to the offer, Adeyanju urged them to give him more time to think it over.

'There is no need to rush into a decision,' said Adeyanju. 'Although the Ogboni fraternity has no say in this matter, I made the messengers understand that because of the late priest's standing in the occult circle, it is imperative that the ogbonis are pacified into agreeing to the freedom of Morilewa. The bi-annual convergence of the Ogbonis is soon, so I asked them to give me until then before expecting a decision. Meanwhile, I will sleep over the matter and tell you my decision in two days.' With the prince's conclusion, the meeting was over.

Adeyanju could not sleep afterwards. He was wide awake for the rest of the night, thinking about how to find his way through the developing situation. In his private thoughts, he knew the agreement would fall apart the moment Morilewa was granted the royal pardon. The so-called friends of Morilewa would backtrack on the agreement the moment they realised that the Morilewa they were after was not the person who was supposed to be serving time for the death of the priest.

Adeyanju concluded that the only way to save the agreement was to let the so-called 'friends of Morilewa' meet the Morilewa of their desire. He began to see the sense in the words of oracle, that he must complete the ritual of truth. The oracle offered a better bargain if he could return the item that belonged to the crown back to the palace. The priest said that finding the *ejigbaileke* will lead to the liberation of Oluweri without losing Odinjo or any part of Ijowaland in the process. He weighed his options and chose the path of the oracle.

Two days later, all the chiefs were at the palace before sun up, waiting for the prince's decision.

'I have taken time to give the issue serious thought and I have decided to proceed with the agreement,' he said. 'That means the first step is to seek out Morilewa, and make a fresh agreement with him. *Balogun* and *Ajiroba* will set about meeting the elders of the Omomose family and discuss the conditions for total freedom for Morilewa.

In the meantime I will set about performing the ritual prescribed by the oracle. The ritual requires that I travel down to Inukan.'

'How long will it take to complete the ritual?' *Otun* asked.

'According to Fakorede, it will take me at least five days of seclusion in his shrine at Inukan to complete the full ritual prescribed by the oracle. I would like to shed more light on the nature of the ritual, but the oracle forbids, so I dare not.'

While Adeyanju and the Ijowa chiefs were deliberating over the offer of the 'friend of Morilewa' in Ode-Ijowa, *Akogun* Ologundudu, the supreme warlord of the Akete army, was marching a reinforcement of four hundred men into Oluweri. Upon arriving at Oluweri, the first thing *Akogun* Ologundudu did was to instruct *Agba-Eso* Ojikutu, the former commander of occupation army, to increase the presence of Akete's warriors along the three major boundaries between Lower-Oluweri and the rest of Ijowa.

Ologundudu began his second full day in Oluweri by conducting a security assessment tour round the boundaries of Lower-Oluweri with the rest of Ijowa. He rode the entire Awoyaya riverbank that separated Lower-Oluweri from upper Oluweri and the rest of northern Ijowa. The tour did not end until late in the afternoon, and he was back at the fort before sundown. On the third day, he led a band of Akete warriors through the forest on the western boundary with Oko-Oba. The general's tour through the forest took a long time due to the terrain, and and he did not return to the fort at the seafront until dusk. On the fourth day, he was on the eastern side, the boundary with Odinjo, and went through same process as he had the previous day on the western boudary.

He stayed in the fort all through the fifth day, not because of tiredness, but to begin working on the strategy to counter possible offensive by the Ijowa warriors. By the end of his fifth day at Oluweri, and after a comprehensive assessment of the security situation, the war general had come to the conclusion that even with an adequate supply of arms, it would be difficult to prevent a force of up to six hundred moderately well-armed men from breaching the wide boundaries of the occupied area. He considered the fact that Oluweri was still under the control of Akete as mere luck, and if care is not taken, it was about to run out. He had the view that preventing the Ijowa army from reclaiming Oluweri was not essentially a factor of men and arms, but of intelligence. So his first action was to set up an intelligence-gathering team of fifteen men, led by *Agba-Eso* Ojikutu. He named the team *owuye* (the whisperers), and their major task was to seek information about the activities of the Ijowa army.

'Every bit of information about the enemy will go further toward ensuring victory, and none should be considered too trivial to ignore,' he instructed the spying team.

Furthermore, the general decided to strengthen the defence of the western boundary with Oko-Oba by adding two more response posts to the existing three and increasing the number of warriors stationed at each post from fifteen to fifty. The length of the eastern boundary with Odinjo was less than half of the one with Oko-Oba on the west, so he did not create a new response post on the eastern side but still increased the number of men at each of the two existing posts to fifty. A hundred warriors were stationed at the fort and the remaining fifty were assigned for random patrol of the communal and residential areas of Oluweri and the market places by the Awoyaya riverbanks.

On the sixth day, he was officially introduced to the the rank-and-file of civilian matters at Oluweri. The activity took him to Ago-Oyinbo for the first time since his arrival. The warlord was well aware that Wontsay was not in Oluweri at that moment, but Ojo was introduced to him by Ojikutu as the person Fadahunse had left in charge while he was away. Knowing the importance of being on the right side of the warlord at such a crucial time, Ojo allowed unrestricted access into the inner perimeter of Ago-Oyinbo. He honoured Ologundudu by inviting him into Wontsay's private quarters as Wontsay would have done and offered him special wine. He further humbled the guest by leaving Wontsay's chair vacant and insisting on sitting on a lower stool. He told the visiting warlord that such was the protocol when the *oyinbo* was hosting 'a very important person'.

Despite his humility and respect toward Ologundudu during his visit to Ago-Oyinbo, Ojo's position and authority in Ago-Oyinbo were too significant for the warlord to ignore. He was curious to know how such a young man could be Wontsay's favourite, and be in charge of Ago-Oyinbo in his absence. The next morning, Ologundudu sent for Ojikutu and demanded to know more about him.

'His father was an Ijowa man from Kuluso, but he grew up in Gbajumo,' said Ojikutu. 'He used to be a canoe man, carrying people and goods from different parts of the Awoyaya river and the seafront. He helped Fadahunse to safety after the infamous *ijamba obo*, and the *oyinbo* showed his gratitude by employing him as part of his exploration crew. He became Fadahunse's favourite employee by virtue of his skill on the *agidigbo*. He is hard working, known to be usually busy and always running about in Oluweri to do the bidding of Fadahunse. He spends most of his time in Oluweri, except when he was probably travelling with the explorer.'

The fact that an Ijowa son of the soil was acting in such a capacity in Ago-Oyinbo raised a small security concern for Ologundudu.

'I want a detailed report of his activities. I want to know about his friends in Oluweri, and families outside Oluweri,' Ologundudu instructed Ojikutu.

'I will do as you wish my lord, but I can assure you that there is no cause to worry about the young man.'

'You do what I ask you to do, and leave the worrying to me,' Ologundudu replied curtly.

On the seventh day following his arrival in Oluweri, a man came to the fort and requested a private audience with Ologundudu. The man claimed he had vital information about the enemy and was willing to discuss it personally with the commanding warlord.

'I understand you have information about certain decisions made in the palace at Ode-Ijowa.' Ologundudu wasted no time getting to the purpose of the meeting.

'My name is Lagemo. I have no connection with the palace at Ode-Ijowa, and I have nothing to tell you about the Ijowa war plan. I only made those claims to have direct access to you, as what we have agreed to offer in support of the Akete army is too sensitive to be passed through a third party.'

'When you said 'we', who are you referring to?'

'We are friends of Morilewa. I am talking about the Morilewa who was wrongly accused of killing the *ifa* priest here in Oluweri about sixteen years ago. The *Onijowa* and his idiotic chiefs at Ode-Ijowa believe that the killing of the priest was part of the greater conspiracy to pave way for the attack that led to the loss of Oluweri. Our friend was found guilty and sentenced to twenty-five years on the king's farm. He was said to have died two years later at Igbodudu, where the palace claim he was being treated. But we know better. Our Morilewa was never sick in the head, but was confined to Igbodudu in order to prevent the public from hearing his side of the story. The loss of Oluweri to the palace at Aromire is our only consolation for the injustice done to our friend and we have since his death vowed to put our resources against any effort by the palace at Ode-Ijowa to reclaim this part of Oluweri. The friends of Morilewa consider it a lifetime duty to ensure that even the future *Onijowa* pays for the injustice done to our friend.'

'What have the friends of Morilewa agreed to offer in support of the Akete army?' Ologundudu, understandably, was only interested in what Lagemo and his so-called friends of Morilewa had to offer and cared very little about the tragedy that had befallen Morilewa.

'We have access to vital resources that could play a decisive role in the battle over the seafront of Oluweri,' Lagemo replied with confidence. 'I expect you are familiar with this type of gun.' Lagemo produced a revolver and placed it on the floor between them. Olugundudu picked up the weapon carefully and examined it for a considerable time.

'This is an *akerekoro* with six chambers,' Ologundudu

replied as he placed the gun more gently back on the floor.

'That is what the friends of Morilewa have to offer in support of the Akete warriors. We have fifty of those with us and more than enough bullets to defeat Ijowa, as long as the Akete army is willing to defend Oluweri. But there are only seven friends of Morilewa. Just as the best cutlass cannot cut the grass on its own, so the best of guns cannot fire itself. As you are well aware, an *akerekoro* is only worth its value and more if handled by somebody adept at using it. That is why we have decided to make ourselves available to train sellected men on how to use it.'

Ologundudu could not have agreed less. Efficient as they are, an *akerekoro* could be fatally counter-productive in the hands of an unskilled user.

'You have come with a very valuable offer for which you require nothing in return, and I commend your loyalty to the king for that,' said Ologundudu. 'While I see no reason why this gesture by the friends of Morilewa will not only be accepted by the king but well appreciated, you must understand that as a matter of due process, I will have to discuss it in the palace before I can accept this generous offer.' Lagemo had been expecting such a condition to come up, and already had his response ready.

'If you ask me, I would strongly advise against that,' he said.

'Are you suggesting that I should not make the king aware of this discussion?'

'I am not suggesting, I am only advising,' Lagemo replied calmly. 'You may be wondering why we decided to come to you in the first place, rather than directly to the palace at Aromire.' He did not wait for Ologundudu to respond. 'My answer I guess you must know, but you will not openly admit it. Both palaces are as porous as sponges. They leak secrets like fishing nets leak water. I can assure you that whatever part of our discussion gets to the palace at Aromire will also be known at Ode-Ijowa in a matter of days. I don't need to be a warrior to know that this would be counter productive. So it has nothing to do with my suggestion. It is about the choice between victory and defeat. It is about the result you desire for yourself and the Akete warriors.'

'Then I don't see how our discussion can go any further. I would be risking a charge of treason against the king and the people of Akete, because, even if I keep quiet about it, I cannot guarantee that the men you will be training will do so.'

'That is why I said selected men,' replied Lagemo. 'Though you are likely to deny this, I am certain that, in your profession, and by virtue of your position, there should be at least thirty of your men who owe their first loyalty to you, and not the king. Those are the ones we will privately engage in training.' Ologundudu understood what he was talking about. No warrior can rise to become the supreme commander of such a strong and influential army as that of Aketeland without having an inner following among the ranks, those who like other warriors will pledge their allegiance only to the king, but in a critical situation, will betray the king to protect their general.

'I do deny that,' Ologundudu replied. 'However, I agree it is the end that matters and not the means. But, to ensure the matter proceeds as intended, it is important that I let my deputy, Ojikutu, into the affair.'

'I have no objection to that as long as you can trust him to keep it to himself,' Lagemo replied. Then Ologundudu clapped trice and a moment later his footman entered the room with two full calabashes of palm wine and placed one in front of each of the men.

'In that case, how soon can you and your friend be available for this purpose, and what arrangements do you want made ready before your arrival?' Ologundudu asked as soon as his footman was out of the room.

'We will be here in about three or four days,' Lagemo replied. 'There is nothing much to arrange. Just a simple shelter in the fort and among your loyal warriors.' He picked up his palm wine and finished the full calabash in one gulp. Ologundudu made to refill his bowl, but he declined. He stood up, bid the warlord farewell and left. He left Oluweri neither via Awoyaya nor any of the land borders, but on a single manned canoe via the sea, rowing east towards the Akete waterfront.

Under normal circumstances, the ideal strategy was for a warlord to spread his most loyal men across all formations, and that was what Ologundudu did when deploying men to the five outposts and the fort. But the day after Lagemo's visit, he carried out a major redeployment of his warriors to be compatible with his plan. At the end of it, all forty warriors deployed to the fort on the seafront were the men he trusted most.

On the fourth day after the meeting, Lagemo and six other men arrived at the fort on the seafront of Oluweri. Lagemo introduced them as friends of Morilewa who would be staying in Oluweri to begin training the Akete army on the use of the revolver.

CHAPTER 14

On the sixteenth day after Adeyanju and the Ijowa chiefs consulted the oracle, the *ifa* priest was again at the palace in response to an urgent message from the *Aremo-Oba*. 'I have decided to follow the path of the oracle and complete the ritual,' Adeyanju told the priest. 'I understand that I have to do this alone, and I have worked out how I am going to go about it, but I will need your assistance in certain areas without compromising the conditions for the validity of the ritual. The proper ritual will begin with my exit from Inukan. The tricky part will be the journey from Inukan to Oluweri and back. That I have to do alone, privately and essentially on foot, in order not to draw attention. Now what I want you to do between now and the next *ojoru* [fourth day of the week] is to make arrangements for a safe and discreet place where I can stop for the night between Inukan and Oluweri without being disturbed.'

'How are you going to enter Oluweri unnoticed?' Fakorede asked.

'I did not tell you this before, but I actually had to be somebody else during the ritual of truth.'

'I don't understand what you mean,' the priest said, visibly confused.

'I had to assume a different identity during the ritual,' Adeyanju replied.

'That is a problem solved then,' Fakorede said after thinking briefly. 'It is the *Aremo-Oba* who will find it difficult and dangerous to enter occupied Oluweri, and not whoever you were during the ritual.'

'That's right. But I will still need your help.'

'I need to remind you that it is a self-administered ritual,' said Fakorede.

'I know, but even then, *Baba* Fatunbi – may the gods soften the earth inside which he was wrapped – did assist in certain ways. I will not be demanding your support beyond that given by *Baba* Fatunbi.'

'I think that should be acceptable by the gods,' Fakorede agreed. 'Did the departed priest knows the name you assumed during the ritual?'

'Yes, he did. In fact he suggested it.'

'Then you must tell me the name, but rest assured that I will keep it to myself the way the departed did.'

'Morilewa,' Adeyanju answered reluctantly. 'That was the name I assumed while performing the ritual.' He was afraid Fakorede might probe further, but was relieved that priest did not seem to make anything of the name.

'Did he know about the item you forgot in Oluweri?'

'No, he did not.' This time, Adeyanju had to lie. He had been performing traditional functions with an imitation *ejigbaileke* and not the real one of *Aremo-Oba*. He could not bring himself to tell the priest that for the past fourteen years he had been performing both the spiritual and ceremonial duties of an *Aremo-Oba* without the authentic traditional beads. The *ejigbaileke* of the *Aremo-Oba* was like the crown of *Onijowa*. The *Onijowa* could not and must not perform the duties of the king without his crown. Hence it was considered a taboo for an *Aremo-Oba* to act in his capacity as the heir apparent to the throne without the *ejigbaileke*.

Upon his return to Inukan, Fakorede set about making arrangements for a safe and discreet place for the prince to stop for a night during his journey from Inukan to Oluweri, and another night on his return journey. Finding a place for a traveller to stop and rest for a night in any village is not a problem, as villagers often have places they let for the constant flow of *alajapa* (travelling traders) who travel from one market to another. However, finding a place that would not only guarantee the prince's privacy but be available for at least five nights at a stretch could be a problem.

The priest considered either Olokoto or Oko-Oba as the ideal midway stop for Adeyanju on the way to Oluweri from Inukan. In his quest for an ideal place, his first stop was Olokoto, and he was fortunate to find the place that matches the exact specifications he was after. It was an isolated farmhouse on the edge of Olokoto. Ironically, it was the quest for a secluded place that made the need for longer duration easy to satisfy, as most travellers tends to prefer to stay within the community.

'I am a travelling trader and I am not stopping in Olokoto during this trip, but my brother will be stopping here on his way to Eti-Osa market, so he asked me to get a place for him in advance,' Fakorede told Lagun, the man whom he was directed to approach for the property. 'I asked around and was told that a farmhouse on the route to Gbajumo is usually available for that purpose. I was also informed that the said farmhouse is owned by your family, and you have the anthority to rent it out to travellers.'

'Yes, that is true. I have the last say on the entire Bojuri estate,' Lagun replied with pride. 'What is the name of your brother, and for how long will he be using the farmhouse?'

'His name is Morilewa and he will be arriving in Olokoto two days before the Eti-Osa market. He will stop for a night on his way to Eti-Osa and another night on his return journey about four days after market day.'

'That means he will only be using the place for two nights.'

'Not exactly. He had some wares from previous trading at the Inukan market which he will be leaving behind until his return journey, so he will be using the place until after his return journey. That means we are talking about six days.'

'I normally let out the place for travelling traders for fifteen cowries per night. Your brother will be engaging the place for six days or nights, which amounts to ten less than a hundred good cowries. But I will only charge him for five nights.'

'That is very generous,' Fakorede agreed. He took out his cowrie pouch, counted out seventy-five cowries and handed them to Lagun. 'My brother is a quiet person and values his privacy. He does his cooking by himself, so it will be very appreciated if he is not disturbed during his brief stay.'

'That will be no problem at all,' Lagun replied. This kind of arrangement was not new to him. It was a general knowledge that male traders often travelled with a secret mistress or concubine, hence the need for privacy.

From Olokoto, Fakorede returned directly to Ode-Ijowa. The priest travelled overnight and arrived at Ode-Ijowa toward sundown the next day. The prince was all set and waiting for him when he arrived at the palace. The next dawn, without a single escort, the prince and the priest rode on horseback out of Ode-Ijowa towards Inukan. It was twenty-one days since the prince had received the messengers from the 'friends of Morilewa'. It was already dark before they arrived at Inukan, and the prince's presence in the village was not known beyond the priest's household. Upon their arrival, Fakorede gathered his immediate household and briefed them about the prince's purpose in Inukan.

'The *Aremo-Oba* is here to engage in a private ritual, and it is imperative that his presence in Inukan is kept accordingly,' he said. 'That is why we planned our arrival at the village to be at this hour. Even the *Baale* is not aware of his presence in the village. We will be leaving for the shrine tonight after I have collected a few things. He will be staying at the shrine during the course of the ritual, and he is not to see or talk to anybody except me until it has been concluded.'

The ifa shrine at Inukan was built in the forest on the edge of the village. The prince and the priest slept at the shrine, but before cockcrow, they were well out of Inukan and almost halfway to Olokoto.

By sundown, it was clear that Adeyanju would easily reach Olokoto before dark. At a fair distance from the Awoyaya river, he stopped and waited while the priest went to survey the riverbank, to be sure that it was devoid of fishermen and commuters. The priest then went and drew out a canoe he had arranged days before. When all was set, Fakorede signalled to Adeyanju to join him. The priest rowed the prince across the Awoyaya and stopped on a part of the riverbank close to the route to Olokoto.

Every other month, the young men of Gbajumo went hunting, and they could be away in the forest for days at a stretch. On this occasion, the reward for the first two nights was frustratingly meagre, so they decided to extend their range right to the limit of Gbajumo and slightly into the farmland and small settlements that lay between Gbajumo and Olokoto. In the late afternoon, after they had roasted the quarry they had taken the previous night to preserve the meat and were resting before the next hunt, Bogunde excused himself, saying he needed to relieve himself. While searching for a convenient place, he spotted two men talking under a tree a few steps off the path into Olokoto. One of them was dressed in the regalia of an *ifa* spriritualist, while the other wore noble attire. On instinct Bogunde dropped to the ground and hid under a cluster of cocoayam leaves to avoid being spotted.

Bogunde was unable to hear what transpired between the two men. From where he hid, he watched as the nobleman stripped and changed into an ordinary *buba* and *sokoto*.

'This is as far as the oracle permits me to be involved in this ritual, else it will be void,' Fakorede told Adeyanju. 'From now on, you are Morilewa, and you have to complete the journey to Oluweri as you would have done in the past as Morilewa. You should be in Olokoto before dusk. The place I have arranged for you at Olokoto must have been vacant for the past two days. It is a fairly isolated farmhouse, but easy to find. Just follow the directions I gave you.'

Adeyanju listened attentively as he stripped himself of his royal garb and changed into a clean but slightly tattered *buba* and *sokoto* which the priest had carried along for him. At a crossroads, the prince and the priest parted ways.

'I will be waiting for you by the riverbank in about five days,' Fakorede said before he began his return journey back to Inukan, while Adeyanju continued towards Olokoto.

Bogunde was on his way to join the rest of the group when he met Kotun, the leader of the hunting party. Kotun had been heading to the river to hastily clean himself before the hunting began for the second night, and Bogunde joined him. When they were only a short distance from the river, Kotun sighted an antelope by the river with its back towards them. The antelope was grazing on the lush grassland, but it was obvious that it was in pain as it limped about in search of the greenest patches. They could see that a small part of the antelope's backside had been torn open, and a chunk of flesh was held on to its body by a flap of skin. The antelope must have had a recent and painful encounter with a predator, possibly a leopard. Kotun reckoned they stood a fair chance of catching up with it if they crept as close as possible to it before the chase began.

When the chase did start, it was a long pursuit through the forest and then into the plains and farmlands that lay between Gbajumo and Olokoto. They eventually managed to get within range of the wounded antelope and killed it with pebbles propelled from their slings. They could only bask in their victory for a short moment however, having realised their hunt had led them to lose contact with the rest of the group. Stumbling in the slight light of dusk, sharing the load of the huge antelope with Kotun, who brought up the rear, Bogunde attempted a path through dry bamboo only to have splinter drive itself into his right foot. Bogunde yelled in anguish as the pain travelled through his veins.

As he examined the injury, Kotun tried to calm his junior to avoid alerting any wild animals. Judging by the way Bogunde was writhing with pain, Kotun was sure the splinter was fairly long and had pierced deep into his ankle. He tried helping him to remove the splinter, but it went even deeper than it looked, and in the process, it broke off, leaving almost half of it still lodged in Bogunde's foot. Kotun soon realised that he had no choice but to seek help. They were very close to Olokoto, but it was getting dark and he could not leave Bogunde alone in such a state in the middle of the forest. Kotun partly carried and partly supported Bogunde across the plains that separated the residential part of Olokoto from the forest. As they were nearing the edge of the plains, Kotun noticed light coming from a farmhouse nearby and decided to approach the occupant for help.

It was getting dark by the time Adeyanju arrived at Olokoto. The hut where he would be stopping for the night was well separated from the main residential area of the village. It had been specifically chosen by the priest to ensure that the prince would not be disturbed.

The restless journey from Ode-Ijowa to Inukan and now Olokoto had left him beyond tired and hungry. He lit an oil lamp that he found by the door and went into the now almost dark interior. As Fakorede had promised, the hut had been stocked with all he could need during his brief stay. There were three yam tubers on a wooden rack in the corner of the hut. He picked one of the yams and went outside to make a fire to roast it.

Adeyanju was just taking out the roasted yam from the fire when Kotun arrived with Bogunde. It only required a brief observation for him to realise they needed help. He took them in to examine Bogunde's injury, whilst Kotun explained how they had found themselves in the situation. 'There is still a sizeable part of the wood inside your leg, and the quickest way to remove it is with a knife and hot oil,' Adeyanju said, rising. 'It will be very painful, but that is your best bet if you are relying on your legs to take you back to Gbajumo. I have got the fire and the oil, but I will need a sharply-pointed knife to drop the hot oil right into the heart of the injury.' He turned to Kotun. 'You will have to go into the village and ask for one,' he said. 'The nearest place is the Bojuri compound and this hut belongs to the Bojuri family. Go there and say you are from Morilewa, the *alajapa* who is stopping for the night at their farmhouse.'

The longer the stick stayed inside Bogunde's leg, the more intense the pain, and his ankle had swollen by half its size before Kotun returned with the knife. Adeyanju carried the oil he had heated as he waited for Kotun inside. He took the knife from Kotun and went back out to hold it over the flame for a moment. Upon his return, he set about using the knife to apply the hot oil to Bogunde's leg. Occasionally, he would probe at the area of insertion with the knife. Adeyanju was by no means skilled in healing and Bogunde had a substantial part of his injured foot burnt by stray hot oil, and the use of the knife was far from delicate. Bogunde's discomfort soon began to ease, though, after the hot oil had pierced the wound and the splinter was eased out with the knife.

'Travelling back to Gbajumo in your condition could still be very painful,' Adeyanju told Bogunde after he was satisfied that the splinter had not broken off in the removal process. 'I advised you look for a horse to take you back. You can sleep in my hut tonight and find one to hire in the morning. I should be gone before any of you is awake. I rented this place for six nights. If anyone question your presence here, tell them you are with Morilewa, the *alajapa* (travelling trader)'

Being the leader of the group, it was not long before Kotun's absence was noticed, and Bogunde too was later found wanting after a brief headcount. The group conducted a thorough search of the area they had been resting in, and then extended their search as far as the river, but found nothing amiss. They scrutinised the grasses and shrubs to see if any area had been disturbed by conflict or struggle, but the vegetation was all as fresh and natural as any could be. The only hunting they could do that night was for their missing friends.

Adeyanju set off for the last leg of his journey to Oluweri at the crack of dawn without waking his guest. He left a small pouch full of cowries by the oil lamp, and beside the sack he placed a bunch of grass. This was a simple coded message that the cowries were meant as payment for hiring the horse. The young men were amazed by their host's generosity, but it also rekindled the mystery that had been clouding Bogunde's mind since his first encounter with their host by the riverside. The irony was that his profile during the brief period before he changed from his regal attire seemed to overshadow the long duration he had seen him in ordinary attire. The more he viewed him as a noble rather than a commoner, the more certain he was that he had seen the generous stranger somewhere before.

Bogunde and Kotun were so tired that neither woke up until the brightness of the day was penetrating through a gap in the bamboo wall of the hut. They immediately set about looking for a horse to hire, but neither of them knew anyone in Olokoto they could present as a guarantor. It took lot of explanation and persuasion, and they had to pay enough to hire three horses, before the hirer would release a single horse. So it was already mid-morning before they finally set off for Gbajumo. They were met midway by their friends, who were just extending their search towards the settlements around Olokoto.

After all efforts to make Ojo marry one of the many maidens he was courting across Ijowa and Akete had failed, Lalonpe decide to take the matter into her own hands. Before travelling down to Oluweri to visit him, she always sent a message via the canoemen to check if he would be in Oluweri and available to host her. But this time around, for strategic reasons, she risked the journey to Oluweri without prior notice, and with a maiden whom she and *Iya* Mojoyin would be ordering Ojo to marry.

Since their reunion, except when he and other native handymen had to travel out of Oluweri with Wontsay on his unending expedition deep into the jungle, Ojo had never let two consecutive markets at Gbajumo pass by before visiting his mother and child. But Ojo had been fully occupied by the demands of managing Ago-Oyinbo, combined with the stress of Oluweri politics, so much so that three markets had passed since the last time he had seen his mother and son. So while Kotun and Bogunde were trying to hire a horse in Olokoto to take them back to Gbajumo, and Lalonpe, acompanied by the ageing *Iya* Mojoyin and a young maiden called Moladun, were boarding the canoe at Gbajumo to take them down to Oluweri, Ojo, on horseback, was on his way to Gbajumo. Following the instruction of his superior, Eso Ojikutu had assigned three of the *owuyes* to monitor Ojo's activities and movements and report back to him daily, so when they saw him leaving Ago-Oyinbo before daybreak, they secretly followed.

Ojo arrived at his mother's house around late noon, but the yard was empty and the front door was locked. He went around to his mother's neighbour to inquire.

'She left this morning for Oluweri with *Iya* Mojoyin,' Gbekeyide told him. 'She said she was coming to your place.'

'She did not tell me she would be visiting. I left Oluweri this morning purposely to come and see her.' Ojo found it unusual that his mother would travel down to Oluweri with *Iya* Mojoyin without informing him beforehand. 'I hope there is nothing wrong?'

'Not that I am aware of,' Gbekeyide replied regretfully, and Ojo believed him. The first thing he knew about Gbekeyide was that she was totally incapable of holding back on anything. If she knew, she would tell. But the fact that Gbekeyide had no explanation for why his mother was travelling down to Oluweri unannounced worried him.

'What about Bogunde and Malaolu? Where are they?'

'She left Malaolu with me, and he is having his lunch

in the house. Bogunde was away hunting with friends, and they are not expected to be back for another four days.'

'Well in that case I had better be returning to Oluweri.'

'Don't you think it is too late to start a journey to Oluweri? Why don't you sleep over and have a fresh start in the morning?'

'Thank you, but I would rather set off now and stop for the night at Olokoto or Oko-Oba, then continue in the morning, so I will be able to get to Oluweri before midday tomorrow,' Ojo replied, then mounted his horse and left.

Adeyanju arrived in Oluweri just as the sun was beginning to set. Although he had not been inside this part of Oluweri for over sixteen years, it was easy finding Ago-Oyinbo and the house of Ojo Kekewura. On getting there, Adeyanju was met by a person who claimed to be looking after the house for the owner.

'I am here to see Ojo Kekewura. I believe this is the right place?'

'Ojo Kekewura is the owner of the house. My name is Tori. I look after the house whenever he is away. Who are you?'

'My name is Morilewa. I travelled down from Igisogba purposely to see him.'

'All the way from Igisogba? Did he know you were coming?'

'He is not expecting me, but he will be delighted to see me.'

'Unfortunately he is not at home at the moment. He left Oluweri two days ago.'

'It is very important that I see him. Did he say how long he will be away?'

'He was not specific, but I expect him to be back within the next two days.'

'That means I have to wait for him. I cannot afford to return to Igisogba without seeing him.'

'I am not sure he will be pleased if I allow you to stay here without clearing it with him,' Tori said apologetically.

'I quite understand your point, and I will not suggest you go against your landlord's order. What I will request of you is to arrange a private place on the outskirts of Oluweri, where I can stay until he returns. You will be well rewarded for it.'

'That I can do. It will be getting dark soon, but I will try my best.'

The sun had gone and dusk was descending before Lalonpe and her companions arrived at Oluweri. It is poor strategy for a matchmaker to let a not-so-willing partner suspect their intention until it is necessary, but at the same time, it would be totally out of order, and could be very embarrassing, to deny Ojo prior notice before presenting Moladun. So when they arrived at Oluweri, Lalonpe suggested that *Iya* Mojoyin and Moladun should wait for her some distance from Ago-Oyinbo while she went to inform Ojo of their presence and purpose in Oluweri.

As usual on her visits to Ojo, Lalonpe stopped at every house in the outer perimeter of Ago-Oyinbo to greet other residents before proceeding to the old house. It was very unusual for her to visit when her son was away, and the housekeeper started panicking the moment he heard of Lalonpe's sudden arrival. He had yet to find a place for the visitor to stay, as most landlords on the outskirts of the village were yet to return from the farm. He reckoned that it would be better to alert Lalonpe about the situation than to wait for her to come down and find a stranger in the house.

Tori waited for Lalonpe to finish the usual round of social courtesy and approached her before she reached the house.

'Welcome mama. How was your journey?'

'Thank you, it was fine. But I was very disappointed when I learnt Ojo is not around.'

'Yes, he is away. He left for Oko-Oba three days ago.'

'Did he say when he will be returning?'

'He only said he could be away for a few days, so I expect he should be back soon.'

'That is no problem. I will wait,' Lalonpe proceeded towards the house.

'Mama, I think you will have to help me solve a little problem,' the housekeeper said as they walked towards the house.

'What is it?'

'It is about the house. A visitor has come all the way from Igisogba to see Ojo. He said it is important that he sees him before returning to Igisogba. I have been trying to find a place for him to stay without success. I don't know how your son will react if I let a stranger stay in the house without his consent.'

'Did you say the visitor came down to Oluweri purposely to see Ojo?'

'That is what he said. He said Ojo would be more than delighted to see him.'

'You don't seem to have much choice. If you cannot find a place for him, then he will have to stay in the house. It would be cruel to deny him shelter.'

'I will put him in the back room. That is where I sleep whenever I come down to look after the house for Ojo. I will be all right in the corridor for the night,' Tori said.

'I also came down from Gbajumo with guests, but the middle room should be all right for us,' Lalonpe assured him. By this time they were at the house.

The housekeeper went inside to inform Adeyanju about the new development. 'You can stay the night in the back room,' he said. 'I will set about finding a suitable place for you in the morning.'

'That is very nice of you,' Adeyanju replied as Tori led him to the back room.

Lalonpe began a quick inspection of the house to ensure that it was in a good enough state for a visiting bride-to-be. Her inspection soon led her to the back of the house. Adeyanju was in the back room, looking through the window into the back yard. From where she stood, Lalonpe had a good side view of him. She stood rigid in shock for a brief moment, then slumped on the ground, knocking over some farm tools that were neatly arranged beside the wall.

Adeyanju was deep in thought, and oblivious of Lalonpe and the fallen hardware. But from the front yard, Tori the housekeeper heard the crash, and rushed to the back of the house. He helped Lalonpe to her feet and supported her to the front of the house.

'Mama, are you all right?' The housekeeper asked as he fanned Lalonpe.

'I am fine now,' Lalonpe replied as she tried to stand steadily on her own. 'It must have been the stress of the journey. I only need to take a little rest and I will be fine.' She was trying her best to hide her fear.

'Would you like some water to calm you down?' Tori suggested.

'Yes, that would be nice,' Lalonpe replied, and Tori left to fetch the water.

'What is the name of that visitor in the back room?' Lalonpe asked the housekeeper casually when he returned with a calabash of water.

'He says his name is Morilewa,' The housekeeper replied, and had to stop Lalonpe from falling again. He noticed that she was sweating profusely. 'I think you need a good rest. Let me help you into the front room so that you can lie down.'

'I am fine now,' Lalonpe said. 'All I need is a bit of fresh air. I want you to escort me down the road to the fishmonger's place. There are guests waiting me there. I want to go and collect them.' She reckoned that the farther she was away from the visitor, the better it would be for her.

'Why don't you let me go there and bring them down while you take a rest?' Tori suggested with concern, but Lalonpe insisted. He helped her back down to *Iya* Mojoyin and Moladun. Lalonpe asked the housekeeper to take Moladun back to the house and settle her down in the front room.

'Listen, and listen very well mama,' Lalonpe began the moment she was sure the housekeeper was out of sight. 'I am not sure whether I am awake or dreaming.' Lalonpe stopped to be sure *Iya* Mojoyin was following. 'Are you listening mama?'

'My ears are with you, my daughter, and I can assure you that you are very awake and not in slumber,' *Iya* Mojoyin replied, and Lalonpe told her what she had just seen.

'Remember, we travelled to Egbejoda and we met Morilewa's family,' replied *Iya* Mojoyin. 'They confirmed his death at Igbodudu.'

'Yes, I remember what we were told. But the man I saw inside my old home, and who also calls himself Morilewa, was the man I met and knew by that name, and *Baba* Fatunbi was witness to our union. But how could the man who was supposed to have been dead suddenly appear in the last place I saw him seventeen years ago? That is what I want to know. Lightning doesn't strike the same spot twice. It is you elders who say something must be amiss if a mosquito returns to bite the same spot on the same night.'

'Lalonpe, I think you need a good rest,' Mojoyin suggested. 'Your imagination might be playing tricks on you.'

'I don't need a rest. What I need is an answer to a question. That man in my old house, the man I strongly believe to be Morilewa, has the answer.'

'What makes you think he is Morilewa? Maybe he just looks like him. There are two copies of every person in this world.'

'I do not think, I am sure. The housekeeper confirmed that the man introduced himself as Morilewa, and said he had come to see Ojo.'

'And Ojo did not mention anything about this?'

'No he did not, and you were well aware of my purpose in Oluweri at this particular time.'

'That is very strange indeed,' *Iya* Mojoyin agreed, in the absence of any other credible explanation.

'Now you can understand my concern when I said I am not sure whether I am awake or dreaming.'

'There must have been a mix-up somewhere. There is only one way to sort it out, and that is to go across to the house and confront him. There is no harm in confronting him for clarification.'

'Mama, what if it is Morilewa's ghost?' Lalonpe was shaking with fear.

'I can assure you that if it is the ghost of Morilewa, then he will have disappeared by the time we get there. Anyway, ghosts are no longer strangers to me. Most of my friends are now among them, and I have been closer to them in recent years. We are like housemates.'

Adeyanju had moved from his position by the window and was sitting on a mat laid for him by the housekeeper in the corridor of the house when Lalonpe returned with *Iya* Mojoyin. She waited outside while *Iya* Mojoyin entered the house to confront Adeyanju.

'Sorry to disturb you, but I only came around to have a look at my grandson's house. Then the housekeeper told me he has a lodger in. He told me your name is Morilewa.'

'That is right. That is my name,' Adeyanju replied.

'The Morilewa from the Omomose compound in Egbejoda?'

'Yes, the same Morilewa.' This time Adeyanju replied cautiously. He reckoned the old woman must have known something before checking his identity, and hoped her question was not leading to something he was not prepared for.

'What we heard was that you were responsible for the death of the priest and that you were mentally ill during your trial, then you died while receiving treatment at Igbodudu,' said *Iya* Mojoyin.

329

'But I am here now. That should be enough to tell you that I am not dead.'

'I made enquiries with your family at Egbejoda and they confirmed your death,' Lalonpe said as she stepped into the house. A silence descended on the corridor as Adeyanju struggled with the sight of Lalonpe, having not expected to see her. The astonishment on his face was mirrored by the disbelief in hers. The silence continued as something Adeyanju would later recognise as a nostalgic pining, welled up within him.

'Well, I am convinced you are not a wandering ghost. Though that does not add light to this inexplicable event,' *Iya* Mojoyin said, choosing to break the silence before she too was shaken by the tension.

'My family were bound to secrecy,' Adeyanju said, returning to the conversation. 'And they still are. Even if you go there now, they will still tell you the same story.'

'Even a toddler does not need to be told that some explanation is in order. That is what mama is asking you to do,' Lalonpe demanded unpleasantly.

'I was wrongly accused of being involved in the death of the diviner. Apparently, somebody who was aware of my closeness with *Baba* Fatunbi used my identity to lure the diviner into the old shrine where he was later found dead. Many witnesses claimed they were there, when a messenger came on my behalf to *Baba* Fatunbi. They swore the priest had retreated to the old shrine supposedly to meet me. I did not have a leg to stand upon because unfortunately, I was not at home when the *ilaris* [civil enforcers] came from the palace at Ode-Ijowa. They laid siege to my family compound at Egbejoda, and upon my return, I was taken to Ode-Ijowa for questioning. I was charged and found guilty for the death of the priest. I was sentenced to twenty-five years of labour. But I never stepped into any of the king's farms. I was just fortunate that I did not pay the ultimate price for a crime I did not commit.'

'So what happened afterwards? I mean how did you manage to clear yourself and gain your freedom?'

'I am not supposed to tell you this, but between the three of us and the silent walls, I escaped on transit between Ode-Ijowa and wherever I was being taken to serve my sentence,' Adeyanju replied.

'How then did you get to Igbodudu, and how come your family confirmed your death?'

'Can you imagine how embarrassing it would have been to the *Onijowa* and the chiefs if it became public that such a high profile convict had managed to escape on the way to the king's farm? I was declared insane, and an *alanganran* [deranged person] was taken to Igbodudu under my name. I was pronounced dead upon the passing of the *alanganran*. The head keeper at Igbodudu who knew about the *alanganran* was led to believe that I was serving my term in one of king's farms and the *alanganran's* purpose was to prevent anyone attempting another rescue. My family had no choice but to confirm the death story, as it was the price for my freedom. Look at me. Do I look like somebody who had received treatment in Igbodudu, or spent even a month on the king's farm?'

Lalonpe scanned Adeyanju from head to toe. 'No you don't,' she said. 'Where have you been all these years then?'

'It took almost a year of living under another name in Igisogba before my wife could join me.'

'What name is that?'

'In Igisogba I am known as Ekisola. Now I hope I have cleared up the mystery for you.'

'Yes, sort of. But I still cannot believe that I am not dreaming. To think that for years I thought you were dead, only to find that you have been a free man all along.'

'Yes, quite unbelievable.' Adeyanju was genuinely excited to be seeing Lalonpe for the first time after so many years. 'You are the last person I expect to stumble upon here,' he lied. Although he had expected to meet Lalonpe again, and had prepared his story for the meeting, he was surprised that she was not expecting him and knew nothing about Ojo's visit to Ode-Ijowa.

'And you are the last person I expected to see alive,' Lalonpe replied. 'Even while in hiding in Igisogba, I indirectly contracted people finders and expended some of my meagre resources to look for you within and around occupied Oluweri, but there was no sign of you.'

'That is true, I did not return to Oluweri. We were in Gbajumo when the war started, and it was in Gbajumo that I was taken captive and separated from Ojo. I have been living in Gbajumo since after the war.'

'If you had returned to Oluweri, maybe they would have found you. Despite the fact that your house has been destroyed and most of the land taken over by Ago-Oyinbo, I continued to employ men to look for you around Oluweri until...'

'Until when?'

'Until I risked marrying another wife, who before the turn of the year gave birth to a son. Soon after, my first wife conceived and gave birth to twins. Since then my wives have not stop bearing children,' Adeyanju replied.

'I am happy that you were able to get beyond that,'

Lalonpe replied without any hint of bitterness. 'So what brought you to Oluweri at this time, and to this particular place?'

'To be honest with you, I did not come here on my own account. My presence in Oluweri and in this particular place is because I am on an important errand. But it has turned out to be a double blessing.' Adeyanju continued with his well-rehearsed story.

'What errand?' Lalonpe asked, but Tori interupted before Adeyanju could reply. It was getting dark inside, so he lit an oil lamp and brought it into the room.

'Four days ago, the *Balogun* of Ijowa came down to Igisogba on behalf of the palace,' Adeyanju continued after the housekeeper had left. 'He came with an offer which he said could guarantee a royal pardon and a safe return to my family home in Egbejoda. The *Balogun* assured me that the *Aremo-Oba* would grant me a royal pardon, and all the chiefs would unite in ensuring that I have a peaceful return to my family compound in Egbejoda, if I can travel down here, and to this house to meet a certain person called Ojo Kekewura. Now I think telling me your reason for being here will also be in order.'

'My presence here at this particular time and place, has absolutely nothing to do with the possibility of meeting you here, either living or as a wandering ghost,' Lalonpe replied. 'I am here because my son Ojo lives here now. He rebuilt the house about four years ago. That is why I am here.'

'I remember that your late husband's name was Iyanda. But tell me, is your son Ojo Kekewura?'

'Yes. Kekewura is the family name,' Lalonpe replied. 'My late husband was Iyanda Kekewura.'

'I don't know if I heard you right, but I believe you said something about rebuilding this house.'

'Yes.'

'You mean we are standing inside the same house that was destroyed during the war?'

'That is what I mean. Ojo rebuilt it just over three seasons ago.'

'What an amazing coincidence!' Adeyanju was sincerely surprised and at the same time excited. His hope of locating the spot where he had left the precious beads and stones took a sudden leap. 'I had never once linked the name to the little Ojo I knew, or this place to be the site of your old house.'

'What is going on between Ojo and the Ijowa chiefs?' said Lalonpe. She was petrified. The implications of her son being involved with Ode-Ijowa at such a high level and at this sensitive time could be tragic.

'I don't know,' Adeyanju replied. 'Only Ojo himself can explain what is going on. All the *Balogun* said was that I should come back with evidence, a sort of *aroko* [coded message] as proof that I actually met and talked to Ojo.'

'Ojo is at present out of Oluweri, but I am sure he will be back soon. He cannot be away for too long because he is in charge of Ago-Oyinbo while Fadahunse is away.'

'The *omo'nkere* [housekeeper] said he should back in a couple of days. I have no choice but to wait for him to return.'

Iya Mojoyin excused herself to rest and left Adeyanju and Lalonpe to discuss the missed years and their chance reunion, though few words were exchanged between the two. For Adeyanju's part, there was only so much he could say about his 'life' as Morilewa – he felt there was more security in asking Lalonpe's affairs. Lalonpe did most of the speaking, briefly detailing her life, but leaving out Bogunde and the *ejigbaileke*.

Darkness had completely set in when Lalonpe eventually offered to send the housekeeper down with something Adeyanju to eat, thus ending their conversation. She bade him goodnight and left, leaving Adeyanju deflated but immensely relieved that so far everything was going as he had intended, and better.

CHAPTER 15

Ojo did not stop at Oko-Oba but continued through the night towards Oluweri. As it grew darker and quieter, it was becoming impossible for the *owuyes* to follow him undetected. They had to suspend their mission, but not before they were certain that Ojo was on the way back to Oluweri.

They spent the night at a small settlement on the outskirts of Oko-Oba, but Ojo rode through the night and arrived at Oluweri just before dawn. The moment he rode into the outer perimeter he was intercepted by Tori, who had kept vigil in front of the house. He had been specifically instructed by Lalonpe to ensure that Ojo saw her before he reached the house or saw the visitor.

'There is a visitor waiting for you in the house,' Tori said as he helped Ojo to unmount from the horse. 'He arrived yesterday. He says his name is Morilewa and he has travelled down all the way from Igisogba to see you.'

'Did you say Morilewa?' Ojo was visibly shocked, and

despite the semi-darkness of the breaking dawn, Tori could not help but notice that his reaction matched his mother's when she had heard the name of the visitor.

'Yes, that is what he called himself,' Tori replied. 'Your mother also arrived yesterday. She travelled down with *Iya* Mojoyin and a young maiden. She stumbled upon the visitor. They seem to know each and they spent a long time talking.'

'Yes I know. I stopped at Gbajumo on my way and was told she had left for Oluweri.' Ojo spoke as calmly as he could, but Tori could sense that he was suppressing his excitement. 'Take my horse into Fadahunse's yard while I go and see mama and the visitor,' Ojo said, handing the reins to Tori.

'Your mother is not there with the visitor. She initially planned to sleep in the house, but changed her mind after meeting him.'

'Where is she now?'

'She retired with her companions to her friend's house, but left strict instructions that you must see her before going to meet the visitor.'

'You go there and tell her that I am back,' Ojo said, taking the horse back from Tori. 'Tell her I will be waiting inside Fadahunse's yard.' Ojo follow the path to the inner perimeter of Ago-Oyinbo while Tori went to fetch Lalonpe.

Ojo waited anxiously in front of Wontsay's house. 'What is going on?' Lalonpe asked as soon as she arrived. 'You knew Morilewa was alive all this time and you kept it from me!'

'What brought you to Oluweri in the first place?' Ojo asked, sitting at a bench outside the house and gesturing to his mother to join him. 'You normally send a message to me before coming.' He had been suspicious of his mother's unannounced presence in Oluweri when Tori told him she had arrived with a maiden.

'When two trees fall upon each other, the logical way to sort it out is to first remove the one at the top,' Lalonpe replied. 'At present the issue of Morilewa is the tree on top. We will talk about my original purpose in Oluweri later.'

'What exactly do you want to know, *mama*?'

'It is not about what I want to know. It is about you telling me everything that is going on. So I want you to tell me everything, as I will not be content with you just providing answers to my questions.'

'It was less than a month ago when I learnt from *Baba* Olubi that *Baba* Morilewa could be alive, but I did not want to raise your hopes until I was sure,' Ojo began. By this time the dawn had broken to the point where the veins of the palm trees were visible, and the sky had cleared of early morning dew. I told *Baba* Olubi that *Baba* Morilewa was my late father's trading partner and had been very supportive of the family after my father's death, but I did not mention anything about Bogunde. *Baba* Olubi assured me that *Baba* Morilewa never set foot in Igbodudu, and could still be alive and serving time on one of the king's farms. It was his idea that we could negotiate for the freedom of *Baba* Morilewa.' Ojo went on to tell his mother about his journey to the palace at Ode-Ijowa and the meeting with the *Aremo-Oba* and *Balogun*. We only went to the palace about fourteen days ago. The *Aremo-Oba* said he would need time to lobby the Ogbonis to agree to *Baba* Morilewa's freedom. I never expected him to be free this soon.'

Ojo knew there would be many questions for him to

answer, and his mother was only waiting for him to say all he wanted to share with her before demanding what she wanted to know.

'Upon what did you negotiate Morilewa's freedom?' Lalonpe asked slowly and quietly. 'What did you promise the *Aremo-Oba* in return for this favour?'

'I am bound by an oath of secrecy not to let this matter be known beyond those directly involved.'

'The world has hidden you from me for so long. You will not hide your world from me. I am not an outsider in this affair, unless you are disowning me as your mother.'

Lalonpe was invoking the sacred maternal sentiment to get an answer. Ojo was certain his mother would not relent in the pressure she was putting on him to disclose everything, so it would be waste of time to continue attempting to deny her.

'We promised to disclose vital information about the Akete security apparatus in Oluweri, that would enable Ijowa to reclaim the occupied territory with minimum casualties,' he told his mother plainly, as though there were nothing incredulous about what he had just said.

Lalonpe paused for a second and stared at her son. She felt disbelief well up within her, but the Morilewa's return from the dead was all the proof she needed that Ojo was involved in such a grand scheme. Disbelief was soon replaced by concern.

'What about your future in liberated Oluweri? What are you going to do about that?' It was a question Ojo had been anticipating.

'*Mama*, I told you we made two demands. The second is that Ago-Oyinbo remains as it is.'

'Don't play dumb with me son. I know you and your

fellow planners cannot overlook the fact that after a successful campaign, your future in liberated Oluweri and Ago-Oyinbo will be at the mercy of the prince and the Ijowa chiefs. Unless you are the biggest fool of your generation, which I am sure you are not, you must have something up your sleeve to safeguard you against that risk. What are you going to do if the *Aremo-Oba* refuses to honour the agreement?'

'*Mama*, I am not taking any risks. On the contrary, I am using the only resources I have for now to safeguard my future in Oluweri. Going to Ode-Ijowa and negotiating was an opportunity that should not be wasted. What I know, and what I shared with *Baba* Olubi, will not remain a secret forever. It might be later rather than sooner, but the prince and the Ijowa chiefs will eventually learn what I have to tell them and consequently reclaim Oluweri. I stand a better chance in liberated Oluweri by switching to the other side.'

Ojo was relieved to see that his mother seemed to be growing content with his reasoning.

'You have talked with *Baba* Morilewa. What did he say about all this?' he asked.

'He also said he never stepped into Igbodudu, but escaped on the way to the labour farm. He truly does not in any way look like somebody who has just been released from any form of incarceration.'

'Have you told him about Bogunde?'

'No I have not. At least not yet. My priority is to know exactly why he is here in the first place. I want know exactly what is going on before revealing that to him.'

'What about the beads? Did he mention anything about them?'

'No he did not. I have no doubt that his primary reason for being here is what you have just told me, and he was not in the least expecting to meet either of us here.'

'What should I tell him if he asked about them?'

'He told you the beads were meant to be a surprise gift for me, didn't he?'

'Yes he did.'

'Then tell him exactly how it is, that you eventually passed them on to me as intended.'

'What about the missing two? Do you think he will not notice them?'

'You don't need to worry yourself about that. If he wants them back, he will have to come to me first, and if he has any queries, they will be directed to me.'

The sun was high overhead, but Adeyanju was still asleep when Lalonpe arrived with Ojo at the old house.

'I am not alone in this scheme, and there is a strict limit to what I am permitted to disclose to you in this meeting,' Ojo told Adeyanju after the initial excitement of the reunion. 'My associates have access to certain information that the *Aremo-Oba* and Ijowa chiefs need desperately, and are willing to negotiate with the palace for it. I volunteered to be the messenger on the condition that your freedom is included in the negotiations. Your freedom is just the first step towards a larger long-term agreement, but that is outside what I am permitted to disclose to you. We promised to proceed with our side of the agreement the moment you are granted a royal pardon, and your freedom is made public. The *Aremo-Oba* said he would need time to consult the Ogbonis and persuade them to support the decision.'

'The *Balogun* told me that the matter had already been discussed with the *Oluwo* [occult leader]' said Adeyanju. 'He has no objection to my freedom, but he has a crucial reservation concerning the process. He cautioned that only the king can grant a royal pardon, hence he will only support the action if the pardon is decreed by a crowned king. He said that your associates, whom he believed to be my friends, will understand why the position of Ogbonis leaves the continuation of the agreement depending on their willingness to wait until the prince is crowned before my freedom is officially granted. So the chiefs sent the *Balogun* to persuade me to come down here as proof that your offer has been accepted in principle by all concerned.'

'*Baba*, are you suggesting that I tell my associates to carry on with the rest of the agreement without waiting for your pardon to be made public and official? You will agree with me that you are truly free only when it is possible for you to return to your family home in Egbejoda.'

'Yes I know that. You said my freedom was just part of a long-term agreement with the prince. I don't know the duration and extent of your agreement, but I am sure that the arrangement concerning the coronation of the *Aremo* as the next *Onijowa* is a top priority to the chiefs and all those concerned at the palace in Ode-Ijowa. For over fifteen years I have been in exile, but a discreet one. I can endure a few more weeks, or even months.'

'Well, if you are comfortable with that arrangement, I will advise my associates to proceed to the next stage of our agreement.'

'I must say that I am very moved by this gesture,' Adeyanju said after Ojo had finished. 'Very few people would go to the lengths you have for their loved ones.'

Despite the fact that he was a first-hand witness to all Ojo said, and had heard it before at the palace, he was even more touched to hear it from Ojo. 'But there is one question which is very important, and I will implore you to tell me exactly what the answer is.'

'What is it?'

'I don't know the detail of your negotiations with the palace at a Ode-Ijowa, but I am going to ask you. My question however is, are you sure your associates can deliver what you promised the *Aremo-Oba* and Ijowa chiefs? I am seeking this confirmation because things could be worse not only for me, but also for my family at home in Egbejoda, if you fail to honour the agreement. The last thing I want now is to be on the wrong side of the *Aremo-Oba* who will soon become the *Onijowa.*'

'Yes, we can deliver,' Ojo replied without hesitation. 'Tell the *Balogun* that the friends of Morilewa will accept this meeting as a temporary alternative to the royal pardon and sufficient proof of the palace's willingness to engage with us. Tell him that the friends of Morilewa will do what is expected within the next twelve days.'

'The *Balogun* demanded that I must return with a message that will be proof of this meeting.'

'You have only one word to say to the *Balogun*, and he will be assured that you have made the journey and meet the right person.'

'What word?'

'*Akerekoro.*'

'Just that?'

'Yes just that, and your part of the task is over.'

'You people sitting before me are not friends but family of a special kind,' he said to Lalonpe. 'You are family made by destiny. How I wish our short relationship had turned out the way we had hoped.' Adeyanju sincerely meant it. If he were not a prince, or better still the name of Morilewa was not connected with the death of the priest, he would have told Lalonpe and Ojo the whole truth about himself. 'Anyway, enough of the past, let us talk about the present.'

'Yes, but the present I want to talk to you about must take us back to the past. Our past.'

'Our past?' Adeyanju asked.

'Yes indeed. Our past. Yours and mine,' Lalonpe replied. 'You left me in a certain condition for nine months. You left me in a condition which resulted in the purpose which you strongly desired. I believe you understand what I am saying.'

'Are you saying you have a child by me?'

'Yes, in the middle of the war I had a son for you,' Lalonpe replied with pride.

'You were pregnant and you did not tell me?' Adeyanju was visible shocked and could hardly speak.

'I did not know I was pregnant. Remember, the war started a week after your last visit. I travelled to the Omomose compound in Egbejoda and confirmed that the man who was supposed to be the father of my child was being held for the murder of the diviner. How were we to know that you were only hiding - that you were out there alive?'

'But why did you keep that from me last night?'

'Because I wanted to be sure that you are the real Morilewa, and not a ghost. Besides, this meeting was so sudden, and I did not know if you were the same man. It was not until Ojo explained how you came to be here to me that I felt it safe to speak to you.'

What was implied was clear to Adeyanju. Whilst he knew her doubt of Morilewa's innocence had been slight, it was doubt nonetheless. Doubt, which had not been ameliorated by the news that he had spent most of their time apart as a fugitive.

She could not readily believe his story. Whilst he wished she took him at his word that he (Morilewa) did not kill the Baba Fatunbi, it was difficult to trust a fugitive. However, if the decision makers at Ode-Ijowa truly did believe he was guilty, they would have hunted him in years ago and would not have gone through extreme lengths to cover-up his escape. Nor would they so quickly promise to release him based on the promises of Ojo and Olubi. Now that Ojo had corroborated his story, only now was Lalonpe satisfied that Morilewa was still a man Bogunde could be proud to call his father. Before that certainty, she did not want him to have any claim to a son she would be wary to associate with him.

'Where is the boy now?', asked Adeyanju. 'I mean, the man? It is almost seventeen years. I must see him! I have to take him back with me.'

'His name is Bogunde. He lives with me in Gbajumo, but he is presently on a hunting expedition with his friends.'

'When will he be back?'

'They may be away for ten days. They have been gone for five days now, so they are expected back in about four to five days' time.'

There was nothing Adeyanju would have wished for more at that moment than to meet a son that he had never known existed until now. The result of his ritual of truth! If he could have had it his way, he would there and then have proceeded to Gbajumo and waited for Bogunde, regardless of consequences, and revealed his identity to his son the moment he was on friendly ground in Gbajumo, but he knew it was not that simple. There were many issues that had to be resolved along with it. The first and most important was to do with the fact that Bogunde, as his eldest son, should by rights be the next in line to the throne after him.

Then suddenly everything became crystal clear to him. According to the diviner, the exact words of the oracle were that he had left something that belonged to the palace. He had automatically assumed it must be the beads. How was he to know that the oracle was referring to an heir to the royal family? What else could belong to the palace more than a child from his own loins? Yes, the necklace also belonged to the palace, but if found they would eventually be handed over to the next *Aremo-Oba*, a position which, given what he now knew, if right was done according to tradition, would be occupied by Bogunde in the very near future. Beads can be replaced, but an heir apparent cannot be substituted except in the event of death.

Adeyanju was convinced that his relationship with Bogunde had strongly influenced Ojo's decision to include Morilewa's freedom in the agreement. It was the quest to free the father of his younger brother that had compelled him to shift sides and put his future in Oluweri at risk.

'How I wish I had time to go to Gbajumo immediately and wait for him to return from hunting, but the *Balogun* is waiting for me at Igisogba,' said Adeyanju. 'Anyway, I would prefer to be a free man before meeting my son for the first time. I will come down to Gbajumo for a worthy reunion the moment all this is over.'

'There will be plenty of time for a proper introduction

and reunion after all this is over,' Lalonpe agreed. 'I will leave you two alone while I go and see to your breakfast.' she advised as she left the room.

Ojo had envisaged that upon gaining his freedom, there was a high possibility that Morilewa would enquire about the beads. But after further reminiscences about the past and the events that led to their reunion, he had not mentioned them, and Ojo was beginning to wonder if *Baba* Morilewa even remembered them. Adeyanju on his part had strategically refrained from asking Lalonpe about the beads before checking with Ojo. His reasoning was that if he had retrieved the beads, he must have passed them on to his mother. He had deliberately held back on the subject in order to back up the story that he would never have been in Oluweri but for the sequence of events triggered by Ojo's visit to the palace. After the revelation about Bogunde, the quest for the beads became secondary, but he saw no harm in asking about them anyway. However he had to find a way of getting round to the subject without appearing to be too interested in the beads.

He was just about to bring them up when Tori interrupted with their breakfast.

'Do you remember the last time I came to your house, just before the war started?' Adeyanju asked after they had finished breakfast.

'Yes, I remember,' Ojo replied, anticipating Adeyanju's line of enquiry.

'We hid a sack together in your mother's backyard. Do you remember?'

'You mean the one you said contained a surprise present for my mother?'

'Yes. But the next morning I had to leave in haste and

forgot to either retrieve it or tell your mother about it. I did not even remember about it until I got home. I came back here shortly before the war to retrieve it, but it was not there. I thought maybe you had taken it and given it to your mother.'

'Yes, I took it and then passed it on to mama eventually. She did not know anything about the beads until our reunion four years ago. I did not give them to her before the war started as I did not want to spoil the surprise. I know you would prefer to present them to her yourself, so I held onto them with the intention of giving them to you on your next visit.'

'They were never meant for your mother,' Adeyanju said regretfully. 'They were a charm of protection against misfortune.' He began the story he had prepared since returning to the palace and realised he had forgotten the beads. 'There was slight damage to the stringing, and my plan was to stop at Inukan and hand them in for repair on my return journey to Egbejoda. I had to keep them away from your mother because they would lose their potency if handled by a woman. I decided to hide them in your backyard and retrieve them later, but you caught me in the act. That is why I said they were a surprise present for your mother.'

'But my mother has already been in contact with the beads. Does that mean they are no longer potent?'

'That I will have to find out. My problem began the moment I disengaged from those neckbeads. I strongly believe that there was more to my indictment over the death of the priest than met the eye. So as soon as I settled down in Igisogba, I consulted an *ifa* priest for divination in order to solve the mystery. The oracle revealed that it is due to the beads I misplaced. The deities demand that the beads are recovered before all my problems due to the death of the priest, can be over.'

'Come to think of it, contrary to your experience, my contact with the beads has always been associated with misfortune,' said Ojo. 'I only held on to them because of my hope for this kind of reunion.'

'Misfortune? How do you mean?'

'Yes. It started with the war and my separation from my mother. This house was burnt down and I had to search through the rubble years later when I came to retrieve it. My imprisonment on Akala Island started on the night I returned with the beads to Eti-Osa. The house where I left it was burnt down before I returned from Akala, and I again had to search through the rubble to retrieve it. That was when I became suspicious and decide to keep it away from me. I kept it in the forest until my reunion with mama about three years ago.'

'So the beads are with your mother now?'

'Yes, but I insisted that she must not keep them close to her.'

Later, Adeyanju asked Lalonpe about the beads and the latter confirmed her son's account. She told Adeyanju that they were being kept safe somewhere in Gbajumo.

Ojo urged Adeyanju to stay another night in Oluweri, but he declined. He knew he had already pushed his good fortune by coming to Lower-Oluweri and sleeping overnight inside Ago-Oyinbo. He considered that an unavoidable risk, but he could not afford to stay longer than necessary in Oluweri. For one thing he would be as good as gone if just one of the Akete royal guards or administrative staff of *Oba* Lagbade in Oluweri recognised him. Secondly, his presence in Oluweri at this sensitive time could be misread by his subjects as secretly pursuing the offer of Oluweri for Odinjo. Such a misconception would throw the palace into disarray and could trigger unpredictable action from the people of Odinjo.

'I probably should not stay longer than necessary because *Balogun* is waiting for me in Igisogba for the feedback,' Adeyanju said regretfully. 'The quicker I return to him with the feedback the better for everybody. Like your mother rightly said, there will be plenty of time for a proper reunion when my pardon and freedom are official.' Adeyanju left Oluweri that evening saying he would come down to Gbajumo as soon as his royal pardon had been made public.

After he had seen Adeyanju off, Ojo returned to the house where his mother, *Iya* Mojoyin and of course Moladun, were waiting and ready to address their original mission in Oluweri. With a little persuasion Ojo yielded to his mother's wish, but made her understand that he would not be able to travel to Gbajumo to meet Moladun's parents for about three weeks, when he would have been done with the issue at hand.

'Three weeks is too long,' said his mother. 'The issue at hand does not prevent you from making a brief visit to your future in-laws and personally registering your intention to marry their daughter. Unless there is more to your arrangement with the *Aremo-Oba* than you have revealed to me.' Ojo knew his mother would not let him off until she had achieved a certain level of compliance. He reluctantly agreed to make the visit.

'I will come down for a brief introduction, but I have a

very important meeting to attend in Oko-Oba tomorrow,' he said. 'I will not be able to come down to Gbajumo for about six days.'

'That is fair enough,' Lalonpe conceded. 'But make sure you keep the date, as I will need to make your future in-laws aware you are coming.'

Having achieved the purpose of their visit to their satisfaction, Lalonpe and company left Oluweri for Gbajumo the day after Adeyanju left.

Lalonpe returned to Gbajumo to find Bogunde at home due to his injury. He was still unable to stand or walk on his own without support. Their neighbour Gbekeyide, who had been tending to the injury, was with him when Lalonpe returned from Oluweri.

'What happened to you?' said Lalonpe, petrified. Bogunde explained how it happened.

'We were fortunate to find a travelling trader who was stopping in one of the farmhouses on the edge of Olokoto,' he said. 'He helped to remove the bamboo splinters from my leg and sheltered us for the night. The man was so kind that he gave us more than enough cowries to hire a horse to bring me back to Gbajumo.'

'That is very generous of him. I wonder if he could be traced so that I can thank him,' Lalonpe said. 'Did he mention anything about his origin? I mean where he lives?'

'No, he did not, but his name is Morilewa.'

'Did you say Morilewa?' Lalonpe asked.

'That is the name he told us to mention in case anybody question our presence in the farmhouse he rented.'

'Really?' Lalonpe was genuinely surprised. What a coincidence, she thought. 'Can you describe this man? The name sounds very familiar,' she said, and Bogunde did not have to go into the details before Lalonpe was sure that the person they had met was Bogunde's father.

'The man who helped you was actually coming all the way from Igisogba to see Ojo,' Lalonpe told Bogunde after Gbekeyide has left.

'Did you say he came down from Igisogba?'

'Yes, purposely to see your brother,' Lalonpe replied.

'That is strange,'

'What is strange about it?'

'Never mind, it just something that crossed my mind.'

'You just tell me what is strange, and leave me to decide whether to mind it or not.' Lalonpe was sure that her son was on to something.

'Nothing in particular, except that I have seen him earlier by the riverside in the forest between Inukan and Olokoto. That is clearly off the route of somebody coming from Igisogba. He must have been coming from an Ijowa village on the upper side of the Awoyaya, but definitely not from the north or any of the routes to Igisogba.'

'He is a travelling trader, and the route he chooses could be influenced by commercial considerations,' Lalonpe replied.

'I cannot say I have met him, but I have a feeling I have seen him somewhere before.'

'There are two copies of every person in this world, so it is possible you might have come across somebody who resembled him in the past.'

Lalonpe was so excited about the unexpected reunion and the associated coincidence that it took a great effort to resist the impulse to disclose the essential facts about the kind stranger to Bogunde. Two days later she was again unable to resist the temptation to question Bogunde on the incident that had led to his injury and the events that followed.

'The man that helped you and Kotun at Gbajumo. Did you have a good look at him?'

'Yes of course,' Bogunde replied from his stool in the front room, where they sat that afternoon.

'Would you recognise him again?'

'Why are you asking?' Bogunde, replied with a raised eyebrow. He had been curious about his mother's demeanour since she returned from Oluweri. Although he did not consider his mother to be stricter than an average mother, since returning from Oluweri she been livelier and somehow unusually over excited over almost everything. She tended to take every opportunity to lead discussion to his accident, which always eventually ended with the man who had helped him at Olokoto. In fact she seemed to be more interested in talking about the man than his injury.

'Just answer my question. Will you recognise him again if you see him?'

'It depends, mama.'

'On what?'

'It depends on how he dresses,' Bogunde replied. 'When I saw him earlier that evening? He was wearing noble attire and was with another man who looked like a diviner. The diviner handed him a *buba* and *sokoto*, which I saw him change into. For some reason which I cannot put my finger on, he seemed familiar to me before he changed his clothes.'

Adeyanju's return journey to Ode-Ijowa was uneventful. It was already dark and raining when he arrived at the farmhouse on the edge of Olokoto. He was so tired that he wished he could just lie down and sleep, but he was also very hungry. This was one moment when he appreciated the luxury of being a prince. He made a fire inside the house and roasted some banana, which he ate with palm oil and soon fell asleep.

The next dawn, he set off on the last leg of his journey as Morilewa. He was met by Fakorede, who was waiting for him at the place by the riverside where they had parted four days earlier. The priest, who had since the prince's departure been shuttling between Inukan and the agreed spot on a daily basis, was very relieved to see him. He had with him all the attire and paraphernalia that would transform Adeyanju from an ordinary townsman back into a crown prince.

The priest was eager to learn of the outcome of the prince's journey, but cautious enough to know that it would be grossly improper to start such a sensitive discussion in a place where they could be overheard. Even when they returned to Inukan he considered it unethical to probe, but waited until Adeyanju was ready to talk about it.

It was already dark when they arrived at Inukan. Adeyanju did not stop at the priest's place but went directly to the house that had been made ready within the *Baale's* compound in anticipation of his arrival. He bade the priest goodnight without saying anything. The priest was not offended by the prince's silence. He acknowledged that the prince must be tired, and resigned himself to the fact that he would have to curtail his excitement till next morning. Then he certainly would not be guilty of being disrespectful by asking, and the burden would be on the prince to make it clear whether he wished to share or disclose anything about the outcome of the journey.

The next morning, after he had washed, Adeyanju told the *Baale* that he would like to have his meal in private, but sent for the priest to join him for breakfast in the *Baale's* compound.

'The oracle is right,' Adeyanju told the priest. 'Not only do I now know where item the oracle was talking about is, but I was reunited with the person I left it with. To cap it all, by virtue of my journey to Oluweri, I came across certain information which confirms that we are heading in the right direction and the prospect of reclaiming Oluweri could not be brighter.'

'I am very pleased to hear that. All you now need to do is to return the item to its rightful place in the palace, and the ritual will be concluded and accepted by the gods.'

'I said I know where it is, not that I have recovered it.'

'Why?'

'That is a bit complicated. It will take some time before I can return the item to Ode-Ijowa.'

'But knowing where it is not enough. The oracle clearly indicated that the item must be returned to the palace before the ritual can be concluded and accepted by the deities.'

'The gods demanded that I know the truth upon which I set about performing the ritual. Just three days ago at Oluweri, I learnt something concerning the purpose for which I set about the ritual of truth seventeen years ago. That is the truth that the oracle was talking about, but which I never imagined existed.'

'It is good that you learnt a truth which you never knew existed before. But have you fulfilled the obligations and responsibilities attached to the ritual?'

'That is the complicated part. The truth ends with

355

finding the item, but fulfilling those responsibilities begins with returning the item to the palace. Unfortunately, I don't think I will be able to bring the item to the palace until Oluweri has been reclaimed.'

'*Aremo* Adeyanju, it is essential that you fulfill those responsibilities. The oracle will not prescribe a condition unless it is vital for achieving a specific purpose. I don't know what you learnt on your journey to Oluweri that gave you the assurance that you are on the right path towards reclaiming it, but if the end plan still involves armed confrontation with the Akete warriors, I strongly advise against it, because it will end in disaster.' With these words of warning, Fakorede departed.

Adeyanju returned to the palace and informed the chiefs that he had successfully completed the ritual demanded by the gods. The *Balogun* then updated him on the issue of finding Morilewa.

'I told the elders of the Omomose family that the decision to grant a royal pardon was part of the last wishes of the departed king. I told them that the late *Onijowa's* wish was that all his last words be executed before the enthronement of a new king. They admit having knowledge of Morilewa's present abode and promised to present him the moment his freedom is made public.'

'The friends of Morilewa are not expecting a decision before the Ogboni convergence began. But we are not going to just wait,' Adeyanju said, and then turned to the *Balogun*. 'I want you to make our warriors ready to launch an attack within three days of receiving the arms they promised.'

So far, everything had been going according to Adeyanju's plans. He had been able to convince Ojo about the customary technicalities attached to the freedom of Morilewa. The so-called friends of Morilewa would not be expecting any developments about Morilewa's freedom until after a new king had been installed. There was still about sixteen days before the bi-annual convergence of the Ogboni fraternity. Although, the occult meeting would last for another sixteen days, the chiefs would expect Morilewa's freedom to be announced midway into the convergence. Ojo gave his word that his associates would deliver within the next ten days. Hopefully, the weapons would have been delivered even before the Ogboni convergence began. Then it would be safe to make a royal pronouncement on Morilewa's freedom.

CHAPTER 16

The sudden appearance of Morilewa made it imperative that Ojo should set off for Oko-Oba immediately and inform Olubi of the development, so as soon as he had seen his mother off, he returned to Ago-Oyinbo, mounted his horse and departed. He was oblivious of the *owuyes*, who were following at a discreet distance on two horses. Ojo arrived at Olubi's house before sundown, and the *owuyes* assumed he had reached his destination.

It was the sixteenth day after their meeting with the Aremo-Oba. Ojo updated Olubi on the latest developments the moment they were alone. Although Olubi was waiting for this development, it had come much earlier than anticipated and in quite an unexpected way. That night, after they had been through the details of their next action, Bopo interrupted to inform them that some men, believed to have followed Ojo into Oko-Oba, were discreetly enquiring about him and his purpose in the village.

'Have you discovered the reason?' Olubi asked.

'We have not taken any action yet. They do not know that they have become the hunted and it seems better to keep it that way until we consulted you,' Bopo replied.

Olubi stroked his chin for a moment then turned to Ojo.

'My immediate thought is that they were acting on the instructions of Ologundudu, but we will soon find out,' he said with a sinister half smile.

The *owuye* kept vigil around Olubi's house, partly hoping that Ojo had reached his destination, and partly anticipating further travelling the next day.

The next morning, they watched Ojo as he left the compound and began tending to his horse. They watched discreetly from a distance as he fed and groomed the horse and cleaned her hooves. The *owuye* were sure he was preparing to leave Oko-Oba but, to their horror, Ojo suddenly slumped to the ground by his horse. The housekeeper ran out of the compound, in panic and fanned Ojo awake with his hand, then helped him sit up. He went back inside and returned with Olubi and together they carried Ojo inside the house and he was not seen outside again for the rest of the day. It was a different person who tended to his horse in the evening and then led it back into the compound. However, that night after Bopo confirmed the followers were still taking turns observing the front of the house from a nearby unused shed, Ojo and Olubi snuck out of the compound from the rear entrance that leads into the yard. They silently skirted a path through the low shrubs until they arrived at the outskirts of the village, where one of Olubi's men was waiting for them with two horses.

'It is very important that we know their sender before you return to Oko-Oba,' Olubi told Ojo as they rode out of Oko-Oba. 'In case they decide to give up the watch before we return, I have instructed Jonpe and Sunmade to engage in a counter-surveillance operation.'

The *owuyes* were completely fooled. They truly believed that Ojo was very ill and likely to be bedridden for at least another day, the next morning, they decided to take a break and return to Oluweri. Jonpe and Sunmade successfully followed them there.

'His name is Olubi,' reported one of the *owuyes*. 'He is a well-known debt collector at Oko-Oba, but my strong suspicion is that Ojo is using his influence in Ago-Oyinbo to engage in a kind of illegal trading which could in the least undermine the king's revenue in Oluweri.' Ojikutu was not particularly alarmed. Such clandestine trade practices were common even among the Akete chiefs and nobles.

'He is an outlaw in Aketeland and wanted by the palace at Aromire,' the second added excitedly, while Ojikutu was mentally struggling to put a face to the name.

'He's what?'

'An outlaw. He was the principal agent in the incident that led to the destruction of the Obatala shrine at Paramole a few years back.'

'Where is Ojo now?'

'We think he is going to be in Oko-Oba for a few more days. He collapsed yesterday morning at Oko-Oba while tending to his horse. His unconscious body had to be carried into the house. That is why we decided to take the opportunity to come down and report our findings so far.'

'That is good. You two can go and have some rest,'

Ojikutu said after a brief pause. 'Meanwhile, get Idowu and Tegbe to keep a constant watch around Ago-Oyinbo. I want to know exactly when he returns.'

Jonpe and Sunmade successful followed the *owuyes* into Oluweri and saw them go directly to Ojikutu's house. Unlike the *owuyes*, the counter-espionage team sent by Olubi were not detected, as their mission did not require them to talk to people. All Olubi asked them to do was to find out to whom the *owuyes* would be reporting. To be certain of their findings, they waited until the *owuyes* left Ojikutu's house. They waited long enough to see Ojikutu leave his house shortly after and head for the fort at the seafront.

Two days later, just before sundown, Olubi and Ojo arrived at Ode-Ijowa and went straight to the house of *Balogun* Odebode. This time they did not seek the audience of the prince, but gave the Ijowa warlord specific instructions from the 'friends of Morilewa'.

'The friends of Morilewa understand the complexity involved in the case of Morilewa, and have chosen to carry on with the agreement, pending the time when it will be possible to make his freedom official,' Olubi told the *Balogun*, like a messenger who had been instructed to pass on a specific message and nothing more. 'To this end, we are ready to deliver the seventy *akerekoros* along with four hundred rounds. For our own reasons, we will not be able to make the delivery to Ode-Ijowa, but to Upper-Oluweri. We will set the delivery time to be the wake of the next Oluweri market in eight days' time. The prince is to direct a delegate of his choice to the house of the *Baale* of Upper-Oluweri when dawn breaks.'

The men politely declined the warlord's suggestion of passing the message to the prince first hand, and left without even a sip of the water offered to them. They again travelled through the night, and arrived at Oko-Oba around late noon of the second day. They were met by the horseman, who had been waiting since daybreak at the outskirts of the village.

'They believed the story we fed them about Ojo's condition and left the next morning,' he told Olubi. 'Jonpe and Sunmade followed them as you instructed.'

'Where did they come from, and who sent them?'

'Jonpe said they went as far as Oluweri. I am sure he knows the person they were working for, but decided to keep that information for you alone.'

Later in the house, after they had eaten and rested a bit, Jonpe and Sunmade gave a detailed account of their mission to Olubi and Ojo alone.

'My guess is that the surveillance was just a random act. It is very likely that Ologundudu will sooner than later ask you about your activities in the last few days. He will only become restless and suspicious if there is any discrepancy between your reply and what is reported to him. We are certain he knows that you have been here, and it's safe to assume that he knows who you have been meeting. But your activities while you are here in Oko-Oba can not be rightly reported to him. He will be under the impression that you are still bedridden in Oko-Oba due to your illness. So it will be safer not to return to Oluweri until we have clear information about his reaction. In fact I would strongly advise that you stay away from Oluweri until it is absolutely necessary.'

'Actually I am not planning on returning to Oluweri

right away. Remember, I told you that my mother was in Oluweri with a young maiden she wanted me to marry. I promised her I would be in Gbajumo to meet the girl's parents as soon as I could.'

'That is fine. But make sure you are back here in Oko-Oba in time for our engagement with the *Baale* on the eve of the Oluweri market. I believe you understand what I mean.'

'Yes I do.' Ojo nodded in agreement.

Despite the tension brought about by the looming confrontation between Akete and Ijowa, the usual influx of people and *alajapas* (travelling traders) into both sides of Oluweri had begun in the days before the market. By the eve of market day, both lower and upper Oluweri were as usual bustling with activity as potential sellers and buyers engaged in the usual *oja anosile* (pre-market bargaining).

It had been twenty-one days since Lagemo and the other six 'friends of Morilewa' had arrived at the fort to begin training the men selected by Ologundudu in the use of the *akerekoro* (revolver). Just before sunset, while Lagemo was updating the general on the progress of the trainees, a messenger who claimed to have set off from Isheri that morning came with glad tidings for Lagemo at the fort; his newest and youngest wife had given birth to a baby boy. The news ended Lagemo's meeting with Ologundudu as it naturally called for an immediate celebration. Lagemo made a brief dash to his hut within the fort and returned with five of the other 'friends of Morilewa' and an unopened bottle of rum. They were joined by Ojikutu, and all converged in front of the general's hut. Lagemo handed the rum over to Ologundudu to bless as custom demanded, but the general refused, for a valid reason.

'Don't get me wrong, I am more than happy for you on the arrival of the newborn,' he said. 'Correct me if I am wrong, but I remember the bearer of the good news mentioned something about the gender of the child.' Ologundudu did not need to to say anything further, as his audience had already got the message. The messenger had said that the baby was a boy, and the general was implying that one bottle of rum would not be acceptable for this 'double fortune'. Lagemo made another quick dash to his hut and returned with another bottle of rum.

They were still on the first bottle of rum when a young man came with a medium-sized gourd of palm wine. 'The *Ajele* heard the news of Lagemo's newborn and asked me to bring this here for the celebration,' he said. 'He said he will be joining you soon.' The bearer placed the gourd gently in the centre and left.

Meeting their own end of the agreement was not as Olubi and Ojo had made *Aremo-Oba* Adeyanju believe. On the eve of the market, just as the sun was beginning to set, fifty men led by Olubi and Ojo, all armed with spears and daggers, set off from the seafront at Oko-Oba in a convoy of seven large canoes and headed east toward Oluweri. In each of the canoes were sacks of sponges that had been saturated with palm oil. On an ordinary day, such a transit towards Oluweri might seem out of place, but not on the eve of Oluweri market day.

It was already dark before the convoy arrived on the Oluweri seafront. It stopped on a secluded part of the coast that was nearer to Ago-Oyinbo but far from the dock. Olubi and Ojo disembarked and walk the shore until they were some distance from the convoy, then lit an oil lamp. After a moment another oil lamp lit up some distance away, and they headed towards it. They were met by Tamedun, who talked with them briefly. After the conversation, Olubi returned to the convoy, whilst Ojo, along with two other men, followed Tamedun back the way he had come towards Oluweri.

It was already dark, but the village centre, as is on the eve of every market, was still lively. The influx of traders from different routes into Oluweri, which would continue until late into the night, was at its peak. Ojo had not returned to Oluweri since the *owuye* had followed him to Oko-Oba, so when they were within sight of Ago-Oyinbo, Ojo and the other two waited while Tamedun went ahead to observe if any of the *owuye* where waiting for Ojo's return.

'Both of them were at the entrance to Fadahunse's yard,' he reported. 'I saw them sitting on a bamboo bench by the entrance to the inner perimeter.' Ojo was relieved by this news because his problem was not about accessing Fadahunse's house. His problem was getting access to the old house, which was within the outer perimeter.

The four men sneaked into the outer perimeter and Ojo and Tamedun went straight to the old house while the other two proceeded to a secluded section of the outer fencing. With experienced hands, they quietly removed about eight of the bamboo poles from the fencing, creating a space just wide enough for one person to pass through at a time. They left via the gap and returned to Olubi on the seafront. Through this gap, twenty-five of Olubi's men will enter Ago-Oyinbo and, subsequently, Oluweri unnoticed.

Not long after Ojo and Tamedun had arrived at the old house, five men came to knock on the main door, and it was instantly opened from within. The men entered, and Ojo handed each man a small leather sack, inside which was one revolver and twenty rounds of ammunition. The men checked and verified the contents of their sacks, loaded their guns and put them back into the sacks, which they expertly concealed under their *agbada* (large garment) before leaving the house. They left the house as quietly as they came, but through the back door. Then the next group came via the front door, collect their sacks and also left via the back door as soon as they had counted their cartridges and loaded their guns. The movement continued till the fifth set of men had come and left.

The first two groups headed towards the eastern boundary of Oluweri with Odinjo, while the third and fourth went in the opposite direction towards the western border with Oko-Oba. The fifth group followed the path that led to the fort, and mingled with a gathering of travelling traders who usually spent most of the eve of the market chatting and socialising under a big *odan* tree, located within sight of the fort entrance that opened towards the village. Soon after, Ojo and Tamedun and the other two, each carrying a sack similar to the kind popular among *alajapa* for packing goods, also exited Ago-Oyinbo via the gap to the seafront.

In the first two sacks, carried by Ojo and Tamedun, were twenty-five loaded revolvers. In the other two sacks were twenty-five small leather pouches, each containing twenty cartridges. At the seafront, a revolver and a sack of ammunitions was handed to each of the men. Olubi, Ojo and twenty men then followed the coast in the direction of the fort. Tamedun and the remaining five men returned to the village. Tamedun returned to the fort, while the five armed men melted into the many groups of farmers, produce buyers and sellers and traders of general goods who were busy engaging in pre-market transactions on the banks of the Awoyaya.

At the fort, the merriment had been growing livelier, and at its peak it almost escalated to a full-blown celebration. The two bottles of rum had long been consumed, and more gourds of palm wine were arriving from 'well wishers'. Lagemo, Ologundudu, Ojikutu, the *Ajele* and five other 'friends of Morilewa' had been drinking and celebrating the newborn so long that the best drinkers were far from sober. The *Ajele* was very drunk, and had partly lost control of his mouth and limbs by the time Tamedun returned to the fort and joined the party. He was not all steady on his feet, and when his throat was not swallowing liquor he was blurting out nonsense, much to the embarrassment of the war general and people around. It took a mixture of persuasion and command before Ologundudu was able to convince him that it was time to quit and return home to sleep.

The *Ajele* was the Akete king's 'eyes' in civil Oluweri and did not live within the fort. He arrogantly put up feeble objections to being assisted home, but the general insisited that he must allow two men to support him back to his house. The work of Olubi men waiting at the *Ajele's* house was made easy when they saw the state he was and the manner in which he was brought home. He was partly carried and partly dragged to his doorstep. His wives and children were all asleep, but they had left the door open for his return. The carriers could not wait to deposit the old man on a mat in the front room so they could hurry back to the fort before the last of the gourds of wine ran dry. They simply closed the front door after them and did not bother to wake any of the family to secure the door behind them as they sped off. which was careless, especially on the eve of market day, when there are many strangers in the village, and the risk of burglary and stealing is very high.

Moments after his helpers had left, five armed men creeped into the *Ajele's* bedchamber, gagged him and bound him tightly with rope and into a large sack before carrying him out of the house. The now unconscious *Ajele* was carried through the village like a sack of farm produce and dumped into a large canoe at an isolated part of the Awoyaya river, under the watchful eyes of the five men covering the riverside.

Agba-Eso Ojikutu had been in charge of security at Oluweri since the occupation began. His family had joined him there and were living with him within the fort before the turn of the second season into the occupation. In anticipation of the arrival of *Akogun* Ologundudu, Ojikutu had to vacate the official residence of the fort commander to make way for him. Instead of moving into a smaller shelter within the fort, he thought it wise to move his family out of the fort to another house within civilian Oluweri. He reckoned that with the reinforcement, the fort would be overwhelmed with young warriors and unsafe for his three adolescent daughters. As soon as they had deposited the *Ajele* in the canoe, his abductors proceeded to Ojikutu's home and abducted his family, while the head of the house was still drinking inside the fort.

Akogun Ologundudu was not much of a drinker and he knew his limit. Although he stayed much longer than the *Ajele*, he drank much less. The supreme warlord was fairly sober when he retired to his house, leaving Olubi and the rest to continue with the celebration. Until their job was completed, the two personal aides of the *Akogun* had to refrain from drinking alcohol, and they were grateful when the warlord finally decided to leave. As soon as they had seen him to his house, they hurried back to the centre of the fort to catch up with all they had been missing.

Soon after the two aides of the *Akogun* had returned to the celebration, Lagemo excused himself on the account that he needed to relieve himself and was joined by three other friends of Morilewa. They withdrew to a corner as if to urinate, and none of the gathering noticed them as they slipped away and quickly but stealthily crossed over to the general's quarters.

Lagemo and his party, now with heads wrapped with clothing like the Fulanis, stormed the bedchamber of the *Akogun*. Unlike the *Ajele* and Ojikutu, Ologundudu was on temporary deployment to Oluweri due to the tension. He had not come down to Oluweri with his family, so no one except the target was disturbed by the intruders. It was not as easy for them as it had been for those who went after the *Ajele*, as the warlord was sober, and put up a gallant resistance. It took a while before he was finally subdued, and it was not before he had inflicted a serious injury on one of his attackers. The little commotion made during the struggle went unnoticed by his aides, who a short distance away were greedily drinking to make up for the missed cheer.

The *Akogun* (supreme warlord) of Akete army was gagged and bound and locked in the inner room of his quarters. As a further precaution, one of the attackers stood sentinel in the dark corridor to prevent any attempt by the general to escape or make a noise that could attract unwanted attention.

The entire ground of the fort was surrounded by

palisades, with two entrances. The entrance on the north, generally referred to as the front entrance, opened into communal Oluweri, while the back entrance to the south opened onto the seafront and the dock. The security at the northern entrance had been heavily reinforced in anticipation of an attack due to the passing of the *Onijowa,* but anybody with any experience in warfare would conclude that it would be foolish and futile for the Ijowa army to attack via the seafront. A large army would have to wade the water against a rain of missile weapons only to have to cut through the palisades. The fatigued and depleted force could be massacred by a troop a quarter of its size. Hence, the level of security on the southern exit was designed to deter thieves and armed bandits from looting the goods in the produce safe house. The only defence against unauthorised access via the southern entrance was a large gate, manned from within the fort by a team of six men who stood sentry in turn on a two per shift basis.

Soon after Lagemo and his company left to 'urinate', Tamedun and the remaining two friends of Morilewa announced that they were done with drinking and would be retiring to their shelters. By this time it was well past midnight, and except for those on normal security duty, most of the warriors had either retired to their sleeping places or were outside the fort partaking in the eve of the market commercial activities. Tamedun and his company went to the southern entrance to the fort and with practised precision attacked and neutralised the guards on sentry, then went on to open the southern gate. The sandy stretch between the fort and the coast was normally devoid of security patrol when there was no trade ship in the dock and none was expected. Olubi and twenty men, all in hoods and armed with swords and *akerekoro*, crept into the fort without making the slightest sound. They split into four groups and headed off in three directions.

There were altogether seven structures within the fort. First there were the residence of the *Akogun*, the armoury and the produce warehouse. These three structures, built from ground to roof with mud, bricks and stones, were among the first to be erected by the occupying forces. Then there was a cluster of four large shelters where the warriors lived, out of which only one was built with mud and stones. The other three were built with wood, bamboo and raffia, and had been hurriedly put together to accommodate the reinforcements that came with *Akogun* Ologundudu.

The first two groups headed for the warriors' shelters, the third to the building that served as the armoury, and the fourth to the storage house. The ground surrounding the buildings was strewn with sacks of palm-oil-soaked sponges, and upon hearing a signal shot from Olubi's *akerekoro*, they were set alight simultaneously. The Akete warmen were rudely awaken from slumber by multiple fires set upon their shelters. They started screaming and running out of their shelters, only to be met from every direction with multiple gunfire from the *akerekoro*.

The residents and traders were naturally alarmed by the sudden outbreak of fire. On instinct, they began running towards the fort to get a clear view of what was happening, but they soon reconsidered their action when suddenly there was outburst of sustained firing from within the fort.

Olubi's men laid ambush around the burning armoury and shot the warriors who were attempting to enter and salvage some weapons. Those who thought it wise to negotiate with their limbs by trying to escape from the fort via the entrances were confronted with more fire from the men stationed inside Oluweri, who had been undertaking the kidnappings.

The thick smoke from the fire at the fort was soon carried by the wind out of Oluweri and into the neighbouring Ijowa villages of Oko-Oba, Odinjo and across the river in upper Oluweri. The flames triggered the expected response from the Akete warriors on sentry duty at the boundaries with Oko-Oba and Odinjo. The border warriors reacted as anticipated by Olubi; they left their posts and began trooping towards the fort. The reinforcements from both boundaries were ambushed and intercepted midway to the fort. The sudden hail of bullets from ten *akerekoros* at the same time was more than the Akete warriors were prepared for. They broke ranks and took flight.

The darkness, the broken chain of command and the lack of weapons, left Akete army disoriented and in disarray. Now that the head of the snake had been cut off, it was only necessary to avoid the final thrashing of the body and wait until it was dead. The occupation army was reduced to a mob, and soon the instinct for personal survival overcame their loyalty to the king. It was easy for Olubi's men to target and gun down as many as possible as they tried to flee the fort or the nearby the outposts. Many of those who managed to leave the fort via the front entrance were picked up by Olubi's men as they scrambled out of the fort, like rats fleeing their holes when a snake visits. Some of them were captured alive, many were killed and a few managed to escape via land, sea and river.

With a death threat on his family, *Agba-Eso* Ojikutu

was made to order the disarmament and surrender of the few trapped in the fort. All happened in dead of night. Neither Ojikutu, nor any of the surviving, surrendered or captured Akete army had any idea that the attack has anything to do with Lagemo and the friends of Morilewa.

As previously instructed by the messenger from the 'friends of Morilewa', *Balogun* Odebode arrived in upper Oluweri on the eve of the market hoping to receive the arms. He stayed in the *Baale's* house and all through the night, heard contradictory reports of the developing events in Lower-Oluweri. The initial report was that it was a rebellion, carried out by disgruntled elements within the ranks of the Akete army. An 'eyewitness' who claimed to be close to the fort when the shooting started said he was sure some of the invaders had their heads shaved in patterns similar to those of the *Ilaris* (civil enforcers) of the king of Abatan.

'The invaders were faceless and with my very eyes I saw fire coming out of their palms,' said another 'eyewitness', who strongly believed that the fort and the Akete army had been attacked by spiritual warriors of Yemoja, the sea goddess.

Before dawn, Oluweri had fallen to the invaders, and Ojo crossed the Awoyaya to meet the *Balogun*. At upper Oluweri, Ojo demanded a private meeting with the Ijowa warlord purposely and solely to deliver the 'message from friends of Morilewa.'

'The friends of Morilewa have done that which the *Aremo-Oba* and Ijowa chiefs strongly desired' he said. 'As I am speaking with you, the land and waters of Oluweri, right from Awoyaya river to the seafront, is no longer under the control of *Oba* Lagbade. Not a single Akete warrior is standing in Oluweri. It is upon this development that the friends of Morilewa ask me to convey the following message to the *Aremo-Oba*. The palace at Ode-Ijowa now has authority over all the lands and waters of Oluweri. The *Aremo-Oba* is now at liberty to appoint whoever he deems fit as the *Baale* of Oluweri. He can, as he wishes and without fear, proceed with the traditional rites that will see him ascend to the prestigious position made vacant by the passing of his esteemed father. Finally, and of equal importance, the *Aremo-Oba* and Ijowa chiefs must be advised not to dishonour the agreement with friends of Morilewa concerning Ago-Oyinbo and Fadahunse.'

The meeting was brief and Ojo left immediately after delivering his message, but it took a while before the *Balogun* was able to comprehend his words. When he did, he found himself before a dilemma regarding the action to take. On one hand, it would be out of order to take any action on such a sensitive development without proper consultation with the *Aremo-Oba* and fellow chiefs at Ode-Ijowa. But on the other hand, it was politically imperative that he (on behalf of the prince and the palace) should take immediate responsibility for the victory in Oluweri by declaring Lower-Oluweri to be free of occupation and back under the control of Ijowa. Even then, he had to be be very careful about his statement, as whatever he said in upper Oluweri would be widely accepted as the true situation across Oluweri.

Ojo was already crossing the Awoyaya back to Lower-Oluweri before *Balogun* was able to make up a convincing story.

'The invaders were a secret army raised by the *Aremo-Oba*, and the takeover was orchestrated from the palace at Ode-Ijowa,' the *Balogun* finally announced to the eagerly waiting *Baale* and elders of upper Oluweri.

By noon on what was supposed to be have been just another Oluweri market day, more than two hundred battle-ready Ijowa warriors, that had been stationed in Upper-Oluweri, led by *Balogun* Odebode, had crossed the Awoyaya to Lower-Oluweri to formally take over the defence and security of Oluweri and its seafront. The incoming forces were expecting to be received by a band of proud and victorious men, but all they found in the fort were ruins, destruction and scores of tied and bound Akete soldiers. As the first batch of Ijowa warriors was crossing the river into Lower-Oluweri, Olubi and half of his men, along with the the corpses of four of his men who had fallen during the confrontation, were leaving Lower-Oluweri for Oko-Oba. They left via the seafront, in the same canoes that had brought them the evening before. The other half melted into the throngs of long-displaced residents from upper Oluweri who had been pouring into Lower-Oluweri since the news broke that Ijowa warriors had reclaimed Oluweri in what was now being tagged the '*ogun ainitumo*' (mystical battle).

'The aim is to create a kind of mystery and illusion around us, and so far it's working very well,' Olubi said to explain his decision to pull the men out of Oluweri. 'The strategy is to prevent the other side from having an idea of our capacity and capabilities. That is one of the ways to ensure that the decision makers in Ijowa respect and honour our agreement. They know we have the best of firearms, but they do not know our human capacity. An outsider would estimate that this feat could not have been performed by less than three hundred men.'

'Hmm, you're right,' said Lagemo. 'That means that henceforth the relationship between the palace at Ode-Ijowa and the friends of Morilewa will be like that of the proverbial hen and the tight rope. It is up to the hen to be still and calm while on the rope, else neither the hen nor the rope will be at ease.'

'Exactly. If the 'hens' at the palace in Ode-Ijowa wants a peaceful reign over Oluweri, then they had better be careful with the 'rope' of the friends of Morilewa.'

Three days later, an *Ajele* (sole administrator) appointed by the *Aremo-Oba* and accompanied by a team of officials including the *ilaris* (civil enforcers), market leaders and rate collectors arrived in Oluweri.

Due to the unexpected development, the bi-annual convergence of the Ogboni fraternity that was supposed to commence in Ode-Ijowa about six days after the liberation was moved forward, and the arrangements for the coronation of the new *Onijowa* were of the utmost priority. The fifth day after the liberation was another market day at Ode-Ijowa, and the chiefs decided to choose that day to announce that the kingmakers had decided to begin the process that would elevate the *Aremo-Oba* to the exalted throne of his ancestors. The familiarisation tour that would mark the beginning of the coronation process was scheduled to commence in twenty-one days. In the same communiqué was news of the palace decision to grant a royal pardon to the six longest-serving convicts on the king's farm. According to Ajiroba, the decision to free Morilewa and five other convicts was part of the late king's last words and should be respected.

'We heard that Morilewa had a mental breakdown and died while receiving treatment at Igbodudu,' said somebody in the crowd.

'Yes, you heard right,' replied Ajiroba, revealing part of the truth as agreed with the chiefs.'But Morilewa was never sick in the head and never went to Igbodudu. Certain information received by the palace on the grapevine indicates that a group sponsored by the palace at Akete were planning to free Morilewa by force. The Igbodudu story was deliberately made up to thwart the plot. The *alanganran* that was taken to Igbodudu was a diversionary tactic to confuse the enemy.'

Market gossip spreads like forest fire in the dry season, and the news of the amnesty granted by the palace to Morilewa and five other convicts had reached every corner of Ijowa by noon on the second day. Ojo was on his first visit to his mother since the liberation of Oluweri when the news got to Gbajumo, and it came as a welcome surprise to both of them.

'This is sooner than expected. *Baba* Morilewa said the Oluwo raised a concern that only a king can grant amnesty for the kind of crime he was accused of,' Ojo said. 'I was not expecting this good news to come until a new king had mounted the throne.'

'Whatever the case, the important thing is that he is finally free,' Lalonpe said with delight.

Each of the freed convicts was escorted to his home village by two palace aides and officially handed to his *Baale*. The message from the palace to the *Baale* of each village was that the freed convict should be received and accepted into the community without reservation. On the fifth day after the amnesty, one of the freed men, who was from Gbajumo, was brought into the village by two palace aides and handed over to the *Baale*.

'Morilewa should also be back in Egbejoda by now. That means we should be expecting him here or in Oluweri in a few days,' Lalonpe told *Iya* Mojoyin.

CHAPTER 17

Ojo felt something between disappointment and anger when ten days later, Morilewa had not visited as he had promised, and there had been no word sent in explanation. So far, the prince and the Ijowa chiefs had respected all other parts of the agreement following the liberation of Oluweri. He saw no reason why there should be a problem with Morilewa's freedom. Six days before the *Aremo-Oba* began his familiarisation tour across Ijowa towns and villages, Ojo made the decision to travel to Egbejoda to find the reason.

On arriving at the Omomose compound in Egbejoda, Ojo asked the first elderly person he met. The woman told him Morilewa was presently not in the compound. 'I hope he has not travelled out of Egbejoda, because I also came down from afar to see him,' said Ojo, fearing that Morilewa might have finally find time to leave Egbejoda for Gbajumo or Oluweri.

'That I cannot say,' The woman replied. 'He has had a

very tight schedule since his return. You will need to see the *olori-ebi* (family head) to be certain.' She led Ojo to the house of the family head. He greeted the elderly man and began the story he had taken time to prepare for this purpose.

'My name is Ojo. My grandmother was a trader in Oluweri before the war and *Baba* Morilewa was a regular customer. He was a generous man and used to bring gifts for me and other children in the market. So when I heard that he had been pardoned and released from the king's farm, I decided to come down and rejoice with him.'

The incumbent head of the family, whom Ojo later learnt to be Morilewa's uncle, replied. 'Yes, he has been freed. He came back twelve days ago and we are all excited about it. The *Baale* asked to see him this morning. He has been there since *iyaleta* [mid morning] and should be back at any moment.' Ojo was relieved that his journey to Egbejoda was not in vain.

'So you travelled all the way from Oluweri purposely to see Morilewa?'

'That is right *Baba*. I have a personal gratitude towards *Baba* Morilewa. I was still a *majesin* when I met him, but during the short period I knew him he taught me a skill that helped me through the most difficult times of my life. He taught me the secret of playing the *agidigbo*.'

'That is strange,' the *olori-ebi* said, slightly confused. 'I had no idea he could play the *agidigbo*.'

'Oh yes he can. Although I cannot say he is the best I have met, but he was very good at it. He also bought my first *agidigbo* for me, and since then I have not stop playing it.'

'Nonetheless, it is very respectful of you to come and

show your appreciation. I wonder what is keeping him so long in the *Baale's* house,' the *olori-ebi* said after a while.

'Maybe he has finished with the *Baale* and returned to his yard,' Ojo reasoned.

'I expect him to return here and give me feedback after the visit,' The *olori-ebi* said with the authority of his position as family head. He then looked through the window and called out a name, to which somebody responded.

'What do you say your name is again?' the *olori-ebi* asked Ojo. Just then a little boy entered the room.

'My name is Ojo,' Ojo replied. 'Ojo Kekewura.'

The *olori-ebi* turned to the boy. 'Go to Morilewa's yard and see if he is back from the *Baale's* place,' he said. 'Tell him that a visitor from Oluweri called Ojo Kekewura is waiting for him in my house.' After the boy had left, the *olori-ebi* excused himself for a call of nature and left Ojo alone in the front room.

Morilewa had left the *Baale's* place and was back in the Omomose compound, but he stopped at his own house for a quick meal before proceeding to his uncle's yard. He was just finishing his food when the boy arrived.

'The *olori-ebi* asked me to tell you that a visitor from Oluweri called Ojo Kekewura is waiting for you in his yard,' said the boy

'Ojo Kekewura from Oluweri?' Morilewa repeated the name, more like a question directed to himself than a clarification from the errand boy.

'That is what *Baba* called him,' the boy replied. Morilewa thought the name sounded familiar, but could not readily put a face to it. 'Tell baba I am on my way.'

Upon arriving at his uncle's yard, Morilewa was duly informed by one of his housewives that the family head had just gone to the yard to relieve himself. The man whom Ojo was supposed to be waiting for entered the front room, they greeted each other passively and Morilewa sat waiting for his uncle return.

When the *olori-ebi* returned, he was greeted by both his nephew and the supposed guest of his nephew. He had no intention of stopping, but only return to the front room to check if Morilewa is back and has seen his guest.

'I will give you time to attend to your guest, then we will discuss your visit to the *Baale*,' The *olori-ebi* said and made to leave the room.

'*Baba*, I think there is a misunderstanding here,' Ojo said to the *olori-ebi*. 'It is *Baba* Morilewa that I have come to see.'

The *olori-ebi* was visibly confused. He looked at Ojo, then at Morilewa and then back at Ojo again. 'You have not seen Morilewa in seventeen years. Are you sure you would recognise him again?' he asked.

'Yes *baba*, I will recognise *Baba* Morilewa when I see him,' Ojo replied confidently.

'Then you need to open your eyes properly. To the best of my knowledge, the person sitting before you is the only Morilewa in this compound, and the only person who has just been granted amnesty by the palace.'

'With all due respect, *baba*,' Ojo said with a slight grin. 'It might have been a while since I last saw him, but the person sitting before me is not *Baba* Morilewa.' He was sure that for some reason access to Morilewa was still being controlled by his family, and the third man in the room, the one presented as Morilewa, was just part of the precautions for his safety. The *olori-ebi's* confusion was immediately replaced by a deep thought. He walked across the room and sat on the stool in between both of the men and exchanged a knowing glance with Morilewa. They realised this man held the secrets of the impersonator who had been responsible for the death of the diviner.

'Young man, the person you seek is the greatest enemy of this family,' said the *olori-ebi*. 'The man you seek was responsible for my nephew's incarceration for seventeen seasons. You are here with good intentions, and it will be against good judgement to make you a victim of his actions by unleashing our anger on you, because his action damaged us.' He looked at his nephew in a manner that invited him to speak.

'The *olori-ebi* has said it all,' replied Morilewa. 'It would not be fair to display anger or resentment against you. However, there is one thing I want to clarify from you. You say your name is Ojo Kekewura. Is your father's name Iyanda?'

Ojo was reluctant to answer, as he had no idea of the implications of an honest reply.

'You don't have to fret,' said the *olori-ebi*. 'I can assure you that your reply will have no adverse reaction from us.' Ojo knew he had no choice but to answer. Despite all his peaceful and calm utterances, the *olori-ebi* could by a simple glance through the door commandeer enough men to force him to talk. He wished he had come better prepared. An *akerekoro* would have put him in a more assuring position, he thought regretfully. But how could he have imagined finding himself in this situation?

'Yes, my father's name was Iyanda.' Ojo replied but visibly on the edge.

'And your mother's name is Lalonpe?' Morilewa asked.

'Yes, that is my mother's name.'

'And your story about this person you knew as Morilewa being your grandmother's customer is not entirely true. Am I right?'

'Yes, you are right.' Ojo replied. He had been confronted with so many new realities in a very short time that he had given up any effort at guarding his response.

'You have nothing to worry about,' Morilewa reassured him. 'I knew your father. He was my friend and trading associate until his unfortunate death. As for the impersonator, may the deities help me. One thing I desire to achieve during my remaining years above the soil is to find him and bring him to justice. Justice not only for the years I spent on the king's farm, but of equal importance, justice for the late priest.'

Ojo was dumbfounded. 'I will need time to think and make sense of what is going on,' he said. 'I strongly believe that there is a misunderstanding somewhere.' He rose to indicate that he was ready to leave. Morilewa invited him to stay and eat something before setting off for his return journey to Gbajumo, but Ojo declined.

'I know some things about this impersonator, but not enough to find him,' Morilewa said as he escorted Ojo out of the compound. I can understand your position. You have nothing against him, so I would not expect you to disclose anything about him under these circumstances. However, I owe it to the spirit of your late father to warn you and your mother that you may not have seen the last of him. He must have been looking for either you or your mother, and I consider both of you to be very lucky that he has not found you yet. He is after a certain item he gave to your mother before the war. If he is still alive, then he could still be looking for her.'

'How do you know that the other Morilewa gave my mother a certain item before the war?'

'I have been generous in warning you. The other things I know about the impersonator will have to remain with me until you agree to share whatever you know about him with me. We stand a better chance of finding him if we work together. But we cannot do that, because we are seeking him for different ends.'

'You don't understand, *baba*. Although, it is our desire to see him again, we are not desperate to find him. Yes, we have something that belongs to the other Morilewa, but he handed it to us personally, and we are not hiding from him. It might be more difficult now you are free because he can no longer risk claiming to be Morilewa from Egbejoda, but I am sure he can reach us whenever he decides to recover the item.' Ojo looked Morilewa straight in the eye. 'But if you have never been mentally ill and taken to Igbodudu for treatment in the past seventeen years, if you have not been incarcerated on any of the king's farms for the last seventeen year but have been living as Ekisola in Igisogba, then I must also warn you that you may not have heard the last of your impersonator.'

He paused to allow Morilewa to respond, but the latter just stood silently, as if he had been strucked by a bolt of lightning. Ojo was certain he had struck a chord. He continued, seeing that Morilewa was in non hurry to respond.

'If that is the case, then I will advise that your problem is not about finding the other Morilewa. Your problem is how you can prevent him from using your identity again in the future. I don't know how, but the other Morilewa seems to have the ability to use your identity, and also manipulate your circumstance to suit certain purposes.'

This time Morilewa responded by requesting, almost pleading, that Ojo should return with him to the *Olori-ebi* and continue the discussion.

The *Olori-ebi's* mouth gaped open in disbelief when Ojo repeated what the family head believed had been a well-guarded secret for over sixteen years. Morilewa confessed to Ojo that he had neither been to Igbodudu nor been incarcerated on the king's farms, and most importantly, that he had truly been living in Igisogba for the past seventeen years.

'The other Morilewa knows the circumstances surrounding the death of the priest,' said Ojo. 'He knows the verdict passed upon you by the palace. You may not believe this, but I am telling you now, as a matter of fact, that your pardon and your presence in Egbejoda today as a free man have the fingerprints of the other Morilewa all over them. You have not told me how you managed to escape the king's farm, but I can assure you that he has something to do with it. So if you want to find Morilewa, your only option is through the person or people responsible for your escape between Ode-Ijowa and the king's farm at Ayefele.'

'The person responsible for my escape had never met the impersonator before,' replied Morilewa. 'He held me for almost a month, and put me through rigorous interrogations and tests, before he was convinced that I was not the man he was after but a victim of impersonation.'

'How do you know all this?' The *Olori-ebi* finally managed to ask.

'*Baba* Morilewa offered to trade information with me. But he is yet to answer the question that prompted me to disclose all I said.' He did not shift his eyes from Morilewa.

'How do you know that the other Morilewa gave my mother certain items before the war?'

'My helper was also after the impersonator for the item. I don't know how, but he believed the impersonator had plenty of them, and gave some to your mother. He organised my rescue with the hope of demanding those items as payment for his service.'

'Less than a month ago, the other Morilewa met up with me at Oluweri after seventeen years,' said Ojo, finally disclosing the information he had been holding back. 'He told me all that had happened to you, and knew you would soon be granted a royal pardon.'

Despite his anger and displeasure at the impersonator, Morilewa was alarmed and scared by the extent to which he had been able to get regular updates about his life. Despite his freedom, he realised his position was as precarious as it was when he was a fugitive. It was well into sundown, and by the time they had finally decided to put a hold on their talks, Ojo was too exhausted to leave Egbejoda until the next day.

Ojo returned to Gbajumo to face the unpleasant task of reporting the outcome of his journey to Egbejoda. Lalonpe was not at home when he arrived, and Malaolu said she was at *Iya* Mojoyin's place. Malaolu suggested he should run along to tell his grandmother that his father was around, but Ojo chose to go down there himself.

'*Mama*, I don't know where to begin or how to describe my experience at Egbejoda,' Ojo said as soon as he had settled down.

'What could have happened there that you find so difficult to describe?'

'I went to Egbejoda and then to the Omomose family. I met the Morilewa who was release by the palace, but he was not the Morilewa we know.'

'What are you talking about?' she asked as if her son was playing a prank.

'*Mama*, the person we know as Morilewa, the person who came to Oluweri less than a month ago, is not the Morilewa who was freed by the palace. He is not the Morilewa of the Omomose compound of Egbejoda. He is not the man that was friends with my father.'

Lalonpe stared at her son worryingly.

'Ojo, I am concerned all the events of the past few weeks are taking their toll on you', she said after a brief pause.

'*Mama*, I know it is unbelievable, but you just have to accept it,' Ojo told her, growing slightly frustrated. 'You needed to have been there in Egbejoda to have an idea how confused I was, when it finally dawned on me that all the while we have been chasing a shadow. Even as I am talking to you, I still cannot make any sense of why Baba Morilewa chose to deceive and mislead us this far.'

'If your tale is true, then who was the person who was released?'

'He is the true son of the Omomose compound. Apart from his physical appearance, all other claims by our Morilewa about his life since the time we first knew him until the last time we saw him were the same as the Morilewa I met at Egbejoda. Our Morilewa claimed to be a friend of the late priest, as was also the real Morilewa. And after a long exchange, he admitted in confidence that he had all these years been living in Igisogba, and had neither been in Igbodudu nor been taken to any of the king's farms. Now here is the interesting part. The Morilewa I met at

Egbejoda said he was a trading associate of my father, and also limped slightly on his left leg. He said his injury was due to the same unfortunate expedition that led to the tragic end of my father.'

'That was exactly how our Morilewa introduced himself at our first meeting,' Lalonpe confirmed. 'This is strange. Very, very strange. It is a mystery.'

'It is strange, but I see no mystery. Our Morilewa used the identity of the real Morilewa to get to you. *Baba* Fatunbi himself is the vital key to this puzzle. Apparently, it was from the priest that our Morilewa got all the information he needed to impersonate the real Morilewa.'

'But why did they have to use somebody else's identity? Why did *Baba* Fatunbi agree to such a diabolical deception?'

'Mama, I pondered hundreds of similar questions during my return journey from Egbejoda, but I was unable to come with any sensible answer or explanation. At this stage, I am not really sure what to believe and I have given up with conjectures. The only person who can solve the riddle, apart from the priest himself, is our own Morilewa, and I don't think he will be coming back now that the real Morilewa is around.'

'I am sure he will be back,'Lalonpe said.

'I don't think so. I believe he had all his actions properly worked out and I am certain this is the way he expected it to turn out,' Ojo said. 'Remember, he still has to answer for his role in the death of the priest.'

'I agree he may not plan a permanent reunion. He might not have intended to see us again, but that was before he learnt that he has a son.' Lalonpe was optimistic.

'Why then did he continue to lie to us after knowing he had a son? Why did he keep away even after the real

Morilewa had been released, knowing full well that we were bound to go looking for him at Egbejoda?'

'Yes, it is plain that he had his plan carefully worked out, and it did not include returning to us. I cannot say if he will be back or not, but Bogunde's existence came as a shock to him. That must affect whatever plan he already has in place. But he must first make a retreat to think about how to deal with the change in circumstances.'

'But how did he have access to information and events that were meant to be limited to a very few people in the palace at Ode-Ijowa, and in real time?' replied Ojo. That is the mystery. That is what enabled him to accomplish this grand deception. He must be very close to the powers that be in Ode-Ijowa or even one of the core decision makers in the palace. He knows too much to be an outsider. I am beginning to suspect that all these years, he was never at any time in the dark about our situation.'

'Yes, you are right,' said Lalonpe. 'That explains some aspects of Bogunde's account of their encounter at Olokoto. According to Bogunde, before their meeting, he had spotted him earlier that day, in the process of altering his appearance from that of a noble to that of an ordinary town person.'

Iya Mojoyin, who had all the while been listening to the exchanges between mother and son, then spoke for the first time. 'Now that you know exactly where to look for your Morilewa, you may never find him.'

'Mama, are you telling me that I will not be able to recognise the father of my son if I see him?'

'Seeing and recognising him is one part of the problem. Finding him is another.'

'What is the difference between seeing him and finding

him?' Lalonpe asked, visibly confused.

'You will recognise the father of your son when you see him,' said *Iya* Mojoyin. 'If Morilewa is an ordinary townsman, we can find him if we know where to look, and when we do find him he will just be Bogunde's father. But to have access to the information that made it possible for him to accomplish all these deceptions, your Morilewa must be somebody of influence in the palace at Ode-Ijowa, so finding him will no longer just mean seeing the father of your son. It will become finding the person responsible for the death of Fatunbi. It means finding the person who is to blame for the loss of Oluweri. Are you with me?'

'All my body and soul is with you, mama.'

'If indeed your Morilewa is as influential as I strongly believe he is, then the question now is, will your Morilewa ever admit to knowing you? Will the father of your son be in a position to accept your claim and the implication that goes with it? It is the answer to those questions that will determine whether you will ever find him or not.'

ND - #0180 - 270225 - C0 - 203/127/26 - PB - 9781861519290 - Gloss Lamination